SHE JUST CAN'T HELP HERSELF

OLLIE QUAIN

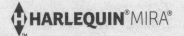

HARLEQUIN® MIRA®

First Published in Great Britain 2016
By Harlequin Mira, an imprint of HarperCollins*Publishers*
1 London Bridge Street, London, SE1 9GF

She Just Can't Help Herself © 2016 Ollie Quain

ISBN: 978-1-848-45394-4

58-0616

Our policy is to use papers that are natural, renewable and recyclable products and made from wood grown in sustainable forests. The logging and manufacturing processes conform to the legal environmental regulations of the country of origin.

Printed and bound by
CPI Group (UK) Ltd, Croydon, CR0 4YY

To Eddie. The purriest. The furriest. The greatest.

One

ASHLEY

Of course, there are times when I think to myself, 'WHAT *AM* I DOING?' But when you work in fashion, it's essential that every so often you do to try to retain some perspective. After all, in this industry we have a tendency to lose ourselves when witnessing a 'moment'. From the arrival of Karl Lagerfeld's cat on Twitter to the return of the consciously unkempt eyebrow, it's easy to get over-excited about stuff when everyone in the 'bubble' is ramped up too. I know a blogger who had to breathe into a paper bag when Balmain announced a diffusion line for H&M. It can get pretty ridiculous. But no one questions this ridiculousness out loud. If they have to, it is to an audience of one. (This guarantees the option of total denial later.) Because there is a rule: *don't prick the bubble.* It mustn't burst.

'I want to *feel* the true essence of Noelle during your interview…' my Editor, Catherine Ogilvy, gushed at me an hour ago in the foyer of the hotel, shortly before the main party was due to start at 3pm. 'She is such an alluring dichotomy of sophistication and quirk. The designer's muse who was happy to 'sofa surf' on arrival in New York…paying her hosts in 'styling tips and personal artwork'. But let's overlook that makeover show she presented, the one for the ugly teens…'

'It never existed. All tapes have been destroyed,' I deadpanned, trying to decide whether a) I liked Catherine's pussy-bow-neck silk polka dot blouse and b) if I had time for a quick (private) drink in the lobby bar. Just to take the edge off. I'd come straight from a non-work-related meeting.

'…of course,' she added. 'You must touch on *that* break-up, which Noelle handled with such bravery and fortitude.'

'That relationship only lasted three months, Catherine.'

'They were *en route* to marriage.'

'No, he was *on tour* with that painful emo rock band he plays with, Barbed Wire. So called because anyone with ears would clamber over all forms of skin-lacerating high-security metal spiking to avoid one of their shows.'

She giggled. 'Tsk. Come on, that poetry she wrote after the split was very dark. Real inner-demons stuff.'

'Yeah, she's like Sylvia Plath for the Snapchat generation…' I muttered, and looked over Catherine's shoulder to check my hair and make-up in the mirror behind her.

Both were as they should be, ie, not too done. I never like to appear as if there has been a deliberate focus on *getting ready*, even if there has. Crimes Against Fashion No. 9: continual obvious use of a '*glam squad*'. Guilty: Rita Ora.

'…well,' I added. 'Thank goodness Noelle managed to get over the worst in time for Coa-*fucking*-chella. Heartache and purposefully frayed denim have never worked well together.'

'And neither does being clever with not exactly Mensa-eligible celebrities. No messing about tonight with Noelle. Just remember why we're all here: to get a better understanding of the woman herself in order to celebrate the launch of her book…'

By 'her book', Catherine was referring to *This is Me* by Noelle Bamford. Not exactly a traditional autobiographical tome, this cobbled-together collection of text-message screen grabs from Noelle's sycophantic pals, Polaroids taken on shoots, fridge-magnet life advice, the odd stanza of the aforementioned poetry (only made *just* literate by a hapless copy editor) and a guide to her favourite hip hang-outs…had resulted in a £400,000 publishing advance. I said we should swerve giving the book anything but minimal attention in the magazine. Even better, we should be seen to be *choosing* to ignore it. Catherine disagreed, calling the book a 'zeitgeist moment in celebrity-slash-fashion-slash-self-reflexive publishing' and a) offered to co-sponsor a launch party alongside the design house, Pascale, who make the perennially popular 'Noelle' tote-style handbag, which was everything Noelle was *not*: chunky and useful. And far, *far* worse b) asked Noelle to be on the cover. *And* almost un*bear*ably c) invited her to be our Guest Editor too.

Catherine clocked my expression.

'Don't be like that, Ashley! You know that now more than ever the fashion magazine industry has to indulge in some vigorous back slapping. Actually, that should be *cupping*, no?' She laughed, but when my expression did not change, she wagged her finger at me. 'Word of advice, Ashley…you need to stop taking things so seriously.'

I hated that she had a point. I hated that I was aware of doing this a lot recently. I'm a fashion journalist, reporting from the front *row* not the front *line*. I needed to lighten up. But first, I needed that drink.

So I had one. Then another. And now, here we are. At five to four in the elaborate Renaissance-style function room of the Rexingham Hotel in London's West End. Noelle is wearing an A-line pinafore dress, shirt with a Peter Pan collar and her signature shoe, the brogue (which she has paired with—I *swear*—pompom socks). I am in a white top and skintight grey leather trousers. I have had the latter for years. The former, a recent purchase. Originally on Net-A-Porter at five hundred quid, there was no way I could justify buying it. I didn't even try. The first sale price of £299 prompted me to make a pros-and-cons list, but the biggest con on my list (both figuratively and literally) was the first round of fees from my solicitor. Finally, the top dipped below two hundred pounds and I pounced. Or rather PayPal-ed. Was it still *wrong* to spend that much on deconstructed cotton viscose mix with raw edges? No. Two words: Alexander Wang. *Right?*

Anyway, Noelle and I are sitting opposite each other on an elevated podium surrounded by white lilies and expensive candles in front of a carefully collated audience of fashion insiders, hipster celebrities and the cooler journalists from the broadsheets and Sunday supplements. Slick waiting staff have been on hand since the doors opened, offering the guests trays of elderflower blinis and mauve macaroons (the canapé equivalent of a pompom sock) to match the pastel-purple cover of Noelle's book. The blinis were disgusting. They tasted like…*hedging*, so I had a couple of vodkas (on the rocks with a splash of grapefruit juice). Also in attendance are some of Noelle's fans, who have won their invitations by entering a competition on her app. They are properly young. The sort of age where they would have no appreciation of Galliano's fifteen years for Dior. Only a vague memory of a fifteen-second BBC3 news story on his sacking. I wonder if they have ever bought a copy of *Catwalk*. I wonder if they have ever bought a magazine.

Thus far, my interview with Noelle has covered 'that' rela-

tionship split (*'I learnt so much, honey...'*) and the possibility
she will be launching an eponymous perfume (*'something
dynamic yet delicate, yeah...'*). Then we touched on how
she felt when she hit two million followers on Instagram
(*'hashtag humbled...'*). Now we're on 'fame'.

'Fame, honey? I guess it means something very different
to me, now I am like, *famous*. Before I thought it meant,
well...' She ponders her answer for a few seconds. '...free
stuff! I'm kidding. Well, joking aside...it does. But you do
have to pay in other ways. The lack of privacy...' Her voice
becomes serious. '...is a *major* cost.'

'I can only imagine.'

'Exactly. You're lucky. You can only *imagine* the cost.
I have to pay and keep pay*ing*,' she sighs. 'Do you mind?'
She grabs her Hello Kitty-customised mobile from the coffee
table in between us and waves it at me.

'Be my guest.'

She raises the mobile at arm's length to her face, pouts
at it, then taps.

'Then,' she continues, 'you also pay the price of like,
responsibility. Knowing my fans look *up* to me...' She looks
over and then *down* at them. '...see me as a role model, on
like a very basic level, *want to be me*; it's important I don't
short-change them. They mean so damn much to me. Every
'Like' I get on, like, social media is, like, reassurance that
I'm, like, doing okay. I'm like, *liked*!'

Giddy, grateful whoops are offered from the 'civilian
pen'. I gaze round the room. My hands are clammy. Not
from nerves. I've done this type of public promo many times
before. I used to relish putting Ashley Jacobs on display. But
today, I'm not sure who people are seeing. Her or *me*? No...
her, definitely her. I tell myself I am clamming up because

we are having an Indian Summer. It's the beginning of September but very mild. Last night at the pub, I was wearing Havaiana flipflops. The original white-and-green ones with the Brazilian flag motif, *obviously*—I wouldn't wear any other colour. I'm like that with Converse, too: I only wear the classic model; not the zipped ones or the rubber ones or the skate ones or the low pump ones or, heaven forbid, the wedge ones. There should be a ban on all major brands and designers adding wedges to leisure or sport footwear. The ONLY exception being Isabel Marant's wedge trainer, which is a classic in its...

I realise Noelle has stopped talking.

'So, Noelle...'

She leans forward. 'Yes?'

'You're erm...now based in the States...that must be...so much going on for you...is it hard to stay grounded?' This is the sort of question Catherine wanted, wasn't it? 'To not change...to be true to yourself?'

'You would have thought that, but no, honeeeeey. Actually, you know what? If—and it's an if I hope *never* happens—I started to become full of myself, I would soon get told off...' She sits forward and gives me a weird smile. '...by my parents. They sacrificed so much to get me where I wanted to be in my career. We never went on holidays abroad and stuff like that so I could go to stage school...even though they hated celebrity razzmatazz. It was because *I* wanted it. They're really private people. That's why I took my nana's maiden name—to keep t'ingz on the DL. Whenever I see them now, it reminds me how lucky I am. Their support, their love...it's unconditional. I owe them everything...' She smiles again. 'But I guess we *all* owe our parents that.'

I realise why her smile suddenly feels weird. It's genuine.
It makes me uncomfortable.

I let her blather on. *Yadadadadadadadadadadadadadada*.
I take a sip of my drink and swallow hard. I do not listen
to what she is saying, only how she is saying it. This is the
longest she has spoken without using that ridiculous accent
which travels to Hollywood via a Hackney council estate
(apparently, she is from a chocolate-box village in the West
Country). I look over at Fitz, the Senior Features Writer on
Catwalk, wearing his favourite Friesian-printed sweatshirt
by Moschino, embossed with the words: CASH COW. (He
dies for a fashionably ironic logo.) He is checking his phone,
so I would bet north of a thousand quid he is on Grindr. Or
Hornet. Or Scruff. Next to him is Noelle's agent. She is
wearing a Foo Fighters tour T-shirt and a flat tweed cap. Band
merchandise with 'country manor' millinery? Ugh. *Please*.
Her name is Sophie Carnegie-Hunt, but Fitz calls her Gopher
Hag-Needy-C*nt. Hahahahaha!

Am I laughing out loud?

'Ha! *No*. No, we don't. Not at *all*.'

Noelle peers at me. 'What don't we do?'

'Pardon? I didn't say…anyth—…I…' DID I? The room is
suddenly so quiet I can hear my watch ticking. It's vintage. I
reckon seventies. It has no designer name on it. The face is
huge. Big faces are so *in* now though, aren't they? I mean,
look at Gigi Hadid's. She's made a fortune out of hers.

Okay, THAT was funny.

'Wasn't it?'

'Wasn't what?' asks Noelle.

'What you were saying.'

'I wasn't.'

'No, you weren't. But what *I* was about to say was…'

I realise I am not in control. And this feels odd because I am Ashley Jacobs. She is not so much a control freak... more of a control *drone*, remotely operating herself to enter, attack and win over all areas of life always with great success. Being like that has enabled her to get everything she has ever wanted, *by herself*. The job she wanted. The flat she wanted. The clothes she wanted. The cat she wanted. The husband she wanted.

Whatever she wants to do, she gets on with it and does it. She does not churn it over in her mind. There is no cogitation. No procrastination. No deliberation.

Shit.

'Like, *so*?' Noelle rolls her eyes at her agent.

'So...' I swallow again. 'Your book! THE BOOK! Yes, that book. Tell me...*Why?*'

She smooths down her fringe. 'Mmm...well, gaaaaad. Obvz, it was because I *had* to. I wanted to take some control back. Some*one* some*where* writes some*thing* about me *every* minute of *every* day. There is no way I can see all of it, even with Google alerts. I mean, I'd be spending all day reading *about* me, and not *being* me. No one should suffer that kind of life. So, I thought, you know what, *I* will give *you* and *them*...*me*.' She beams earnestly at those closest to the podium. 'Hence the title, *This Is Me*. And it is *all* of me too. I don't hold back. You probably think that's like, crazy. *Surely*, I would want to keep at least part of 'me' to myself? It's not like I have much left to give, but it wouldn't have been me, then. The *real* me...'

As she talks, I focus hard on her mouth moving, so I don't roll my eyes too. Because all I can hear is bullshit. I know that if everyone else in the room was listening *individually* to what she is spouting that is what they would be hearing too. A gushing fountain of brown (which will NEVER be the new black! EVER!) bullshit. But we're in the bubble, aren't we? No one has any perspective. Not her. Not us. Not the kids in the pen. Even though we *all* know that Noelle is *not* the Noelle in *This Is Me*. In my meeting earlier, I wasn't me either. I was pretending to be someone else.

'Surely?' prompts Noelle. I'm not sure how many times she has said this.

'Oh, yes. Surely, Noelle. *Surely.*'

'...but it's what my fans deserve. That's what I have given them.' She waves a hand towards the pen. 'It's my gift to you.'

The competition winners screech in adoration. I hear extra appreciative 'yo yo yo!'s added by Jazz. She works at *Catwalk* too. Her title is Contributing Associate Editor. Although, since Catherine employed her, I would sum up her contribution thus far as simply, *irritating.* Her writing is whimsical and she has a habit of bringing trays of overpriced, overdecorated cupcakes into the office. What's wrong with a packet of biscuits? I spot her standing—no surprise—next to Catherine, who is doing her trademark breezy nodding gesture. It's the same one she uses when telling me she's leaving the office early (again) because there's an issue with one of her three children that 'simply can't be dealt with over the phone'. I decide I do *not* like her silk shirt. Polka dots are verging on *twee* territory. You need to wear them with something tough and she's opted for a skater skirt.

'But by writing about yourself, Noelle,' I comment, 'you're only encouraging *more* to be written about you. The less you put out there, the less will be commented on.'

Immediately, Fitz looks up from his phone.

Noelle gives me a pinched smile. 'True, I *suppose*. But ultimately, I want to be heard. *This Is Me* is about who I was, and how and why I have become the me I am today. It is my story.'

'And it is a *story*, isn't it?'

'What do you mean, honey?'

Now Fitz is sucking in his cheeks. He knows where I could be about to take this interview, if I had the balls to prick the bubble. It's where any proper journalist would. No, *should*. A discussion about Noelle's notoriety has to include—if not revolve around—one subject. Her weight. Because *that* is the only reason Noelle has become so well known. As her BMI has plummeted, she has rocketed to *cover* star. Yeah, she's cultivated one of those hipster careers: *the model-come-DJ-come-It girl-come-presenter-come-entrepreneur-oh, come off it!*, but she is not globally recognised for a single one of those jobs. She is famous because her inner thighs have not met since 2013. Type her name into a search engine and the first most popular associated word which pops up is: THINSPIRATION. Given the world she lives—no, *subsists*—in, it's obvious *how* she manages to 'skip the odd meal'.

I take a deep breath. Fitz mouths 'YOU SHREW!' at me and makes a sort of strangled face as if I am about to do something really stupid. And I am, aren't I? I am about to prick the bubble.

'What I mean, Noelle,' I begin, 'is that your book is not *all* fact, is it? The person in the book can't be who you *actually* are.' I flip open the copy I have on my lap at a Post-it note I slapped in it last night. I was in the wine bar round the corner from the office. (Before I went to the pub.) '"*So, when me and my mates have had a, like, big night out in NY, yeah, and are really feeling it the next day, we cab it to any of the wikkid authentic Jewish hang-outs and pig out, stuffing ourselves to the max. My fave is Ben's*

Kosher Deli. Boom! Check this bad boy."' Next to this bit of copy (in a wacky speech bubble) is a picture of a towering sandwich made with thick white bread, filled with cold cuts and oozing with relishes. I show everyone in the room. Then Noelle. 'Seriously, can you *honestly* tell me you've eaten that?'

'Of course, I have. I erm…*love* ham.'

I don't skip a beat. 'It's a strict orthodox restaurant, they don't serve swine. So much for *pig*ging out.'

She fiddles with her Peter Pan collar. 'But I, erm…'

'…have been a little liberal with the truth?' I feel dizzy but focused. Unpredictable but in control. Deep despite the shallow content of what I'm saying. So, *this* is what it's like to prick the bubble! 'There's also a quote from you saying that *all* women are beautiful, no matter what shape or size.'

'I *do* think that! I've just been *hashtag* blessed with a fast meta-meta-metabolicity.'

'Metabolism? So that video which went viral of you having your fringe trimmed whilst giggling that your ex-boyfriend's new—no more than a Size Ten—girlfriend, "*probably has to take her selfies by satellite…*" was a one-off lapse of judgement?'

A sharp and collective gasp emanates from the room. Noelle looks up at me, her usually pallid cheeks now flushing. I watch the colour lift…then my eyes dart from one fashion insider to another. Everyone knows what I have done. They grip onto their champagne flutes and stare at me, their eyes googly with shock as if they can see the metaphorical pin in my hands. But I don't acknowledge them or Noelle for more than a few seconds. Or the fact I have pricked the bubble. I am thinking about the meeting I had earlier. The reason why I needed that first drink. And then the others. It was with a woman I only met eight weeks ago, although I had her number for a month before that. Now she contacts me almost every day.

ME: So, how are you?

HER: Fine. I thought we would go through that paperwork I posted you, first. As thus far, I haven't heard back.

ME: The postal service round my way is a nightmare.

HER: I also emailed it to you. As an attachment. Twice. You've already told me about your postman.

ME: Did I? Ah. He's a good guy. But bad at delivering letters.

HER: (Leaning forward.) Ashley, I am concerned that we are behind with things. Look, I'm telling you this because— and please, excuse the hackneyed expression—but time is money. My time is your money. I was thinking, maybe it would be useful—and cheaper—if we all sat down together and went through everything. It's often the best way to get things finalised. You say what you want. He s—

ME: No. There's no need for us to do that.

HER: But it will get you there quicker. (Pausing. Giving me a look. It's Look Two.) Ashley, has anything happened outside of this situation? You're distracted.

ME: Mmm…I agree.

But actually, I am recalling the high-necked low-sweeping black Gothic ballgowns worn by the Olsen twins at the Met Ball a while back. Vintage Dior by John Galliano. Fuck-*ing*-hell. What a moment. Add their trademark louche grooming and the gowns took on another, more modern but equally theatrical story. Couture for the people. *So* different to their own label—The Row—which is…pared down, almost *anonymous* luxury. Too Park Avenue for me.

HER: Ashley? You agree you're distracted?

ME: Sorry?

HER: I said, has anything happened? Outside of this situation?

ME: (Pausing.) Nothing.

HER: Nothing?

ME: Nothing which can't be dealt with. But I don't need to deal with it right now. That's the thing with real shit, it's always there. It isn't going anywhere, is it?

HER: But you want to get there quicker?

ME: Where?

HER: The end.

I hear my watch ticking again. Fitz has his phone clasped to his face, trying not to laugh. Noelle's agent is heading towards the stage. I catch Catherine's eye. She draws her index finger sharply across her neck. I no longer feel any sort of buzz; merely an intense sense of fucking up. And drunk. I turn back to Noelle. Suddenly, she screeches.

'Oh, my gaaaaaaaaad! Guys, know this, yeah. Without the genius over there…' She points at the door. '…the 'Noelle' tote would totes not exist.' The assembled guests gasp again, as if this thought was too ghastly to contemplate in this soft candlelit light of the afternoon. 'Saaaaafe, crewdem!'

I twist round to see Frédéric Lazare, the boss of RIVA, arriving. RIVA own Pascale as well as numerous other clothing, cosmetics, fragrance, accessory and footwear brands. As befits a fashion conglomerate big wig (*literally*—Fitz *swears* that's a hairpiece on his head), he is flanked by two security guards dressed in (last season) suits from one of his labels. Frédéric waves a heavily ringed hand at Noelle, then an obscenely handsome long-haired Latino—presumably a model from a current campaign—appears from behind the heavies and steps forward with a huge bouquet of purple flowers. The room breaks into applause. I lean across to Noelle. I *could* be about to apologise—could I?—but then Sophie Carnegie-Hunt arrives at the stage, flapping her cap at me.

'Wrap this up, *now*!' she snaps.

Gopher Hag-Needy-C*nt. Hahahahaha!

I ask Noelle if she would like to leave her fans with something.

'Yes, I would *like*, like that…' she says, her voice still quivery. 'I guess I want to say thank you.' She doesn't look in their direction. 'You're like the bomb diggity and have made this whole ride, like, a *trip*. This book is for you…' Now she turns to them. '…and is available from midnight at all the usual online retailers and my website—obvz! Oh, and in booky-type-shop thingies from tomozz. Nuff said! So remember *hashtag* ThisIsMe, yeah? Let's get this mo fo trending!'

And on that subtle marketing plea, the audience shower Noelle with further applause, and purple confetti is released from the ceiling, which I guess is appropriate given we have just witnessed the perfect marriage between meaningless bullshit and PR nonsense. But as the lavender-scented hearts rain down on us, I know that I am the one coming out of this stinking. Noelle doesn't look at me again. She steps down from the stage and lurches into Sophie's arms, as if she has just been released from a long-term hostage situation. I jump down too, but before I can go anywhere, Catherine approaches and grabs my wrist. She marches me to the back of the room.

'What the *hell* was all that about?' she whisper/snaps at me. 'You're going to get *slaugh*tered on social media. My god, Ashley, teenage girls are like terrorist cells. Brainwashed, angry and ready to blow things up! Don't you remember being one?'

I'd rather not. I focus more on the typical clunkiness of Catherine's extended metaphor.

'And as for the damage to our relationship with Noelle! I am stunned…I hope you're sorry.'

I nod. I *am* stunned at my behaviour and, yes, I was almost sorry a few minutes ago too. But similarly to how I was feeling at the end of my meeting earlier, I am now indignant.

'Well, Catherine,' I retort, 'I guess I was *also* stunned *and* sorry that you asked an illiterate personality vacuum whose Twitter feed proves daily that the rule about whether to use 'your' or 'you're' is entirely dependent on how many characters she has left, to guest edit *our* magazine to champion *her* book…i.e., next month someone who can't write will be overseeing what we are writing about what she didn't write. We used to have a distinct editorial voice *of our own*. We didn't need anyone else's.'

Catherine sighs. I am sure there is a part of her—that part which belonged to the forward-thinking editor she used to be—which agrees. She shrugs, then steps closer to me.

'Have you been boozing?'

I almost smile, because her rhetorical tone indicates that she doesn't think I have. She would consider me someone who could 'take it or leave it'. If you really think someone has a problem with alcohol, you never ask this question wanting a legitimate answer. It is pointless. All you can do is listen at school when taught First Aid instruction on how to put a patient into the recovery position. And act appropriately when necessary.

'*Ashley?*'

'Of course I haven't been drinking. Look, I'm sorry,

Catherine. I didn't mean to put the magazine in a difficult position. I'm merely concerned about the direction we are taking it.' *Or is it me?* Is it the direction I am moving in that is of concern? Maybe everyone and everything else is *FINE*. I feel clammy again. 'Anyway, you know I would never purposefully embarrass you or *Catwalk*.'

'It worries me that you failed to see the importance of today. We are lucky Noelle chose *us* to promote her book. We could have lost out to the mainstream market leaders: *Elle*, *Vogue*, *Grazia*, *Stylist*, *Instyle*…look!' She gestures over to the stage. 'Everyone wants a piece of her.'

We watch as Sophie manoeuvres her client through the journalists to answer their questions, subtly making sure the big-name hacks get priority. On the outskirts of the throng are the 'second round invite' guests, i.e., writers from the 'lesser' publications; the tattier tabloids and London freebie papers. As Noelle chats animatedly to the style writer from the *Guardian*, I see a woman at the edge of the pack wave at her. She has her back to me, but I can make out Sophie looking the woman up and down, pursing her lips, then elevating her clipboard and turning to cut off any potential contact. I wince. That has got to hurt.

'You see?' says Catherine. 'Noelle is "it".' She leans in closer to me. Admittedly, "it" doesn't have a specific talent, but you and I both know the days where that was a pre-requisite for media coverage are long gone. To pretend otherwise is foolish. Even more foolish is to not use this to our monetary advantage.'

'Sell out, you mean?'

'Keep your voice down.'

'You know I'm right.'

She sighs another semi-reflective sigh. 'This conversation stops right here, Ashley. You should leave before you say something *else* you regret. I wouldn't want you to talk yourself into dismissal territory.'

I nod as if I am taking her seriously, but Catherine won't sack me. I am the backbone/life blood—insert essential body part or function here—of the magazine. My column is always the most-read page when we do a focus group, she wouldn't dare drop it. Besides all that, if I wasn't around it would present Catherine with the worst possible scenario at work: *she would have to do some.*

As if reading my mind, she continues. 'It would do you good to remember that you're the Deputy Editor of the magazine. You're not *the* magazine. You're part of a team and your main role within that is to support me. Something that I will need a lot more of in coming months.'

She cocks her head at me. Another of her trademark mannerisms in recent years. She usually reserves this one when informing me she is off on a non-essential PR jaunt. She never used to do that, but these days her buzzwords are: invitation, complimentary, gift, expenses and freebie. Preferably all in relation to the Maldives.

'You're off somewhere?'

The angle between Catherine's shoulder and neck decreases. I picture the hut on stilts with aquatic views from a window in the bedroom floor. I hear a woman behind me order a glass of red wine.

'Intermittently, yes. And then next year, well, for a little longer. I'm pregnant…'

The sound of a cork popping. Then liquid pouring.

'…due mid-Feb, but I'll be booking in for a Caesarean at the Portland on the eleventh; sadly, the anniversary of

Alexander McQueen's tragic passing. But a rather lovely tribute, I thought?'

'Maybe a little McCabre.'

Catherine playfully wallops me on the shoulder. 'Stop it, I'm still furious with you. But yes, four kidlets! Ridiculously greedy, but Rhuaridh and I always planned on having a large family. He's an only child and you should see the pile his old dear rattles around in. There's an awful lot of—excuse the pun—reproduction furniture that will need to be divided up eventually. As you know from last time, and the time before, and the one before that, I don't enjoy the easiest of times in the early to mid-section of my pregnancies.'

I hear the woman thank the barman for her drink. I never used to drink red. Where I grew up it was considered poncy. But recently, I've been drinking it at home after work. I get into my (secret) Snuggle Suit and pour a glass. Then another. Staying in is safer.

'Ashley?'

'I am listening. Erm…congratulations. *Congratulations*. Sorry, I should have said that first.'

'Thank you. But, anyway…' Her voice is serious again. 'The reason I wanted to tell you about my pregnancy is that if you would like to take a holiday, sooner would be better than later.'

'I can't take any time out soon. London Fashion Week is in a few days.'

'You won't be attending LFW.'

'Excuse me?' I physically recoil. '*Are you having a laugh?*'

'Calm down. Come into the office as usual tomorrow, attend the features meeting, but then…home. And stay there. Your entry pass will be disabled. I'll deal with any other details and email you what I need done.'

I grip onto the bar. 'Whaaaaat? But you…I mean, I can't not…for Christ's sake, Catherine…' As soon as she has finished with me, I'm going to order a glass of red. 'Are you insane?'

'No, I am not, and don't for one minute assume that I am setting these measures in place because I think you're heading that way. You're a mentally robust woman, Ashley, but…' She pauses again. 'I think you could do with a little me-time. I've been concerned for a few weeks, but have kept this opinion on the down low because I didn't want to, well… add to any of your problems. Today's incident has established that I should step in and say something.'

'To confirm, then, you're not asking me to take a holiday…' Maybe I'll leave now, buy a bottle of Merlot on the way home. 'You're suspending me.'

'Not officially. But I am insisting on you having a short break…a few days, that's it.'

'What for? To come to terms with pricking the bubble?'

She peers at me, confused. 'No, whatever that is. To come to terms with your *divorce*.'

That's when my Alexander Wang gets it.

Two

TANYA

I stare at the red stain spreading like a bullet wound across the white top. Simultaneously, I can feel my usual purple heat rash creeping across my chest. It's my body's default reaction to a—okay, most—situations where I could potentially become involved. *In a situation.* I never look for a 'situation'. Heaven forbid, set one up. If I find myself in a situation, I usually attempt to vacate it as promptly as possible. Gripping onto the empty wine glass, I don't dare look at the woman's face. I know that pain and shock will be etched across it as if she has actually been shot. After all, this is a fashion party, and that won't *just* be a top.

I glance to the side. A man charges towards me, stuffing a macaroon into his mouth. He grabs a pile of napkins and waves at the barman.

'Water! Barman! Quick. We need help…!' he shouts, spraying purple crumbs. 'We need white wine!'

'Leave it,' I instruct. 'Use a rub of Vanish later.' I almost laugh at how pedestrian the words 'rub of Vanish' sound in this environment. 'For the moment, rinse it through…as quickly as possible.' Then I find myself adding—*clearly, to expose myself as living a life of comparative suburban*

Ollie Quain

mediocrity where dealing with the removal of marks on fabric is part of my daily drudgery even though it isn't and I would OBVIOUSLY take it to a reputable dry cleaner…—'Time really is of the essence with stains.'

On the 'st' of stains, my 'victim' shuns the barman's soda gun and the handful of serviettes her friend is flapping at her. She growls at him to buy her a T-shirt from American Apparel: 'Men's. Extra small, deep V-neck, not round or a scoop', then spins round and strides in the direction of the toilets. I follow her. Which might not make sense, as oversee-ing the removal of a potentially ruinous stain on someone else's designer top through to the end is a textbook 'situation'. But another thing about me is that if I do get myself into a 'situation', I don't like to come out the other side thinking I could have done anything differently. Guilt is not something I like to feel, *on any level*. It's the combine harvester of human emotions. It breaks you down, churns you up, spits you out, but then spreads…and grows. *Faster.*

Inside the loo, the woman wriggles out of her top with no concern whatsoever about anyone else hanging around by the sinks touching up their make-up or doing their hair. I'm not surprised by her lack of inhibition. She has exactly the type of body you would expect from a fashionista. A deep-caramel pigment to her skin—the result of a blood line, not a spray booth—and a tiny, hard body. She probably picks at processed snacks and smokes cigarettes but is also a gym rat. And combines that with Bikram yoga, some sort of combat training, Cross-Fit, weights and Barry's Bootcamp…girls like her don't get the results they demand from doing one form of exercise any more, do they? They 'mix it up' so that all parts of their bodies are toned, honed, shrunk then stretched in order to achieve that perfect combination of muscular fragility. Then they are prepared for any sort of trend as soon as it arrives *on the* catwalk, or more specifically in…

…*Catwalk*.

Oh, my God. I grip onto the sink. Frozen, I watch as the woman's head frees itself from the neckhole. A dark mop of glossy ethnic hair springs out first, then the delicate, fragile features which are at total odds to the personality I know lies within.

It's *her*.

Her eyes are closed. When they open, she immediately focuses on the soap dispenser. She pumps some liquid onto the top.

'I'm fine, you can go…' she says, turning on the faucet.

I don't move. I cannot say anything. Not even her name. Or mine. My purple heat rash is burning my chest.

Her mobile phone bleeps. She grabs it from her bag, checks the caller ID, adjusts it to speaker setting and goes back to holding the exact area of fabric directly underneath the gushing tap.

'Yeah?' she barks at her phone.

'*Hey…*' A man's voice. He clears his throat.

'I said 'yeah' …I'm here.'

At the sink next to her, another party guest finishes washing her hands, wrings them and turns on the dryer.

'…you'll have to shout. It's noisy in here.'

'*I need to talk to you.*'

'About what?'

'*Maybe we could meet.*' The man continues. '*No. We, erm, ought to meet. Now…*'

'I'm at a work thing,' she replies.

'*It's important. The, erm, report…you know…look, I'm at*

our…well, your…the flat. Can you get back here soon? We should go through it…'

'Now? You think I won't read it? Christ. Relax. I *will…'*

'Seriously…we have to speak.'

She tuts, grabs her phone, turns off the speaker setting and puts it to her ear. With the other hand, she pulls her top away from the tap to check it. Just a cloudy mark remains. The dryer comes to the end of its cycle and the other guest leaves the room. She is quiet for a few seconds, then she calmly switches off her phone, squeezes out the remaining moisture from her T-shirt, puts it back on and stares ahead in the mirror at herself. Finally, she turns. Her eyes flicker up towards mine.

She sees me…flinches and gasps; but it is only a short, sharp inhalation—then her face becomes emotionless. The last time she looked at me like this, we were in the reception of the building where *Catwalk* is based.

It was a few weeks after I had finished my degree. I was about to start an internship at my favourite magazine. I'd bought *every* copy ever published. I was addicted to it from the first issue. I'll never forget the launch copy. My best friend showed me it. The lead fashion shoot—set in a dilapidated mansion—was a glossy homage to what eventually became known in the tabloids as 'heroin chic'. The models—dressed in flimsy, sheer, de-constructed fabrics—were draped across broken beds and chairs or lying on the cracked marble floor, as if they were abandoned garments themselves. But the ten-year-old me didn't look at the pictures and think, 'Yikes, they've had a heavy weekend on the skag…'. I didn't even know what narcotics were, other than that they could possibly be disguised as fruit pastilles, as my father constantly told me: 'NEVER ACCEPT ANY SWEETS FROM HER (my best friend's) FAMILY—THEY COULD BE DRUGS!'

We—my best friend and I—stared at the shoot. She fell in love with the clothes; how everything looked on the surface. I loved what was going on beneath; the way each model was captured by the camera. Each one had a story to tell. But it was a secret.

The receptionist at the front desk puts a call through to the magazine.

'Good morning, your new intern is waiting in reception. Shall I ask her to wait for you down here?' He smiles at me from behind his sponge mouthpiece. 'The Editorial Assistant will be right down.'

'Ah, okay…' I feel my purple heat rash spring across my chest. My dream job. This was *actually* happening. After everything that had happened. *Life* was about to happen.

'Don't look so worried,' says the receptionist, mistaking my excitement for nerves. 'She's new too.'

But she wasn't new to me. As the lift doors opened, I saw her before she saw me. Unquestionably pretty, petite—almost imp-like—and dressed casually but coolly in ripped skinny jeans, a grey T-shirt and Nike Air Max. Her hair was in a mussed-up high pony tail. I had ironed mine into a poker-straight bob. Typically for her, she looked at my shoes first. She stared at my 'office smart' kitten heels as if I had dragged in a rotting animal—no, *human*—carcass. I used this time to gather myself. It was only a few seconds…it was not enough. But an hour would not have been enough. Nor a day. Nor another year. And it had already been five. She gave me her trademark impenetrable stare. Her face was emotionless.

RECEPTIONIST: Ah, you two know each other? Well, that's nice, isn't it?

But it was not nice. Not for me, Tanya Dinsdale. Or her, Ashley Atwal.

Trance-like, she nodded at me to approach the lift. I walked over and got in. The doors shut but she did not press any buttons. I stood by her side. Should I say something? Should I say nothing? No. Yes. I should say…

ME: I don't know what to s—

HER: (Interrupting. Voice flat.) Have you seen The Devil Wears Prada?

ME: (Confused.) Erm…yeah, of c—

HER: (Interrupting again.) You know that montage? Which loops together the makeover scenes? It starts with the Style Director taking Andrea—the awkward, shy intern—into the fashion cupboard and lending her a poncho? Then she borrows more and more clothes, and as she does she grows and flourishes into a confident, well-rounded member of staff who fits right in? Well, this scene and the rest of the movie—is a pile of crap. It is about as far removed from the reality of life doing work experience on a fashion magazine as you can get…and even further from the reality of what your life will be like at Catwalk. *There will be no development of your personal storyline, no actual job to be retained or offered at the end…and you can bet every penny you have—I hear that's a fair bit these days—that at no point will you be taken into the fashion cupboard by a kindly gay male member of staff to help get your look on point using all the latest designer clothes.*

Firstly, you will already be in the fashion cupboard—and trust me, 'cupboard' makes it sound far more glamorous than it actually is; it makes the communal changing cubicle in an out-of-town discount-designer outlet resemble Coco Chanel's Parisian apartment. It has no windows. The iron and industrial steamer are on permanently. Your pores will open up like craters.

Secondly, we do not have any 'kindly' gay male members of staff. All three who work here are caustic. But that said, nowhere near as brutal as the straight women. And as for being tasked with anything to do with the Editor; in respect to her life on the magazine or private world, forget it. You won't even meet her. In fact, you won't get as far as that end of the office because you will spend seventy-five per cent of your time in the aforementioned leper's cave of a fashion cupboard, another ten per cent by the photocopier and the other fifteen per cent tramping round Central London, running personal errands for senior staff. This could be anything from picking up dry cleaning to buying cashew nuts. And if you do, for fuck's sake don't buy salted, honeyed or roasted. Plain. Always plain. They won't touch a modified nut. It also goes without saying that if you consider Anne Hathaway's kooky fish-out-of-water shtick as endearing...then I suggest you don't simply keep that opinion quiet, you keep it locked and hidden in a dark vault in the recesses of your mind, never to be unlocked. Remember all of the above and you should be able to last the twenty days you have been pencilled in for. It is essential to note the word 'pencilled', as you are only here as it suits us. There is no contract. No cosy back-up from HR. No pay. You are here or not here because we do or do not want you to be. By 'we' I mean 'I'.

She gave me that flickering sideways glance. Because to look at me directly would be giving me too much when she felt I deserved nothing.

ME: You.

HER: Yes. Me. Are you in? Or out?

She raised her finger and hovered it over the button for

the fourth floor. Out. I was out. Our relationship was about to be over for a second time. I left the lift and vacated the building. I did not turn round.

This time, it is her who doesn't turn. I watch the door swing shut as she leaves, then face myself in the mirror. I am wearing a shirt under a jacket with trousers and boots. All Reiss. Not too edgy. Not too conservative. Not too high street. Not too expensive. But not too cheap either. Solid middle-ground shopping choice. Everything in black. A quick glance in my wardrobe and it could be assumed I was a funeral director or a mime artist. Black is the perfect colour for being present but not drawing attention to yourself. You can be *there*, but not 'HERE!'. Unless, that is, you were invited to one of those toe-curling-ly *cringe* Z-list celebrity weddings on a foreign beach, where all the guests are asked to wear white (*and* go barefoot).

I breathe in very slowly. Then exhale. And continue to stare. This is me *now*. Not the me she knew. I am finished with both of them.

'Hon-*eeeeey*!'

The only reason I am here flies through the door and gives me a perfunctory peck on the cheek.

'Noelle! How are you?'

'How am I? Duh! Not exactly happy. That *bitch*!'

'What bitch?'

'The bitch who interviewed me. Ashley some-one-or-other.'

I realise Noelle has not recognised her. Not surprising. She was a small kid when everything happened. A concerted effort was made to 'keep her out of it'.

'Sorry, I got here late. Was at the hospit—'

'You missed the whole thing?'

'Not on purpose. What's the matter?'

'I got trashed out there,' continues Noelle. 'I've never been so embarrassed in my, like, *life*. If Frédéric hadn't arrived… well, quelle doomage! Anyway, why didn't you come and find me?'

'I attempted to. But was prevented from doing so by a lady holding a clipboard and wearing an *I'm-so-special-I could-eat-myself* hat.'

'Oh, you mean Sophs. She was only making sure I saw all the right people first. No, like, offence. There were a *lot* of serious national journalists out there. Internationally, if you include Internet hits. I mean, the Web has become even more important than print these days, yeah.' She adds this as if she was revealing a prize nugget of information gleaned from years studying the development of digital media.

I don't engage. 'You're okay then?'

'I'll pull through, I think. I *have* to. I've got to hang with Frédéric, sign some like, shit—I mean *books*—ha! for my fans…then go to another party.'

'I meant, *generally*, are you okay? I keep getting missed calls from you at weird times of the night.'

She shrugs. 'Soz. Only tryin' to catch up and t'ingz. Time-zone issues. But, yeah, I'm more than okay. Honeeeeey, believe…this bitch is *fly*.'

'Good, because I was…' I stop myself. There is no point voicing concern. 'We can still do a picture?'

'Yeah, I'll get Sophs to arrange it.'

'What's there to arrange? All you have to do is stand in front of the display of your books by the podium.'

Noelle scrunches up her face. The bones underneath don't so much jut as *project*.

'Thing is,' she says, 'Sophs, is a bit funny about who snaps me these days.'

'Noelle, *you* snap yourself every day on a Hello Kitty phone. You're not Nick Knight.'

'Don't get on my grill. That's different. Insta, innit! Let me see what I can do. It is, like, *you*, after all. Wait there. I need a pee.'

She disappears into the toilet. I see the tips of her shiny patent brogues poking towards the gap beneath the cubicle door. Then she flushes and turns round. Now I can see the backs of her shoes and pompom-socked ankles. I know what she is doing. Sure enough, I hear the sound of a card being tapped quickly and violently on the cistern, followed by a long drawn-out gutteral snort, which she attempts to drown out by flushing the loo again. But frankly, she could have carried out that little routine by the Niagara Falls and still be heard. Also as expected, I gag.

Even after I had grown up enough to realise that my father had *not* been joking and that Class A and B drugs did in fact look like *many* sweets (Sherbet Dip Dab, Toblerone, Love Hearts etc,) but *not* fruit pastilles, I avoided them. Therapy had given me mental stability. Well, more of a plateau of not feeling anything, which suited me fine. I did not want to see where a pill or powder could 'take me'. I did not want to *go* anywhere.

At college, people would question my lack of adventure and tell me I didn't know what I was missing out on. But Dr Google gave me a pretty good idea: '*A brief, intense high and rush of confidence that is immediately followed by depressive thoughts, anxiety, a craving for more of the chemical, heart palpitations, insomnia, hyper-stimulation and paranoia…*' And all that was only in the *short* term! Oh, and it gave you terrible diarrhoea; I witnessed both verbal and gastric. The latter of which I think Noelle is now experiencing because she is flushing the loo again. Either that or she is doing another line. I gag again.

'Noo-Noo! Nooooooooooo-Noooooooooooo!'

A clipboard appears in the doorway, followed by the peak of a tweed cap and the enticingly punchable face of Noelle's agent.

'She's in there.' I point at the correct cubicle. 'Testing out the efficiency of the plumbing.'

Sophie walks in and knocks on it. 'Noo-Noo, we need to do one last circuit and then get you down to drinkalinks at the Serpentine. I want your arrival to be circa the same time as Paltrow or Palermo. And *Harry*. Styles not Windsor. We're okay-ish for the moment, Loopy's just radioed through…but we really should bloody chop chop.'

'I think she's already done that,' I mutter.

Sophie ignores me. Noelle unlocks the cubicle door and beams at us. Her eyes are glassy and wide. Her top lip sweaty. Her smile skewed. As on the last few occasions I have seen her like this, there is part of me that wants to take her aside and tell her exactly what I am seeing. But then the other part of me speaks up to remind me that Noelle isn't fussed by what I see. Only how she is *seen*…by people she doesn't even know.

She goes to the sink and starts washing her hands. 'Sophs, I've promised this honey…' She nods at me. '…I'll do a snap, yeah?'

Sophie crinkles her nose. 'Eh? We're not doing any pics today, Noo-Noo. It was part of the deal with *Catwalk*; they get the exclusive on *all* the party images to go up online overnight. I know nothing about any other requests.'

'It's for my own personal website,' I explain. 'I have a blog.'

'A fashion blog?'

'More of an on-going study about the relationship between women, image, marketing, reality, art and social media.'

The look on Sophie's face tells me I may as well have asked, '*WOULD YOU LIKE TO ROLL IN SOME FOX FAECES WITH ME?*'

'How nice,' she says. 'But not today. Maybe another time. Pending on your hit scores, we could tie it in with something for charity. I'm all about getting bad ass on bullies. And STDs, obviously.' She adds nonsensically and passes Noelle a make-up bag. 'Noo, blow your nose, get some slap on and meet me back by the bar.'

As Sophie departs, Noelle grimaces at me. Her pupils are even more dilated and blacker, like the liquorice swirls we used to love. She shakes the water from her hands.

'Don't get ants in your pants, honeeeeey,' she shouts. 'I'm as, like, gutted as you are. I, like, really mean that, yeah? But I guess, if I've learned anything from this situ it's that I'm now at a point in my career where the smaaaaa-llest request has to be, like, put through my agent? Bonkers, I know, but then everyone knows where they stand and I'm not disappointing anyone. Espesh peeps who I like, really care about, yeah? Because you know that's not who I am. I'm a people-pleaser not a, like, people-letter-downer. I mean, yeah, if the request gets like turned down, they'll still be disappointed, but Sophs will do the disappointing for me, you know? It means I don't have to carry that, like, burden.' She does a ducky-mouth pose in the mirror and captures the moment on her Hello Kitty mobile. 'But, hey, at least you got to come down and get a little taster of how cray cray life is for me right now, huh…I mean, that bitch out there was just jealous of my success, right? My fans still love me. Like I give a, like, fuck about the haters.' She shrugs off their imaginary hate. 'It's *always* women who are having a pop at me. Remember that show I did in the States…*Check Me Out, Sista!*? Feminist wackos basically said that by making over lonely teenage girls using fashion, make-up and haircuts inspired by the most popular celebs that we were like, not only taking away their individuality…but moreover underlining the homig-homug-…'

'Homogenisation?' I interject, only because I want to correct her.

'Yeah, the homogeni-wotist of, like, female youth erm… culture, yeah. That's it. I was like, "*Whatever, go laser your bikini line*…" It sucks! I *really* don't need those negative vibes.'

'Not when you've got a book to sell, eh?'

'I'd also *like* an MBE…at some, *like*, point.'

'I'm going to go home now, Noelle.'

'All that way? Bit of a trek, honey. Why don't you crash in my hotel? We could hang tomozz…I've got fittings for fashion week at Tory Hambeck—I'm doing 'da c-walk' for her—but that's, like, it. I would invite you to the Serps but it's totally invite only. I mean, I *could* ask Loops if she could get in contact with the peeps running t'ingz, see if she can track down a spare ticket, but I can only i-*mag*-ine the waiting list. It starts in an hour.'

'I imagine it would be easier to locate, purchase and install a new lung before then. Not to worry. I can't stay in London, anyway. I'm going to a gig…at The Croft.'

'That old pub by the station?'

'It's been revamped.'

'*Sweet!* Awww, I can't do gigs any more, they remind me of Troy too much. Coachella was like twisting a, like, Sam-Sam-Samo-…a big knife in my heart. Sometimes I wish Loops had screwed up my Access All Areas pass for Reading so I'd never met him. It probably would have been better…' She sniffs loudly with dual purpose; to halt her runny nose and demonstrate how upset she is at the memory. 'So your boyf is still singing? That's cute. God loves a try-er!'

'Yes, he is still singing…*because he is a singer.* I emailed you a link to his most recent demo. It's an acoustic set…' I cringe at those two words. It find it impossible to use music terminology without sounding pretentious. 'I thought that maybe you could help, with your connections…'

'Email it again, honeeeeey. Probably landed in my junk. I permanently have major storage issues.'

I can't help laughing. 'Sure you do. Bye, Noelle, it was great catching up. I'm glad I came all this way.'

'I'm glad you came too! Hey, you know what…? I think Sophs is right. I should do more charity work.'

'Well, you know where they say charity starts…'

'Who does? Where does it?'

Add *inability to detect sarcasm* to the paranoia in short-term effects of cocaine. I hug her goodbye and go out into the foyer. The room where Noelle had her launch is still buzzing. The guests will all be 'going on' somewhere soon. Either to that do at the Serpentine or some other bash for more customised cocktails and loosely themed finger food. On the steps of the hotel, I bump into the man who sprayed the macaroon crumbs. He is holding a bag from American Apparel.

'Excuse me,' he says. 'My name is Fitz Martin…I work at *Catwalk.*'

'Get you.'

He squints at me, confused at my reaction.

'My friend, the one who…with the Wang. Is she in there?' he asks, worriedly, as if he was arriving at hospital to witness her last rites. 'Can't believe that top was Wang. *Unworn* Wang.'

'I know. It was a shame. But…' I pause and look up and down the street on both sides, pretending to gauge the activity. '…thank goodness, the world is still turning.'

I lift my hand to hail a taxi. It's a confident departure… which is the only way to navigate clearly out of a *situation*. Not 'out there' or 'up for it' or 'in-your-face' confident, but 'quietly' confident—which is more believable. Anything more than that is obviously a front. I am fascinated by how much 'fake' confidence people—especially women—project these days, especially on social media. It's why I started my blog…to examine how women present themselves on the various portals. There is a *lot* of faking extreme confidence going on. You know that for every smug #nofilter #nomakeup 'selfie' posted, there are forty-seven rejected images—taken in umpteen different locations (ploughing on through successive breakdowns over choice of outfit) until the most flattering light is found—sitting on their camera roll. That for every '*Wooooooooooo!* PARTY TIME!' status update, there are double the amount of lonely nights in, spent reaching the depths of despair (and a carton of pecan-fudge ice cream) that never get flagged up. That for every sobering, wise and self-aware proverb 'meme' posted, there has been a spate of pissed, stupid behaviour that they live in fear of being reminded about.

But I understand. Truly, I do. Faking it is the only way to move forward. Pretend that everything is okay. The good news is that if you do this for long enough, you'll start to believe it. Whatever happened in your past will not affect you any more. I never thought I would get to that point. But I have. A base line of aggressive therapy helped but, after that, it was all me. I didn't quite realise how far past that point I was until about twenty minutes ago. But seeing her…how can I put it?

I loathe Disney animation. The heroines all have craniums bigger than their waists. It's the first registration point for any girl wanting to sign up for self-esteem issues later in life. But today I am going to paraphrase Queen Elsa: *I have let it fucking go.*

And I never swear. *She* did. Not Elsa. *Ashley*. She swore a lot. But today it feels right. No, good.

Three

Tanya Dinsdale. *Tanya Dinsdale. Tanya FUCKING Dinsdale.*
She was never meant to factor in my life. I took one look at
her and thought, 'Nah, no *way*'…even though I was actively
on the lookout for a new best friend. I had been forced to
ditch my last one because she'd developed a habit of stealing.
When her parents found a load of clothes from a selection of
mainstream mall brands under her bed, she stitched me up,
saying *I* had nicked the lot and had forced *her* to hide them.
I didn't know what was more offensive…the fact her parents
believed that I was a thief or that I would have thieved such a
bland and impact-less array of 'stretch jersey basics'. Within
seconds of meeting Tanya Dinsdale in the school canteen, I
could tell she was one of those girls who liked to act as if she
was born with a silver spoon in her mouth, even though the
cutlery in question was more likely to have been one of those
plastic forks which come free with a Pot Noodle. Even worse,
she was wearing Mary Jeans and culottes. No, worse, she was
wearing them *proudly*. I should have walked away then.

I let myself in the front door, ignoring the photo on the
sideboard, and walk into the lounge. Zach is layering a large
cardboard box with bubble wrap. He is wearing his gym gear.

I hadn't realised he was working out again. He jumps up to hug me, but we end up giving each other a nervous head lock. I add a handshakey-matey-back-slap, as if I am welcoming him onto my own chat show. As he pulls away, I sense him scanning my face.

'Sorry I had to drag you away from your work thing, Ash, but it's imp—'

'Yeah, so you said. Whatever. I wanted to leave, anyway. That magazine is doing my head in…and before you suggest I put my feelers out to see whether a decent position is coming up on another one, I would *know* if it was. No one wants to budge. The magazine side of the industry is getting smaller and that means it's less fluid—not an environment you take risks with your income. Not if…' I stop rambling.

I am about to say *not if you have reproduced*—as many of the women in the top spots have done—often multiple times. They need their solid salaries to pay for the painfully expensive day-care bills, that probably hurt more than giving birth itself. But I don't approach this topic. Not in front of Zach. *Shit, I forgot to buy any red wine.*

'…not if you can be totally sure that the magazine is secure, i.e., supported by other products…' I continue. 'And that would mean going to a publication which is part of an umbrella company and, trust me, those jobs are hard to come by because applicants for the second-job-down nearly always come from the inside.'

Zach nods. In a few seconds, he will give me the same half-understanding/half-tolerating look he has been doing ever since I started to talk *at* him, as opposed to *with* him. He knows there is no point trying to engage because this is a rant, not a discussion. Everything I say to him I have already made up my mind on. He reaches back down into the cardboard box and straightens up a batch of records even though they are stacked perfectly. Zach used to own a ton of vinyl, most of which he stored along the walls of our flat—literally, *sound insulation*—but sold most of it in the New Year because we would be 'needing the space'. I told him he would regret selling his collection (mainly rare remixes of classic pop songs) because he started it when he was a kid. But he went ahead and bunged pretty much all of it on eBay as a job lot. All those tunes he had meticulously chosen and added one by one over the years…gone in three days and seven bids. It made me uncomfortable. I felt as if he wasn't so much preparing for the future, as forcing it.

He looks up at me. But the look I was expecting is not there. I can tell he is nervous.

'Is Kat Moss okay?' I ask quickly.

'Yes, yes…she is fine.'

'Still establishing her territory?'

'Mmm…almost there, I think.'

'But she's getting back into her usual routine of late nights and sleeping all day?'

'Yeah…'

'Well, you'd still better not have a Chinese takeaway any time soon. Not until she's totally settled in. MSG is feline crack. She might get involved in something she'd regret. I can only imagine what her police mugshot would look like, all dilated pupils and bushed-out tail…'

Zach manages a smile. '…and hanging from her mouth, the bloody remains of an urban rodent only identifiable from its dental records.'

I laugh. So does he, but then we both stop. Abruptly. Zach clears his throat again.

'Ash, the reason I called you tonight…'

'…was because you needed to show me your financial report for the…' I don't say it. The D word. I don't call it that. If forced, I replace it with a generic term that covers the legal aspect, like 'process' or 'arrangement' or I simply trail off. 'I heard you. Give me five minutes.'

I need to go to the off licence. The only booze in the fridge is my three-week-old half-drunk public 'decoy' bottle of Sauvignon Blanc that I keep there to pretend I can have it in the flat without drinking it.

'No, *no*, Ash…I said that so that you would come back home as soon as possible. I need to tell you something.'

I blink hard. Six very average words. *I need to tell you something.* But how they are spoken makes all the difference. Quickly, short spacing…the something is Some Thing which may affect part of your day. Slowly, wide spacing… the something is The Thing which will affect your whole life.

'Sorry?'

'I.' SPACE. 'Need.' SPACE 'To.' SPACE 'Tell.' SPACE. 'You.' SPACE. 'Something.'

'What.' No intonation.

'Your mother…she's passed away.'

I look down at the box of records. The only visible one is an (I'm imagining *appalling*) house remix of *Don't Speak* by No Doubt. I was never a big fan of Gwen Stefani's fifties rockabilly look when that song came out. The overtly punk style that came afterwards lacked authenticity. And then the geisha thing was too…well, it had been *done*. (Madonna, Kylie, Janet Jackson…who *hasn't* put their hair in a bun and sweated through a video in a silk dress with a dragon motif?) But now…*wow*. Stefani is a street fashion icon. Okay, it's structured, expected, formulaic almost…

'Ash?'

…but *no* one can deny that she hasn't been hugely influential on the general look of girl groups from the Pussy Cat Dolls to Little Mix. Or as Fitz calls them, Wind in the Willows. Ha!

'*Ash.* I'm so sorry. I don't know any of the details but when I was here, a woman called and left a message on the answering machine about the memorial service. She must have thought you already knew.'

MOLE. BADGER. RATTY. TOAD.

Zach steps forward. I step back.

'I didn't mean to shock you but the last thing I wanted to happen was for you to listen to the message on your own and th—'

I interrupt him. 'She had a husky voice…the person who left the message. Right?'

'Yeah.'

'Her name is Sheila. She ran the pub next to the block of flats where I grew up. She had white-blonde hair and always wore skintight shiny black clothes. Not leather…PVC. She always laughed—chestily, in fact, thanks to a forty-a-day Lambert and Butler habit—in the face of breathable fabrics. I lik—'

Now he interrupts. 'Rewind. How can you be sure it was her?'

'Because I already know.'

'*What?* You know *what*?' He manages a double intonation.

'I know that my mother is…' Another D word. Another one I—or anyone would—want to think about. Let alone, articulate.

'And you didn't tell me?'

'No. Look, it's not as if it wasn't…' Around the corner? Bound to happen? A matter of time? I pause, knowing I sound like an automaton, but I don't want Zach's sympathy because he feels *obliged*. '…you know the relationship she and I had. And let's face it, you and I are in a difficult situation too.'

'Come on, Ash. Don't be like that. How long have you known?'

'Two months.'

'*Two months!*'

'Yes, Zach, two months. That's what I said. Look, you don't have to feel guilty. You weren't to know this was going to happen.'

'Guilty? You think that's why I want to be there for you?'

'Well, it is, isn't it?'

'Ash, don't be so brutal. I'm here because I care about you. This is a massive thing to have happened—irrespective of the timing and irrespective of your relationship with her. This must have—must still be—bewildering for you. I think "bewildered" would be totally understandable in this situation. How did it happen?'

'All that coconut water. It's a lesson to us all. Clean living gets to you in the end.' I squirm at my wholly unnecessary joke. 'It was liver disease, Zach. Sheila told me that there are around seven thousand alcohol-related deaths each year and sixty-five per cent are because those livers have just said, "Nope. No *more*. E-fucking-*nough*!"'

He shakes his head, sadly. 'I can't even begin to imagine how I would be feeling if it were my mother.'

'Don't make me look bad by personalising the conversation. It's a slightly different situation. I have not seen mine once in the last decade. You speak to yours every day. *At length*.'

Zach's mother has a lot to say about everything, but little of her commentary is necessary. It's always coated with middle-class concern over what other people might think, even when she doesn't need other people to know. She randomly emailed me the other week to say, '*I've told Barbara and Tim from next door that it was decided shortly after Easter you would be going your separate ways...*' As if her neighbours had been glued to the *Sky News* ticker tape during the summer waiting for an update on mine and Zach's marriage.

He sighs at me. 'I know that Mum will be really sorry for you when she hears the news, Ash.'

I ignore this comment. He ignores my lack of response.

'So, will you go to the memorial? Because if you do decide to, I'll come with you. I can drive us there.'

He clears his throat. Another one of the mannerisms we both seem to have acquired recently. Whenever we are discussing something on the phone, either he or I or both of us suddenly seem to have something obstructing our oesophagus.

'Don't be silly. You've got that pitch coming up.'

'It's tomorrow. We finished the prep a couple of days ago, thank God. There's been a lot of late nights in the office with Keith and...the team.'

'Lucky you.'

Keith With The Bad Teeth is Zach's business partner. He refers to women as 'poontang' and rides a pimped-up eighties BMX along the pavements of East London into work. As Noelle Bamford would say, 'Nuff said.'

'Seriously, I appreciate the offer, Zach, but I'll be more than capable of handling this.'

'"Handling this"?'

'Yes. Handling this,' I repeat. It sounds even worse third time.

'Well, when you decide what you're doing...you know how to get hold of me.'

'Through your solicitor?' I joke weakly. 'Please, can we not talk about this anymore.'

He manages to smile too. 'Okay. Hey…look, until I heard the news about your mother, I wasn't planning on being here when you got back. You'd said you were going to be out late tonight, so I would have made sure I was gone by nine-ish. I want you to know I wasn't breaking the agreement we made.'

That being whilst things are being sorted out on the legal front, it's best we are not in one another's company. We talk or text when necessary but we avoid face-to-face encounters, especially at our homes. I haven't even seen the place that Zach has rented, even though it is only a ten-minute walk.

'Don't worry about it,' I tell him. 'It doesn't matter if we crossover occasionally. Obviously, you're going to need to pack up the rest of your stuff and, besides, it's still your flat.'

'Nah, it's *your* flat now.'

'Maybe we should refer to it how Prince might: "The Home Formerly Known as *Our* Flat".'

We both emit a short burst of uncomfortable laughter again.

'Well, I'll, erm…finish off this box and then maybe we could grab some dinner,' suggests Zach. 'I know it's also against the rules, but I don't like the idea of you being on your own, thinking about all of *this*. Let me take you out for a Chinese. I won't tell Kat Moss. Unless you've erm… got a hot date coming over later, then of c—…'

'Actually, *yes*, I have!' I interrupt, almost manically brightly. 'I would quite like you to meet him. Nice guy. City trader, got a faintly experimental haircut and zips around on a Vespa…but despite that, isn't a wanker. Although, I haven't seen his bike helmet yet. If it's emblazoned with a Union Jack or a Mod target in the colours of the Italian flag, then we'll know he is indeed a massive *tit*!' I pause, my unhinged laughter hanging in the air. 'Sorry, I was just trying to l—'

'Lift the atmosphere?'

'Yeah.' I clear my throat. 'That.'

'No need to apologise. I started it by making a joke about you having a date…which wasn't necessary.'

'Mmm…' I flop faux-casually down onto my giant bean bag—the first piece of 'furniture' I bought for the flat. 'True. It wasn't. I can't recall seeing anything on the initial paperwork sent from either of our solicitors instructing us that from now until the decree absolute is signed, one of us has to be the official 'Lifter of the Atmosphere' whenever we are in an enclosed space together.'

He smiles at me. It is more relaxed this time. 'Actually, we should probably take it as an encouraging sign. Apparently, a reflex desperation to lift the atmosphere is perfectly natural. One of the account managers I work with said that when they were in the early throws of getting a…' He is as unwilling to use the D word as I am. '…well, breaking up with their partner, they went into this strange entertaining mode every time they saw each other.'

'That sounds horrific. We'd better nip this in the bud right now then, or Christ knows where we could end up. Juggling, unicycling, fire-eating, angle grinding, puppetry…' I prod him with my foot. 'From now on let's promise to only communicate with cold stares, monosyllabic replies and signatures in the appropriate places. Deal?'

Zach reaches over with his right hand to shake mine, but I feel as if he has punched me with it. He is not wearing his wedding band. This is the first time I have seen him without it since we took our vows. We both decided to wear our rings on our right hand. Him because he's left-handed. Me because the ring was too big for my left hand and I didn't want to get it fixed. I wanted to wear it as soon as he gave it to me, and then I never took it off. I still haven't.

I clear my throat again to stay 'in situ', but I am not here... *now*. It is December 24th last year. I am lying on the bean bag next to Kat Moss. She is the world's coolest cat. She is the cat that all other cats want to be. She makes being a cat look utterly effortless. And she knows she's the best. Her meow sounds like she is saying, 'Meeeeeeeeee...'.

Kat has been grooming herself intensely. My face is now pressed against her fur, I am inhaling it, wondering if there is a finer smell in the universe than 'eau de freshly washed feline'. Instead of heading out for my final festive knees-up with Fitz, I've come home straight after work to get changed. Zach and I are going out to dinner...*to continue talking about* '*it*'. I look up as he enters the lounge. I had left the house before he got dressed that morning so I assess what he is wearing: Stone Island wool coat, a ridiculous Christmas jumper which was given to him by his team at their work party the week before, True Religion jeans and, as usual, hi-tops. I like how the laces are tied as loose as they could be whilst still maintaining enough grip to walk in. He has perfected 'louche lacing'.

HIM: How's my Number One girl?

ME: Good, thanks.

HIM: I didn't mean you. I meant Kat Moss. (Picking up our cat. Cuddling her.) But I am also open to hearing how you are too given that although you don't have the subtle, come thither allure of Ms. Moss—or the impressive whiskers—you're still very sexy, Ash.

ME: I know that. But it's nice to hear that you think that too.

HIM: And I will always think that. Even when you're knackered, moody and swollen in places you never knew existed! (Laughing.)

I swallowed. I had not realised we were laughing about 'it' yet. I thought we we were still talking about it. And would be doing more of that tonight.

ME: What?

HIM: (Not realising I am not laughing.) Oh, yeah, my Mum told me all about how things just...swell up. Apparently, your sock elastic will feel like you've been caught in a wire hunting trap, bra straps will give you welts and you may even need your wedding ring removed with a blow torch. You'll be forced to live and work in your Snuggle Suit.

I paused and considered whether to pursue the joke to see how it felt.

ME: But being skinny is my thing. I'm the annoying girl everyone hates because she eats crap and never puts on weight.

HIM: You'll find a new thing.

ME: So might you. A new play thing.

HIM: Maybe. But I promise that if I do, it will only be while you are chubby. When you've lost the bulk again, you and I will be back in business. (Putting Kat Moss on the sofa, then checking his watch.) Now, get that soon-to-be huge ass of yours into the bedroom. We've got a good hour before you need to faff about in order to make yourself look as if you've just got out of bed...even though you will have done exactly that.

I sprang up, grateful of the diversion.

ME: So you know, Zach, there is a difference between bed hair and 'bed hair'. The latter is not a literal effect of the former. (Walking through to the bedroom, stripping off my

T-shirt and trousers, jumping onto the bed in my underwear.)
It takes tongs. And clips. And effort.

HIM: *(Appearing at bedroom door.) And just so you know,*
Ash, I was kidding. There will never ever be anyone else
but y—

'Deal. Yeah, it's a deal.' He rubs my shoulder brusquely
as if I am a 'pal'.

Immediately, I am back in the now, staring numbly at him.

'Ash? Talk to me… you don't have to hold all this in,
you know.'

'I'm not. I've been dealing with it. I am dealing with it.
I will deal with it. But at the moment, I told you…work is
pissing me off.'

He sighs, knowing he will not get any more out of me on
anything more important.

'Then I really do think you should look at some options.
A change of scene may do you good. At this rate, when you
do quit, the HR department won't give you a carriage clock,
you'll be presented with Big Ben.'

'Well, maybe some of us find it a little easier than others to
fuck off,' I snipe, and am immediately embarrassed. 'Sorr—'

'Don't apologise.'

'No, I shouldn't have.'

'You should.'

He smiles again, but his smile is different *again*. There
is warmth, worry too…but also pity. I don't know what's
worse. The fact he thinks I need it or the fact that he clearly
sees himself as the stronger one in this situation.

Some more clearing of throats. I tell him I'm going to get
changed. As soon as I step into my walk-in wardrobe, I feel
myself levelling out a little, because it's *my* space. Zach has
never even been in there. No one has but me. And the bloke

who fitted it. And Kat Moss. It was the first building work I had done as soon as the sale of the property had gone through. The cost meant I couldn't afford a new boiler or a fridge, but a lack of the former meant it was cold enough for me not to need the latter until the summertime. Besides, what was the odd game of 'dairy roulette' with a carton of milk kept on the window sill, when I had my *own* wardrobe next to my *own* bedroom in my *own* flat?

Everyone said it would be impossible for me to buy my own place when I was earning so little—at the time I was still only a junior at *Catwalk*—but I was determined to save up enough for a mortgage deposit. So I made some changes. I moved into a two-person room share *within* a house share. I worked nights in a sauna. Weekends in a club. I only bought food and beverages from (the economy range in) supermarkets and not from any form of restaurant or 'snack' emporium; especially coffee shops. I had to think of a daily visit to Starbucks as the equivalent of grinding up a five-pound note in a percolator. I didn't go partying. I'd seen enough of all that. I wanted my own home. One that no one—mortgage company withstanding—could ever ask me to leave.

My walk-in wardrobe is not packed full of clothes. Yes, I am obsessed with fashion but I don't relentlessly throw money at it. Although, recently I *may* have been PayPal-ing a little more than I used to. But it's not as if I'm one of those girls who buys 'outfits'. That's too expensive and too *obvious*. Crimes Against Fashion No. 23: a head-to-toe look (unless sitting front row at the *actual* designer's show. Or it's your *own* label, e.g., Stella McCartney.) Guilty: The Kardashians. All of them. *Plus* Caitlyn Jenner. Girl really does need to be *way* less matchy matchy. Everything I own is carefully and *eclectically* selected from all spectrums of fashion retail: designer, vintage, high street, market and online then combined to achieve a look I would *hope* could be classed as edgy statement chic. I look after each item. I either dry clean or I hand wash, rinse, dry, iron, fold and place back in the allocated spot. My mother's wardrobe started out like that…she said you should respect clothes as if they were your friends. 'Because many of them will be in your life a lot longer.'

I reach up to get a fresh Snuggle Suit off the top shelf. On the level above is my collection of *The CR Fashion Book*. Carine Roitfeld is a genius; and that is not a word I bandy around lightly. In a world where so many are told they are fabulous…she actually is. No one does edgy statement chic like her. Almost mannish but oh-so-sexy. And subtle. Fitz gave me a framed photo of Ms Roitfeld to place on top of my accessories cupboard, just to remind me that a *little* more is nearly always *too* much. But there is not much chance of me over-accessorising at the moment as I can't open the bottom two drawers. There is a fake Louis Vuitton suitcase lying on the floor which I have no other room to store. It was sent to me last week by Sheila. I don't need to open it because I know what is inside. Exactly what was in there when I unzipped it all those years ago. I was so excited I couldn't wait to show my best friend. But the second I flipped the lid, she turned to me.

*

I looked at her face. I knew this face almost as well as my own. With its wide, wise, eager eyes which looked even bigger when she scraped her hair up into a messy top knot, which I had recommended she did as it was classic 'off duty model'. Much better than the overly straightened, overly hair sprayed bob which was her go to style. I'd told her many times. Crimes Against Fashion No. 28: chemical processes during grooming clearly evident. Guilty: Christina Aguilera (the *Genie* years).

*

Suddenly, a mottled rash spread across her skin.

*

HER: I need to tell you something.
   ME: What? What do you need to tell me, Tanya?

Four

I can hear the band playing as I leave the station. They're doing a cover of that Mumford & Sons track which sounds as if it should be played in a village square on May Day by locals drinking scrumpy and wearing neckerchiefs. The lead singer's voice is raspy. *Sexy*. He doesn't quite manage to hit the high notes with full precision, but this inevitably makes him sound even sexier, because *maybe* he is too cool to care. As I open the door, the band attacks the final chorus and the vocalist clutches his microphone stand. His faded (purpose-fully crumpled) grey T-shirt is patchy with sweat and clinging to his torso. His hair is also damp and hanging messily in his eyes. He glances down into the audience; a mixture of local twenty- and thirty-somethings on the tail end of a drink-up after work. Most of them would have been in the pub drinking anyway, even if they hadn't known there was going to be some sort of musical entertainment. They've stayed, which is a positive thing. But it's unlikely the majority of them had the gig diarised on their mobiles…even though a few are being held aloft in video mode. The frontman acknowledges these 'fans' with a nod, then wipes his brow. The chunky man bracelet he is wearing flops forward then back to his wrist.

I can see in his eyes that the situation isn't perfect for him. He'd rather be looking out across a sea of fans at the O2 who have bought tickets—months in advance—specifically to see him play *his* music. I admire him for still having that kind of, well, *hope.* Because, let's face it, at this stage, ambition alone is not going to make him—my true love—a star.

Set finished, he jumps down from the makeshift stage onto the floor. I go over to give him a kiss. As he leans down, I think I can smell cigarette smoke.

'I wouldn't do that if I were you, babe, I'm well sweaty.'

'Don't care.'

I plant a smacker on his mouth. Yes, he's been smoking. I sense other women in the bar looking in our direction. They were looking at him, but now they are looking at us together; assessing our compatibility. Greg has become *very* good looking. To me, he always was, but over the last couple of years, I have noticed that a *lot* of—almost *all*—women do as well. He *finally* quit smoking marijuana, lost two stone and toned up to the point where you can see the sinewy outer line of muscle tissue through his clothes—which consequently, took on a more streamlined edge. I was surprised when he told me it was time 'to hit the gym'. Previously, he'd been more the type of guy who would only look at the cover of *Men's Health* if he was ripping it up for roach material.

I kiss him again and come away from his face with a sticky chin.

'Eww.'

'So, what did you think of the set?' he asks, pulling away. 'Personally, I thought it went pretty well…' He lowers his voice as the rest of the band start dismantling their equipment '…except for the Oasis tribute. The two new guys were on point but Jez fucked up the riff at the beginning of

Wonderwall. I mean, seriously! You could give a monkey a banjo for half an hour and I guarantee it would be able to strum that out, no problem. Did you hear me do my solo on the guitar?'

'Sorry, I've been running late all day.' I had to wait for ages to get my procedure done at the hospital. 'I've only just got here. Was it an, erm…acoustic…' I cringe. '…spot?'

'Yeah. Then the two newbies came in at the end. Nothing went wrong vocally or instrumentally, not surprising considering that numbnut wasn't involved.' He glances over at Jez. 'Am thinking we need to have words. I don't see how the band can progress with him as part of the unit. Don't get me wrong, I love him as if he were a brother, but I already have a brother, and I choose not to see him, so I don't need another holding me back. You wouldn't want another sister, would you, babe?'

'God, no.'

He kisses me again. 'You know I hate going on about it, but I don't suppose she's…erm, managed t—'

'No, no, she hasn't. You don't need her though. You need talent and that's what you have. That will bring you success.' I say this as affirmatively as possible. 'You've got it, Greg.'

'Mmm…' Greg gazes at the punters, no more or less excitedly guzzling their drinks then they were during the gig. 'Shall we do the offski?'

'Are you not cashing up tonight?'

'Nah. If I hung around till closing, I'd explode the rock-'n'-roll mystique for my "fans"...' He raises an eyebrow. '…that in *real life*, I manage a gastro pub and the only instrument I usually carry around with me is a portable chip-and-pin machine, not an electric guitar. Have a drink whilst I grab my stuff.'

I order an orange juice and chat to the new barman. He's 'cute', but I've never been attracted to boyish good looks. I like *men*. Greg is manly. And like I said, there was even more man at the beginning. He was solid physically. That was what drew me to him, because on a very basic level, I was looking for someone who was solid *mentally*.

The night I first saw Greg, it was a Thursday. As we did on this day every week, Suze, Maddie and I would go to The Croft after work for some drinks. Suze saw him first, then Maddie and then me. With almost choreographed perfection their eyes swivelled from him to me, as if to say, '*He's SO your type!*', which was a fact, and I suppose *quite* sweet of them. But I could already sense the patronising exchange that was about to follow. *It did.*

'Go and talk to him,' said Maddie.

'Don't be ridiculous,' I replied (only semi-)sarcastically. 'I can't do that. It is considered highly inappropriate for clientele frequenting drinking establishments to speak to the staff working there…except in extreme circumstances, like *ordering a beverage.*'

'…and don't attempt to distract the situation by making shit jokes,' said Suze, snorting.

'This could be fate,' added Maddie. '*He* may have been sent to *our* pub for *you*. Everything happens for a reason.'

I rolled my eyes at her. 'You know who started that expression? The fairies at the bottom of the garden. They came up with it shortly after finishing off that day's *twelve* horoscope predictions which would apply to the world's population of *seven billion*.'

Another snort from Suze. 'Whatever, T, get on with it. When was the last time you dated?'

'I went on a date last week.'

'I mean, *seriously* dated.' She rubbed her chin. 'Actually, I remember…it was before Jasper had taken his exams for prep school. In fact, you came to his last sports day with the guy you were seeing. Jasper bit his teacher. She had to get a jab. Then Evie threw your bloke's car keys into the swimming pool.'

'You're right, Suze, I forgot you had a calendar in your kitchen which correlates your children's advance through the education system with my love life.'

Suze laughed.

'We only want you to be happy,' added Maddie, who had recently made things official with her boyfriend, Kian.

I rolled my eyes at her. 'Surely it is a given that everyone should want that for everyone else as *standard*. But for some reason, as soon as a woman becomes part of a couple, she automatically morphs into this beatific altruistic creature who roams the land wanting happiness for all women. Maddie, suffragettes *died* on *your* behalf so that our gender could flourish in their lives without being reliant on men for anything, least of all happiness.'

'Until you start thinking about kids,' she replies. 'If you want to have a baby, you'll need a man. It's a simple fact. And you'll need one that you can *rely* on.'

I stiffened. Suze sensed my reaction immediately. I know this because a second later she was replying to Maddie so I wouldn't have to.

'Bullshit, you don't need to *rely* on a man to have a child. You only need one temporarily.'

'You mean a donor?' Maddie shook her head. 'I don't know whether I could do it. Not from a moral point of view, of course, it's not for me to cast judgement in *that* sense. I mean, plan on being a single parent. I'd find it overwhelming.

Within a day of meeting Kian, I knew I wanted him to be the father of my children. Two months in, I still do. But I want to wait until I am absolutely sure that the environment I am bringing that child into is right. Would it really be fair if I didn't?'

'Fair?' I blurt out. 'On who?'

Maddie shrugs. 'Well, the child.'

'If you are intending on having one out of love, it doesn't matter how many people are involved. One or one hundred!' My voice rises. 'And who are *you* to say what environment is right or wrong?'

'I was only saying that I think it would be tough doing it on your own…and that the better scenario is a two-parent family. It's a wider support system. You must agree with that?'

I tutted at her for being so…well, so typically Middle England Maddie. But deep down, I agreed with her. Of course, it would be tough doing it on your own. It would take a brave woman to do that. If you were a scared girl, forget it.

Suze clocked my expression and stepped in again.

'Anyway, I think this is all getting a bit *Loose Women*. Are we going to get a drink or what? At this rate I'm going to die of thirst…' She reached into her bag for her purse. 'Oh, and if I do drop dead, you can have one of my children *each*. And then, trust me, neither of you will ever want one of your own!'

So, Suze got the first round. Then Maddie got the second. They found out the new barman was called Greg and had been posted here by the brewery from another pub across town. I kept quiet. There were so many variables that simply weren't in my favour to do something as rash as speaking to him. For a start, it would have been too *obvious*. And, therefore, embarrassing. And, consequently, awkward for both of us. And then, painful for *any* of us to come back to a pub which had been our regular hang-out for years. Ultimately, I would be creating a 'situation'. The girls knew this was how I would be thinking, so after two drinks they stopped badgering me. The following Thursday, we arranged to meet at our usual time…but when I turned up (five minutes late), they weren't there.

I saw *him* though. His back was to me as he changed an optic on a bottle of vodka. I knew it was him as I had stared at every part of his anatomy so hard the previous week, I could have given *Crimewatch* an exact E-fit of the nape of his neck. I was about to spin round and leave when a text pinged through from Suze:

If you walk out you're officially a TWAT. FYI Maddie is with me, so don't think about calling her.

I approached the bar, purple heat rash prickling.

ME: Erm…hi.

HIM: (Turning round.) Hey.

It was a generic I-don't-recognise-you "hey".

ME: I'm Tanya. I was in last week. You were talking to my friends, Suze and Maddie. We're here every Thursday, but they haven't turned up yet s—

HIM: Oh, right, yeah. How's it going?

ME: Great, in fact. You?

HIM: Yeah…good.

ME: That's, erm…good. Really…great.

Move over Dorothy Parker.

HIM: That's all decided then. I'm good and so are you. No, you're—in fact—great. What do you want?

He smirked. Negatively? Positively?

ME: Oh, God, erm…nothing really. I got here early, so

*thought I would say hello, since I was in here. Waiting. For
Suze and Madd—*

HIM: I meant, what do you want to drink?

ME: Right. Of course. Prosecco?

I HATE PROSECCO!

HIM: Coming up. So, tell me, Trisha…

ME: Tanya.

HIM: Sorry…Tanya. What do you do?

ME: I'm a content writer for corporate websites.

HIM: Ah, cool.

ME: It's not. But I have a crazy boss who is obsessed with
Star Wars. *It's really funny, he does impersonations of Yoda.*

Yeah, he's a lunatic. Because not even the vaguest sci-fi
fan does that, do they?

*HIM: Sounds it. Hey, maybe you could do a new website
for my band? Pretty please!*

ME: Band?

NOT what I wanted to hear.

*HIM: Yeah, I'm a singer. The band is pretty successful,
but I like to work behind a bar still. Keeps me grounded. I'm
just hoping that I get to enjoy this sort of freedom for as long
as possible before things sky rocket and we l—*

*ME: (Interrupting to tie up the conversation.) Well, that
sounds like you're keeping it, erm…real. The fans must
appreciate that.*

I physically recoiled at my use of muso speak.

HIM: I'm sure they would if I had any.

ME: What?

*HIM: I was winding you up! The band…it's a hobby.
We play covers at weddings…not original material on the
Pyramid stage at Glastonbury.*

ME: OH! (Warming to him again.) So, erm…what kind of traffic do you get on your current website?

HIM: Traffic? (Rubbing his chin.) Well, metaphorically speaking…you know if you take a left at the roundabout before Lidl, and then go right past the old recreation ground and take that spindly lane which snakes round the back of the church up towards the farm which is basically only used by the occasional agricultural vehicle? That's pretty much the type of traff—

ME: Yep, I do. Actually, my parents use that lane too… they live just off it.

HIM: Poor them. That's where Howard Dinsdale lives, isn't it? In that mock-Tudor monstrosity. His company bought the youth club I went to as a kid and turned it into luxury flats. He's an arsehole…

ME: Try having him as a father.

HIM: Ha! Nice attempt at getting me back. Now you're winding me up. (Peering at me.) Oh. Shit. Oh, shit.

I smiled at him. He smiled too. At that moment, my stomach didn't simply flip. It did a full-on exquisitely executed Olympic-level triple flickflack into a double backwards somersault with a twist. One which had been perfected by a dedicated Russian gymnast who had spent her entire childhood in a Moscow training camp, but who knew if she nailed a flawless routine she could move to the United States once the Games were over and be free to watch Miley Cyrus pop videos. And visit the Dash store. And eat Ben and Jerry's.

I disappeared to the toilets and shut myself in a cubicle to call Suze. I told her everything Greg had said. Everything I had said. She informed me that she and Maddie were on their way, and ordered me to go back out to the bar and talk to him until their arrival. I left the cubicle. At the same time, another girl vacated the other cubicle and we both went to the sinks to wash our hands. As she rinsed hers, she stared at me. She was an Eva Mendez-esque exotic beauty with sloping features and olive skin. There was not a dab of make-up on her face—not even a very light mineral veil or BB cream. (I know my subtle cosmetic camouflage, they are the only products I use.) But she didn't smile back, and left the lavatory without drying her hands. When I returned to the bar, she was sitting on a stool, chatting to Greg. He waved at me.

HIM: Hey, Tanya, this is Sadie. (He passes Sadie a pint of beer.) Sadie, meet Tanya…one of the regulars here.

Sadie raised her glass and gave me a look. This look told me that she'd heard every word I'd said in the toilet. It also told me everything about her relationship with Greg. But moreover, *my* relationship with *my*self. She knew I wasn't going to compete with her, as I was the type of girl who avoided competition. The sort who lived within the remit of her capability but didn't push herself further than that. She was right. My approach to life since my late teens had become: *get through it*. Full stop. Not, *live it*! Certainly not 'to the full' or 'to the max' or with the pressurising pre-cursor, of 'you only have one, *so*…'. And that is what I had been doing, getting through it. No highs. No lows. Anything to avoid…*feeling*.

'Do you think I should call myself something else, babe?' Greg asks, as we pull out of The Croft's car park and head home.

He is driving. I had a silly spate of fainting a while ago, so I don't feel fully comfortable behind a wheel. Besides, I like watching Greg drive. It says a great deal about how sexy he is that he is *still* sexy when zipping about in my Ford Ka.

'Eh? Why on earth would you do that?'

'My name is so lame.'

'How can a name be lame?'

'When you're called Greg. There can't be many more inappropriate monikers for the front man of a band. Just say we make it—and I am obviously being stupidly optimistic here, as our most recent demo is probably being used as a coffee mug coaster in all the record companies we sent it to—and not even on the A&R guy's desk; it'll be his assistant's assistant, or the reception—'

'Stop it, something *will* happen.' I interrupt, to tell him what he needs to hear. 'Think of how far you've come in the last couple of years.'

'Playing covers in pubs as opposed to marquees? Mmm…I can almost feel my fingers closing round that Grammy.'

'Shoosh. Anyway, you don't need to change your name. Besides, I like it.'

'That's because *you* like *me*,' he says, laughing, 'but, I'm sure, if prior to us meeting, you had been presented with a list of ten men's names and asked which one belongs to a rock star, "Greg" would not be your number one choice.'

'It depends who else was on the list,' I say, looking at him as he changes gear then indicates.

'Okay, so on this list…' He continues. '…*other than Greg*, are the following; Jon (without the "H"), Kurt, Axl, Mick, Bruce, Gene, Eddie, Freddie, Jim…and Bono.'

'Ha! But you don't want to be called a name that is already associated with an established star…especially a dead one. Or worse, a smug one. Besides, you have to think that some singers aren't necessarily born with the coolest name. They make the name cool themselves. I mean, what's that guy called who fronts the, erm…Killers?'

'Brandon Flowers.'

'There you go!'

'An isolated case…and to be fair, he's not really that rock'n'roll. He's a Mormon.' He reaches across to rub my knee. 'Hey, I've been thinking about your birthday…you know I was meant to be working? Well, I'm going to organise some time off. I need a break. That place is doing my head in. Why don't we go somewhere? Have a long weekend. Manchester, maybe? See a band…'

'Awww, that sounds brilliant…' I lie. *Live music! Drugs! Enforced wild abandon!* No, thank you. '…but I've got a really important meeting on Monday morning at work and I'll, erm…have to prepare. My boss is on my case about it.' Another (half-)lie. I do have an appointment first thing that day but it's not in any way related to my job. And no one would ever be on my case about anything because I'm always a consummate professional. 'You know me, I hate being unprepared.'

'Life on the edge, babe.' He laughs.

'Yep, I'm all about that periphery. Ha! Anyway, Suze and Maddie wanted us to do lunch. With Rollo and Kian, too…' I add, in attempt to make it sound more appealing for him.

'But we did lunch with them last year…'

'That's because they're my best friends. Suze, Maddie and I always see one another on our birthdays. Besides, you get on with Rollo and Kian, and at least you and Suze can go off and you know *what*…' I poke him.

He brakes and changes gear jerkily as the road twists.

'No, *what*?'

'God, sorry! Didn't mean to make you jump. I meant, *smoke*. She's the only one left out of everyone who still does.'

'Oh, right. Yeah, I guess she is.' He stares straight ahead. 'But I'm not smoking any more…'

'Which is why it's so strange you smell of fags, not to mention unfair, when you've put in so much hard work.'

'Very funny.' He exhales loudly. 'Okay, o-*kay*, I had a couple tonight before the gig. I needed the nicotine hit. It gets me hyped up. And, more importantly, *stops me caning crisps*.'

'I still fancied you when you ate salty snacks. What happened to the electronic cigarette thing I bought you?'

'It's at home. I look like such a dickhead puffing on it.'

'You'll look even more of a dickhead when you're hooked up to immobile medical apparatus so you can breathe.'

'I know. I hear you. I'm so sorry, babe. I'll try harder.' He glances across at me briefly. 'To quit…'

I laugh. 'Stop it! You sound so tormented. I'm not angry with you, Greg…just concerned.'

'…and you're right to be concerned. I shouldn't do it but, in the moment something sort of takes over.' He rubs his forehead. 'But I'll make more of an effort, I promise…'

He takes his hand off my knee to change gear and his man bracelet jangles. I gave it to him and had it engraved on the inside: To my T. T = TRUE LOVE. I wrote this in code to a) make sure that other people did not know what it said as I hate relentless public celebrations of togetherness. (There is a whole section on my blog about the horror of 'Insta-couples') and b) because it was such a huge statement from me. I knew I would see it every day. In code, it was less likely to be a glaring reminder that the love I'd experienced before had been so *false*. It was a lie. The worst kind of lie. The type that breeds more lies.

Let it fucking go.

I find myself emitting a short gasp. It is a breath of realisation. Because it is time. Time to admit it to myself. Time to tell him. It is, isn't it?

'Babe?'

I jump. We are parked outside the house. Greg waves the car keys (attached to his mini-Fender Stratocaster keyring) at me.

'Are you going to get out of the car?'

'Wha— God, sorry.'

'You all right?'

'Uh huh.' I click off my seat belt. 'Greg…'

'That is my name, *yes*…unfortunately. Ha!'

I don't laugh. 'I want to talk…'

His face tenses. 'Right…'

'About something good! The last time we discussed it, I wasn't sure, but now, I think it will be fine. Fine! What a ridiculous word to use. I've been going round in circles in my head, not wanting to commit to a decision for so many reasons. But then I thought, what am I doing? In practical terms, we now have a house so it will not be *that* much of an upheaval as we have *way* more space. God, I'm sure the noise will still be a shock but you can't hav—'

'Awww, babe!' He interrupts me and plants a kiss on my cheek. '*Thank* you. I knew you would see the light eventually. It's not as if we ever park the car in the garage anyway. Trust me, the guys will be over the moon. And please, do *not* worry about the noise. When Jez had his studio in his ex's garage, he egg-boxed the whole thing for sound insulation. Sounds crazy but it works…you need a *lot* of boxes, so you can't really do it with the dozen boxes you get at the supermarket. I'll go to that posh farm shop up the road from your parents'. They'll have the big trays. Unless…' He takes a deep breath then gives me one of his Olympic-flickflack-inducing smiles. '*Unless*, we do it properly and get your old man to get some of his builders to soundproof properly. Yeah, I know, I know…

you hate accepting anything from him. I do, too, but he did ask if you wanted help renovating when we first moved in and you said, "No," so, the offer was there. All we need to do is clear out all the rubbish in there. What *is* in there, anyway?'

I consider whether to reboot the conversation. Are we actually talking about the *garage*?

'Babe? Are you listening?'

'Yeah.'

'I asked what was in there.'

'Oh…erm…you know, stuff…'

'Like what?'

'Old clothes. Magazines. Letters. Things like that…'

…let it *fucking* go.

'But nothing important?'

'No, nothing important.'

'Fantastic! So, you can ask Pops and we'll be good to go. Right you…out.' He opens the car door and jumps from his seat. 'I'm going to show you my appreciation in the only— but the best—way I can: N to the O to the O to the K to the I to the E. NOOKIE!'

Seconds later, I am tapping in the alarm code. Minutes later, we are in the sitting room. Greg's kit is off already. *As usual*. He can strip fast. My true love is a *very* sexual being. He wants to have sex every day, multiple times if possible. He starts by pumping me against the leather armchair. The force shunts me and the furniture across the room. It is good. It is sooooo GOOD. No, it's great. GREAT! GREEEEEEEEEEAT. Aghhhhhhhhhh! We edge past the coffee table, manage to traverse a pot plant my mother gave me, then head towards the CD tower racks from my old flat. Each one is ordered alphabetically. The corner of the chair slams into the nearest tower (A–F). An Arctic Monkeys live album, Biffy Clyro's debut and *White Ladder* by David Gray (tsk—that should be under G–L!) and all of Coldplay's studio work shoot out onto the floor. Oooooh, that's hard. It's getting harder. TOO HARD! OW! OW! OWWWWW! NO, I've chaaaaanged my mind. *MORE!* I WANT IT HAAAAAAAAAARDER! I hear a nasty crunch and know that *Parachutes* will need replacing. A few more shunts to the left and three whole towers tumble. All the albums which land on the floor are 'some bloke' acts… every one a quadruple platinum-selling television-advertised sensation that I purchased because it was what 'some bloke' I was dating was into. Ooooooooooh…that's the spot. That's the SPOT. Mmmmmmmmmm…oh, Greg, YOU ARE SUCH AN ANIMAAAAAAAAAAL! There was a string of these men. Including the slightly more longterm one who got bitten by Suze's daughter, Evie. I remember her teeth sinking into his arm. I remember the exact pattern of the marks she left as Suze unhooked her jaw. I remember we waited in A&E for three hours. But right now, I can't remember his name either. Was it Steve? Stephen. No, Stephan. Or was it St—it doesn't matter, because…oh my god, oh my god, oh my god, oh my god, OH MY GOD! We move to the hallway, then the utility room—but change our minds because we both value our coccyges—and end up in the master bedroom. I lie underneath Greg, looking at his face: contorted with pleasure—his eyes screwed shut, accessing *that* place. A private, hidden place. He does this sometimes, not just in relation to sex. He sort of zones out. Some people can do that, can't they? *Remove themselves.* I am not one of those people. Not any more. I was when I used to buy all those magazines that are in the garage. When I used to wear those clothes which are in there. When she wrote me that letter which is lying in the first issue on the opening-double-page spread of the heroin-chic shoot. Oh, yeah, I was one of those people then. But now I am very much in the moment. And at *this* moment, I am about to have…no, I am having, I AM HAVING AN ORGAAAAAAAAAASM! Oh yes, oh yes, oh yes, oh yes, oh yes, oh *yes*! YES! YES! YES! AND ANOTHER ONE! YAHOOOOOOOOOOO! *YES!* I'M COMIIIIIIIIIIIIIIIIIIIG!

Mmmmmmmmmmmmmmmmmmmmmmmmmmmmmmmm mmm…

Greg does too. Then collapses on top of me. As I lie underneath him, panting—deliriously satisfied to the point that he could ask to convert the whole freaking house into a production studio and I would say *yes*…then even re-mortgage to pay for Pharrell Williams to show him how to use all the equipment—I pray that he and I will always have 'nookie' like this. Even if that nookie becomes nookie for more than pleasure's sake. Even if that nookie is a means to an end. Because that end will be a new beginning. I would never want to be that woman who has nookie and *physically* is going through a wide variety of motions, but *mentally*, her only thought is…

…*I want a baby.*

Five

'So, Noelle's shoot for her Special Edition issue…' Catherine turns to our Fashion Director, Wallis. 'I had a chat with her agent at the party and she has confirmed that Noelle will be picking her five favourite key pieces from the new season.'

'Her stylist will, you mean,' says Wallis, as she repositions her headpiece—a stuffed swallow attached to a metal band. (No one batted an eyelid when she walked in wearing it this morning). 'You know every single look of hers is put together by Kenny Chong? My girlfriend cuts his hair. She said Kenny introduced Noelle to brogues too.'

Jazz glares at Wallis. 'That's absolute rubbish, she's always worn men's shoes. She's into androgynous dressing. It says so in her book.'

'Then it must be true,' deadpans Fitz.

He glances over at me and rolls his eyes. I roll mine back, as standard. Jazz is irritating on the best of days, least of all on my last few hours before suspension. She *worships* Noelle and is always suggesting we should feature other *model-come-DJ-come-It girl-come-presenter-come-entrepreneur-oh, come off it!* celebrities in the magazine. As a rule of thumb, the least obvious the talent, the more likely Jazz will be a fan. I'm convinced this is because she feels less exposed by these sort of people. Before *Catwalk*, Jazz hadn't been employed *anywhere* before. That winning dual combo of über-rich parents and ultra-fast WIFI had meant she could fill her days being a blogger. Not too long ago, blogging would have skulked under HOBBIES AND OTHER INTERESTS at the bottom of a CV. But to Catherine, the fact that Jazz was a whizz at uploading pictures of *people attending events* and had even managed to get one of Noelle in the VIP tent at some shite rock festival with an early prototype of the 'Noelle' tote was more than enough reason to give her a job. Her first one. *At twenty-fucking-nine years old.* The same age as me.

'…so, yup, five outfits and Noelle's favourite on the opening-double-page spread,' says Catherine. 'That's the Tory Hambeck neoprene tunic in olive from her debut collection. We should champion a new British designer.'

Wallis bristles. 'Tory Hambeck is British but she is *not* a designer. She is a reality TV star who has employed a very good design team…*from* America. Hambeck doesn't even know how to stitch let alone sketch.'

Catherine ignores her suggestion. 'She *can* draw. Her PR tweeted one of her sketches last week.'

'Actually, Catherine's right,' says Fitz, seriously. 'I've got it right here.' He holds up his notepad, where he has drawn a stick person in a triangle dress.

Everyone laughs, including Catherine, because she knows no one will be changing her mind.

'Look, it's essential to put Hambeck at number one, then we'll get an exclusive interview when she launches her perfume at Christmas.'

'What?' Bronwyn, the Beauty Editor, balks. 'But we've never gone *near* celebrity perfumes. *Catwalk* beauty is about catwalk—with a small c—*creativity*, not about A, B or C List vanity projects.'

'Absolutely,' says Fitz. 'If we're going to do a feature on Hambeck, it should be about how her designs are manufactured and marketed…who the *real* minds are behind it. Let's talk to industry insiders, not her. She'll only spout the same insipid waffle that all the celeb so-called *designers*—who have never even approached a work bench let alone pattern cut—do, about wanting to 'empower women'…when actually all they are asking of the female population is to *go shopping and make me richer*! At least be honest. It's a business. Real designers are not afraid to say that, they are proud. So they should be.'

'He has a point, Catherine…' squeaks Dixie, our Talent Editor. 'A more investigative angle is way more in sync with our readers. Yes, we include famous people in the magazine, but we're not a fanzine.'

Catherine cocks her head. 'We are a business too! And we need to compete by getting more readers who like the other angle as well.'

Fitz throws his hands up. 'But that dilutes our brand. If we give this type of coverage to Hambeck, where do we stop? She is *not* the brains behind the label. And label makes it sound a far more complex operation than it is. She does shapes, no *actual* tailoring. Ashley's cat could have cobbled together her last season's look with a tube of Pritt Stick and a basic set of instructions.'

I blink at him as if considering what to say on the matter, but I'm not thinking about Tory Hambeck's designs. I'm remembering the collection of the first designer I knew. She specialised in what she called 'rave togs'. The whole range she did was unisex: sweatshirts, T-shirts, dungarees, hats, vests. Each piece was emblazoned with neon lettering, swirly patterns or smiley faces as if it been manufactured in a toy factory.

ME: Mum?

HER: Ashl-eeeeey! (Voice sing songy.) Where are yooooou?

ME: (Shouting back.) In my room, I'm reading that new magazine you bought.

HER: Oh, that. It's shit! *(Sticking her head through the door, tripping slightly as she does.) Where's your Dad?*

ME: Gone to get the van fixed. Again. Why don't you dump it?

HER: Because it's got history. Like I always say, you were quite possibly conceived (slightly slurring on the double 's' and the 'c') in that van en route to some rave-up in a field. Or on the way back. Ha! Maybe parked up behind a service station. (More slurring.)

ME: I think I prefer the shtory of the shtork.

She either did not hear my joke or she chose to ignore it.

HER: You're an aciiiiiiiiii-ed baby!

ME: Aghhhhh…don't do that!

HER: I'm only having a laugh with you…(Plonking herself down on my bed next to me.)

I could smell the Red Lion on her.

HER: …Gawd, I worry for your generation. You think THAT (pointing at the photo shoot in the magazine) is the future. Fashion should be fun! That's just depressing.

ME: It's called 'heroin chic.'

HER: I make clothes to dance in, not die in.

ME: It's what's selling in London. (Clocking her expression.) Sorry. I wasn't saying that it is better.

HER: No.*(Voice darkening.)* But you were THINKING you know better.

ME: I'm ten, Mum. Why would I think that?

HER: Because a lot of people round here do. Think they know better. Think they are better. I was just saying that to Sheila in the pub—this estate is split into those who LIVE here and those who want to LEAVE here. And the latter don't have any respect for the former. I mean, look at your little buddy, Tanya...she's always round. You're never over there. Have her parents ever invited you or us? Nope.

ME: Have you ever asked Mr and Mrs Dinsdale over?

HER: Only because they wouldn't come. They're snobs. Boring ones at that. I bet the closest they've ever come to a warehouse party is paying for some flat pack furniture in Ikea...ha! And as for their clobber! Cheryl is drip-dry, and have you seen the shoes Howard wears? Docksider boating shoes. For fuck's sake, he lives on a housing estate an hour and a half away from the nearest harbour. What? Has he got a yacht moored in Plymouth? The new St. Tropez, eh? What a penis. *(Rubbing my head. Suddenly, bright again.)* Hey, you know what shoes your Dad was wearing when I first met him?

ME: What?

HER: Kickers.

ME: Never heard of them.

HER: *(Sighing.)* Well, one day—when you're old enough to appreciate that not everything has to have been featured in a glossy magazine to be a significant trend—I'll explain their social impact. Believe me, those shoes meant something. You can always judge a man by his shoes, Ashley. It will tell you everything.

Last night, Zach was wearing new trainers. Zach is not *that* vain but he is obsessed with 'old school' sneakers. He buys them from a Japanese website that sources rare originals. Since 'it was decided' I have not seen him sport any new footwear, but he was wearing box-fresh Travel Fox the other night. He was wearing Travel Fox when we met. It was in a bar round the corner from here…

Fitz is eyeballing me. Should I be speaking? I look away.

'Either way, it's not happening,' confirms Catherine. 'To wind up Hambeck's management would be like kicking a hornets' nest wearing peep-toe sandals and pedal pushers. We'd be guaranteed to get stung.' She turns back to Wallis. 'So. Neoprene. Tunic. Olive. And here is a list of the other designers I want you to use…' She peels off a Post-it note and passes it to her. 'Right, last on the agenda: the *Catwalk* twentieth-anniversary party. It's been moved forward to fit in with our sponsors. Invites will be going out via email in the next week or so. Now, if we're all happy…' She doesn't pause. 'That's it. Actually, Ashley…I'd like a word.'

Christ. WHAT NOW? Everyone troops out.

'Are you looking forward to a quiet few days?' she asks me. 'Time to relax but also reflect on, you know what.'

'No, I am not. And to be honest, Catherine, I would prefer it if we didn't discuss my…' I *consider* using the D word to see how it feels, but back off. '…*issue* in the office. You wouldn't even know that I was in *the process of one* if I hadn't sent you that message by mistake.' Hungover one morning last month, I emailed her an update on mine and Zach's living arrangements, instead of the mortgage company. 'What happened at the book launch was a minor blip.'

'To you, maybe, Ashley. But certainly not to Noelle, her fans or her agent. But, most importantly, Frédéric Lazare.'

'With all due respect, who gives a monkey about Frédéric Lazare? None of RIVA's brands and products, and yes—I am including Pascale's 'Noelle' tote in that—are right for *Catwalk*. It's not as if Lazare's labels would ever attract boundary-pushing talent. The 'new' Olivier Rousteing, JW Anderson, Thomas Tait, Dion Lee, Jonathan Simkhai, Esteban Cortázar, Michael van der Ham, Sally LaPointe, Mary Katrantzou, Carly Cushnie, Michelle Ochs…would not touch RIVA. Lazare is the living evidence of money not being able to *create* or *sell* style.'

She sighs at me—almost nostalgically, like she did at the book launch.

'But, some of that money contributes to a *portion* of our advertising and will be paying for our party in its *entirety*, so I suggest you keep that opinion very much to yourself. That aside…' Her eyes dart furtively. '…when you get back from your break, you need to knuckle down and prove yourself. Looking further ahead with my pregnancy, I need to know that when I am out of the office, the magazine will be safe. I need to leave someone at the helm who won't rock the boat, and right now I don't see you as a particularly reliable captain.'

'That's unfair and you know it. I've covered for you three times and each time everything has been kept…shipshape.' I pull a face as I elaborate on her nautical metaphor. 'There is no one else here who could do it.'

Is there?

I look through the glass window at the five longest serving members of our editorial team at their desks. All of them are perfect in their current roles, but not as Editor. First, Fitz, currently wearing a pink custom-made sweatshirt with WHAT WOULD DONATELLA DO? embossed on it in metal studs. He's witty, insightful and blunt verging on tactless. Exactly what you want from a fashion writer and a mate. But as a leader, he would quite happily admit he lacks patience, empathy and tolerance. In fact, he would be *livid* if you implied that he did have those qualities. Then there's Dixie, our Talent Editor, who is as loud as the clashing vintage prints she wears. Her excited squeal can reach such a piercing level that when she manages to secure a top interview, dolphins in the Irish Sea are also made aware of the scoop. She's too hyper. Bronwyn is the opposite. Like a lot of beauty journalists, she always sports a crisp white shirt (usually Ann Demeulemeester) and is smug verging on "shit-eating". A beauty writer's self-satisfaction is usually directly correlated to how clear her skin has become thanks to the endless unctions and treatments she is invited to test. Bronwyn has been at *Catwalk* for eight years. (That's a *lot* of peptides.) Besides, a Beauty Editor would *never* be made Acting Editor. It does not happen. It's not how the publishing chain of command works. And there's no way Wallis—despite being one of the most respected Fashion Directors in London—would be given a chance either. She's too much of an eccentric and wholly anti-establishment. She may not be able to keep a lid on her views during meetings with corporate advertisers. Oh, and her hairdresser girlfriend has a habit of rocking up to the office unannounced to pick fights. Wearing a scissor belt.

Catherine must be planning to bring in someone from the *outside*.

She gets up from her chair. 'Nothing is decided yet, I'm simply letting you know that there is a lot for you to think about over the next few days. You're going through a period of change at home, maybe you need one *at work too*. It could be good for you.'

'What could?'

'To spread your wings and fly…make a new nest.'

'*A new nest?* You want…'

I distract myself from the enormity of what Catherine is saying by examining her oversized corsage-style brooch pinned to her chest. Crimes Against Fashion No. 21: Obvious tributes to Carrie Bradshaw. Guilty: thirty-something females on a Monday after a weekend of watching *Sex and the City* repeats on Comedy Central.

'…me to leave?'

'I want what is best for you, Ashley. Think about it. It could be good for you.' Her voice becomes thicker, more serious. 'You're talented. That talent will always be yours. You could do and go wherever you want. I knew that when I first employed you. Don't forget that…with all your drama going on. No matter what happens here, you…you…oh, aaaaaa-nyway…' She claps her hands together, as if stopping herself elaborating. 'I'll be out for the rest of the afternoon. Bit of a problem with one of the little ones, and the new au pair's English is still somewhat left of centre. You'd have thought three months in Barnes was enough for anyone to grasp the essentials. Clearly not. Oh, and can you ask Jazz to meet me in my office in five mins…thanks, Ashley.'

She walks out, en route rubbing my shoulder with about as much sincerity as Naomi Campbell's anti-fur campaign for PETA. I stay seated. We have never had a conversation like this in the entire time I have been at *Catwalk*. We started at the same time. Her at the top. Me at the bottom…an intern.

It took me two years to be offered an internship at the magazine. I lost count of the times I sent in my curriculum vitae, each time including an elaborate missive about the power of fashion to Polly, (then) the Editorial Assistant. I rang her too. But my letters and calls were never returned. Thinking back, it was a stupid thing to have done—going down the 'this is me' route. Polly had a double-barrelled surname and by listening to her answering machine message you could tell she bled Malbec. There is always at least *one* Polly type on the staff at *all* magazines. You just have to pray that she is not in charge of sifting through the CVs, as all of them are notorious for only giving work experience to their own people. Or rather, 'peeps'. After I had clicked that this was the case, I sat down and wrote a fresh CV with a few mild embellishments.

First up, my surname. I went from Ashley Atwal to Ashley Jacobs. I chose Jacobs for no other reason than it also belonged to Marc Jacobs—who the magazine were ob-*sessed* with back then and were very likely to always be. Next, I said I lived in Fulham. Benenden School in Kent was where my education had now been spent (*literally*—their website said it cost over twenty grand a year). My hobby was importing beads from Thailand, which I sold on the Portobello Road. I bought a Pay As You Go mobile so my number was different from my original application—and sent it off. Polly called me within a week. Within a fortnight I started.

Today, Catherine deigns to delight us with her presence until 3.36pm. Everyone else leaves two and a half to three hours later. By quarter to seven, it's only Fitz and I in the office. We're sitting at his desk, flicking through the new issue which has just been delivered from the print house. He sticks his head over the top of the partition to check we are alone.

'She's in seed, isn't she? Ogilvy…'

'How did you know?'

'She was on the San Pellegrino at the launch, she's rearranged the party date and I totally clocked some bloat in the features meeting. Thought she'd been overdoing it on granola. But no, *another* being has taken root in her womb. *So* Sigourney Weaver! Does she need another one? It pisses me off how women who make a *personal* choice to have so many children have a ricochet effect on other women—and men!—who work hard because they WANT or NEED to, enforcing them to work harder with no extra pay…whilst the breeder continues to be rewarded with their higher salary on maternity leave, which pretty much amounts to a paid holiday. And one which when it *officially* finishes, doesn't *actually* finish…because their work share will continue to be offloaded to other staff during half-term and other school holidays, parents' evenings, and random departures from the office when precious has fallen ill or off their pony…' He flops back into his seat. '…or quadbike. Don't you think?'

I shrug and stare down at my lap. I am wearing a pair of Rag & Bone ripped and faded jeans. They are skin tight. I've worn denim like that since I was teenager. My mother always wore a pair of voluminous dungarees, even though she was smaller than me. They made her look like a farmyard cartoon character. That look put me off *non*-snugly fitting denim for life. Whenever bell-bottom flares or a sailor-style cut reappear in the collections, I say *no*.

'That said,' continues Fitz, 'at least with Ogilvy out the way for a few months, we might start getting some decent material in the mag again. Don't you think this issue is even *more* vanilla than the last? There's not one piece I was excited to see in print. Your column is funny, *naturally*, but the subject matter…I mean, seeeeeeriously, Jacobs, you shrew. I used to DIE for all of it.' He flips the issue open at my page and runs his finger down it. 'Latex as daywear, Russian doll surgery, grime chic, Caroline Vreeland and the rise of the multiple-threat Insta girls—*okay, fair enough*—but knuckle tattoos, stylist lexicon, spike epaulettes, the new mephedrone and e-cigs? *E-cigs?* I am choking! But I am deffo *not* dying!'

Even I cringe. 'Catherine wanted the topics to be more mainstream.'

'And you didn't argue the toss? We're playing too safe. There's no grit. We're turning into the magazine equivalent of Miranda Kerr; looks fabulous—no denying that—but the personality, well…' He sucks in his cheeks. 'I find it astonishing that our sales haven't slipped.'

I shrug again. 'Yeah, well…they haven't, *so*…' I sigh. 'Anyway, does it matter?'

'Does it matter?'

'Or rather, do *we* matter anymore, Fitz? We put out *one* magazine every *month* to share our collective views, but each one of our readers has a way of expressing their unique point of view *in every single moment of every day.* Our generation was the first to grow up with the Internet—we were meant to be in control of it, but we're not. And it's going to get worse. I thought it would affect us, but we could never have predicted *this*…I am starting to feel like *what is the point*? Is there a point to it? *Us?*'

Fitz leans back and eyes me as he chews the end of his biro. 'Woah! Where has all this come from?'

'They're trying to prick us from the outside, you know,' I mutter. 'We're not safe in the bubble.'

'O-*kaaaaay*.' He laughs. 'I've got two qwezzies for you, Jacobs. The first is not one I like to ask anyone, as it always gets misconstrued, but, are you okay? I've been concerned. Ugh. There. I've said it.'

'Why are you worried?'

'I said, 'concerned', not worried. Worried would imply

this is about *you*. But this is about *me*.' He raises an eyebrow at me. 'Recently, you've not exactly been full of the joys of Spring/Summer or Autumn/Winter. 'I'm *concerned* because how you are acting is affecting my general enjoyment in the work place. The truth is, you've been behaving in a peculiar fashion. Not fashionably peculiar. You have been and are being... *boring*. I can see a pattern of said banality forming both in the flesh and online versions of you. Your Instagram account used to be a relentless and shameless exercise in showing off without ever quite making you look pleased with yourself. No mean feat. And as for Kat Moss, she could have been the new Choupette! In person, you haven't instigated a round of the I DIE FOR game in an age and now this... questioning the essence of who we are? We *are* fashion, Jacobs. Don't ever question that. Something is definitely up. Where has my vicious shrew gone? Spillez les haricots, pronto.'

I crumple a piece of paper in my hand. I am acutely aware that it could be considered odd I have not told the person I am closest to (other than my husband) that I am in the middle of a separation. Indeed, that the 'process' is already at the stage where our legal representation are conferring and are sorting an 'arrangement'. But it's not as if I have lied, I've simply been airbrushing the truth. I throw the crumpled-up piece of paper at Fitz.

'I'm perfectly fine.'

'Prove it, then,' he says. 'Prove you are *not* a fun sponge.'

'How?'

'Come to a party next Saturday. I introduced myself to Frédéric Lazare's *painfully* fit PA at Noelle's launch. Get this...he's called Jesus! Talk about if the cap fits...if He is the Second Coming, it was well worth the wait. Anyway, he told me, Lazare's having a twenty-four-hour bash next weekend at his penthouse on the river. Expect a crowd of acerbic fashion whores off their tits on whatever dirtbag narcotics they can get on speed dial by tapping their acrylic fingernails against limited-run chrome Samsungs…then dancing the night, following morning and possibly the next arvo away to a re-*lent*-less disco beat. In other words, it'll quite possibly be…'

'…the best party ever?' I suggest. This is one of our in-jokes. Every industry bash *always* has this potential revered status.

'Up for it, Jacobs?'

'Maybe…'

'Bring Zach, obviously.'

'Ah, I doubt he would be able to make it. He's still preparing for that big pitch at his agency,' I say, quickly. 'Oh, and let's not forget he absolutely loathes disco.'

Fitz tuts. 'Yawn! Straight men really are a strange breed, aren't they? I can just about understand them not wanting cock. But glitter balls?'

I force a smile, but I am already imagining about what would happen if I went to the party. I'll drink, get drunk… then sober up way too quickly. When I do, I'll be looking in a mirror, in a bathroom, in a home I have never been in before. That's when I have to face myself because the reflection never lies.

'Jacobs?'

'I said, *maybe*. Anyway, what was the second question you had?'

'Ah, yes. That dizzy cow who chucked her drink over you at the book launch. She threw me such shade as she was leaving. I mean, serious attitude! Is she *some*one?'

'No. She is *no* one.' I say, very slowly. 'No one at all.'

'Anyway, did the Wang recover?'

I exhale deeply, collecting myself. 'The dry cleaners are going to do what they can, but they couldn't give me an answer for sure. You can never tell what the long-term effects will be after that sort of damage. I should know more in a day or so. Best we can both do is let the experts do their thing…and pray.'

Fitz laughs. 'That's better, darling. *Almost* funny. Keep this up and I may not replace you. I was even considering Bronwyn earlier as my new office bf.' He throws the paper ball back at me, then checks his watch. 'Right, I'm off. Am nipping to that do which Oil Denim are putting on. They're celebrating the release of their new ethically sourced boyfriend jean. That would be nice, wouldn't it? An ethical boyfriend…oooooh, I bet Jesus has a social conscience. He'd have to…with a name like that.'

'I'm sure he does a *lot* of volunteer work,' I deadpan.

'Totally. Heart of gold!' He giggles. 'Actually, I might *casually* ask him to pop down. Right, I'll text you later, when I am nicely pissed and the night feels full of possibility. And then again, when I'm eating my feelings in a kebab shop and considering a Reece's Pieces Nutrageous chaser. Oh, and Jacobs, remember…' He swings his jacket round his shoulders. 'Cheer the *fuck* up, you SHREW!'

I go back to my desk. My screen saver of Kat Moss is partially covered by my email inbox. During the time I was with Fitz, I have received twenty-three new messages. Around half are tagged with a little red exclamation mark—a 'screamer', as we call it—signifying that the contents require reading urgently. But I can tell from the subject boxes most of these are not even verging on 'pressing', let alone anywhere in the ball park of urgent. Sample sales, product launches, label re-branding, model-agency parties, designer-high street collaborations, new clubs and bars, store openings, store revamps, store invite-only evenings, and bloggers asking for interviews…not exactly *real* newsworthy events. But honestly, *all* of that used to excite me. It's what the industry is all about. *Image*. But right now, I can feel my own image slipping. *I* am slipping.

I stare at my computer screen. A new email pings through from *gillian@bellsolicitors.co.uk*. How ironic that hers are always free from any exclamatory tags yet they are the ones which make me want to scream. I click on it.

Ashley,

I've received notification from your husband's solicitor regarding the status of your mortgage and house accounts. Please call me to discuss. I shall be at the office until 8pm tonight.

Kind regards, Gillian

I check that Fitz has left and reach for my iPhone. I've got two missed calls. One from Sheila. Another from Zach. I dial 901. The disembodied voice kicks in.

You have one new message. To return the call, key five. To replay the message, key one. To s—…I key 2 and save the message. *The next message is four…minutes…long.*

Zach's mobile has rung me by mistake. This happens a lot because he only uses code-less Nokias made between 2003 and 2008 and never puts the lock on. He thinks smartphones are naff. I listen to the message. I can hear music, mate-y joshing, fruit machines…the background hum of a pub. Then the noises become clearer. I assume the mobile has been removed from his pocket.

ZACH: Still can't believe it. (Excited.) We hit that out of the park. Smashed it in the back of the net. Insert your own triumphant cliché here...

A WOMAN'S VOICE: I knew we would get it.

I don't recognise her. She must be a colleague. Probably one of the fancy dress enthusiasts. Zach's office is full of them.

A MAN'S VOICE: Just between us, I was shitting myself.

I recognise him. It's Keith With the Bad Teeth.

Properly shitting myself.

THE WOMAN: Charming.

KEITH: You were too, Zach. Admit it.

THE WOMAN: He didn't come across like that during the pitch.

ZACH: Well, that's good to know. Hey, where are the toilets in here?

KEITH: Told you!

ZACH: D'you always have to be so low rent, Keith? It's amazing how you've become even more uncouth since you've stopped drinking. You used to be a one-man wave of tastelessness...

KEITH: ...and now I am a tsunami! Even better, the next morning I get to remember all the chaos I've caused. Bogs are up the stairs to the left...

ZACH: Cool...watch those files for me, please.

THE WOMAN: That's a lot of paperwork you've got in there.

ZACH: Yeah, it's for the...(Stops.) We're not exactly doing our bit for the conservation of the planet.

WOMAN: God, don't. Pete and I must have destroyed a good few acres of the rainforest before our decree nisi was issued.

KEITH: I would prefer not to be listening to this conversa-

tion. It's depressing. As you both know, I am very recently engaged…

    ZACH: How that happened, I have no idea.

    KEITH: Me neither!

    WOMAN: Well, if it does go horribly wrong, my advice is to be reasonable at all times. Pete and I started out being more than civil, but then he got nasty, so I did too. It was tough. At times I wondered if it was going to be worth it, but I just kept repeating to myself a joke my best friend told me.

    ZACH: Go on…

    WOMAN: What's the difference between getting a divorce and getting circumcised?

    KEITH: What's the difference?

    WOMAN: When you get a divorce, you get rid of the whole pri—

The message clicks off and the disembodied voice returns.

To return the call, key five. To replay the message, key one. To save, key two. To delete, key three. For message details key eight.

I key 8. The message was left six minutes ago. I imagine Zach washing his hands at the sink in the toilet, looking into the mirror. He is content with his reflection. Why wouldn't he be? Zach never fucks up. That's Zach. A justifiably shame-free zone. I think about the way *she* looked at *me* in the mirror at the hotel. After looking at me she looked at herself. She was staring at her face until I left the room. It was expressionless. There was no shame. I wonder how long she gazed at herself for like that. How could she? How *dare* she? After what she did…

…Tanya *fucking* Dinsdale.

Six

'Happy birthday to y—'

'MAMA! Jasper's being MEEEEEEEEEAN! I haaaaaaaaaate him! I want to go shopping!'

'Happy b—'

'Whatever, Evie. You ugly anus pig face.'

'Jasper! E-*nough*. Where did you learn that dis-*gust*-ing expression?'

Greg leans down and laughs in my ear. 'His eye-wateringly expensive private school, probably.'

'MAMAAAAAAAAAAA! Owwwwww! Jasssssper! MY ARM! He's got my AAAAAAAAAARM!'

'Happy birthday, dear Taaaaany—'

'Can't we go to the shops? OWWWWWWWWWW!'

This particular squeal is so blood curdling I drop my fork. One decibel higher and there could be potential perforation of an ear drum. Judging by the expressions (ranging from marked annoyance to *Chitty Chitty Bang Bang* Child-Catcher-style loathing) worn by the other customers eating in The Croft's alfresco area, they feel the same. Across the table, Maddie and Kian, look stoically—and a little smugly—at each other. Kian is bouncing their baby, Carter, on his knee.

Carter has not murmured since we got here, whilst Suze's children have not stopped swearing and screeching whilst locked in combat. Her eldest, Jasper (my godson), has always been rough with the younger Evie (Maddie's goddaughter), to obtain information or his own way but, recently he's started treating her way outside Amnesty guidelines, purely for fun.

'Jasper! *NO! I said, NO!*' shouts Suze.

'Listen to your mother,' adds her husband, Rollo, without much volume or losing focus on the remaining section of his cheeseburger. 'Maybe I should put them in the car…'

'Don't be silly,' I reassure him. 'They're only playing.'

'…cut to Evie being disembowelled,' says Greg.

Suze shoots him a look. But then, another squeal. This one more cochlea-penetrating than the previous. Suze jumps up from the table and marches over to where Jasper is yanking Evie across the grass by her left wrist. With one swift action, Suze separates both kids and drags them towards the car park, where they will stay until she 'effing says so'.

'How long is an effon, Mama?' asks Evie, as they are shunted off. 'I want new shoes. With a heeeeeeeeel! Flatties make your legs look gross. You get cankles! FACT! Is an effon longer or shorter than a minute?'

'You can work that out whilst you're sitting in the car, can't you?' seethes Suze. 'And by the time you have, we'll be leaving.'

Jasper blows a nonchalant raspberry at his mother. 'Like I care. Sooner we get out of this lame *hole* the better. Can we go to Nando's on the way home? Food here is crap. I want peri peri chicken. To take away. I'll eat in my room, then smash the shit out of *Call of Duty*.'

Greg bursts out laughing. 'To be fair, I often think that when I come here to start my shift…'

I smile at my boyfriend again, relieved that he is not simply making light of the situation but actually enjoying himself *and* making sure everyone else does too. I know he wasn't expecting to have a good time at my birthday lunch today. I noticed a box-shaped lump in the back of his jeans as he was tapping in the alarm code before we left the house. *Cigarettes*. Or as they shall henceforth be known: *sperm destruction sticks*.

Suze returns to the table with dots of sweat on her forehead. She dabs at her face—she has applied a fair amount of make-up today—and gives Rollo the type of look usually reserved for violent criminals in the dock.

'What was that for?' he asks her, dipping the last piece of his brioche burger bun into a pot of aioli. 'I haven't done anything.' He swivels his eyes at Greg and Kian. 'Did I do anything? No, m'lud, I didn't.'

Suze claps her hands to her cheeks and makes a skew-whiff 'O' shape with her mouth, briefly resembling *The Scream* by Edvard Munch.

'I think that may have been the issue, Rollo, mate,' mutters Kian, chomping on his dressing and cruton-free Caesar salad (Maddie has put him on a diet) whilst goo-gooing at his five-month-old son. 'Never *ever* admit to *not* doing something.'

'Who taught you that?' asks Rollo.

'You. When Suze got preggers for the first time.'

Everyone laughs, even Suze. She sits back down at the table next to her husband and he puts his arm around her.

'Sorry, sweetness.' He squeezes her. 'If it makes you feel any better, I too wish our son was not so sadistic nor our daughter so materialistic, and that we could leave them both at an enclosed educational institution *all* year round. As soon as such a place is set up—that is not strictly a prison and has flexi but not compulsory visiting hours—I assure you, you will never have to see them, unless you want to.'

Suze manages a smile back at him. 'You promise?'

'As I am also your barrister, I'll get some legal papers drawn up.'

'Thank you. Oh, and remember you also promised to drive back.' She kisses him on the cheek then takes a restorative gulp of white wine. 'Right, shall we try and sing "Happy Birthday" to Tanya again?'

I wave my hand at them all. 'No! God, really, you don't h—'

'Yeah,' agrees Greg. 'Probably not the *best* idea. I think it's safe to say the rest of the beer garden know we're here now.'

Suze glances across the table at me, eyes narrowing. I pretend I haven't seen her.

'…so, what are you lot doing next Friday?' continues Greg.

'Erm, that's when we're round at my parents' house for their anniversary. *You* reminded *me* the other day.'

He pulls a face. 'Oh, shiiiiit, yeah. Only, there's a band playing in Camden I wouldn't mind having a look at. A sort of experimental indie collective with a retro-seventies Hendrix feel.'

I pull a face back at him. I've been to gigs with Greg before, where the boxes marked CAMDEN, EXPERIMENTAL and COLLECTIVE have been ticked. And you can guarantee if they have been, so will the ones marked HOT, SWEATY, NOISY, SMELLY AND ABSOLUTELY JOYLESS. But with the addition of the word HENDRIX? That's a fresh kind of hell that I have not even visited in my darkest nightmares. Suddenly, sitting across the table from my father for a couple of hours feels more appealing.

Greg clocks my expression. 'Don't panic, I meant a boys trip.' He nods at the guys. 'We could get up there early doors, have a few drinks, do the gig, go to a club…stay overnight. It's been God knows how long since we all went out on the lash. What do you reckon?'

Like highly strung barn owls, Suze and Maddie's heads rotate round towards their partners.

Rollo laughs. 'Well, I think that's your answer, mate. Sounds great, but it's the aftermath I can't handle…that noise you heard earlier, imagine that when you're hungover. *All* day. It's torture.'

'I hate to tell you,' Suze adds, 'next weekend it will feel more like an actual torture *chamber*. Eves and Jasps are having a sleepover weekend at ours with four pals. Imagine the first *Saw* movie with elements of *Hostel* thrown in.'

'Oh, sweet Jesus, *no*…' moans Rollo.

'You'll have to count me out too, Greg. Sorry…' Kian apologises. 'Obviously, I can't leave Maddie overnight.'

'What with her being a fully functioning adult and all that,' jokes Greg.

I don't laugh as I know Maddie is staring at me.

'He means leave me *with the baby*,' she says. 'It's still early days, and besides, *Greg*, the last time Rollo and Kian went out with you overnight, Kian came back with a black eye, his arm in a sling and a cracked tooth.'

Greg sighs. 'Come on, that was an isolated incident.'

'It wasn't that bad, Maddie,' I add, sticking up for Greg. 'They didn't leave him on the pavement. A night in Casualty and Kian was good to go.'

'Good to go *straight back to bed*, where he remained for two days,' says Maddie. 'And he couldn't do a feed either.' She nods at Kian. 'Forget it, you're not going.'

'Jesus, you're so pussy whipped, mate.' Greg laughs.

'Yep,' smiles Kian, quite happily. 'That pretty much sums it up.'

'What about Jez?' I suggest. 'He'll want to go…'

'Nah, not his thing. Too edgy. Jez doesn't like to veer too far from the status quo. The concept or the band,' he mumbles.

I can sense he is getting irritated.

'Tell you what,' I suggest. 'Why don't *you* go to the gig and stay over? I'll go to my parents on Friday night, then meet you in London on Saturday morning, and we can spend the weekend there…do something *fun*. By "fun", I mean something in no way involving trippy guitar music. And nothing experimental or, heaven forbid, *experiential*.'

He smiles at me. 'Yeah…why not? You've got yourself a date, babe.'

I smile back. If there was ever a perfect time for us to have The Baby Talk it will be on a 'mini-break' (not that I would call it that out loud because I hate all that couples parlance). I'll splash out, book us into one of the luxury suites at The Rexingham, that posh hotel where Noelle did her book launch. Greg and I will be in our room—which will be a textbook lover's playground of squishy pillows, his'n'hers dressing gowns, a fully stocked mini-bar and a remote-control docking system—lying in bed after having 'nookie'…and start talking. I will pre-empt the conversation by saying that at no point during our future life as parents will we be like *them*. 'Them' being Suze and Rollo, Maddie and Kian or any other couple who reproducing has turned nuts. Or boring. Or both. He will laugh. So will I. And we will both know that we are in this together. It will be as far removed from what happened before as it is poss—

I jolt.

'I'm gasping for a fag,' says Suze. She puts her knife and fork together and glances up at her husband. 'Can you go and check on the little shits? They might be hot wiring the Range Rover. Greg…cigarette?'

I scan his face for a vague hint that he could be considering it, but he doesn't flinch.

Suze looks at him. 'You've given up?'

'Yep, it's all behind me now,' he says. 'I'm a reformed character.'

'That's…*good*. Good for you,' mutters Suze, pulling a Marlboro Light out of her pack. 'I'm the only one still up for it, then?'

'Looks that way,' he confirms.

I stop myself from looking too pleased.

'D'you mind not having one at the table, Suze?' Maddie grimaces at Suze. 'I know we're outside, but with Carter here…' She reaches over and strokes her baby's cheek. 'Actually, we're going to need to make tracks soon. My precious boy needs a nap.'

'Yeah, I'm exhausted,' says Kian, downing the remainder of his pint.

Maddie tuts at him. 'I meant Carter, you idiot. I hope he doesn't go bananas again when we put him in the car seat. It's the only time he really screams. You don't mind if we sneak off, do you?' she asks me.

'Erm…no, of course not.'

'I mind,' says Suze. 'Not all of us are ready to leave yet.'

I tap her arm. 'Relax, it's fine, Suze…we can stay.'

She rolls her eyes. 'It's always the end as soon as someone leaves,' she snaps. 'Jesus, Maddie, if you go slightly off schedule for *one* day, Carter is not going to grow up to be a serial killer.'

Maddie looks wounded and says nothing.

'Why don't you go for a cigarette?' I suggest to Suze, to diffuse the situation. 'Let me say goodbye to these two and I'll catch up with you. Greg, you don't mind, do you?'

'Nah, I'll go and help Rollo.'

Suze eyeballs him. 'Why would you want to do that?'

'Because it's fun watching over-indulgent middleclass parents being relentlessly poked at and abused by their own offspring.' He grins at her as he wanders off. 'It's a modern and *far* less upsetting form of bear baiting.'

After watching Maddie buckle a suddenly inconsolable Carter into the back of the car, I find Suze at the bottom of the beer garden next to the pond.

'What was all that about?' I ask her.

She drags on her Malboro Light. 'I thought we were going to be making a day of it, that's all.'

'No, not that. Getting at Maddie.'

'Oh, right…she's bugging me at the moment. It's as if she's produced the first baby to crawl the earth and *everyone* has to be reminded of this *every* second of *every* day. When I first had Jasper I was not like that. I was a *lot* more relaxed…'

'You were stoned, plus you had your sister *and* your mum—a hugely experienced GP!—on hand twenty-four hours a day to help.'

Suze pulls a sheepish face. 'Yeah, okay, I hear you. Hey, maybe the reason why my children are so out of control now is because I was too effing chilled out then? They're rebelling against their incense-infused, Portishead sound-tracked babyhood.'

I smile. 'Nah, they're going through a phase…one which

I have to say, you're dealing with incredibly well. I'd blow a gasket if mine started acting like that.'

'Oh, I'm only dealing with their behaviour thanks to Philip Morris and endless boxes of picnic wine from Lidl.' Suddenly, she stops. She is making her Munch face again. 'Sorry, what did you say? '*If mine started acting like that...*' T, you're not *preg*nant?'

I shake my head. 'No, no, god no...but...'

'Thank fuck for that...I mean, th—' She stops herself again. 'Sorry! *Sorry*. I was only thinking about what it would be like, erm...*for me*...to have another one. So...you've decided you want a...*baby*?' She drains her glass and swallows hard. 'Are...you...are you sure?'

'Uh-huh. Pending on everything working downstairs— I've had tests at the hospital and I'm seeing your mum for the results, so I need to wait and see. I'm sure everything will be fine. It was so long ago that...but, yeah, I'd like to get pregnant as soon as possible.'

'But...' begins Suze. 'B—'

'Oh, I know...' I interrupt her. 'I do *not* want to be one of those women who act as if it's like organising an Ocado delivery slot.'

'No, that's not what I was going to say...'

'What were you going to say?' I peer at her. 'Suze?'

She stares at me for a few seconds then gazes out over the pond. 'Are you *really* ready though, aft—'

I butt in again. 'Yeah, I am.'

'But even a few years ago, you still didn't know what you wanted, and now...you're sure?'

'Yes, I'm sure. I'm not a mess any more. Not a single part of my life is. Everything about me is in order. My home, my job, my friends and most importantly, the man I want to have children with.'

'You mean Greg?'

I shrug. 'Well, I did consider that "cute" new barman who started here last week as a potential father. Obviously, your husband too, but then thought, no. Even though we *know* he has good swimmers, it might be a bit weird for our friendship group. Definitely not Kian either. But more because his head is a weird shape. Carter was very lucky not to have inherited that.' I growl at her. 'Of course, I mean Greg, Suze. Greg is my boyfriend. If I am going to have a child with anyone it will be Greg.'

'Right…'

'Yes, *Greg*. Greg is *my* Mr Right. And you *can* blow fag smoke in my face for rolling out that mawkish old chestnut.'

'Look, T…' She is still looking out over the pond. 'I'm not saying Rollo is the ultimate catch. I mean, I look at him when he is doing that trick with the cereal and think, *how the hell did I end up with someone who thinks spraying cornflakes out of their mouth and all over the kitchen in the style of a burst New York fire hydrant is funny?* But you know what, the kids find it funny. They love how funny he is. They love him. And he loves them—despite their clear lack of respect for anyone bar the waiting staff at specialist chicken restaurants or the sales assistants at Schuh. And he loves me. He always has. From our party-mad years right through to the staid, middle-class perjury we serve now, he has loved me. And I know that when we are old and dec—'

I interrupt her. 'Why are we talking about Rollo? I've already said I think it would be odd if he sperminated me.' I continue the joke, purely to give Suze a chance to re-consider what she is about to say. But she doesn't.

She turns back to me. 'You know what I am getting at.'

'Would it be the same thing you were getting at about twenty minutes ago, when you shot me a look after Greg was reluctant to sing "Happy Birthday" again?'

'Well, it's not as if he's gone out of his way to make it a very special day for you, is it, T?'

'That's unfair, Suze. He doesn't have the funds which Rollo does. He works at *a* bar, your husband works at The Bar…it pays a lot better.'

'I'm not talking financially, just in terms of effort.'

'Hang on, it was *your* idea we came to The Croft because of the outside space for Jasper to re-enact a hunt-to-kill mission on Evie. Besides, we've got our weekend away in London to look forward to.'

'Only because *you* suggested it about five minutes ago. He was quite happy to be going on a piss up with the boys— totally disregarding the dinner you had arranged over at your parents', I may add. The addition of some time with you—romantic or otherwise—was an afterthought, of *yours*.'

I growl at her. 'Whenever you have a couple of glasses of wine, you cannot wait to start carping about Greg.'

'That is not true,' she retorts, then laughs. 'Let me assure you I carp about him when I haven't been drinking too, but behind your back.'

'Suze! This is serious. You're my best friend. He's my boyfriend. It's going to stay that way. I'd really like it if you could build a proper relationship with him. There must be *some*thing you like about him. You've shared enough cigarettes with him over the years.'

'I'm not saying he's a bad person, T. All girls are meant to faintly disapprove of their best friend's boyfriend.'

'But it's more than that with you…'

She pauses again, then takes a deep breath. 'I guess it's because of…because of everything you went through. I saw you go through it.'

'…and "through" is the operative word. I am over it. Partly thanks to you, because you were there for me *through*out. Why are you being like this, Suze?'

She swallows hard even though she has no wine left.

'T…'

'What?'

'I want you to be sure.'

'I am sure. I've been sure for a while. But the other day…' I swallow hard too. 'I saw her.'

'Who?'

'Her.'

'*Her?*'

'Her.'

Suze sucks in her cheeks. 'What the *fuck*? Where?'

'In London…at a launch I went to for my blog. *Catwalk* were sponsoring the party. I had no idea.'

'Shitting hell! What did you say?'

'Nothing. She didn't say anything either.'

'And that was it? T! This is HUGE!'

'It's not.'

'T! You saw Ashley Atwal? *You saw Ashley Atwal?* YOU SAW ASHLEY ATWAL?'

'Shooooosh, keep your voice down. *Please*. Look, it happened. It's over. It's done.'

Suze's face contorts as she digests the information. But then she shakes her head at me.

'And this apparently *non*-event has changed your mind about everything?'

'Of course not! For God's sake, Suze, you *know* me…I'm

not the kind of person who makes decisions without thinking things through so thoroughly I even bore myself, but seeing her forced me to examine whether I was ready. *Truly* ready. Not because I want to change the past. Because I am living in the present.' I highlighted this sentence in one of my psych books on cognitive therapy. I found the books more helpful than the therapists. 'Do you understand?

'Mmmm, and I'm…'

'I think the word is 'happy', Suze. *You* are happy for *me*.'

She pulls me to her. Our embrace is stiff. As I pull away, I hear a guitar being strummed. I twist round. So does Suze. Immediately, both of us gulp for air.

Her sudden need for oxygen is down to shock. Mine is down to a overwhelming sense of love. Okay, *and* shock. Greg is standing on top of the table where we had eaten our lunch and is playing his acoustic guitar. Within seconds, everyone in the beer garden has stopped talking. They are staring at Greg. But he is only focused on one person…*me*. He starts to sing a song I don't recognise, but when he hits what appears to be the chorus, there is one word I am familiar with; Tanya. *Tanya*. TANYA. He makes it rhyme with 'I want ya'. From beside me, I hear Suze mutter, 'Move over, Ed Sheeran…'. The other punters are swaying in time to the music and offering Greg encouraging whoops. By the time he has got to the chorus for the second time, a few of them have a go at joining in.

Oh Tanya, Tanya, Tany-aaaaa
I want ya, I want yaaaaa
Sometimes I find it hard to show it
But Tany-aaaaaa, I want yaaaaa
To know it
The way I feel

Is reeeeeal, yeeeeeeah!

I stay sat, staring back at him. This is easily the most romantic, creative, unexpected, well-planned and personal gesture he has ever made for me. But it is also the most public. I would like him to stop immediately. I am acutely aware that anyone who isn't looking at *him* is looking at *me*. I attempt to focus on his bracelet jangling around as he plays, in order to remind myself that he is my 'true love' and as such, I should be thrilled by this torture. I mean, *gesture*. But my purple heat rash starts crawling. It is more intense than usual; spreading over a greater surface area—a wisteria of self-consciousness. I force a smile up at Greg. He is now scanning the garden as he sings. Suddenly, he lets his guitar drop so that it is dangling across his shoulder by its strap, then he raises his hands above his head. Clapping out a beat, he encourages all the other customers to join in and together they sing the next chorus a cappella.

Oh, Tanya, Tanya, Tany-aaaaa
I want ya, I want yaaaaa
Yeah Taaaaaaaaaaanya
I want…
…yooooooooooou!
It's the way I feel
For reeeeeal…

The way I feel for real is MORTIFIED. But I smile at Greg. No, I *beam*. Because that's what other girls would do. They would dig this, wouldn't they? All this…*attention*. This is why so many movies end with a *public* declaration of loving intent by the leading man. It's what we're brought up to believe is the ultimate romantic scenario: if other people are watching it makes it even more special. Not for me though. I don't want flash mobs or billboards or kiss-cams or orchestras or sing—

Yeah, Tanyaaaaa

It's true.

It's you.

On the 'ou' of 'you', he gives his guitar a sharp slap and drops his head. *It's over.*

'Jeeeee-sus,' says Suze, flatly.

'Cheers, everyone!' shouts Greg, wiping his hair off his face. 'If you didn't think that was too painful, my band play right here at The Croft a couple of times a month. We usually put up some flyers around the pub the week beforehand for you all to ignore, so please, make sure you don't give them a second glance…'

With that, my boyfriend jumps down to the ground. His crowd jump up; laughing, cheering and applauding…and then, thank-the-Lord-Jesus-Christ-and-the-Holy-Ghost they return their attention to drinking and eating. I get up and walk over to Greg. As I do, he reaches into his left back pocket, which I know has that illicit pack of cigarettes in. For the first time in my life, I consider smoking one. But then I stop. He has not pulled out a pack of Camel Lights from his jeans… it is a black velvet box. He lifts the lid.

I stare at the contents until my vision becomes fuzzy. Then the voices around me become dulled. My head feels as if it is being compressed. The only part of my body I can feel is my burning chest. I grab the box and slam it shut. I know I am about to faint. And like always, as I am losing my balance and the ground is hurtling towards me, I remember standing at the top of the yellow tower. The one which looked like dirty Lego.

ME: I've missed you so much…

HIM: (Mumbling into my hair.) Oh, Tanya...I missed you too. So, so much. I'm sorry we haven't been able to meet for a bit.

ME: A bit? It's been thirteen days. I've been going out of my mind. Seeing you but not talking to you. Not holding you. Not feeling you. I don't know how much more I can take. We've got to work out a pl—

HIM: A plan. I know... (Taking a breath.) That's what I've been doing. A mate of mine, he's managing a club in London. He might be able to give me a job. Promotions. Warm-up DJ-ing. Bar work.

ME: Will we be able to afford a flat?

HIM: Ha! No. We'll have to get a room share or something. Worst-case scenario, we've got the van until we get ourselves sorted.

ME: You have no money?

HIM: I can't take the savings that are in the bank. There's only a few hundred quid. I couldn't do that to...to either of them. But I'm going to start saving now, put some cash aside for us every month.

ME: Every MONTH? For how many months? A whole year? Two? THREE?

HIM: (Flapping his hand.) Stop it, Tanya. Keep your voice down. Do you think that it has been easy for me?

ME: No, b—

HIM: Look at me. (Grabbing my head.) I promise you that I will do it. You've always known it was going to take some time and it still is. I can't just up sticks and neither can you. We'll both hurt people.

ME: But there is no going back on that now. They'll be hurt whether we are together now or in a month or a year...

HIM: Trust in me, Tanya.

ME: I'm trying, I'm trying.

HIM: Good. (Voice softening). Let's focus on the future. We're strong enough to get through this, but on the days when you aren't feeling so strong, this... (reaching into pocket, pulling out a small box)...this should make it easier.(Opening it.)

ME: (Seeing the ring. Gasping.) Does this mean...

HIM: (Kissing me on the mouth.) It means I'm yours.

ME: (Kissing him back. Placing the jewellery on my finger. Staring at it. Taking a breath. Then another.) The only problem is...it may not fit for much longer.

HIM: (Smiling.) Oh yeah, I forgot. Your mum does have a reputation as the estate 'feeder'. Why does she cook so much fucking f—

ME: (Interrupting.) No, not because of that. (Looking up.) I'm pregnant.

HIM: What?

ME: (Scanning his face but finding nothing to read.) I'm pregnant...and scared. (Crying.) So scared.

HIM: Shooooooooooosh, Tanya. It's okay, it's okay. Breathe. (Exhaling deeply. Rubbing my shoulders.) So...how...how did this happ—?

ME: (Shrugging.) I don't know. I'm on the pill. I mean, there was that time I had a bug and she said that you sh—

HIM: (Sharply.) Who said? Who have you told? Who is 'she'?

ME: My doctor. Dr. Lyons.

HIM: Dr. Lyons? That's that girl Suze's old dear, isn't it? Are you insane? Her husband is a copper and she used to hang out with... (Gritting his teeth.) Does she know you're up the duff? Tanya, ANSWER ME!

ME: Please, quit with the questions. It doesn't matter HOW it could have happened. It's happened and is now

happenING! (Getting hysterical.) And no, no one knows.
Please, I don't need you interrogating me. I need you to tell
me not to be scared because everything will be okay.

HIM: It will. It will…I'll be there for you. I won't let any-
thing happen to you. I'll look after you. Promise.

ME: (Wiping snot away from my nose with my sleeve.)
We'll go to London?

HIM: Yeah. No one will know us.

ME: When?

HIM: Next week.

ME: (Managing to smile.) But what about needing to
save?

HIM: Let me worry about that. We'll only be down there
for a couple of nights, won't we? I'll be able to scrape
together enough for a hotel room and the clinic.

Clinic. As those final two syllables hung in the air between
us, snow started to drift down.

I sense Suze by my side. She is bellowing.

'T! Answer me. Back off, everyone…nothing to worry
about. She's having one of her turns. T! I know you're alive.
You know you're alive. Wakey-wakey. One, two, three…
WIDE AWAKE!'

I wait a while to open my eyes, my body is rigid with
embarrassment. Whenever this used to happen and Suze was
there, she always made sure to get rid of the gawpers so I did
not wake up in a 'situation'. She wipes my hair away from
my forehead and holds up two fingers close to my face, as if
flicking me a 'V' sign.

'What does this mean?' she jokes, just like she did the first
time I fainted at college in the student mini-market.

'Fuck off,' I mumble.

'And this?' She holds up a middle finger.

'Fuck you.'

'Yep, you're fine.' She smiles. 'It's been a while since you did that. I'd almost forgotten what that thud sounds like. There is no other noise quite like that of a human being slumping to the floor. I told Greg to go and get you a Lucozade *immediately*. D'you remember at college, I always kept a bottle in my bag just in case y—' She is distracted by the black box which is lying next to me. 'What's this?'

Before I can answer, she opens it. As soon as she sees the ring she inhales sharply. Touching it, she shakes her head from side to side, seemingly baffled.

'Wh-what does this mean? T? What does this mean?'

I cannot put into words what this means. Which is ironic because, in my early teens, I had my views on marriage totally sorted. I remember ranting to Ashley (which I would do a lot—she would call my outbursts 'Tanya Tirades') that I would not get married.

'Marriage is just a piece of paper, isn't it? And who needs more admin? A marriage contract takes the mystery out of a relationship and redefines it as a business deal. I've always survived independently of anyone and always will do. That said, if in the future my partner wanted to get me a ring, I would accept it. It could mean what it wants to us, because ultimately that's all that matters: what we think of each other. Not how the legal system views us. Once you introduce that kind of outside influence, it's going to affect you in some way. I mean, everything could be tickety-boo at the point of acceptance, but what if we hit a rocky patch at some point? If we did we should attempt to ride it out because we still want to be together, not because we are financially bound together by a pair of signatures. I don't see why people don't just be.'

Ashley laughed at me and said, 'Fuck that!' …she already

knew what she was wearing. She'd found a picture on the
Internet of these vintage Versace frocks, so now, all she had
to do was find a husband. And then she added that if I ever
got married, I should expect to be divorced on the spot if I
used the word 'tickety-boo'.

Suze is still staring at the ring when Greg crouches down
by my side. He passes me a glass of fizzy orange liquid.

'Sorry, we only had Tango behind the bar. Are you all
right, babe?'

'Yes,' I tell him. 'And, yes…'

'*Yes?*' He smiles at me. 'Does that mean..?'

I smile back. 'Yes.'

It also means that I need to apologise to…*her*. I don't
even know where she is living now. But I will find her and
say sorry. One last time. *Yes*.

Seven

It has not got colder, merely gone drizzly and muggy. Humid. I hate humidity. Anyone who works in fashion does. Humidity sounds the death knell for any look other than 'easy separates' with a baseball cap. Even Catherine—who *never* turns down a freebie—refused to attend Hong Kong Fashion Week as the guest of a billionaire merchandiser. I glance up at my outfit for the memorial which is hanging in cellophane off the storage rack on the train. Acne cream silk shirt and Joseph leather joggers. In my vintage Miu Miu bag, I have some Giuseppe Zanotti heels. (All bought on Outnet at a reasonable reduction.) Only *looking* at the joggers is enough to bring on the clamminess. Three hours of broken sleep and an acute hangover—the type which doesn't come in waves but compresses your frontal lobe with no let-up—is adding to the usual churning nausea I knew I would feel returning to my home town. I felt it the last time.

I faff on my iPad; mainly second-hand designer discount websites and archive interviews with the Olsens. Why sit with your own thoughts for three hours when you can learn how Mary-Kate gets her hair so perfectly tousled for a major event? (Dry shampoo, no more than five hair pins. *Ever*.)

Or buy a barely used off-white hidden chain limited-edition millennium lambskin flap bag for just shy of one and a half grand. Okay, so *yeah*, it's quilted. But it's not a cliché. It's Chanel. I PayPal the fucker, then log onto Instagram.

Catherine has made her pregnancy public with the ubiquitous scan upload.

Stork ETA NW3 mid Feb! #4

The first person to congratulate her is Jazz.

Maje congratz! Totes happs for U n all the fam-a-lam.

This is typical Jazz. Her tweets make Noelle's look like those of a linguistics professor. Below Jazz's congratulatory message is a link to her latest Instagram entry, a photo of her about to leave for work in a sequinned mini-skirt (pretty sure it is Sass & Bide), faded grey sweatshirt and vintage Vivenne Westwood buckled pirate boots. I reluctantly approve of the mix in textures, eras, effort, cost and labels. No Crimes Against Fashion are being committed. Catherine has also given this look the thumbs up.

@missjazz LOVE! You MUST do the Westwood boots at LFW! Best of British!

LFW. Their meeting after my meeting. Jazz is taking my seat on the front row at all the shows during London Fashion Week. Isn't she? ISN'T SHE? I try to stay calm. But now an even more hideous vision is projected into my mind. The magazine team are sitting round the table in the boardroom, ready to discuss features for the first issue since Catherine has left for her maternity leave. Jazz walks in, places a box of pastel iced, crystallised jelly-topped cupcakes on the table, before uttering the dreaded words, '*So, as the new Acting Editor, my vision is…*'

CHRIST!

Is Catherine grooming Jazz to take over when she's on maternity leave?

I have to hand it to her, Jazz has been playing a good game. Presenting herself as some sort of software soothsayer, luring Catherine into believing she will not be able to survive without her knowledge of the digital future. I don't know why Catherine is encouraging it. If anything, it encourages buyers not to engage with the tangible magazine. She'll regret it when she's replaced by a *hologram*.

I flick to my own Instagram page and look at my last post...from the beginning of the summer. Christ, in Insta-time, I may as well be dead. It's a great picture though: a 'throwback Thursday' snap of Cara Delevingne on the runway for Giles Deacon. She was filming *herself* on her mobile as she walked. I remember fashionistas around me were literally gasping in delight and awe at this dazzling alchemy of technology, branded sponsorship *and* lightweight knitwear. It's a great shot. Undisturbed by the back of any-one's head. It ever so subtly whispered, 'Front row, baby...' Jazz hadn't taken one anyway near as impressive because she hadn't once been put on the 'frow'. Every picture she had taken had been obscured by a flamboyant hair-do or some elaborate millinery. I posted it—*yes*, admittedly *very* smugly—on the way home. I smiled. Then I sniggered. Then I laughed. I laughed so loudly that I could see I was making other commuters on the bus uncomfortable. But I didn't care. I was laughing again. The laughter felt good.

I try to laugh now, and it makes me feel even queasier. I think I may still be pissed.

As soon as the train gets in, I march straight to the public loos and vomit, hard...until my insides feel raw and only flecks of stringy, sticky, yellow bile are attaching themselves to the toilet bowl. Sweating but shivering too, I walk up the road to the nearest pub, buy a pint of iced (full-sugar) Coca-Cola, neck it, then use their cloakroom to clean my teeth. Then—for the first time ever—I place my wedding ring on the normal hand. I don't want to face any awkward questions. Saying you are married is the neatest, most finite answer when in strange company. Anything else initiates further conversation. I will not be staying for long.

I get a cab number from the barman, and order one to take me to the King Edward pub. The driver drops me on the road outside as the car park is packed. A fresh wave of nausea washes over me as I arrive an hour late for my mother's memorial.

'…as I said at the start, today is a celebration of Yvonne and all the good times she had. We *all* had. When we were teenagers, she made me promise that if she died before me, there would not be a funeral, as it would put everyone on a, I quote, "massive downer"…'

My mother's best friend, Sheila, is talking. She is exactly how I remember her: a monochrome sensation in a black pleather dress with her hair bleached through from root to tip. I creep round the edge of the pub. It has been decorated with balloons and streamers. At the back, there is a DJ set up with old-fashioned record decks.

'So, I want to leave you with an image of the Yvonne on the day I met her.' Sheila smiles. 'It was the first of January 1988. I'd ended up at a random chill out at her parents' gaff. She showed me her portfolio and said she was off to fashion college to become an award-winning designer. I told her I was going to be a fancy restaurateur. In that moment it all seemed *so* possible. That feeling of being able to *unquestionably* achieve your dreams…the direct result of having youth *on* our side and boyfriends who sold mind-boggling ecstasy pills *at* our side!'

Most people in the pub laugh. I vaguely recognise some of them as part of the original 'crew' who lived on the estate when we did. When I was a kid, our flat was always full of my parents' friends. There was a lot of music, a lot of dancing and *vast* quantities of weed. A bloke from Social Services did pop round once, but ended up sharing a spliff with everyone and enthusiastically listening to a 'bangin'' mixtape.

Sheila chatters on, recalling the crew's halcyon years: orbital raving, pork-pie hats, road trips, sooooorted, 1210s, Shoom, nice one, cheeky halves, wheels of steel, Oakey, loved up, Ku, head rubs, mental-chicken oriental-radio rental, galloping beats, warehouse, Vicks vapour rub, glo sticks, hands in the air, Garys, Jimmies, Terry and June, chooooon, what's-your-name-where-you-from-what-you-on?, nauuuuughty, large it, have it, love it…BUZZING! With each Acid house-related piece of terminology she spouts, the man standing next to her appears more confused. I wonder whether this is—*was*—her second husband. He is wearing a black three-piece suit. Either a fairly expensive off-the-peg one which has been altered to fit well, or a bespoke by a decent local tailor. The shirt is also well made. You can make a five-thousand-quid suit look cheap with a bad collar. Ditto the cuffs. This theory works vice versa as well; a premium quality 'chemise' can upgrade a cheap tux. But I can tell both of his are investment pieces. He looks comfortable in it too. Her first husband did not own a suit and tie. He saw those that did as being sartorially shackled by society.

I walk round to the back of the room and slip into a booth. The table is sticky to touch and has that distinctive tangy smell of booze that has saturated into the wood over years of service. Or maybe the tang is coming off me. I am sweating. The man in the suit steps forward to say a few 'final words'. The expression on his face is now lost. I cannot look at it.

Zach's became like that, the longer time went on. I pretended I couldn't see it. But it was all I saw. He knew it too. Bizarrely, he chose our local Chinese restaurant to tell me.

ME: What's that face for? You feel guilty about Kat Moss? Oh, come on, just don't tell her I'm having prawn balls. Say I went for the vegetarian stir fry. She will be way less, 'Talk to the paw, beeyatch!' With plain rice, not the egg one. She likes that too. Or the special fr—

ZACH: (Interrupting.) Ash, we need to talk.

ME: About our cat's increasing consumption of monosodium glutamate? Or mine? Yeah, I know I've been eating crap recently. Well, more crap than usual. My arteries have already had a quiet word.

ZACH: No, about us.

ME: (Laughing.) Are you winding me up? And can you please stop looking at me like that!

ZACH: (Expression not changing.) Why would me asking to 'talk about us' be a wind up?

ME: Because it's such a cliché.

ZACH: It's not a cliché, it's what normal couples to do.

ME: But we're not a normal couple, are we? And that's a good thing. (Waving a prawn ball at him.) You have got to eat one, please. I've had five already.

ZACH: I'm not hungry.

ME: O-kay, now you're freaking me out.

ZACH: (Sharply.) You don't think I'm freaked out?

ME: By me? Zach, what the fuck are you going on about? If I've done something wrong, th—

ZACH: You've done nothing wrong. You've done nothing.

I glanced around the restaurant, it was half full. Zach and I had been here a zillion times before but I had never noticed the quantity of clientele before.

ME: Then what's your poi—

ZACH: (Interrupting. Again.) That is exactly my point. You've done nothing. You've said nothing. You've felt nothing. That's the point. That is my point. THAT IS MY POINT, ASH!

I chewed super slowly on my prawn ball. This was the loudest Zach had ever spoken to me.

ME: Sssssshhhhh…

ZACH: No, I will not sssssshhhhh…'

ME: You're making no sense. What do you want me to do? To say? To feel?

HIM: I have no idea. Something. Anything. You should need me.

ME: I do need you.

HIM: It doesn't feel like that.

ME: (Smiling nervously.) I'll try harder.

HIM: You shouldn't have to try to need me.

ME: I've got an idea. Why don't YOU try to STOP doing, saying and feeling…why can't you just 'be'? Why do I have to be the one in the wrong? Why do I have to need anything?

All the other diners were now craning to get a better view of our table. So, I made a decision to shout so that if they couldn't see, at least they could hear.

ME: WHY CAN'T WE MOVE ON? I will not fuck up my life—or let you fuck up yours—for one that NEVER. EVEN. FUCKING. EXISTED. Or is that what you want?

HIM: (Calmly.) No…no…I'll tell you what I want. What I want is… (Pausing, looking around the restaurant.) What I want is…the bill. (Pulling out forty pounds from his wallet, throwing notes on table. Getting up. Leaving.)

'Ashley! You came…'

'Sheila!' I smile at her, but I can feel another wave of nausea building. 'You look great…and so does the pub.'

'Ah, I gave it a face lift a couple of years ago. Could only afford one of us. It was either this place or me!' She slides into the booth next to me. 'If *I* look just about passable it's because I knocked the old fags on the head. Had to. Lungs would have shut up shop if I'd carried on. Never mind walking up stairs, even pulling a pint was making me wheeze. You're not going to believe it, but I do Zumba now.' She envelops me in a hug. 'Oh, it's ruddy brill to see you, Ashley. Honestly, I would have understood if you hadn't wanted to be here today. It must have been a difficult decision.'

'No, not at all.'

'Is your husband here with you?'

'Husband?'

'Yvonne said you'd got married.'

'How did she know?'

Sheila shrugs. 'I'm not sure. Bet he's well dishy. You always bagged yourself the hot boys in the estate. Is he a good man, though? That's what's important.'

I exhale slowly and clasp my clammy hands together. 'Yeah, yeah, he is.'

'Well done. You deserved the *total* opposite of your f—' She stops herself. 'So, things are going well in the fashion world, for you, I hope.'

'Mmm...' I mumble.

It makes me uncomfortable that Sheila managed to find me all those months ago. Or rather, the fact she had to put in such effort to do so because I had changed my surname. It made me look as if I was hiding.

'It's such a wicked job,' she continues. 'Really, I'm so impressed.'

'Well, it's not as if I'm saving lives. Although, you could say I have saved a few people from dying of embarrassment by suggesting they don't ever attempt to copy any of Katy Perry's red carpet looks,' I joke, clunkily.

I think I may be sick again. Or maybe I need a drink. Sometimes it is hard to figure out which direction you need to go in: toilet *or* bar. Sheila misinterprets my mental dilemma.

'I was talking about Yvonne's designs earlier. It's such a shame they didn't take off as she had hoped.'

'Yes, it is but…'

'But?'

'Fashion is a very competitive industry, you can't simply "hope". You have to work at it.'

'Maybe you could have helped her.'

'I tried to help her! I spent most of my childhood doing that.'

'I meant with her collections. Sorry, I didn't mean to talk out of turn. It's hard to know what to say to you even at the best of times, let alone at a time like this.' She takes a breath. 'Listen, Ashley, I wanted to ask you…it's always on my mind…even now…'

I interrupt. 'Please, stop.'

She ignores me. 'I did the right thing, telling her, didn't I? She needed to kn—'

'Sheila, you're about to rehash the past, and really…'

There's no need? No reason? *Or, no time like the present?* No. There is no need *or* reason. The past is done. My stance on it is very clear; it is not up for discussion. I always imagine that Jennifer Aniston must feel the same whenever the topic of her marriage to Brad Pitt is bought up in an interview. Despite the fact they split back when ecru hemp turtlenecks were unfathomably in vogue (note lower case—they were NEVER in *Vogue*,) she *still* gets asked about her feelings on the matter. Personally, I reckon Aniston feels *nothing* for Pitt any more. Not because he got remarried, but because he starred in that preposterous advertisement for Chanel No 5. In one floral spritz of pompous drivel she would have been over him for good. I don't continue my sentence. I stare back down at the table. The deep grooves in the wood are filled with gunk. I scrape my fingernail down the middle.

'…was she happy?' I blurt out. 'Was she happy before she died? Was she?'

Sheila takes a breath. 'Yes, she was good. Not physically, obviously, but mentally…yes. That was why it came as a shock. I thought if she believed she would make it, she would.' She pauses. 'But the happiest I ever saw her? Well, you know that story I told in my speech…about the chill out? I missed out a couple of facts. Nothing that anyone else needs to know. Only you.' She doesn't wait to see if I want to hear them. 'That day I met her…she told me a *massive* secret. She was pregnant. I was the first person she told. Me! Some stranger she'd met at a party and invited back to her parents' gaff because I had Rizla and none of the shops were open. That twenty-four hours could not have summed up 1987 more perfectly. We talked for hours. She couldn't shut up! I'd thought she'd done the same pills as me: rhubarb and custards. But she'd done nothing. No booze. No chems. She was high on life…*pure* life. Puffing a bit of resin perhaps, but that was it. Her excitement…I could almost touch it. I joked that maybe this was because being preggers would give her an excuse to wear these mental dungarees she had on for another eight months—but she said, *nah*…it was because she couldn't wait to meet you. That was why she wanted to make a success of herself. It was for *you*.'

'Right,' is all I manage. I can feel the irritation rising out of my nausea.

'Obviously,' Sheila grimaces, 'things didn't play out as she expected, but try not to judge her by what happened. Deep down, she really loved you and always hoped for the best. For you. And her. Your relationship.'

'Yeah, well she should have worked at that a little harder too. Then maybe she would have had a career and a daughter.'

'You don't mean that.'

'I do.'

Sheila squeezes my shoulder then eases herself out of the booth. 'Go and get a drink, lovely. Have anything you want. It's on the house. There's lots of food too. Gone are the days where the policy in here was "eating is cheating"! I'll be back with you in a minute, just need a quick natter with the DJ. He lived in your block. Played jungle and happy hardcore back in the day…now my bank manager! Bless you for coming, Ashley.'

After she has walked off, I stay sat in the booth and turn on my phone. Fitz has Whatsapped me. *Jacobs, call me now.* He messages me again, this time via text.

OI! I KNOW YOU JUST READ MY WHATSAPP! I'M CALLING YOU!

My mobile bleeps.

'Fitz.'

'What's going on? Where are you? Why aren't you in the office?'

'Because…I'm in the waiting room at the, erm…' I pause,

to think of something he will not push me for details on. '…
gynaecologist.'

'Ughhhhhhhhhh.'

'Yeah, I've got a couple of days off to deal with some
girl's stuff. I had a dodgy sm—'

'DON'T YOU DARE SAY IT! Bleurgh. God, the mental
picture…I am now shud-*der*-ing.'

'Stop being so squeamish. All they do is get a s—'

'If you say *that* word beginning with S-P-E-C and ending
in U-L-U-M I'm hanging up.'

'Fine, but you wanted to speak to me, not the other way
round.'

'Jacobs! Why are you not prolonging a joke until it is not
remotely funny? Gosh, you are *weird* right now. Anyway,
I haven't got much time, I'm meeting Jesus for a coffee
in a mo. But I'm going to have a green tea. Don't want
rank espresso breath in case he goes in for a kiss. Anyway,
look, you know that list which Ogilvy gave to Wallis? At the
features meeting, on the Post-it…?'

I try to focus. 'With the designers she had to use?'

'Yep. They are *all* affiliated to Frédéric Lazare. *And* he
has JUST become the major shareholder in the company
who manages Hambeck. Not only that, but in the issue that
is going to print, sixty per cent of all the products that Ogilvy
flagged up as *Catwalk DIES For*…guess what? They're all
RIVA brands. In other words, Lazare owns the lot. So I
checked out the previous issue *and* the one before that…
same thing. Ogilvy's getting a backhander, must be. Oh, and
she emailed through the new features list and she's dropped
my piece on Rick Dumont, the accessories designer. And you
know je suis mort pour Rick Dumont. Such a talent.'

'Really? I thought you only wanted to interview him

because he's got an eightpack and lives in Miami on the same stretch of beach as Gloria Estefan.'

'There is that too, but guess who Lazare tried to poach to one of his brands, Pascale, as Product Designer but he refused on creative grounds despite a mega pay packet? *Rick*. Lazare was well miffed. Hell hath no fury like a BALD power-crazed fashion conglomerate owner spurned.'

'You know Lazare is paying for our *Catwalk* party?'

'No! Who told you?'

'Catherine.'

'*Whaaaaaat*? She is up to her pussy-bow-tied neck in it.'

'But who will you tell this to? Her husband owns the magazine.'

'True. We need more facts. Something is going on, I can feel it. Okay, so when you get back into the office after your manky procedure we need to investigate, yes? Okay, am going to run…God, d'you realise I've *never* been on a date before 8pm? A late lunch at an all-day brasserie would be awkward enough, but Caffè Nero at midday? Should I take some poppers just in case? To take the edge off, as you would say?'

'Fitz. That's a ridic—'

But then I stop. The nausea dissipates from my stomach. The irritation that is left thickens then morphs into a solid, impenetrable tar like lump of anger. There. She. Is. Black trouser suit. Hair *trussed* up in one of those donut-bun things which only air hostesses (in uniform) can pull off successfully. Minimal make-up. I hear Fitz shouting my name down the phone, but I hang up and slam it into my bag. Then I barge my way through the room, until I am standing behind her. For a few seconds, I say nothing…because when there is *every*thing to say, it's impossible to narrow it down.

'Tanya.'

She jumps and spins round.

'Oh, my God, what are you d—'

'What am *I* doing here? I hiss. 'It's my mother's memorial. What the *fuck* are you doing here?'

I sense the group of guests chatting by the trestle table looking over.

'Please…'

'Please *what*? Please, can we talk? Please, can I calm down? Please, can you explain? How dare you ask me for anything.'

'I wasn't going to ask you for anything.' Her neck and face are purple. 'In f-f-fact, I have no idea what I was going to say. I didn't think you would be here. Honestly, I would never have come if I had thought there was even a possibility. But it's public knowledge that you haven't seen Yv—'.

'Don't say her name.'

'But Ash—'

'No! Don't say mine either.' I step closer. Her skin is visibly flinching. 'So, what *are* you here for, then? To see that it's finally over? All the drama? Well, I think you can be assured it is. I mean, it doesn't get more final than a memorial. What *you* started is now finished.'

'Stop, stop…' She is welling up. 'I know you don't mean that.'

'I do. I mean every word. And believe me, there are so many more I could say too…'

She swallows and steps back. 'Why didn't you say them when you saw me the other day?'

'Because you're not worth it. I wasted too many on you the time before that. Now. Get. Out.'

'Okay, okay, I'll leave…in a minute.' Her voice is wobbling. 'Let me at least tell you why I'm here. I came to pay my respects to Yvonne. And, yes, I will say her name because that *is* her name. She deserves to have a name and she deserves for me to apologise for last time. I'm getting m—' She stops and takes a breath. 'I'm getting m—'

I interrupt her. 'Just get the fuck out of here. Get the *FUCK* out of here!'

Sheila dashes over, flapping her hands at me. But I do not stop. I am now shouting in Tanya's face.

'GET OUT. GET OUT. GET *OUT!*'

She turns, and as she does, I whack my hand in between her shoulder blades and push her. She stumbles and falls to the ground. Immediately, guests rush to her assistance. I feel another grab me round the waist and pull me away. I see my mother's widower staring at me in bewilderment. I lash out with my arms and legs and wriggle free. The room is now quiet bar the sound of Tanya Dinsdale sobbing.

'Don't you dare do that. Don't you dare cry. Don't you dare try to make me feel sorry for you.'

'I'm not. It is me who is sorry, I'm sorry, I'm so sorry…'

'Sorry for what?' I take a breath and walk over to where she is lying. 'For killing my mother's marriage? Or that she *then* drank herself to death? Which one?'

'Both of course, and so much more. But most of all…'

'Most of all, what?' I almost spit these words.

She raises her head and looks directly at me. '…believing your father loved me.'

*

I get a cab straight to the pub I got changed in earlier. The taxi has no air con. My shirt is damp with sweat and is clinging to my back. I can feel rivulets of liquid trickling down my leather joggers. Inside the pub, there are only a few custom-ers. I march up to the bar. The barman is tapping something into the till. I scan the optics behind him. It calms me.

'Vodka and grapefruit, please. Double. Thanks.'

He looks up. It's a different barman from this morning. This one is fit. Not handsome. Not dishy. Not sweet. *Fit*. The kind of guy that even if you have a certain look you usually go for, you would still admit that he is 'fit'. He chucks some ice into a tumbler.

'Bad day?'

'Yes.'

'You want to tell me about it?'

'No.'

I stare hard at him. His T-shirt could be a more casual cut but at least it is not ironed. He's wearing a crew neck—I prefer a V or a shallow scoop. His jeans are in somewhat of a denim limbo: snug, but not quite skinny enough to be labelled 'skinny legs'. But at least—I peer over the bar so I can get a full-length view—they could not in any way, THANK GOD, be described as boot cut. Shoes are more than acceptable: Red Wing hiking boots. General grooming is on point too: dark hair not too 'finished' but not too purposefully dishevelled either. Nothing worse than a hairstyle on a man that you know has taken them up to forty minutes in front of the bathroom mirror armed with a legion of waxes, gels and pomades to get the desired look. He also has decently cropped facial stubble. It's that purposefully shallow fashion-y length. It's rare to get that on a man in London these days. Especially East. There are *way* too many 'overly sincere' full beards on show near where I live.

'I'm also hungover,' I tell him, my concentration back on the optics. 'And I've been in a fight.'

'Ha! Then you're in the right place. I'm not going to ask anything as cheesy as if you come here often because I've never seen you.' He turns round to hold the glass up to a Smirnoff optic. 'Doubly cheesy, I would've remembered you.'

He knows that *I* know what that last sentence meant without needing to see my reaction. I don't need to see his face either. I reach for my mobile to check my messages. Like I always do when this situation arises. *Just in case.* But no, there is nothing.

'So, what's your name?' asks the barman, facing me again. He passes my drink alongside a bottle of juice.

I add barely a splash. 'Ashley. You?'

A slight hesitation. 'Jared. I'm called Jared. You local?'

I hesitate too. 'Nope. Never been here before.' I drop my hands behind the bar and switch my wedding ring back onto my right hand. The *wrong* one. I gulp back my drink. 'I'm staying in a hotel…down the road.'

Eight

'Tanya? You're shaking!'

'Sorry I'm l-late. I was at a memorial and I…'

'No need to panic.' Dr Lyons checks the time at the base of her computer. 'Only by a few minutes. Infinitely more appealing than being *the* late in that sequence of events.' She smiles at me. 'I'm sorry too, for your loss.'

'Oh. It wasn't…she wasn't someone…but I needed to go. For her. It was Yvonne Atwal.'

'Atwal, Atwal, Atwal…that name rings a bell. God, didn't she have a child at school with you and Suze? Actually, yes, she did! I know *exactly* who her daughter was. Not the most angelic of pupils, if I remember rightly. How decent of you to go.'

I avoid eye contact, because I *know* I *am* lying. Ashley was right, I went for me. Exactly like that first time I visited her mother. I lied then too. Yvonne opened the door of her flat. It was a year since I had been there. With all the rumours of her problems with alcohol that had circulated the estate before we moved, I was expecting her to look worse. She read it in my face immediately and gave me that Atwal impenetrable stare. The one which Ashley had perfected by the time she was ten.

HER: (Leaning in the doorway.) What were you expecting? For me to be hugging a bottle of supermarket gin, wearing fingerless wool gloves?

ME: No, not at all, I…

HER: Don't lie. I know what everyone says. Why are you here, Tanya? Because if it is to attempt another apology, then I'd rather you didn't insult me. Leave now.

ME: Believe me, I would never want to insult you…

HER: Again. Insult me AGAIN.

ME: (Hanging my head.) Again. I'm fully aware of the damage I created and will always, always regret it.

HER: Shame you didn't think that you may eventually develop some kind of conscience the first time you were screwing my husband. Or the second. Or the third. Or all the other times which followed. Hindsight, eh? The ULTIMATE bitch! Get to the point. I'm busy. Contrary to the gossip you may have heard, I do actually have a life. I have a collection to finish.

ME: Oh, that's erm…good. You are still selling on the stall?

HER: I said, 'get to the point'.

ME: (Taking a deep breath.) I can't find Ashley.

HER: (Short burst of laughter.) You've come here to tell me that?

ME: I still have no way of contacting her. She has blocked me from her email, taken herself off Facebook, made all of her social media private…I have no idea where she lives.

HER: And you expect ME to tell you?

ME: Please, Mrs Atwal. Ashley was my life. I did a bad, bad, BAD thing but, believe me, I was punished for it.

HER: YOU were punished? Ha! Tanya…I really do think you ought to leave. (Sighing.) This is now beyond the realms

*of insulting and entering into downright contempt. There is
nothing you can say to m—*

*ME: (Interrupting. Stepping forward.) Ashley was my
family. I loved her as a sister. I still do. I know it is ALL my
fault that she is not here. I drove her away. I can't change
what happened but I CAN tell you how that there is not a
single moment of the day where I do not hate myself for what
I did and I always will do. I don't want any sympathy for this,
but I am begging you to give me a chance…ONE chance…
to see your daughter again. I miss her.*

Yvonne looked at me in silence, but this time not with
the impenetrable stare. Then she lifted her hand. For a split
second, I thought she was going to hit me. She didn't. Instead,
she touched the side of my face.

HER: I miss her too.

'Mmm…death is a bugger.' Dr Lyons smiles and raises
a heavily pencilled eyebrow at me. 'Happens to us all
eventually, though. It's the *one* diagnosis that as doctors we
can absolutely guarantee. Croaking is *not* an option. It's a
certainty.'

I attempt a smile too. Dr Lyons is a great doctor. She is a
conventional one in terms of treatment, but not approach. You
don't feel as if you are on a conveyor belt with thousands of
other patients. She never gives you that disconcerting look
of personal concern underwritten by professional detachment
which most GPs can't help but develop. I guess it helps them
segue kindly but efficiently between a verruca examination to
a Type 2 diabetes confirmation via an anal wart in the space
of thirty minutes. She's also very liberal. When her daughter
revealed she was pregnant at nineteen, she simply said, 'Fine,
Suze. You and Rollo can stay in the house as long as you stay
at uni. And the bong goes.'

I sit down in the chair opposite her, and watch as she pulls a piece of paper from the printer next to her and puts on a pair of spectacles. I'm not sure I like that she needs to *refer* to something.

'O-*kay*, Tanya, shake your shoulders. Relax.'

'Mmmm…'

'I'm pleased you decided to go for the more extensive and invasive check-up as something has made itself known which we need to look at, as it will affect your chances of trying to conceive naturally.'

I need her to repeat what she said but suddenly, I can't find any words. She draws her chair a little closer to me.

'You've got a disorder in your fallopian tube, which means you *can* get pregnant, but you'll have a degree of difficulty. The job of a fallopian tube is to capture the egg after ovulation. Yours is unlikely to be able to do this. Nor will it be able to transport sperm from the uterus to the fertilisation site. It is not an uncommon condition. The positive aspect of this being that because many women have experienced it, we have the necessary stats to make a well-informed opinion on how to overcome it in order to conceive. It is both mine and general medical opinion th—'

'B-but…why? I should be in prime baby producing condition,' I blurt out. 'It's because of *that*, isn't it? Because of what happened…what I did. What I had to do…'

'Please, *relax*.' Dr Lyons taps me on the hand. 'Look, it's a *possibility*, given you came to me afterwards with pelvic inflammatory disease, but let me remind you, I'm *not* saying you won't be able to have a baby. It's my job to provide the relevant information for you to decide on the best way to move forward. Given that we have discovered the state of things *now*, it means we can get the ball rolling much sooner than if you had tried natural methods first. In a sense, you were lucky it even occurred to you to have such thorough tests. Many women try for up to a year—sometimes more—before even considering to investigate any underlying medical issues.'

I stare at her face. As I do, it starts to morph into Ashley's. This used to happen a lot when I was in therapy. I would see her face in the therapists' faces. At first, I was freaked out by this, but then it made more sense. After all, if she was sitting in the room she would have wanted to know the answers to all of their questions too.

'How did you feel when your best friend's father kissed you on your sixteenth birthday?'

'How did you feel in his company in the years building up to that?'

'How did you feel when he asked you to marry him?'

'How did you feel when you realised he only said it to stop you from telling anyone?'

'How did you feel when you told him you were preg—'

'…Tanya?'

'Mmm?'

'I asked if you wanted to discuss options?'

I nod.

'So, let's talk pro-actively. If you want to use the NHS, I can get you an appointment within six to eight weeks. Privately, it will be quicker—you may even get seen tomorrow, but it's the same experts who work across the private and public sectors throughout your treatment so it is entirely up to you. Whenever patients ask me the main differences, I always say much less hanging around and a snazzier waiting room. In fact, there is so little hanging around you don't get to enjoy the snazzy waiting room.'

'Can we rewind, please? Appointment…round…treat-ment…for?' I look up.

'In vitro fertilisation. IVF.'

She says these three letters as easily as she might have said FYI or TBA or ETA. Or LOL. But I know there is nothing funny about IVF. I've read the horror stories. The wannabe mums who get addicted to the hope; cycle follows cycle but the only thing that implants itself and grows inside them is fear and desperation. The ones who lose their partners, money, friends, jobs and marbles. The ones who turn from being rational human beings into insane hormone-fuelled gorgons who forget that they once had a life because only a baby is worth living for. I grip onto the underneath of my chair.

'Tanya…' Dr Lyons squints at me and waves her pen. 'Don't do it.'

'What?'

'Automatically assume this is going to be a drama. Ignore anything you may have seen in the press. Let's face it, "woman gets pregnant after one cycle of IVF" is not going to make the headlines or be worth gossiping about. In the demographic with your particular issue, I'd say the success rate of treatment resulting in a live birth would be around thirty-five per cent.'

'That puts failure at just under seventy per cent.'

'Ahem! What did I say? *No drama.* Let's not turn this into an eight-part special on Sky Atlantic. Why don't you share this information with your partner and come back to see me? I'm happy to see you together. Or if you know IVF is what you want, this afternoon, I can make sure your notes are sent through to the clinic…'

Clinic. CLINIC. *CLINIC.*

'So?'

'Yes. Absolutely, yes,' I reply, robotically. 'I should definitely talk first with my…fiancé.' I try out the word for the first time.

'Oooooh, congratulations! You're *engaged*!'

'Mmm…' I get up from my chair. 'Anyway, I really appreciate you taking the time to see me, Dr Lyons. I'll be in touch. Onwards and upwards.'

She gets up too and rubs my shoulder. 'Tanya, you don't have to revert to that default setting which all patients have, to be as polite and grateful as possible on the way out of a doctor's surgery, irrespective of the gravity of news they have been given. It's *me*! I've known you for years. And I will help you through this. Now, have a look through these…and get back to me.' She passes me a bunch of leaflets. 'I'm here all week but off Friday…Suze has treated me to another spa break. Bliss. So, we'll speak? Yes?'

'Yes. Thank you.' I take the information and head to the door.

'Oh, and one other thing,' she says, as I turn the handle. 'Do *not* leave here and leap onto the Internet to investigate your condition. The Web is a lot of wonderful things but it is not a qualified gynaecologist. Wait until you have seen the qualified experts before you call upon the virtual one. Dr Google has a habit of giving only the worst case scenario to all of his patients.'

Three minutes later I'm sat in the car, tapping my phone. FALLOPIAN DISORDER INFERTILE FOREVER? is sitting in the Google search bar. 592,000 results. I scroll down. There are endless websites dedicated to my problem. And public forums too. I am about to click on one, but then I stop myself. *Do not enter the chat room.* It may as well be a suite at the

Hotel California. You can log on but you can never leave. I tap out a text to Greg.

Need to talk to you. What time do you finish tonight?

I delete it. I don't want to worry him. That sounds as if there is something wrong with me. Which there isn't, is there? Merely something that needs to be put right.

Would like to talk to you. What time do you finish tonight?

I delete that. Now it sounds as though *he* has done something wrong.

We should talk. What time do you finish tonight?

Agh. No. That sounds as if there is something wrong with our relationship. I delete that too.

What time do you finish tonight?X

I press Send. He replies a few minutes later.

Last orders. Why?X

I stare at my phone for at least a minute before typing:

No big issue!

Then I text Suze and Maddie at the same time.

ME: Can you guys nip over after work, early-ish. Food?

SUZE: Today?

ME: Yeah.

MADDIE: Short notice???!

ME: I know. The thing is I

I'm still typing when...

MADDIE: Carter not had good day. Sick earlier. Very vocal after bottle.

SUZE: Acid reflux?

MADDIE: Yesterday too.

SUZE: Rigid when crying?

MADDIE: Don't know. Napping fine now though.

SUZE: Def acid reflux. Evie had it. Made horrific noise.

Sounded like being murdered. They get over it. Can get pills to help. But liquid version much better. Easier to get down.

ME: TONIGHT?

MADDIE: Not sure when Kian is back. Playing squash.

ME: Bring Carter.

MADDIE: Doing essential oil baby massage on him later.

SUZE: Still school hols. Need to pick up Jasper from judo. New instructor other side of town. Evie has play date at cinema. Can't call friend's mother as is lawyer—in court today. Don't have nanny's number. Also, Lidl shop required. Sorry. You KNOW my mad schedule!

MADDIE: Ditto!

I roll my eyes at my mobile.

ME: But Rollo is home?

SUZE: Yeah.

ME: Carter has car seat?

MADDIE: Yes.

ME: This is important. Just been to see your mum, Suze. Will need IVF to have baby.

Well, if they can play the kids card, I'll play my *lack of kids* card. Three hours later, Suze and Maddie are sat at the table in my kitchen.

'Oh, Tanya…what a nightmare. I can't believe it. And you had no idea? I forget how lucky I was.' Maddie looks over at Carter, fast asleep in his stroller. 'How *most* women are. Sorry, *sorry*…that's not helping. Are you okay?'

'I'll be fine. I've got to be, haven't I? Thanks for coming over. I'm heating up a quiche. Nothing quite like the combination of short cut pastry with a savoury custard filling in times of stress. Said no one *ever*.'

'There's no need to put on a brave face, T,' says Suze. 'That sucks. Really…god, I feel for you.'

I stare at my best friends' faces. Maddie looks as if *she* is
about to cry and Suze looks as if she is expecting *me* to cry.
At the island unit, I twist pepper over a bowl of green leaves
which I have tossed in a shop-bought vinaigrette. Maddie
jumps up from her chair, arms outstretched.

'You need a hug…'

'Not yet,' I tell her. 'What I need *first* is for you both
to react how I planned. I was meant to tell you that I am
going to start treatment, then Maddie, *you* were meant to be
incredibly positive, so much so that Suze would have to step
in and remind you that it *could* be a reasonably precarious
process but that ultimately, *yes*…I would still have an excellent chance of conceiving. Something along those lines.'

Now they look at each other. *Sheepishly?* No, awkwardly.
And shiftily.

'…o-*kay*,' I continue. 'So, I guess we'd better use this
supper to toast the end of my fertility and the beginning of an
awkward new aspect to our friendship where the two of you
feel guilty about having children…and I feel even guiltier
that I have forced you to feel that way.'

Suze rips the silver tab off a can of Diet Coke.

'Oh, shut up, T. As if I anyone could make me feel guilty
about anything. More to the point, let's not forget what I
pushed out into the world. Joke! Look, there's no need to
panic. As you know, my sister had both of her kids through
IVF.'

'Your mum never said that…'

'Erm…Hippocratic oath! Look, I'm not going to lie,
those hormone injections did strange things to her. She was
emotional. Empathetic. *Felt things*. I'd go as far to say she
almost resembled a normal human being for a few months.

But she did three rounds and got two babies. Not bad odds. And she was *way* older than you.'

'Why did you give Maddie that look then?'

'Because…' She swivels in her seat at the kitchen table to face her. 'Why did I give you that look, Mads?'

Maddie grimaces and sits back down. 'Have you erm…?' She has a sip of cranberry juice. 'Have you…?'

Suze interjects: '…told Greg yet? About the IVF thing. That's what she is trying to ask.'

'No. I'm going to chat with him tonight. I wanted to do it face-to-face. Why?'

They glance at each other. Suze picks up the conversation again.

'If you decide to do IVF, you're going to need him to be one hundred per cent committed. Not only to the process, but to you.'

'Suze! We. Are. Engaged. How much more commitment do you want him to show me?'

'WHAT?' squeals Maddie. 'YOU ARE ENGAGED! And you didn't tell me?'

'Yeah, sorry…I had some stuff to sort out. I haven't told anyone else. Honestly, it's not as if it's a massive secr-'

Maddie interrupts. 'Clearly, it is!'

'Please, we can discuss it later,' I mumble, before turning back to Suze. 'Whatever it is you're building up to... tell me.'

'Fine. Something has come to our attention. A Greg thing,' she says. 'Well, it came to Mads' attention.'

'It's more of a minor issue,' says Maddie. 'A "thing" makes it sound as if we've been discuss—'

'Discussing the 'thing' at length?' I continue for her. 'Clearly, you have, otherwise it would still be a minor issue and not an actual *thing*. Go on.' I throw the salad servers into the bowl and fold my arms against my chest. 'Give me the lowdown on the Greg *thing*, Maddie. And if you dare hold back on *any* detail to save my feelings because of the IVF *thing* or the engagement *thing*, I'll be able to tell. You know I will.'

'She will,' confirms Suze, apparently engrossed in choosing the right olive from the ramekin in front of her, even though they are all green.

Maddie fiddles with her left ear lobe and takes a deep breath.

'Well, erm…' she begins. 'You remember that weekend you and I had away at the very beginning of the summer and the boys went out on the town together?'

'When Kian started a fight?'

'No, he *tripped* and ended up in an altercation that had already started. But, yes, *that* night. It happened in that club which used to be tolerable after a bottle of wine—each— but then got taken over by that chain—actually, I think it was more of a franchise set-up or someth—'

'She doesn't need to hear the leasehold arrangement of the venue, Mads,' mutters Suze. 'Get to the point.'

'I am, I am,' she insists. 'So, after the incident happened which Kian *got caught up in through no fault of his own*… Greg disappeared.'

'In what sense?' I ask.

'In the sense that he fucked off somewhere,' says Suze. 'He checked Kian was okay but didn't end up going to the hospital with him and Rollo.'

'And?'

'Well, that's the thing, *the Greg thing*…' Maddie squeaks. 'At your b'day you implied that he stayed all night in the hospital, but he wasn't even there at the beginning. The boys tried to find him when they were leaving the club, but couldn't, so they got a minicab and left without him.'

My purple heat rash starts cooking the skin on my chest. I pick up the salad bowl, walk over to the table and plonk it down in the middle.

'I have no idea what comment I made at the lunch. If I said the wrong thing it would be because I'd forgotten what Greg had told me, not because he'd lied.' I am now talking very loudly. 'Why would he lie to me? *Why?* WHY?'

'Okay, okay, can we all calm down, please?' says Maddie. 'Or we'll wake up Carter. Maybe we should leave it there until we know the facts a little better. It's not as if he's ever lied before.'

'We don't even know if this is a lie!' I fume.

'But he has lied once before though... he slept with his ex-girlfriend.' Suze feels it is necessary to point out. 'That you do know for sure.'

'Yes! Because he did not lie about it! He told me. And after that happened, he left her *for me*. That kind of thing happens all the time. In an ideal world he would have been single when we met, but he wasn't. Big deal. Since then we have been together three years.'

'More two years and eight or nine months, isn't it?' mutters Suze.

'Stop it, Suze,' I mutter back, ignoring her (factually correct) dig. 'Your constant low-level hum of disapproval is getting really boring.'

'I do not disapprove of anything you do. *Ever*. Let's get that straight.' She gets up and walks over to the French windows. 'I'm going to have a cigarette.'

Maddie flaps her hands. 'This is getting silly. We didn't

come round here to argue.' She glances at Suze. 'Let's all have some quiche. It smells delic—'

'Forget the quiche!' I tell her.

I step out onto the terrace, where Suze is lighting a cigarette. Maddie follows me.

'Listen to me!' I demand brusquely, so as to convince them both I am relaxed in attack mode. 'I want to be with Greg. Only him. He wants to be with me. Only me. I don't need your approval to be with him. Neither does he to be with me. WE ARE ENGAGED. May I add here that I never vocalise what I see as shortcomings in *your* relationships. For example, I would never point out to *you*, Suze, that you and Rollo never do *any*thing together as a couple. In fact, since he started working from home, you've spent even less time there to get on with whatever it is you fancy outside of it. Anyone can see he is desperate for your approval as a *husband*, not just as a nanny, housekeeper and legal advisor.'

'You forgot to add chef too,' Suze shrugs, apparently not bothered by my remark. 'He's getting very handy in the kitchen.'

I turn to Maddie. '…and certainly I would never tell *you*, that both you and Kian would probably benefit from doing something on your own as individual entities. You are husband and wife. Not Siamese twins.'

Maddie makes a face. 'He prefers to spend time with me. It's not as if I am forcing him.'

'That's *not* what the look said which you gave him at my birthday lunch when Greg suggested a weekend away,' I tell her. 'Look, *no* one has a perfect relationship. Not you and Kian. Not Suze and Rollo. Not even Tom Brady and Gisele Bundchen, and they are officially certified as perfect as individuals. You do not see the Greg I do.'

'Oooooh, the inner Greg,' mutters Suze. 'Bet that's a complex labyrinth of emotions.'

Maddie shooshes her then turns to me. 'We only want what's bes—'

'Please! Don't say, "We only want what's best for you", it's up there with 'we want you to be happy". Actually, you have got to stop being so pious *generally*, Maddie. From the moment you gave birth, it's as if you've been expecting to be lauded as some kind of holy figure, the Virgin Maddie. You produced a baby. You did not perform a miracle.'

Suze laughs and drags on her cigarette. 'T has got a point there, Mads.'

'And Suze, you can be so patronising,' I tell her. 'The whole of the South West knows that you...' I gruff up my voice to do a not half-bad impression of her: '"dropped my first pup before my finals", as if this gives you the right to cast your opinion on anyone who is even thinking about reproducing, or anyone that *has*. Including Maddie.'

'Why? What has she said?' asks Maddie. She spins to Suze.

Suze rolls her eyes at me. 'See what you've started?'

I ignore her. '...and let me remind you, Suze, that when you announced you were pregnant with Rollo's baby, the most you had ever shared with him were Law tutorials and pints of Snake Bite and Black. But I supported your choice. What I am trying to say is this. *I don't know if Greg will be a good father. I don't know if I will be a good mother.* But what I do know is that for the two of you to cast judgement on his and my relationship and our suitability to bring a child into the world—however that may happen—is at best irritating. At worst, insulting. All I ask is that you respect my decision. *Our* decision.' I add, my chest now on fire. Then I exhale loudly.

'*You tell'em, babe!*'

Suze, Maddie and I jump. Greg is leaning against the island unit, a wide-awake Carter in his arms, looking at the three of us. I wonder how much he has heard. Tentatively, I gaze through the French windows at him. The expression on his face—and I am assuming mine too—says that we *both* know this was not an ideal way for someone to find out that their partner is ready to procreate. I smile. I am more relieved than I probably should be when he smiles back. Suze waves at him.

'Hi, Greg. As always, a pleasure…'

'Likewise, Suze,' he replies, equally sarcastically, as he walks towards the open door. 'Oh, and I'll have you know that the inner Greg is indeed a complex labyrinth of emotions. In fact, you'll be excited to hear that under that labyrinth are deep, twisting tunnels of philosophic thought and philanthropic angst. Who'd a thunk it, eh?' He turns to Maddie and passes her Carter. 'Et tu, Maddie? I'm hurt. I thought you and I got on okay-ish. Admittedly, I wouldn't expect you to take a bullet for me, but I'd hope you might give me a nudge if you saw Suze loading a gun and pointing it at my head.'

'Funny,' says Suze, flicking her cigarette butt across the terrace. 'Impressive too, Greg. I never had you down as a classical scholar.'

Maddie giggles nervously as she squeezes her son. 'Eeeeek, sorry, Greg. Whatever you heard, it was only said because us girls are so protective of each other. We've been friends for so long. I'm sorry. And congratulations from both of us…we're really happ—ah! Sorry! I'm not allowed to say that, am I? But we, erm…*are*. Aren't we, Suze?'

She glares at Greg and says nothing.

'We should probably go,' says Maddie.

'Probably,' agrees Greg, glaring back at Suze.

She twists to face me. 'I think you'll find that's up to T. It's *her* house. T?'

'To be honest,' I snap, 'I think that maybe you should. I'll call you later.'

'Are you kidding?' She balks. 'You're chucking Mads and I out of your home when *both* of us reorganised our entire evening to be here so that you can tell us about a problem which…' Her eyes narrow, and I know she is about to say something that she is fully aware she will regret, but is too angry to stop herself. '…*which quite frankly* someone in a decent relationship would have gone to the person they are in *that* relationship with *first*.'

We are both silent for a seconds; the air between us a smog of resentment. Then Suze marches back inside, grabs her handbag off the island unit and leaves the kitchen. A few seconds later we all hear the door slam.

Greg laughs. 'Over-opinionated hag,' he says casually, and goes back inside.

Maddie sighs. 'Oh, God, what a mess. Sorry, Tanya. I should have come to you first before I spoke to Suze. It was merely a passing comment but she latched onto it. I had no idea she was going to blow it up like that. Don't call her later. Leave her to calm down or she'll say something else she regrets…'

'…but would not ever admit to regretting.' I finish her sentence.

'Exactly,' says Maddie. 'You know what she's like.'

'Yeah!' Greg shouts from the kitchen, '…An over-opinionated hag who doesn't know when to shut the *fuck* up!'

Maddie and I can't help laughing. She leans in to give me a kiss over the top of Carter's head.

'I know you hate this expression, but I really *am* happy for you…about the engagement,' she whispers. 'I promise. And hey, apologies if I've been a bit of a nightmare recently, you should have said something sooner.'

'Thanks. I'm sorry too…for calling you the Virgin Maddie.'

'It's okay,' she says, bouncing Carter up and down. 'But I hope for your sake that this little one…' She bounces Carter up and down. '…doesn't grow up being able to turn water into wine or multiply loaves and fishes, because then you'll look more than a bit silly.'

I walk Maddie to her car and spend fifteen minutes helping her to put a predictably *livid* Carter into his baby seat. When I go back inside, Greg is not in the kitchen. I stick my head out of the French windows. He is sitting on the metal bench at the bottom of the garden. Smoking. He looks up.

'Don't even *think* about telling me to put this out,' he shouts, waving his cigarette. 'Suze has driven me to it. Christ, imagine living with her! I bet Rollo keeps a secret crack pipe hidden inside the glovebox of the Range Rover.'

I stroll over to him. 'I don't know why she can't accept you.'

He looks straight at me. 'Bottom line, she enjoys stirring. It's not like she has much excitement in her life, is it? Two untrainable chimpanzees she calls children and a yes monkey of a husband. On a wall somewhere in their house I reckon his balls are in a glass box. On a plaque underneath will be the date he met Suze.'

I laugh, further relieved that Greg has made a joke, as opposed to because of the joke itself. But he isn't laughing. He puffs on his cigarette and pats the seat. I sit down next to him.

'So, are you going to tell me what this problem is, babe? The one Suze was referring to? Because I didn't know we had a problem. I thought we were pretty problem free.' He puts his arm around me. 'But I'm guessing *that* is the problem. You feel that the lack of something—or rather, some*one*—is problematic…'

'That's a positive start,' I deadpan, as I sit down. 'Referring to your potential first born as a problem.'

'Come on, babe, this is a bit of a curveball. Last time we spoke—in fact, every time we've spoken about it, you've s—'

'I know, I know…I've said I'm not ready and I didn't know when I was going to be ready. 'But I am now.'

He exhales deeply. 'Okay…' His voice is calm. Kind.

'Come on, Greg, at least I'm not suggesting something really freaky…like we take up a *hobby* or something. And please don't say, let's j—'

'…just enjoy being married for a while? Actually, I was going to suggest we just enjoy being engaged for a while.'

I whack him and he puts his arm around me. Despite joking, he feels tense.

'Okay, no more kidding about. Tell me what your concerns are.'

He nods slowly. 'I only have one concern. And it's…*that* will be *it*.'

'What will be?'

'The life we have now,' he says, plainly. 'People should *only* have children when they are absolutely sure they have achieved everything they want as individuals *and* together as a unit of two. We both have stuff we want to do. At least, I know I have.'

'You mean…the band?'

'Why did you say it like that?'

'I didn't say it like anything. Greg, having a baby does not mean your life stops.'

He laughs, but it is not a gentle laugh. He removes his arm from round my shoulder.

'Babe, that is *exactly* the sort of bullshit propaganda put out by first-time parents who *know* they went into the game way too early. They think that if enough of them bang on like this they can convince themselves—and others—it is true. "Oh, they end up fitting into your routine…" is the biggest lie told by new parents. *And they know it.* But *obviously* they can't question what they have done—it's too late. Nor can they admit they might be regretting it, so what do they do? They have another baby in a bid to persuade themselves—and everyone else—that they knew *exactly* what they were doing and were so pleased with how their original choice panned out, they've decided to do it again.' Finally, he pauses. 'Sorry. Look, I don't mean to upset you, but I'm confused…I thought you preferred blogging.'

This sounds like a joke but he isn't smiling. I take a deep breath.

'I wanted us to be in the right place. For everything to be exactly as it should be. And it is, isn't it? I've thought about it long and hard every day for…for…*years*. And now, now it's time…'

He says nothing.

'Greg? Say something…'

He gets up, walks up and down in front of me as few times, then speaks.

'Okay, babe. Here is what I *will* say. Yes, I want to be a father—I always said I did…but it is not something I think about that much. I stop myself from going there because my family life was ruined by mine. He made it shit. I think men who have shitty relationships with their father fall into three camps. In the first camp, you have the son who goes through his life thinking that something is missing, and will have a kid as soon as humanly possible to fill the void.' He chucks his zapped cigarette in the flower bed. 'In the second camp, you've got the kid who goes through his teens and early twenties having a pretty good time not really giving a fuck that he doesn't get to tell people that there's nothing better than a pint on Christmas Eve with Dad down the pub. But as the kid gets a little older and life gets more serious and he screws up a bit for the simple reason he doesn't want life to get serious because screwing up usually involves having fun, *other people* begin to assume he is screwing up because of the lack of paternal support when he was young. And these people go on about it…constantly. So, that's when the kid who is screwing up starts to question himself. "Hang on a second, maybe I am screwing up because I am screwed up over my screwed up relationship with my father. Not simply because I don't want to grow up." So, he heads to psychotherapy…and what's the first question he gets asked? "*Can you tell me about your relationship with your father?*". So his assumed screwed-up-ness that did not even exist in his mind before other people started assuming it was an issue now gets underlined by a professional, making the initially entirely non-screwed-up kid now, entirely screwed up adult. That's my brother. He will *never* have children for fear of starting the cycle of doom all over again. And then you have those in the third camp: the guys who *do* want to be a father eventually, but because they want to nurture a child, it's not about anyone else…'

'But it *is*, it's about me too. And I need to know when "eventually" is.'

'I know. Well, I *now* know that, babe.' He crouches in front of me then sighs. 'Listen, I'd better get back to the bar.'

I nod. 'Yes, you should…I appreciate you coming back.' My words sound hollow and inconsequential. 'Why did you come home in the middle of your shift, anyway?'

'You needed to see me *urgently*.'

'How did you know?'

'The delay between me texting to ask why you wanted to know what time I was finishing work and your reply. I knew something was up.' He shakes his bracelet at me. '*To my T*. True love.' Then he taps my engagement ring. 'And *you* are mine. That's why we'll figure this baby thing, I promise. Besides, there's no rush. We've got loads of time, haven't we?'

Of course, this is when I should tell him about the IVF *thing*, but I don't. Because I am remembering something else…

It is the second Bank Holiday in May. Maddie and I are staying in a Center Parcs cabin with Carter, Evie and Jasper. The weekend break is mine and Maddie's belated Christmas present to our godchildren. In addition, looking after Suze's kids for a whole weekend is our early birthday present to Suze. It is also her and Rollo's anniversary, so he has booked her a two-day stay at a detox spa with her mother and sister. Her present to *him* is not having her or the kids around. So, with us girls away, Rollo and Greg decide that on Friday night they should take Kian out 'on the lash', as he hasn't been partying since the baby was born. At midday on Saturday, whilst Maddie and the kids are swimming, I go for a walk in the forest and call Greg.

ME: Well, well, well…good afternoon.

HIM: (Voice sleepy, confused, muffled.) Afternoon? Is it afternoon? Ow, owwwww…my head. Uggggggh.

ME: Mmmm…you sound fresh.

HIM: Yeah, right. Ugh. Are you, erm…having a good time?

*ME: Not too bad, actually. Carter has been pretty chirpy…
and get this, Evie and Jasper have almost been behaving
themselves. They haven't been banned from any activities or
entertainment zones…yet. They even helped each other to build
a log fire without attempting to use each other as kindling.*

HIM: Ha!

*ME: Ouch! You must be feeling delicate. That was a good
joke! So, any idea what time you got in last night?*

HIM: Erm…sort of. About one, I think.

ME: You think wrong. It was nearly five-thirty.

HIM: (Pausing.) How do you know?

ME: I spoke to you.

HIM: (Shocked.) Did you?

ME: Yep.

HIM: What did we talk about?

*ME: We were talking numbers. Or at least, I was. You
were babbling nonsensical drunken rubbish. I gave you the
alarm code for the house. You had entered the wrong one.
Multiple times. The police alerted me to this in a phone call
at zero five twenty-seven.*

HIM: Shit. What did you tell them?

*ME: That before they sent out a car to see whether there
was an intruder, I should check to see whether it wasn't simply
my true love being a pissed up idiot. Which of course, it was.
I called them back to inform them of said intoxicated idiocy.*

HIM: (Exhaling loudly.) Sorry, babe.

*ME: That's okay. I can't imagine Suze and Maddie would
be so forgiving. Can you imagine if Rollo or Kian staggered
in at that hour? For Rollo it would be instant castra—*

HIM: (Interrupting.) Yeah, erm…listen…you'd better tell

Maddie. There was a bit of an incident involving Kian. He got into a fight. Hurt his arm and ended up with a cut above his eye. Not a bad one, but it needed to be looked at. Had to go to Casualty...we all did. Waited for hours and hours and hours...it was getting light when we left.

ME: Good. Pissed up idiots draining the NHS at the weekend should be MADE to wait.

When Maddie returns from the pool with the kids, I tell her what has happened. Tutting, she plonks Carter in my arms and goes out onto the cabin's porch to call Kian. I hear her giving him a lecture about having to be more responsible now he is a dad. But being Maddie, she can't be angry for long and is soon more concerned about whether he has managed some breakfast. Then she starts giggling.

'So much for your big return to The Boys Night Out,' she says. 'Two drinks. Trips over. Gets walloped. Accident and Emergency by ten o'clock. Home by midnight. Rave on!'

He lied. Greg lied.

I follow him back into the house. I focus on his silver bracelet slung round the bottom of his wrist. 'My T'. My true love. The closer I get to the French windows, the stronger the aroma of burnt quiche.

Nine

ASHLEY

From my hotel room I can see where it all happened. The flight of stairs on the block which we all called the Lego Tower. This was where Sheila overheard their conversation. Three levels down, her flat where she told my mother. Then, on the left side of the estate, our home. That was where my mother returned to and drank herself into a stupor. Just outside, the landing which she staggered out to before collapsing. I put her in the recovery position and went to get help. And to the right, the steel railings on the side of the building which she must have climbed up – to this day I have no idea how because she was so drunk. And there, the roof which Shelia and I spotted her on, threatening to jump. The square where everyone gathered to watch the drama unfold, outwardly hoping that it would be dealt with without any major problems…but inwardly squashing involuntary thoughts that the drama could carry on into the night until everyone involved was quite literally on the edge.

Of course, no one else would be able to see all that *now* because a gigantic mall and cinema complex have replaced the estate where I grew up. But I can still see it. I look down. I am high up overlooking the car park. It is full of low to mid-range, sensible silver cars. I'm pretty sure this area would have been the precinct for the old shopping centre. That's where I found out. Tanya told me herself.

I pull the curtains closed.

Two double vodkas and grapefruit juice. One bowl of chips. Three single gin and tonics. But the number I am thinking about is five. That's how many one-night stands I have had since 'it was decided'. I thought it was about to become six, but I misread the situation. So now I am—alone—twiddling my wedding ring, watching a game show on the TV in Room 13 of a small roadside travel lodge. I bought a bottle of Peach Schnapps—it looked refreshing—on the way here, but I haven't touched it as there was 'currently no ice' on the premises. The nice guy on reception is getting some from the adjoining budget restaurant.

It's a shame number six didn't happen. I needed it.

A knock at the door.

'Your ice, madam…'

I open the door. The nice guy from reception is not there. Jared is.

I look at him. I know that this time I am not misreading the situation. I am fully aware that if he steps inside, the door shuts and the lock light turns red, it will not mean STOP. It will mean GO. If I don't want this, I need to close the door. Now. Before we have *shared* anything, not even a kiss. I can leave and I will wake up tomorrow morning; with a murky hangover but a clear conscience. This is what I have told myself at this point on each of the five occasions. *You can leave now*. But why would I, when I can enjoy the silence?

Jared looks at me and steps into the room.

CLICK. The light goes red.

He drops the bag of ice and kisses me. We fall over each

other further into the room. I start unbuttoning my shirt. He yanks it off me. We kiss again, even harder. Teeth clash. He presses me up against the wall, grabs my neck with one hand and with the other reaches round and undoes the clasp of my bra in one quick snap of his fingers.

The first one-night stand after 'it was decided' was an American I met at a record label party. He was a dancer for a famous singer who was performing over here on a chat show. We were both drunk. I told him I wasn't a fan of his boss's music. He told me he wasn't either and never listened to it by choice. When we had sex he played Ariana Grande.

I wriggle out of my bra, throw it to the side and unbuckle his belt. We kiss again, so hard that this time I can taste blood in my mouth. I pull his T-shirt over his head. He grabs the waistband of my leather joggers.

The second was a guy I met having a cigarette (which I didn't want) outside a club. He was a student. We did it in his grim, asylum-like halls of residence on his single bed: the spindliest piece of sleeping apparatus I had even seen in my life. I woke up on the floor, immediately regretting doing 'it'. But not the fact I didn't go to university.

I pull out his belt from the denim loops of his jeans and let it drop to the floor. He puts my left hand over his crotch. I open his fly buttons just using my right and tug down his jeans. He steps out of them, then kisses me as he wriggles out of his socks using only his feet to get them off.

The third was a Tinder hook-up. His picture had been taken with a sepia filter, for fuck's sake! Sepia. Who does sepia any more?

He throws me down on the bed, grabs the waistband of my joggers and slides them down my legs, over my heels and off.

The fourth was an ex-fling from years ago; the last one

before Zach. He'd been stalking my Instagram and as soon as he noticed the decrease in snaps of Zach and me together he got in touch.

I lie still for a second. He stares at me in my g-string and heels. I sit up and stare at the very impressive bulge in his jockey shorts. He smiles. I peel off his underwear and take him in my mouth. He groans. I do too as I feel him descending down my throat. He presses my head into his pelvis.

The fifth was a model Catwalk *used on a shoot with abs like road bumps and the sweetest of natures. He wanted to introduce me to his Nan and make it 'official'.*

I semi-gag but then find my rhythm. He groans harder. I feel his legs shaking. He grabs my pony tail and mumbles something about it being 'too much'. I clamber over to the door and get a condom from the inner zipped pocket of my bag. He pulls me back towards him by the elastic of my knickers. I shove him back on the bed, roll down the Durex and climb on top. He thrusts.

Last night I saw the American dancer again. He was back in London on tour. He wasn't drinking because his boss had just come out of rehab and everyone who worked on her show was being routinely tested. I drank way too much. We went back to his hotel room. He ordered room service to sober me up. Then I passed out. No sex so it didn't count.

We thrust. His eyes glaze over. Mine feel mulchy with running mascara and eyeshadow. He swivels me round. I ride him again then jump off and get on all fours. He slams into me. I slam harder. He comes. I don't. He collapses back on the bed, panting, his hair and face wet. I collapse next to him. We lie there. He is unable to speak. I am unwilling to.

Let me enjoy the silence.

I only get around a minute and a half, maybe two.

'Shiiiiit…' he says.

'Charming.'

'No, I mean shiiiiit, that was…*not* shit. Not *not* shit at all…'

Shuuuuut-up!

'…for me. But for you,' he continues babbling. 'Erm… apologies. I got *way* too over-excited. Can't think why when there really wasn't much chemistry between us at all. Clearly, I didn't fancy you that much. And vice versa.'

'As far as I was concerned it was a one-off mercy shag,' I reply, resigning myself to the lack of silence. 'I felt sorry for you. I can't imagine you get much attention usually.'

Then, I smirk at him. Because this is a tried and tested part of the whole one-night stand thing, isn't it? The post-coital laboured sarcasm in an attempt to normalise the atmosphere, because the reality is you've just been writhing under and sweating over someone *you didn't even know at lunchtime today*. I manoeuvre myself to the top of the bed and yank the sheet up to wrap around me. Another thing you do, isn't? Act a little bashfully all of a sudden. Even though—as Catherine would probably say—the HMS *Modesty* has well and truly sailed.

'Weird, isn't it?' I add. 'How one-night stands are called 'stands', when there is rarely much standing around. You just get on with it.'

'*Night?*' He pulls a face at me. 'You're getting ahead of yourself. I won't be staying the night.'

'Fine by me.'

'You don't want to know why?'

'Nope. Why would I? The precursor to night is "one". So, frankly it's not really here or there whether you sleep here or, indeed, *there*…wherever that is.'

'Oof! Ouch.' He clambers up the bed to where I am. 'So, we're not going to try and see if that chemistry can be improved then?'

'Negative.'

He screws up his face. 'That's a shame. I was thinking from a *purely* scientific stance it would have been interesting.'

'Yeah, well…I live in London. Not exactly handy.'

'Come on, the journey isn't *that* bad; only a few hours.' He bursts out laughing again. 'Did that sound keen?'

'No. *Desperate*.' But I laugh too.

'Cheers. So…' He gets off the bed, picks his jeans up from the floor and retrieves a pack of cigarettes and a lighter from the back pocket. '…what is it you do, apart from luring unsuspecting bar staff into bed and then crushing their self-esteem afterwards?'

'What do I do?'

'Yeah, as a job. It's a perfectly normal question to ask someone after you've slept with them.' He lights a cigarette, and stays in the middle of the room, smoking. Naked. Except for a jangly silver chain around his wrist.

'Isn't it more normal to ask them that *before* you sleep with them?'

'Nah, you're confusing that with names. Names you definitely have to ask before you have sex. That's the only essential. Apart from any relevant medical issues, of course. Occupation, hobbies, phobias, siblings and parents…that's staple information but not of premium concern, so it can wait. Or *not* in our case, as you've put the kibosh on any further contact.'

'What about relationship status?'

'I would hope that isn't a necessary question,' he says, blowing a smoke ring at the ceiling.

'You would *hope*…'

He watches his smoke ring rise. 'But I would not insist on an answer…if it was a one-night stand. But for the record, you're…'

'Single.' Immediately, I regret raising this subject so I change it. '…and in answer to your question, I work for a fashion magazine.'

'God, really?' He raises an eyebrow at me. 'I never would have guessed from those mental trousers you *were* wearing.'

'Pants. They're called pants. Nobody says trousers these days. Actually, they're leather joggers to be precise…and they are not "mental". Far from it. Leather joggers have pretty much become a become a lower half wardrobe basic, like a cigarette pant or a skinny leg pant or a high waisted pant etcetera. But for your information, leather bootcut trousers are not an option. Crimes Against Fashion No.40: Bootcut anything. Guilty: All of us in the nineties and early Noughties… when you you could still say "trouser".'

'Mmmm, I'll take your word for it. Which magazine?'

'I'm not telling you or you'll display further tragic behaviour like buying it every month to feel like we're still *connected* in some way.'

At this point, I force myself to look away from his body because I have been staring at it. It's pretty good for an average guy. But when you're used to seeing the *über* bodies of male clotheshorses trotting down the runway your grip on the reality of a man's physique becomes warped. That said, most models suffer from some sort of body dysmorphia. Even if they are honed and buffed to perfection they see Jabba the Hutt in the mirror. It's clear that Jared is perfectly content with his lot. Especially, his penis. He still hasn't put it away. He flicks some ash in a coffee cup and passes me his half-smoked cigarette. I shake my head.

'Right, Ashley, since I'm not going to see you again, it would be a shame for us not to share our other staple information, don't you think? That way I won't remember you as the girl with the mental *pants* who I didn't fancy that much. I'll start. Hobbies? None really. Do a bit of music. Nothing impressive like making my own sushi…'

'I hate sushi.'

'Wooooo! Me too!' He jump ups and punches the air. His 'appendage' wiggles about. 'This is *definitely* a sign we should see each other again. We're practically soulmates. Go on, then. Your turn. Hobbies…'

'Anything to do with fashion, I suppose. Appreciating the work that has gone into it, knowing what it will work with, then *working* it. I love the characters; the designers, the fashionistas, the models…all of them. I have a cat called Kat Moss.'

'I'll hold back from making a joke about getting to know your pussy a little better. Actually, I'm allergic to cats. They make me sneeze.'

'Really. I'm allergic to people who think that a cat being called a pussy is even remotely funny. Next?'

'Phobias…'

'I don't have any,' I tell him.

'Except journeys between different parts of the UK which may take up a substantial part of the day.'

'Hilarious. Yours?'

'Atychiphobia.'

'Ooooh, fear of failure. Almost interesting.' But I do not let him add anything. 'Siblings?'

'I have one brother. You?'

'None,' I say, emphatically.

'Oooooh, a loner. Lastly, parents…'

'My parents? Well…erm…' I pause. One second. Two seconds. 'They live about forty minutes outside the capital in a suburban cul-de-sac which has a Neighbourhood Watch scheme and a bloke who delivers fresh fish every Friday. My mother is a purser for an airline—she only does short haul these days so she can spend more time in the garden—and my father runs a plumbing business. They are part of a local bridge league which operates during the winter and a croquet one which is summer only. They both used to vote Conservative, but are now staunch UKIP supporters. They buy dairy "spread" not butter. Oh, and they insist on shoes being removed before entering the house. But no padding around in bare feet. Thick socks or slippers at all times.'

That will do, won't it? I know it is a believable answer because I have described two real parents: Zach's. Gwendolyn and William.

Jared smiles at me. 'They sound very…'

'Gwen and Bill? Oh, they are *very*.'

'My turn…'

But then *he* pauses. For the first time this afternoon I can sense a twinge of *real*ness. He sits down on the bed next to me. He is ready to offer up serious information that will take the conversation…somewhere. It makes me uncomfortable. We are here to *do* some*thing*, not to *go* some*where*.

'This game is boring. Let's have a drink…' I suggest.

I swing my legs over him and, pulling the sheet with me, I wander over to the bag of ice lying on the floor. I tip the melting cubes into two glasses and pour Peach Schnapps over the top. I am about to open the curtains again but I pull them tighter shut. Then I stare down into the glasses of alcohol. I am staring for a few seconds. Maybe more. Maybe minutes. Until I feel hands around my waist. I don't turn round.

'D'you want a drink, Jared?'

'No, that's boring too. First, *Ashley*, I am going to demonstrate to you—*in detail*—how a "one-night stand" came to be called exactly *that*. We've established the "one" and the "night" parts. Now it's time for the "stand".'

We have sex again. This time we both attempt to remain vertical throughout the session. At least one of us has a foot on the floor at any point. It lasts a lot longer than our initial session and it's better. Way better than any of 1–5 of the other 'stands', in fact. After it's over, we both crash on the bed. Jared falls asleep, allowing me to enjoy a much longer period of silence. I watch him for a bit. Not in a freaky way. I'm merely fascinated by how heavily he is sleeping. His breathing is deep and easy. It's odd how guys allow themselves to do this. It leaves them so exposed. I could be anyone. A fully formed psychopath, not simply an intermittent liar.

Not that any of the lies I told him could be particularly damaging. The first, that I was 'single' instead of 'separating' barely even registers as a fib, given that both terms mean I am *on my own*. The second about Kat Moss still being mine was simply because I miss her. And, thirdly: Gwen and Bill, they were my in-laws. So not exactly a whopping lie, more an abridgement of the truth. I haven't seen Bill since last Christmas. But I saw Gwen about four months ago. It was a Saturday morning. She had texted me the night before. Her message was written in her usual efficient/officious manner.

Ashley, I'd like to run a couple of things by you (without my son in attendance). Tomorrow morning would suit. Regards, Gwen.

We met at a coffee shop. I ordered a cup of tea. Gwen, an Earl Grey. We sat down by the window.

GWEN: I appreciate you coming to see me, Ashley. I hope it wasn't too awkward.

ME: With Zach? Oh, he'll be fine. I left him doing some work. He thinks I'm at boxing. I'm usually doing that at this time on a Saturday, anyway.

GWEN: Boxing? I hope you weren't doing that when...

ME: (Taking a breath.) Of course not. No sparring. Just circuits...which are perfectly safe.

GWEN: Seems so strange to me that young women today never seem to want to slow down. Even when they get the opportunity to.

ME: (Taking another breath, trying not to let my irritation mount.) All the research shows that there is no need to adjust your fitness schedule until you feel it is necessary. In fact, most stipulates that you should never suddenly stop what you were doing.

GWEN: Is that right?

Please, NO. I do not want to rehash the SAME FUCKING SHIT!

ME: Yes, it is. Anyway, I'm glad we've met up. I was going to suggest we did. I've got something to show you. I'm going to keep it a secret for a bit from Zach, so don't tell him.

GWEN: (Eyes suddenly twinkling.) Is this what I think it is? Oh, Lord! I'm so, so pleased. I didn't even consider for a moment that you would have been thinking about d—

ME: (Interrupting her.) Well, we've got to get on with our lives. So, here...check this out. (I tap my iPhone, scroll down to the picture I want.) Or rather, check HER out.

GWEN: (Putting on her spectacles.) Her? Oh, Ashley! That is wholly unexpected but so utterly lovely you would want to let me see first. I'm really quite overwhelmed. I know we've had our ups and downs but... (Taking my mobile.)... oh my. Oh my. OH MY!

ME: I know! That was my first reaction when I saw her. That is one ridiculously cute...

GWEN: (Dropping my iPhone on to the table)...cat. It's a cat.

ME: No, SHE is a kitten. Yeah, I know we've got Kat Moss already, but Zach adores her so much and I know he will fall in love with this little thing too. She's from the same rescue centre as we got Kat Moss from. I've already told the lady that we're going to take her. On Zach's birthday, she will be exactly nine weeks, so I thought I'd present her to him at home that morning...and then we can have a quiet weekend together helping her settle in and getting her acquainted with Kat Moss.

GWEN: You are giving my son a cat?

She made this one syllable sound like it had seven.

ME: No, a kitten. It's important Kat must feel she is in charge. I'm going to suggest we call her Meowmi Campbell. Get it? Kat Moss and Meowmi Campbell. Ha! I thought it would be the perfect birthday surprise for him. To be honest, I really don't think he wants a big fuss or anything like that. It's cool of you to want to arrange something but maybe just keep it on the quieter side. Just a few peop—

GWEN: A party? You thought I wanted to meet you today in order to discuss a party for my son's birthday? A PARTY. My daughter-in-law wants to ADOPT A FERAL ANIMAL THEN CELEBRATE??

That was when I realised Gwen had thought I was about to show her an ultrasound scan. I couldn't help laughing as I weighed up what was more ludicrous. That she had misconstrued what I was saying or thought I would have shown *her* first if that had been the case. Then I stopped laughing, because I wondered what that would feel like, to have a foetus to show. And I couldn't. I couldn't actually *feel*. I couldn't feel anything. Gwen was still raging.

GWEN: Are you TOTALLY insane? I came here to talk about his current mental state. I wanted to know if you thought he might need some therapy. Over the last eight weeks I have never seen him so low. He's not eating properly, he's not inspired by work, he's not going to the gym. He clearly hadn't shaved the last time I saw him. Good grief, Ashley, it never even entered my head that he would want to celebrate. For crying out loud, you have just lost his baby!

ME: No. WE lost IT.

I slide out of bed and tiptoe round the hotel room collecting my clothes. My shirt and pants are lying by the door. I find one shoe under the bed, the other by the window. My g-string is on the chair. I can't find my bra. But then I see the black strap dangling over the edge of the pillow Jared is lying on. That bra cost me £125 at Agent Provacateur, but I don't even attempt to remove it in case he wakes up. I put on the rest of my clothes, grab my bag, drain one glass of Peach Schnapps and creep out of the room, down the corridor and into the lift. Then I put on my heels. In the foyer, I thank the receptionist for the ice and pay the bill. He gives me a knowing smile as if respecting me for what I have got up to. Lots of men probably use that hotel for an illicit shag, and there I was—a woman—just as much of a player. But I want the game to stop. If I was to use another one of Catherine's clunky metaphors, I don't want another throw of the dice. I want to gather up the pieces, fold up the board, put them back in the box and forget about the scores. No one has won.

Twenty minutes later, I'm standing on the train platform waiting for the last train service back to London. I am staring at the tracks. I can't face looking at any of the other passengers. At this moment I could not feel more *soiled*. My mobile rings. Maybe I can…it's Zach.

'Hey, it's me,' he says.

'Yeah, I know it's *you*. You'll be touched to hear I haven't deleted your number from my contacts list.' I sigh. 'Everything okay with Kat?'

'She's fine. Ash, about that text you sent…'

'What text?'

'You sent me a text last night.'

'Did I?' Fuck. 'What did I say?'

'Listen,' he continues. 'I think we should talk…'

'About what?'

'Everything. Maybe we could meet? If you're about…I'd like to see you.'

My chest thumps. This is the first time in three months Zach has said he'd 'like' to do *any*thing with me. The other times he has requested my presence it has been with an 'ought'.

'Tonight?'

'If possible.'

'Yeah. I'm…at a erm…' *Today didn't happen.* '…at a birthday dinner thing in Zone 5. But I could be over to yours by about…' *How long will it take me to get back?* '…midnight. That's not too late?'

'No. It's important I see you. Bye.'

'Bye…'

Then it starts raining. I don't move. I stand in the rain until I am soaked through. I let it pelt down onto my face, in a bid to wash away—not just this evening—but every night I have regretted during the last ninety days. To what or whoever it was that made Zach change his mind, I am thankful. I am also thankful that I have a change of clothes in my bag, as this is not a movie. And I would have had to sit for hours on a well air-conditioned train in wet silk and leather. The train arrives on time.

'Thank you!' I say it out loud. And then, as the doors whoosh open I find myself looking up into the night clouds and saying it again without even thinking who I am talking to. 'Thank *you*.'

*

At 12.09am, I am outside Zach's flat. I am wearing a tan shearling jacket, black leather leggings and a white vest with Aquazurra suede boots. They were a present from Zach on our anniversary last year. I couldn't justify spending so much money on them when they were originally on sale, but then the entire line sold out. Zach lurked on the Vestaire website for months until someone wanted to sell an unworn pair in my size. Since the day 'it was decided', I have thought about what I would wear when he changed his mind, and this was it. The jacket is slightly too warm for this time of year, but I hadn't foreseen us getting back together so early into autumn. He opens the door. I clench my fists to stop myself from flinging them round his neck.

'You're early…'

'Got a cab. Didn't want to ruin my shoes.'

He doesn't look down to acknowledge their significance.

'Do you want to come in? Or we can go down the road. There's that painful hipster juice bar open late…'

I balk at his suggestion. 'Of course I want to come in. That's the only reason I'm here, to *finally* check out your bachelor pad. You better have a one-hundred-inch HD television with surround sound bolted to the wall in the living room, as well as a mini fridge next to the sofa so that you can grab a can of beer without standing up whilst you're watching the football. And if there aren't pizza boxes piled up by the bin or a load of damp, mildewy clothes sitting in the washing machine that you haven't been arsed to dry properly, I sh—' I stop.

...we kiss again, even harder. Teeth clash. He presses me up against the wall, grabs my neck with one hand and with the other reaches round and undoes the clasp of my bra in one quick sn—

Zach peers at me. *Can he tell?*

'Sorry, I was…'

'Rambling,' says Zach.

'Yeah. I, erm…had a couple of cocktails at the birthday dinner thing.'

Zach nods and rubs my shoulder. 'Well, come in…'

He ushers me into the hallway which is lined with trainer boxes, and into the kitchen. It's got an industrial edge, with freestanding metallic units and a big, battered oak table. Kat Moss is sitting on this, giving herself a vigorous pedicure. She briefly glances over in my direction, her deep brown slanting eyes assessing whether my arrival is worth cutting short her beauty regime.

'Meeeeeeeeee!' she says.

Then she lifts up her other paw, flexing it so that the individual pads are accessible and then gets to work on that.

'Cheers, Kat,' I smile at her. 'You could have put a bit more effort into our big reunion. Have you not seen *The Incredible Journey*?'

I go over. She blinks up at me, signalling she is ready to

let me rub my face against her and breathe in her impeccably groomed fur, but…

'*I'll hold back from making a joke about getting to know your pussy a little better. Actually, I'm allergic to cats. They make me sneeze.*'

I feel my hands go clammy. The nausea returns.

'Shall I get you a drink?' asks Zach.

'Erm…yeah, glass of red would be nice.'

'No booze in the flat, I'm afraid. I'm on a bit of a health kick, haven't had a beer or anything for ages. Except the night we celebrated getting the pitch. Ugh. That got messy. Ended up with the vilest hangover in the morning.'

'As long as that was all you ended up with. Ha!' A forced laugh.

I wriggle out of my bra, throw it to the side and unbuckle his belt. We kiss again, so hard that this time I can taste blood in my mouth. I pull his T-shirt over his head. He grabs the waistband of my leather jog—

Zach doesn't laugh. 'So, how are you doing on that front, Ash?'

'*That* front?' The 'ending up with' men-other-than-you front? 'Christ, Zach. Do you really think we should have this conversation? I don't think it is a good idea, not when we're thinking about g—'

'I was worried. I *am* worried.'

'There is no need. Really. Because…' *Every other 'stand' from 1–5—and now 6—has meant nothing.* I trail off. 'It never means anything.'

'It's understandable, Ash.'

'It is?'

'For sure.'

'I can't believe you're saying that. I thought you would be…angry. No, *livid*.'

He throws me down on the bed, grabs the waistband of my joggers and slides them down my legs, over my h—

'Nah.' Zach flicks the switch on the kettle. 'That's not going to help, is it? Besides, I have no right to be pissed off with you. There is no rule book as to how you are meant to behave at times like this. But I do think you should knock it on the head now. You've had your phase.'

Absolutely. I agree. Thank you for understanding. No, more than that…thank you for accepting me. You have no idea how, erm…'

He grabs my pony tail and mumbles something about it being 'too much'. I clamber over to the door and get a condom from the inner zipped pocket of my bag. He pulls me back towards him by the elastic of my knickers. I shove him back on the bed roll down the D—

'Accept you? Ash, you're being overly dramatic… and you certainly do not need to thank me for understanding. I may have gone down the same route, but that pitch gave me something to concentrate on. Anyway, don't take offence, but I wanted to give you this.' He pulls a card out of his trousers and passes it to me. 'You know Keith did the twelve step programme? Well, he still goes to meetings. As you also know, they didn't manage to stop him being a mouthy git nor will they ever, but they managed to stop him boozing. He says not to be put off by the Higher Power aspect to it, as that doesn't have to mean god, merely a spiritual pres—'

I zone out and look down at the card. Printed on it are a list of places. *Of all the East London branches of Alcoholics Anonymous.* And their meeting times. I almost laugh.

'You want me to stop drinking? *That* was what you were talking about? Me. *Drinking?*'

'Yes. It's a delicate subject but it needs to be addressed. Like I said, I'm not having a go at you, but I know your… *that*…is getting out of hand. You're not keeping up to date with the solicitor's stuff, you're always edgy, you send texts at four in the morning telling me…well, I know you didn't mean to be cruel because you were clearly drunk, but it was still totally out of order.' Zach sighs. 'Look, if you're depressed you need to take control of your feelings. Or at least share them. Drinking is only going to make you lose your grip. I know it's not my business, b—'

'No, it isn't any of your business…' I hiss back. 'But it is your *fault*.'

'Don't say that. I was concerned how it might start affecting your work. You wouldn't want to lose your job.'

'As well as my husband? And my cat? No, that would be very remiss of me.'

His eyes glaze over. Mine feel mulchy with running mascara and eyeshadow. He swivels me round. I ride him again then jump off and get on all fours. He slams into me. I slam harder. He comes. I don't.

I march into the lounge. I can't look at Zach a second longer because I don't want him to see the bewilderment, shame and disappointment in my eyes. I look around the lounge. Nothing about it says 'temporary'. It says, '*I'm here to stay!*'. The way he has kitted it out is similar to the place he used to rent before he met me, but demonstrates how much more he is earning now because all the furniture is vintage, not megastore-bought masquerading as such. There is a man-about-town-retro-chic feel to it. Artfully battered and tattered-leather Chesterfield sofa, velvet armchair, feather lamp, tasselled rug and a round art deco glass coffee table, upon which are a pile of thick hardback books and an antique backgammon board. In the corner is a discreetly positioned and sized television. I look down, keeping the door open is a pair of…

'…are those fucking dumb bells? Ha! What a cliché.'

He walks in behind me. 'Ash, stop. Don't be like that. Let's talk.'

'I thought we'd done that. Or was informing me that I'm an alcoholic only the warm up? I can't wait to hear what you've got in store for me as the main workout. I'm here now, so you may as well go for fucking gold.'

Obviously, I am lying. I don't want to hear what he has to say, because everything about this flat tells me this really is 'The End'. The place where my solicitor said we all apparently *wanted* to get to. I stare at the picture he has over the fireplace. It's a framed record sleeve of a rare twelve inch dance remix of Britney Spears' *…Baby One More Time*. His team at work gave it to him for his birthday. The same one I was going to get him the kitten, but didn't. It used to be on the wall in the hallway at our flat.

'D'you remember you wanted that to go up in the living room as an "ironic centrepiece"?' I ask him, my back still turned. 'I wouldn't let you because I didn't consider Britney ironic. Not even post-ironic. No one can be considered to have ironic appeal after doing Vegas. Then you said that me having that black and white print of Carine Roitfeld in my wardrobe was equally as lacking in irony because *I* genuinely thought *I* was cool for having it there. "*Wooooo! Get me, I've got a cutting edge fashion idol! Ergo; I am cool!*" And then I had a go at you for using the word "ergo" and you said…' I turn round to face him. But his eyes do not meet mine. They dart away. '…that I was a fine one to talk as the day before I had used the phrase "on trend" without any sense of *irony* whatso—'

'Ash…'

'Just say it,' I tell him.

His eyes drop to the floor.

'I said, *say it.*'

'Okay.' He doesn't need to clear his throat. 'I'm seeing someone. It's not serious at the moment but it could get there. In fact, I know it has the potential because we have been getting close for a while now. I know this is difficult for you to hear and wish I didn't have to tell you so soon after your mother passing away, but I wanted you to hear it from me. No-one else. And it's so difficult to keep anything quiet these days. Nothing can be kept a secret. Not that this should be secret because I don't feel I should have to hide it, but what I do feel is that you deserve to be the first to know. It's what I know you would do for me, and by the way, don't think that it won't kill me when you start dating again, because it will. I've been dreading telling you and how *much* to tell you, but I came to the conclusion I should be up front and give you the facts. Those facts are these: she is called Rachel. I work with her. She's an account manager…been with the company for a while. You met her once at a Christmas do. During the time you and I were together I swear nothing happened with her. Or anyone else. The physical side of things only happened six weeks or so ago. It felt strange not being with you. But the weirdest thing – and like I said, this is total honesty – that although it felt strange, I did not feel guilty. I thought I would but I didn't and it made me realise that I am starting to move on. Something I thought would never happen. But I am. That said…' Finally, he looks up, but his line of vision is more directed at the picture behind me. '…I don't want to be endlessly processing stuff between us any more. Not emotionally, practically or legally. We've both been guilty of dragging our feet but we need to stop and step away from each other's lives. Because we are getting a divorce.'

It is the first time I have heard him use The D word, in all its soul-sapping, life blood-draining, hope-annihilating glory.

'Okay.'

'I'm sorry if that all came out badly and jumbled up, but nothing about this situation is good or clear cut, and I did—'

'I said, o-*kay*. Okay, I get it. I get *it*.'

'That's it? You don't want to ask me anything? Because I want to make this as easy as possible for you.'

I stare down at his still box-fresh Travel Fox. 'Then I will also make it easy for you too, Zach. I've also been seeing someone else, actually there has been more than one person. A few. In fact, I was with one of them earlier. As soon as "it was decided", I started seeing other men and like you with Rachel…' I almost spit this word. 'I didn't feel guilty. Not in the slightest. So, like I said, I get it, Zach. I get *it*.'

I look up. He stares at me, this time his eyes do meet mine. They are filled with tears. I feel sick. Sicker than I did this morning. Sick that I have made Zach cry. Sick he is going to bed with someone other than me. Even sicker that he is waking up with them. Sick from drinking all day. For months. Sick that I knew my mother did exactly the same. For years…

I leave the flat without saying goodbye to Kat Moss—I don't want her to see me like this. After her start in life, she would quite rightly think I was pathetic. She had nothing and she made everything of herself. I've done the same, but I've thrown it all away. By choice. My choice. Running up the main road, I can hear Zach shouting my name. I slip down a side street and check the sent messages in my phone. Just before dawn, I *did* send him one.

I would never have gone through with it. That's the truth.

And then I *am* sick. Because I know he would have entirely misunderstood what I was saying. The vomit splashes all over the pavement and my anniversary boots. Which *really* naffs me off. It's impossible to fully remove a liquid stain from suede. You'll always be left with some sort of mark.

Ten

Tanya,
So, here it is. The goodbye letter. I chose a handwritten
'missive' because after a period of silence it felt like
the right approach. The equivalent of a one off couture
Christian Lacroix gown (predictably to be only afforded
by a Hong Kong fashionista) filled with drama and an
almost, I hope, poetic sensibility. An email would have
felt too functional. Too Prada. (NEVER usually a bad
thing—Miuccia is a utilitarian visionary—but today,
not appropriate.) I'm leaving. But not because of you.
It is important for me that you understand that. You
have no effect on my life now nor will you ever. What
you did means nothing. You mean nothing. Of course,
there was a time when you meant everything. We were
more than best friends. We were sisters. But I'm one
hundred percent confident that as the years pass, I will
forget everything I liked about you until there will be a
point where I wonder what on earth I found appealing
about you in the first place. Much like that pair of jeans
I bought and customised with feathers at the bottom.
Remember them? I tried to copy the Gucci ones, but

*the end result looked as if I had strapped a couple of
dead pigeons to my shins. Earlier as I was packing,
I looked at them and thought, why did I bother when
I liked the trousers before? And that is exactly how I
imagine I will remember you; as a badly thought out
bit of customisation to my life—now, easily discarded.
Because let's face it, there will always be more denim.
This does not mean I wish you sadness. I hope you will
be happy. However, the chances are you will never
be happy again. Why? Well, your shame will never
leave you. I'm not trying to be the voice of doom or
anything, simply stating a fact. Whenever you do get the
opportunity of happiness, you will destroy it because
you won't feel as if you deserve it. It will be your fault.
Always. And that will be the truth. In fact, this will be
your ONLY truth. This is because what goes around
comes around. The law of moral causation…KARMA.
Ashley.*

This was all she ever said about what had happened. The day
I told her, she said nothing. Not a word. She nodded, slammed
shut the suitcase full of clothes and dragged it through the
wet precinct, where snow had been brought in from outside.
There was a blast of cold air as the glass doors whirred open
for her to leave. The individual next-door traders rolled their
eyes at one another in seen-it-all-before unison as if joint
stall holding was always prone to minor disputes. I wondered
what specifically *they* were assuming had happened. Have
the two girls had a disagreement over the display? Are there
inadequate float funds? Could it be stock issues? Possibly
a problem with production? I can guarantee that not one of

them even considered the possibility…*maybe she is having an affair with her best friend's father*. Maybe her best friend's mother is finding out *right now*. Even I didn't consider that.

I never read another word she wrote either. Until today. The latest copy of *Catwalk* is in my desk drawer. I bought it on my lunch break and forced myself to look at her column. Her writing has not changed. It still has that confident air of superiority and mocking humour. It made me feel uncomfortable. It still is…having something directly related to *her*, near *me*. I picture the magazine in the drawer, next to my blog notebook, the production schedule for this quarter's work schedule, Chewbacca-emblazoned stationery (a silly gift from my boss when he promoted me), a bottle of Lucozade… and a picture of Greg and I. I keep the latter hidden because I am not someone who broadcasts their life outside of the office. A life that is neatly compartmentalised is what I am happy with. And happiness is what I have achieved, despite everything Ashley Atwal predicted. I have, haven't I?

Haven't I?

*

Greg picks me up from work. The excitable butterflies that I usually get in my stomach when I see him feel more like frustrated moths batting their wings aimlessly against the inside of a lampshade. I get in the car, chucking my overnight bag on the floor. He leans over to kiss me on the mouth. I fully reciprocate, but I am stiff, because I'm looking at him but I'm seeing someone else. I'm seeing a liar. I kiss him again and smile. He smiles back – it's one of his Olympic-flickflack-inducing grins. This time, I'm seeing someone who could have perfectly good reason for lying.

'How was your day, babe?' he asks. 'You look a bit…'

Quickly. 'What?'

'Stressed.'

'Me? Nooooo. I had a great day. My boss has decided that we need to have a more flexible approach to how we work. So now, instead of having the creatives, account managers and copy writers in different sections of the office, we're all going to *mingle* depending on which project we are working on. The excitement keeps on coming, eh? And yeah, before you say anything, he did finish his email by announcing, "Hot desking, the future is!"!' I force a laugh.

Greg laughs (naturally) as he pulls out onto the main road.

'I know that shouldn't be funny, but…'

'It is, I know.' I laugh even harder. 'No one else in the office seemed to think it was, though. I mean, give the guy a break! At least, he's *try*ing to have a giggle. They take themselves so seriously. At least he keeps his *Star Wars* jokes relevant to a digi-marketing business. He came up with a corker the other day. D'you want to hear it?'

'Go for it…'

'Which programme do Jedi use to open PDF files?'

'I don't know. Which programme do they use?'

'Adobe Wan Kenobi. Get it?'

He smiles. 'Yeah, I get it.'

'Then he followed it up with this one: "The *Star Wars* text crawl walks into a bar. 'Get out of my pub!' yells the landlord. 'Why?' asks the text crawl. The landlord points at him. 'Because we don't serve your type in here.'" Get that?'

'Your type? Oh! Your *type*! Ha! Nice one…'

…and on we chatter aimlessly; which is exactly how it has been all week since our discussion in the garden. Getting to the root of any problem is never straightforward. I was tempted to navigate my way straight there after Greg came back from work *that* night, but then I decided the direct approach was not the best one. But the problem with all the other routes I have come up with so far is that they all (bar one)—have to go down Creating An Issue Avenue. Once on that road, you can only go in one direction. It is the dual carriage way of relationship ruin.

'You looking forward to the gig?' I ask. 'Sorry, I mean, are you *hyped*? Or do I mean *ramped*?'

'Yeah, *ramped*! Should be a good one. It's a shame you're not into live music, babe. Seriously, there's nothing like being rammed in the middle of a mosh pit, ears deafened by reverb, drenched in sweat—not just yours—and warm beer.'

'Mmmm…potential claustrophobia, tinnitus and flu.'

'You can't be persuaded then? There are still tickets available.'

'I *bet* there are! No, I'll get Mum to drop me off at the train station early tomorrow. I reckon I should be at The Rexingham by about midday. We could have brunch?'

I balk as I say this. We Could Have Brunch is surely the turning you need to go down in order to bypass that dual carriageway and hit Just Carry On As If Nothing Has Happened And It Will Be Okay Street.

'Yeah, brunch sounds good. I'll make sure I'm showered and have necked a Berocca…and not still in bed dribbling into the pillow.'

'Mmm…sexy.'

'Always.'

He indicates left at the roundabout leaving the centre of town and onto a B road. This takes us to the village which my parents' house overlooks from the hill. On the corner of the village square is Suze's house. Greg clocks me looking at it as we drive past.

'Before you ask, Suze and I haven't made up,' I tell him.

'Oh, right…I wasn't going to.'

'We will though…we always do, don't we? This time she'll come to me, I know she will.'

Greg does not comment. I watch the mini Fender Stratocaster guitar key ring swaying rhythmically from side to side as it dangles from from the ignition.

'Hey, you know she said that her and Rollo were looking after Evie, Jasper and *four* of their friends on a sleepover tonight? Well, apparently, Suze's mum and sister are doing one of their spa things and insisted she join. Maddie said that Suze is leaving Rollo—on his own, no nanny—with all *six* children.'

'Yeah, well, I'm sure Rollo will be fine in the Range Rover with his crack pipe.'

'I think he might need something stronger. God, Suze really does have some front, doesn't she? I don't know how she gets away with it. Actually, I do. It's because even though she has her episodes of behaving like a little madam, upon reflection she *does* apologise if needs be. If she's in the wrong, eventually she'll admit it.'

Unlike Ashley. I picture that letter. I can see her handwriting. The curly loop slightly leaning towards the right, the 'a' styled as if it were type font, the tight spacing between each word. A graphologist would say that the person who wrote it was young and precocious but already professional, focused, secure in her own mind, knows that whatever she is writing is *right*.

Always being right was Ashley's thing. And quite rightly. She was right about everything in those crucially formative years of friendship as we headed into our teens. She was right about never accepting you could not do whatever you wanted. About never getting your hair braided at a street stall.

About never letting other girls assume they were better than you no matter where they came from, what they said or who had told them they were. She was right about never getting a tattoo to prove your spirituality. (Especially a dolphin, dream catcher, shining sun. Or anything written in a language you did not speak or from a country you had never visited or any form of tribal branding.) She was right about never trusting her father because she sensed he was a cheat.

I realise Greg is talking.

'So, yeah. My mind's made up,' he says. 'I'm leaving.'

'I…' I have to push the word out. 'You're *what*? Gr—'

He interrupts me. 'Bit of a curveball, I know. But we both knew the time would come eventually.'

Whenever you do get the opportunity of happiness, you will destroy it because you won't feel as if you deserve it.

'B-b-but…how…wh—' I stare down at my lap. 'Because of what happened the other day? You're l—' I choke, this time too shocked to continue.

He shrugs, almost *casually*.

'Not *just* because of that. We're going in different directions. It's best I walk away now or we'll end up fighting. Then I'll end up doing something I regret.'

Even if you think the destruction is not your fault, it will be.

He slows down at a roundabout and glances at me. I look away.

'Don't look so sad, babe.'

'How do you expect me to look?' I gaze out of the window. My hands are gripping the seat. 'It's…it's…my fault, isn't it?'

'Absolutely not.' He reaches across and squeezes my knee. 'Why would you say that? I've been thinking for a while that I need to go it alone. There's much more chance of me achieving what I want to without being with anyone else who may hold me back. I need the freedom to make the choices I want. You understand?'

And that will be the truth. In fact, this will be your ONLY truth. Your shame will never leave you. Not ever.

She was always right back then. She is right now. I nod. My breathing is rapid and shallow. I am sweating.

'At least it's a clean break. It would have been worse if I'd said to the other two I wanted to carry on with them and only sacked Jez.'

OH! Oh! Oh. Ha! JEZ! GREG IS TALKING ABOUT LEAVING THE BAND! I take a gulp of air and burst out laughing.

'Babe? It's not that funny. Jez was devvo.'

'Sorry! God, sorry, no! It's not funny. He must have been gutted. But maybe the use of the word 'devvo' by a grown man is faintly amusing,' I deadpan, in a bid to make myself sound less manic. 'How did you break it to him?'

'Just said it was nothing personal…that I needed to explore where I could go as a solo artist. But obviously, between you and me, if a record company wanted to fix me up with a band then I'd still go for that. I'd do anything! Within reason. Actually, no…I'd do anything.' He continues to rub my knee. 'God, you feel tense. Mind you, I would be if I was having dinner with your father. Don't forget to ask him about renovating the garage into a cheeky studio space. Pretty please!'

'Let's see.'

'Thanks, babe... hey, can you grab my e-cig out of that Adidas bag in the back?'

'So, you've finally decided that looking like, I quote, 'a dickhead' is a small price to pay for not having to rely on the NHS—as opposed to your lungs—to help you breathe in later life, then?' I twist round and grab a small grey backpack from the seat. 'Why the sudden turnaround?'

'Because I thought it was the least I could do. For you. And me. *For us.* Does that sound cheesy?'

'Yes, but I like it.' I really do. I need the full digestion-baiting board of lactose delights.

'But for the record,' he adds, 'I still think anyone who smokes one looks like a dickhead. Electronic cigarettes are uncool. Fact. Always have been. Always will be…' He glances sideways at me and immediately yanks the backpack out of my hands. 'No! Not that one…it's full of manky socks and shit…stuff I left at my flat. I said the Adidas black hold-all.' He sounds irritated. 'It's on the seat…has the Adidas three stripes running round it. And the Adidas logo by the handles. Under the word *Adidas.*'

'Ok-aaaaay. Calm down. God, nicotine withdrawal!'

'I'm fine.' He shrugs.

I rummage in the correct bag and pass him the e-cigarette. Then I find myself doing something to prove *I am fine too.* I pull out the copy of *Catwalk* from my bag. It is in the same pocket as the IVF information Dr Lyons gave me. I flick through, find the page and read out loud.

'Actually…' I return Greg's knee squeeze. 'You could not be more wrong about these things. They are officially cool. In fact, there is a feature on how cool they have become in this magazine. Listen…' I clear my throat. '"*Admittedly, they were ridiculed at first. E-fags weren't a product that were cool. They didn't suddenly hit the coolest bars, clubs or after parties with confidence, they appeared rather nervously—usually on their own—in a puff of sickly smelling vapour at that lame "do" you'd already tried to get out of a few days previously. Their lame glow made me grateful that I had never smoked if this is what it had come to…*" Then…' I explain to Greg, relishing how wholly unaffected I am by her words. '…it goes on about how models started to use them backstage at shows. Blah blah blah, "*…but, now, e-ciggies in all their insipidly fruit-flavoured, intimate shaver-looking, lamely advertised naffness are…cool. It's official. Why? Ms. Moss has been spotted smoking—or rather clicking—one. That's THE Kate Moss and not MY Kat Moss, who regular readers of this col—*'Owwwww!' I slam into the door as the car swerves. The magazine shoots out of my hands. 'Greg! What are you doing?'

'Shit! Sorry, sorry…' He exhales deeply. 'Sorry…I thought I saw something in the middle of the road. Fox or a rabbit or a…something. Did you see it?'

'I wasn't looking.' I check the road behind us. 'I don't think you hurt anything. I didn't feel a bump. So anyway, yeah, they must be cool…e-cigs, if *she* says so; the Deputy Editor of *Catwalk* magazine. Ash—' I stop. I have not said her first name out loud in its entirety for so long. But now I do. 'Ashley. Ashley Jac—'

Suddenly, Greg lets the vehicle veer the other way towards the white lines. I grab the wheel.

'GREG! What the HELL! Straighten up!'

'Sorry, sorry…' he says. His voice is shaky.

'Your driving is all over the place at the moment.'

'Don't worry, babe. I'm concentrating…now. I only let go of the wheel for a split second. I never lost sight of the road ahead. Promise. Sorry, I'm…' He rubs his forehead. 'Listen, let's organise a night to see your parents next week to tell them.'

'About what?'

'The engagement! Remember? You're my fiancée! Don't do it tonight. I want to be there. We can make it official. It'll be a fresh start.'

'I didn't know we needed one…' I take off the ring and put it in my bag.

'Oi! You know what I mean.'

'Do I?'

'I think you mean 'I do', babe. Get it?'

Not really. I don't. And just like that I am not fine. Again.

*

When we arrive at my parents' house, I ask Greg to drop me off at the end of the driveway. I need some fresh air. As I walk the remaining one hundred and fifty metres to the house, I inhale and exhale slowly, and tell myself that the neurosis I am experiencing has been created by me. There is no solid fact on which to base it and therefore it is not to even be considered, let alone believed. This is the basis of cognitive therapy. Second guessing, predictions, jumping to conclusions, mind reading, assumptions…they are the cattle prods of anxiety, nudging you, then trapping you into an enclosure of depression. I need to exist *in the moment*—not *in my mind*—and only deal with real issues as they arise. The past and the future are out of my control. I need to see what I am doing and help myself. I know that.

I also need *not* to be seeing my family, because that will not help. I know that too.

It takes my mum a few minutes to configure the various alarm systems to let me in. Dad has spent a fortune on security at their house. You would have thought they were living next to a gang-led Johannesburg township and not in a leafy enclave in the outskirts of an English country village.

'Sweetheart, you shouldn't have!' Mum gasps with delight at the gift I present her with. 'Look at *those*. Oooooh, leopard spots…you know I can't resist a bit of animal print. And with my initials too. Really, they're…*erm*…'

'It's a set of covers for your golf clubs, Mum.'

'You mean a set of covers for the metal implements she hacks away at the green with as if she's trying to locate a time capsule,' says Dad.

'I'm not *that* bad,' she smiles, squeezing me. 'What a lovely prezzie. For a second, I thought they were salad-server warmers! Where's Greg? I thought we were seeing him tonight too.'

Dad butts in before I can reply.

'Salad-server warmers?' He snorts, as he tops up his glass of beer. 'Ever the entrepreneur, Cheryl. Good luck with that on *Dragons' Den*.'

'They're monogrammed too,' I tell Mum, ignoring his dig at her. 'Well, since every serious present I've got you on your wedding anniversary you've taken back to the shop because it was 'far too much to spend on me', I thought I'd get you something silly and non-returnable. Dad, I got you some too. They're strip—'

He interrupts me, laughing. 'Cheryl has come to the Den looking for two hundred thousand pounds in return for fifteen percent of her company specialising in keeping summer kitchen utensils above room temperature. After a confident opening pitch she opens the floor to questions from the Dragons…ha!'

I stare at my mother, assessing the fixed smile on her face. But she turns away and busies herself at the kitchen counter where a joint of beef is resting on a wire tray. Like all of her roasts, the centrepiece is of Jurassic proportions. It could feed eight people, even though there are only three of us ready to sit down at the table. To accompany the meat there are pota-

toes, parsnips and swede roasting in the industrial-sized oven
and five different saucepans on the hob. Mum is a feeder. Her
weekly shop is the size of a Red Cross emergency drop. More
food was the first sign that things were changing. We still
lived on the estate, but our new fridge was a lot taller than
its predecessor, 'tea' became 'dinner' and became a sit down
occasion and then, snacking moved to a more aspirational
level. Out went crisps and in came M&S 'nibbles'.

'Okydoky,' says Mum, patting down a length of silver
foil over the meat. 'I think everything is under control. I'm
going to nip upstairs and freshen up.'

As she leaves, Dad helps himself to an olive-oil-and-
rosemary-infused bread stick from a glass on the table. He
dips it in a bowl of houmous. I sip on orange juice and stare
out of the window. I know he is considering what to say. And
vice versa. Conversation never comes that easy between us.
It's always been this way. Even when we lived in a flat with
only five rooms, I avoided the one he was in. He did too.
He would even creep past a room to avoid me. Any sort of
creeping is unnerving.

Greg crept up the stairs the other night when he got back
from The Croft.

*ME: (Turning on light.) It's okay. No need to tiptoe. I'm
awake.*

*HIM: Oh. You're still up? It's gone one. You should be
asleep…ignore me I'll be quiet.*

*ME: I said I was awake. That rain was making so much
noise against the skylight in the hallway…and I could still
smell burnt quiche. First world problems, eh? (Glancing at
clock.) You're late.*

*HIM: Yeah, the bar was really busy tonight…took me ages
to cash up. Thought I was going to be there all night. I'm*

cream crackered. (Taking off his T-shirt, throwing it into the laundry basket, unbuckling his jeans, sitting down on the side of the bed with his back to me to take off his socks.) Babe?

ME: *Yeah?*

HIM: *I'm sorry…about tonight.*

ME: *Me too.*

HIM: *No, you shouldn't be. It's me who should be apologising. I handled that conversation really badly and I regret…I regret not staying with you, to sort it out. I shouldn't have left.*

ME: *Shoosssssh. (Easing his belt belt through the loops on his trousers. Reaching my hand into his jeans.)*

HIM: *(Getting up.) D'you mind if we don't? Like I said, I'm zonked.*

ME: *You're turning down nookie? Actually, when I was watching the news earlier they said that there was a possibility that hell could be freezing over later tonight…*

HIM: *(Turning round. Smiling.) I'll be back in the game tomorrow, babe. I need a long shower and then bed. Just feeling a bit blah. I think it could be my time of the month or something. I'd be up for a cuddle though.*

He showered, brushed his teeth and got into bed. We lay intertwined. I was on my side, head nestled into his shoulder. The side of his head was rested on top of mine. My right hand was on his stomach. His left hand was stroking my shoulder. After a few minutes I tipped my head to kiss him on the mouth. He kissed me on the head.

'Tanya? *Tanya?*'

Dad flaps a bread stick at me. For once he looks as if he knows exactly what he wants to say, there is no consideration needed.

'Oh sorry, I was admiring the gard—'

'So, when were you going to tell me?'

'About what?'

'The memorial service for Yvonne Atwal.'

'Ah, yeah…it was earlier this week. Should I have told you? I thought you would have known about it through local chit chat. Did you want to go? I assumed that…well…'

'And you assumed right! Did I want to go?' He over-enunciates each syllable. 'NO! Of course, I did *not* want to go. My point is, why the *hell* did you?' He sips his beer, not losing eye contact with me. 'And by the way, the reason I know you attended was that you got into a brawl with that feral daughter of hers. *That* I did find out through local chit chat.'

I put my glass on the table. 'It was not a brawl. I didn't think…' I force myself to say her name again. '…Ashley was going to be there. It is common knowledge that she has had no contact with her mother in years. And by the way… that girl is a lot of things, but she is not feral.' I don't know why I add this.

Dad shrugs. 'You still haven't answered my question. Why did you go?'

I shrug too. 'Because I felt like it was the right thing to do, to pay my respects.'

'Your respects? You felt like being respectful *now*? Tanya, are you going doo-lally?' I am sure I hear him mutter 'again'. 'You will *never* be able to claw back what you did in order to show *any* respect to that woman and, frankly, you should have had more respect for the rest of your family to put yourself anywhere near *her* or those people again. Word got back to me within hours. I cannot believe you pitched up there without a single consider—'

I butt in. 'That's why I went. I considered it fully.'

He rolls his eyes. 'Is there something going on you need to tell me about?'

'No.'

'Then why? Why! You have a life now.'

'I was still alive then too, Dad!'

'Don't be facetious, Tanya. Listen to me, your name—*our* name—will always be associated with what happened. You put your family's wellbeing at risk. If we hadn't been able to leave when we did, god knows what may have happened.'

'You're being paranoid.'

'Paranoid!' He grabs another breadstick. 'We were pariahs on that estate as soon as the rumours surfaced.'

'I don't remember our family getting a particularly warm reception before…' I mumble.

'Tanya, you…' He stops and sighs. '…you will never understand what we had to go through because you were busy being sixteen. At sixteen, I only thought about myself too. It's not as if I don't accept that. When you're that age, you can't take responsibility for your actions because you don't know what the true value of responsibility is. But you're an adult now, aren't you?'

He taps his fingers on his chin, indicating this is not a question he particularly wants the answer to.

'Adults still think about what happened to them when they were sixteen, Dad.'

I look out the window again. The view from my parents' house is chocolate-box perfect; rolling hills and old houses. You can't see any of the new build blocks that my father made his money from.

He clears his throat. 'Look, I do not want to draw out this situation any longer than is necessary. I'm not going to tell your mother you went. She'll get emotional. You promised us you would never go near those people or the estate ever again and that would be it.'

'It *is* it. I won't.' My tone is sharp.

'Good girl. I believe you. So let's not discuss it any further and enjoy dinner. Well, the atmosphere anyway.' He helps himself to the last bread stick and passes me the empty bowl. 'We might need some more nibbles. That beast your mother has cooked is looking decidedly animated. God knows *why* she took it out of the oven so early…it's definitely not an improvement on being burnt to a crisp. In the choice between dying from salmonella or ash carcinogens, I'd choose the latter. Get something spicy, will you?'

I take the bowl and walk into the larder. That was a text-book conversation with my father. He gets to put across his point of view without showing interest in anyone else's. Whenever I went round to Ashley's flat on the estate, I was always fascinated with how she interacted with her own father. They would always be rowing. Hardly surprising as Ashley was the type of kid who could start an argument with a hair scrunchie. But what was always surprising to me, was the way that her father reacted. Every hot-headed opinion that was fired from his daughter's mouth, he didn't simply hear…he *listened*. Then he fired back his own opinions at her in his own equally hot-headed way. He disagreed with everything, but to have come to his own conclusions he had thought about what *she* said.

I am opening a bag of wasabi peas when the doorbell chimes.

'Howard! Can you get that?' I hear Mum shout.

He shouts back. 'Who is it, Cheryl? We're not expecting anyone are we?'

'Not as far as I know,' she yells. 'Can't think of anyone who would need to be here right now to help us celebrate. Can you?'

Oh, *great*. I know exactly who it is. So does Dad. I leave the larder to see a wide—no, *joyous*—smile spreading across his face. Mum comes into the kitchen with a newly crimsoned mouth and winks at him. He dashes out into the hallway, voice booming.

'Nelly! My little Nelly! Is it you? Tell me it's you!'

'Hey, Diddooooooooooo!' squeals another voice. Female. *Ridiculous* accent. 'It *is* me! *Me!* No, *This Is Me!* Let's keep it, like, on brand!'

More rapturous shouting from my father and some more self-congratulatory shrieking from the other voice. After some bolt shuffling and electrical beeping, they walk into the kitchen together, arms looped.

'Hi, Mum!'

'Hello, you!' she replies.

'Hi, honeeeeey.'

'Hi, Noelle,' I say. She is holding a dome-shaped holdall.

'It's really her!' says Dad, shaking his head. 'My little Nelly!' He looks across at Mum, there is slight irritation in his eyes. 'How *could* you have kept this quiet?'

'Sorry, Howard. We thought it would be a nice surprise.'

'It was my idea to keep it a secret,' explains Noelle. 'I'm back in the UK for three days. Fashion week shizzle and also having a party thrown in my honour like, tomozz evening, so I couldn't *not* come to see my Diddoo in between commitments!' She puts down the holdall on the end of the kitchen table and unzips it. She pulls out a tiny dog. 'Happy anniversary!'

'Oooooh, well…look at, erm…that!' says Mum, peering at it. 'Is it a hamster?'

'Don't be ridiculous, Cheryl. That's a teacup Pomeranian,' corrects Dad, peering underneath the puppy. 'And a fine bitch at that…'

Noelle hands her to Dad. 'She's from the, like, top breeder in the UK. Her mummy was a Crufts Best of Breed finalist and her, like, daddy won it the year previously. Her show name is Princess Tatiana of Dark Thunder Castle. Loops in my management office has got all the details. I bought her so you so can start your breeding programme, Dad.'

Mum giggles. 'Oh, Howard, you can't be serious. I'll end up having to look after it. You're too busy to be breeding pomegranates.'

'Pomer*anians*.'

'I was obviously joking.'

He still doesn't laugh. 'I need a hobby, Cheryl…and why shouldn't I? I work hard for my money.' He emphasises the solo pronouns. 'Now, let's get Princess some food and water and then I can focus on my *other* little princess.' He smiles at Noelle.

After Tatiana has been gushed over, the rest of us sit down to eat. Or rather Dad, Mum and I do. Noelle piles her plate with food, takes a picture of it on her Hello Kitty phone, then pushes the contents around. It is almost impressive at how she makes all the right clanking noises and cutting motions with her cutlery without a morsel of food entering her mouth. I wonder if she is either coming up or coming down off something. She is even more twitchy and distracted than usual. Whenever I look over at her, her eyes dart away.

Dad beams at Noelle. 'It's wonderful to have you back… even for a fleeting visit. Are you okay?' He leans across and rubs her arm. 'You seem a little left of centre.'

'That'll be the jet leg, Diddoo. I'm like, wired! But hey, that's my job. I don't want to let people down, and part of that is accepting I'll be operating on different time zones,' she replies, as if she were jetting around the globe on behalf of the United Nations, not a cable music channel. 'I was all over the States last week, for this new show I'm presenting about like, the world's biggest teen vloggers. I don't know *how* I feel about all of that whole scene. These people are taking over. Casting directors for like, adverts *and* telly shizzle… can't like, get enough of them. I kind of feel it's unfair, as they haven't really paid their dues. All they've done is banged on about their—as far as I can tell *not-exactly-exciting*—lives, to a camera, uploaded it and they're like, stars. There's no *real* skill to what they do. No training is required. I mean, I had to like, seriously *graft* when I was their age.'

'You were sent to stage school, not down a coal mine,' I laugh.

'Nelly worked very hard,' chides Dad. 'She was utterly dedicated to getting noticed, and look, it paid off. Both artistically *and* financially. I couldn't be prouder.'

'Thanks, Diddoo. But, yeah, as I was, like saying. It's, like, the *normality* of it all,' adds Noelle. 'I mean, do these kids *really* want their own lives reflected back at them? *Booooor*-ing.'

'Maybe they're bored of thinking they need to be better and are stimulated by the thought that being themselves is good enough,' I suggest.

'Honeeeeey! Don't get all, like, bigger picture on me. I'm only saying that it is difficult to understand their motivation.'

'That they want to be themselves and not Kylie Jenner? Yeah, I see how confusing *that* is…' I jab back, unable to help myself revert to the teenage me at family meal times.

'Tanya! E-*nough*.' Dad admonishes me. 'You're being very argumentative.'

Mum tuts at him. 'She's only saying her piece, Howard.'

'In a purely negative fashion. Nelly has come a long way to see us.'

'Awww, don't worry about her, Diddoo,' simpers Noelle. 'She's still got like, ants in her pants about what happened at my book bash.' She gingerly places a small square of beef in her mouth. Her first bite of food. 'This is so yummy. Worth a Transatlantic flight. I love it like, rare.'

'Mine is practically alive,' mutters Dad. 'I don't know why you didn't let me arrange a chef, Cheryl.'

'Because I like to cook,' she replies.

'And we like to eat *your* food, Mum,' I reassure her.

Dad ignores us both. 'What went wrong at the launch, Nelly?'

'Oh, nothing maje. I couldn't do a pic for Tanya's little blog t'ing. Obviously, I would've loved to…' She gives Dad a sugary smile. Or rather an aspartame-y one in her case. '… but a fashion magazine had the *exclusive* and I'm working with them like closely, next month. Sophs says this is a real show of respect from the industry. To be…' She smirks at me. '…guest editor of *Catwalk*.'

I stop chewing. My hands grip tightly onto my cutlery.

'You are going to be *what*?' I can't bring myself to say the words.

'Guest Editor of *Catwalk*.'

Mum nods at me. 'Isn't that the glossy magazine you did an internship at, sweetheart?'

'It was and it didn't work out, did it?' Dad reminds us all. 'Bit embarrassing really, given I set it up personally. Anyway, it's a shame – but understandable – Nelly couldn't help with your hobby.'

I throw my napkin on the table. 'Forget my "hobby",' I tell them all. 'I have an idea. Noelle, why don't you do a *pro-*

fessional blog. You're a journalist now...books, magazines, surely that's the next move for this erudite writing machine.'

'Whatever *that* means, I do *know* you are being sarcastic,' she says. 'Look, it's hard for me to like, say yes to all requests...'

I groan at her. 'I asked you to do one thing. I never ask you to do anything else, *ever*, in any other area of our lives.'

'Yeah, you do,' she says. 'You asked me to see if I could help Greg.'

'Help him do what?' Dad laughs. 'Mix a cocktail? Pull a pint? Change an optic?'

Mum rolls her eyes at him. 'A bar manager is a perfectly good job, Howard.'

I ignore both of them and turn back to Noelle. 'Which you still haven't done.'

'Have, have, have!' she retorts, now fully reverted to the teenage *her* at family meal times. 'HAVE!'

'Bollocks,' I mutter.

Noelle turns back to our father and gives him a 'See what I'm up against!' sigh.

'She wanted me to share Greg's demo with someone in the biz, so I sent it to Angus O'Donnell. He's a like, producer or a like engineer-y type t'ing for Barbed Wire. I used to chat to him when Troy was laying down tracks in the studio. He probs fancies me, so I'm sure he'll reply.'

'I hope you're not still in touch with that Troy, Nelly,' says Dad, entirely uninterested in anything to do with Greg. 'You know I didn't feel that he was suitable, something about him I didn't like...'

'Maybe it was the fact he was an absolute pillock,' laughs Mum.

'Mum!' gasps Noelle.

'Oh, come on, darling, he was. I guarantee he still is and always will be. A case of ingrained pillock-ness! He didn't smell very nice, either. Expensive aftershave and vegan farts.'

'At least he was doing his bit to save the planet.'

'…just not the ozone layer,' quips Mum, glancing at me. I can tell she is keen for me to lighten up.

Noelle stabs another morsel of meat.

'Well, you can't help who you fall for,' she says. 'Besides, it's like, difficult, when you're in my position to find someone who is with you for *you*. With someone equally well known I can be sure that at least they're not after not-not-notori… fame. As the expression goes: "Beware the hungry tiger!" Do you know you said that?'

'The Dalai Lama?' suggests Mum.

'Paris Hilton,' says Noelle, seriously. 'And she should know. She had to be *so*, like, vigilant when choosing her new best friends on those reality shows.'

'Hmmm…' Dad deliberates this. 'I get that, Nelly, but just be careful with *all* men; stars or civilians. I know you have your head screwed on, but I always feel it's worth being vigilant. And let's face it, I've had enough drama to deal with in one lifetime when it comes to my daughter's relationships with men.'

That pretty much brings another fun family supper to an end. After pudding—a crumble that could double as a triple jump sand pit—Dad and Noelle settle down in the cinema room to watch some rushes of her latest show and take selfies with the puppy. Mum and I clear the table, put the leftovers in the fridge and fill the dishwasher.

'Don't let your father get to you,' she says. 'I know he can be an old goat sometimes, but he isn't *all* about "The Noelle Show", he's very much a fan of you too.'

'Oh, Mum, stop it. I can handle being the Un-Chosen One. I wish he would be a bit nicer to you though.'

'He *is* nice! Most of the time. If he does niggle it's only because we know each other so well. Believe you me, all couples get like us eventually. Or at least, that's what we need to tell ourselves,' she adds, as she wipes down the table. 'Don't worry, you and Greg have a long way to go yet. One word of advice, though—actually, five—if you want to prolong a mutually respectful relationship for as long as possible; *never EVER play golf together.*' She laughs, but her laughter tails off into a sigh. 'So…' She chucks the cloth in the sink. 'Everything okay?'

'With what?'

'The two of you.'

'Noelle and I don't do 'okay'. You know that.'

'I meant you and Greg.'

'Why are you asking?' I am unnecessarily snappily.

'I'm not prying, sweetheart. I was wondering why he didn't join us for supper when you said he would.'

'His plans changed. He's at a gig in London.'

'Ah, anyone I would have heard of?'

I appreciate she is making an effort, but I don't feel like engaging. Suddenly, I feel that familiar compression in my head. I grip onto the counter for a few seconds then splash some cold water on my face from the tap.

'What on earth are you doing, Tanya?'

'Sorry, I'm hot.' I tap my face with tea towel. 'Anyway, it's some imitation Hendrix thing…'

'Grim! Bad enough first time round.' Mum shudders. 'Never been a fan of the self-indulgent guitar solo. So, he's coming back tomorrow?'

'What's the big deal?'

'No deal! I'm interested. We don't get to chat that much so I w—'

'I'm going to join him in London. We're staying at The Rexingham for a couple of nights.'

'That sounds very romantic.'

'Mmmm…' I agree, flicking my indicator to turn left down Just Carry On As If Nothing Has Happened And It Will All Be Okay Street.

Mum smiles at me and rubs my shoulder. 'Sweetheart, you've always been such a self-contained soul and you *know* I'm all for that. But remember I am always here for you. You don't have to keep things bottled up. Sometimes it's better to take the lid off intermittently, release some of the pressure. Remember that tomato, chili and red pepper chutney I made, which got all gassy and detonated all over the larder?'

'I thought we'd established that everything is fine?' I feel the snappiness in my tone again.

'All I'm saying is don't be an exploding condiment, sweetheart. It makes an awful mess.' She tips some finely diced cold beef off the bread board onto a side plate. 'Right, let's hope Princess Tatiana of Dark Thunder Castle likes her beef a little rarer than your father.'

'I'm sure he'll let you know if she doesn't. Night, Mum, thanks for dinner. I'm going to bed.'

'Already? It's not even ten o'clock.' She *always* points out the time.

'I know, I'm tired.'

She gives me an understanding shrug but her eyes are downcast. She would do this whenever she knocked on the door of mine and Noelle's room to ask if I wanted to watch something on telly/look round the shops/make a mess in the kitchen with her. I would always say I was reading *Catwalk*, but actually I was thinking…over and over again about the same thing until my brain felt like it was melting.

The same thing happens tonight. I get into bed and stare at the IVF print outs, but I am not reading. I am thinking over and over again about what happened high up in the yellow tower which looked like dirty Lego. 'Let me worry about that,' he said. 'We'll only be down there for a couple of nights, won't we? I'll be able to scrape together enough for a hotel room and the clinic.' I wiped snowflakes and tears from my eyes.

ME: But I love you.

HIM: For fuck's sake, Tanya. Grow UP! We are not going to be together. I'm not allowed to love you.

ME: (Almost hoarse.) What? You just asked me to marry you.

HIM: I know.

ME: So…

HIM: So, I was… (Stopping. Pushing me back.) Look I'm sorry, so sorry, but we never should have started this. Never, ever.

ME: But you just gave me a ring…oh, my God. Oh, my God. You did it so I would keep my trap shut, didn't you? To fob me off! You have no intention of leaving. BUT YOU LOVE ME NOT HER!

HIM: (Hissing.) That's enough. Keep your voice down. Tanya. I love both of them. I can't leave them.

ME: How long do you think it will be before they figure it out? Before EVERYONE figures it out? Because they will. The entire estate will know that baby is yours.

HIM: (Suddenly, gentle again.) They will not.

ME: Don't be so stupid! And you're telling ME to grow up? Ha!

HIM: They will not know the baby is mine because you can't have this baby.

ME: (Gripping onto the wall.) What?

HIM: You know you can't. Think of what you will lose.

ME: But I will gain 'us'. You, me and our child.

HIM: No.

ME: No? NO?

HIM: Yes. Tanya, there is no more 'us'. We both knew that this time would come. You have to get an abortion.

That was when I knew it had all been a lie. I'd lost everything for the sake of a lie. I will not do it again.

I jolt upright, throwing the IVF leaflets into the air. As they scatter across the room, I glance furtively across at my mobile on the bedside table. I grab it, and scroll down my contact lists until I get to the letter 'T'. T = TRUE LOVE. I am about to press Call, but then I stop and drop my phone on the floor. Greg will be pissed. Possibly—most likely—on some badly cut drug too. On a dance floor. Surrounded by people throwing their limbs around, not caring that they may injure themselves or each other, just simply loving how free and entirely lacking in responsibility they feel *in that moment*. Pretty much the worst possible laboratory conditions to address any issues. I peer over the side of the bed. I can reach my phone if I shuffle a little to my left. He won't hear it ring anyway. I could leave a message. Or I could text. Email? I slide to the side of the bed and gr—

Stop! Release the communication device from your hand. *Release it, Tanya!'* I drop it again and switch off the light. But even though the room is now dark, I know it's *there*. I need to be physically separated from it.

Mobile in hand, I make my way downstairs. The house is silent. But just as I reach the first floor, I freeze. I can hear a noise coming from the kitchen. At first I think it could be the Pomeranian scurrying about, but then I see a glow of light. I tiptoe down the final steps and up to the door, then peek in through the crack. Before I even focus on her, I know what she is doing. It started when she was a teenager. It went on for years but I never interrupted her. After all, it was *her* show. I stare at my sister.

She is standing at the fridge, gobbling cold, buttery roast potatoes—each one via a quick dip in a jar of mayonnaise. When the bowl is empty she necks half a pint of juice, then chomps through slices of beef smeared in brown sauce and rolled round hunks of cheddar cheese. More juice. Then she shovels hunk after hunk of crumble topping into her mouth and pours custard—directly from the jug—in there too. The creamy sauce spills gloopily down her face and splats onto the floor. At the same time my phone slips out of my hand and hits the flagstone flooring. She spins round. I jump back from the door and dash into the utility room. Twenty-five minutes later (twenty minutes was always her maximum binge time), I shuffle out. The kitchen is in darkness. I flick on the light. There is no evidence of what may have happened, except a J cloth and some anti-bacterial spray sitting on the table. I check on the puppy in her tent. She is fast asleep in a ball, looking even more like a hamster.

That's when I hear retching. It's coming from the down-stairs cloakroom. *Binge and purge.* I never told anyone about this either. The 'finale' to each show. I pick up my phone and hover in the corridor, about to go back upstairs…but then I take a deep breath and raise my hand to knock on the door. My knuckle is about to make contact with the wood…

'Leave. Me. Alone,' she says.

Eleven

Gillian Bell of Bell & Bell Solicitors has three looks which she gives in rotation. The first is an intense stare whilst she chews the inside of her right cheek for when she is absorbing information. The second is a softening-the-blow hint-of-a-smile combined with a stare that is even more penetrating for when she is giving me information to absorb. And this same stare and semi-smile is mixed with a furrowed brow for when she knows I am *not* absorbing the information. Currently, she is giving me Look Three, because I have been distracted by a post on my Twitter feed.

It is Jazz. She is live Tweeting from London Fashion Week. I stare at the image of her with Noelle Bamford, dressed head to toe in Pascale. The two women have their arms flopped over each other. Jazz is sticking out her tongue and making a peace sign. Which is so paaaaainfully obvious but that said, she is wearing a Gareth Pugh geometric leather-look jacket with Victoriana-style shoulder pads and a corset waist. I have never seen her look so stylish. The entire photo screams, 'THIS IS FASHION!' No, worse, 'I AM FASHION!' Despite this, Jazz has hashtagged it: #noelle #lfw # #tongue #peace #me #lovegareth #catwalk #icon #sistas #styleiseverything…

just in case anyone might be mystified by what they were seeing.

'Ashley?'

'Gillian.' I throw my mobile into my bag. 'You were trying to explain…'

'I was explaining that it would work exactly the same way if your husband had put down the deposit, purchased the property, but after you moved in—and for the duration of your marriage—the mortgage was paid jointly. He would need to raise the equivalent of the share in profit made due to the rise in the housing market, and pay that out to you… as you would have invested in this gain.'

'Yes, I understand that's how it should work *on paper*,' I reply, shifting in the sagging leather chair. 'But that does not take into consideration what it took for me to buy that flat. Gillian, I lived in a room share *within* a house share for *years*. At one point I had three jobs. Five nights a week I worked in a sauna and the other two I worked in a nightclub. During the day I was at *Catwalk*…and I jogged between all three positions of employment. I lived like this so I could save up for my own home. Do you know my most lasting memory of my early twenties is?'

'What?'

'Being really *fucking* thirsty,' I grimace at her. 'And you don't want to know what my late *fucking* teens were like before that. Sorry, I didn't mean to drop two 'f' bombs.'

Gillian smiles. 'Say what you like. Believe me, I've had far worse dropped. It usually starts in the initial consultancy. In fact, if I don't get a few "total arse-wipes" and one "absolute C-U-N-T" I wonder if the client really needs me. If my office had a swear box I would have retired a good decade ago.'

I don't laugh because I have thought of something else. '…

and another thing. As far as the renovations to my flat were concerned, initially, I had only done my walk-in wardrobe, but after Zach moved in I did up the rest of the place…*I* paid, because he needed all the funds he had to start his own business.'

'Do you have the receipts, records or bank statements to prove this?'

'No. It was all cash in hand. The guy I used didn't work for an actual building company. He was my next door neighbour. His main job was knocking out skunk.'

'He *what*?'

'He distributed marijuana—a strong variety.' My fists are clenching. The reality of what I am being told is sinking in. 'And Barry only did the structural stuff. Every spare minute I had was spent stripping, tiling, grouting, painting, varnishing; whilst Zach concentrated on setting up his digital media *thing*. I didn't mind, because we were a team. I never thought that we…' I don't bother to continue.

My solicitor exhales. 'That's another penance box I should have installed a long time ago. The I Never Thought That We…box. I would not only be retired, but I'd be spending said retirement in a Venetian-style villa on Lake Como and regularly nipping round to Clooney's at elevensies for a Nespresso. Look, Ashley…' She taps her fountain pen on the desk. 'I've been through the numbers which your husband's solicitor sent over and to be honest, the final figure—bearing in mind everything you have told me too—does look reasonable. My advice would *not* be to challenge it. I've also had a barrister give it the once over and she was adamant he could have gone for more.'

'But where do I magic this money from?'

'Re-mortgaging.'

'Not an option. My lender is over the whole lending thing. I've already tried. Credit history issues. Over the last few months, PayPal is the only friend I've turned to.'

Gillian grimaces. 'In that case, we could come to some sort of monthly direct debit arrangement until the sum is paid off, which I can negotiate…or…' She leans forward and fixes me with Look Two. 'Or, you could sell up. Cash in. Pay him off. Buy somewhere else.'

She makes it sound easy. But it was hard enough the first time round. Not even with my painstakingly built deposit and a whopping mortgage could I afford somewhere 'on the up' or in the next '*insert name of locale with a Virgin Active and Sainsbury's Local already in situ*'. I was utterly realistic. The sort of space I wanted was not going to be available in a swanky area. This was London. I needed to find an area that was free from hope. One that had no regeneration project planned, where the local amenities consisted of a decent drug dealer and an off licence where the cashier was protected behind a metal grill. If the roads were littered in yellow tape due to being cordoned off for police then it was likely I may be able to afford a place there. I found the perfect property on Day Seven of my search. A top floor end of terrace flat with not a single functioning mod con but it did have a 'pleas-ant view of the local greenery'; the next door neighbour's hydroponics set-up in his loft. But most importantly it had a second bedroom, which although could only serve as a sleeping venue if you slept upright, had the potential for conversion into a walk-in wardrobe. And it was cheap.

Well, it was *then*. No one could have predicted what was going to happen to my area over the last few years. None of the sales negotiators showing me round had bothered to give me any flannel about investment potential. But the regeneration *did* happen. By the time Zach moved in, roads which Barry (the skunk dealer from next door) wouldn't even let his 'errand boys' deliver to at night, gradually began to be cruised not just by police cars and cut'n'shut getaway vehicles but by Foxtons' Mini Coopers. A pricey Prosecco arrived in the off licence. A rapper named his breakthrough iTunes number one selling album after our postcode. It meant one thing. The area was going up in price.

And it kept going. So much so that by the London Olympics, tourists were actively seeing spaces to hire near me. Then the local school—which had once made the one in *Dangerous Minds* look like Eton—leapt up the national performance league table under a new headteacher. I started to overhear the word 'catchment' being thrown around in the local pub (which now sold *freshly made free-fucking-range* Scotch eggs and *artisan fucking goats' cheese* Ploughmans). Last year, Barry wound down his illegal business interests, bunged a massive glass kitchen extension on the back of his house and sold it for over a million to a pair of human rights lawyers. It was official, our area was a Prime Location baiting hot spot. '*Tre*-men-dous buy. You've quintupled your orig investment. Nice!' commented Rupert, a local estate agent, when Zach and I got him round for a valuation. Because we were going to move. To get somewhere bigger.

'Is that something you could consider, Ashley?' asks Gillian. 'Selling?'

I nod and shake my head at the same time. 'Well, I…yes, I suppose…NO! *No*. He's already taken my cat from me. Now my home? It isn't f—'

'Fair? Don't do it to yourself, Ashley. Look, in return for the relatively low figure, all he requires is for us to move quickly in tying things up. As with all matters regarding divorce the quickest route is the most preferable. The longer any financial issues are drawn out…the more difficult it is to draw that definitive line from a personal standpoint too.'

Gillian returns to Look Three. I gaze up at the wall behind her at the certificates of qualification on display. She qualified in 1991. I wonder how many definitive lines she has drawn since then. As if reading my mind, she offers an empathetic sigh.

'This process is never easy, but yours is a pretty straight-forward split. Every time you come to see me—as much as I have enjoyed your company—it is costing you. I don't want you to end up paying for a wing of my Italian waterside retirement home. Your case is simple. Let's keep it simple. Comprendez?'

I am still gazing at the wall. 'My case is *simple*? What would have made it more complicated?'

'That's even more simple.' she replies. 'The C word. The *other* one…'

'A child?'

'That's it!'

That's it, isn't it? That's it.

It is February. Zach and I are in bed drinking Dom Pérignon champagne—a gift from one of the designers show-ing at London Fashion Week, which had finished that day. I was leaving for Milan early the next morning. New York and Paris were done. We'd just had sex. Properly. Giddily. Relentlessly. *Like we used to.* We were lying in each other's arms talking about nothing, but the familiarity of the situation meant *everything*. I filled our glasses again and placed them on the dressing table, then checked my Instagram.

ME: Ha!

HIM: What?

ME: Jazz... she's forced herself to like my throwback picture of Cara Delevigne at Giles Deacon. Trust me, she is hurting right now, having to relive that. Ha! Oh god, I'm such a shrew. I am, aren't I? (Chucking my phone down on the bed.) I'm a common shrew. You know that's what Fitz calls me? It's because they're very territorial and aggressive for their size.

HIM: They're also randy. The adults only live for a year and can have four litters of up to six junior shrews.

ME: Really? (Gently. Bracing myself.)

HIM: Yeah, I saw it on a David Attenborough documentary on insectivorous mammals.

ME: Wow, they can't have much time left for hanging out shrew-style; enjoying the woodland, snuffling the undergrowth and stuff. (Full on steeling myself.)

HIM: (Turning to me.) We are going to try again, aren't we?

ME: Zach...please.

HIM: We need to discuss this.

ME: Why now?

HIM: Because I need to know. I need to know when.

ME: But I don't know.

HIM: You don't know if we will? Or you don't know when?

ME: (Shrugging. Looking away.)

HIM: A shrug is your answer?

ME: Sorry, sorry...no. It's not. I shrugged because it's hard. Hard to t—

HIM: (Interrupting.) Hard to talk to me or hard to make your decision? Neither should be hard, Ash. I'm not trying to start a fight. There will be no prawn balls at dawn, you have my word.

ME: (Turning back to him. Smiling.) I do want to have a

*conversation with you, but you're not listening. You're telling
me what you want to hear. You want me to tell you that I'm
ready to… (Tailing off.)*

    HIM: Of course, I do.

    ME: But that's it. (No tailing off. I stop.)

    HIM: (Staring at me. Unblinking.) That's it?

    *ME: Yes. You know that's how I've always felt. It was how
you always felt too. It was what we pretty much decided when
we first met. It was what we decided for sure when we got
married. That it would be us. You and me. That's it.*

    HIM: (Quietly.) But that was before…

He was right. It was before. It was before 'it'. It was
before 'it' became everything we talked about, everything
we thought about, everything—apparently—we existed for,
despite having lives of our own for years…it was before
all of that. I couldn't tell him that I liked how I was before.
How he was before. How *we* were before. I couldn't tell him
any of that. Because then I would be no better than the one
person who had never wanted 'it' either.

    *HIM:…and now things have changed. We're different
now. You're different. You have to accept that. You are not
the person you were. I am not the person I was but I do not
want to go back there either. I want to be the person I almost
became. I want to be a dad. I want you to be a mum. I want
us to have a baby and be parents.*

    *ME: (No bracing or steeling myself.) It's not what I want,
Zach.*

    *HIM: (Arms still around me.) You were right, then. That
is it. Isn't it?*

THAT'S IT, ISN'T IT? Seven years of marriage. *That's
it, isn't it?*

Abruptly, I get up from my seat.

'Thank you very much for seeing me,' I tell Gillian. 'I'll let you know what I decide to do about the finances. I should head to the office.'

But I don't mean mine, I'm still suspended. I head to Zach's. I don't consider making a mental pros and cons list of going there because there are none of the former. What I am about to do will make my drunken texting look like an amuse bouche of mild embarrassment to the main course of self-inflicted mortification, but I don't care. I march into the foyer and straight past the reception desk towards the lift. Zach's office is on the top floor of the building, which houses eight companies, all digital and media consultancies of some variation.

'Hang on a second,' shouts the receptionist. 'You need a pass. We have security measures.'

'Don't panic,' I snap back over my shoulder, as I jab the metal button to call the lift. 'I'm not working for a terrorist faction who specifically targets those who value Google fucking positioning and offer geeeee-nius fucking brand "solutions"…which my cat could probably come up with. WELL, IF I STILL HAD ONE, THAT IS! I'm here to see my husband.'

The metal doors whir and clank open. I step into the lift and press Level 5. The whooshing sense of elevating up through the floors fuels the adrenaline which is rushing round my body.

That's it, isn't it?

The lift opens at Level 5. I walk around the edge of the open plan working space, ignoring the darting eyes and sharp gasps of the fifteen or so employees. The last time I saw them it was at their fancy dress Christmas party, which *obviously* I refused to wear fancy dress at. It was a few weeks since I'd done the test…no one knew the result except Zach. Oh, and his mother, who had guessed when Zach made it purposefully obvious by telling her I didn't want any vodka *or* Worcestershire Sauce or horseradish in my Bloody Mary when we went over for lunch. The final drink didn't even qualify it as a Virgin Mary. It was basically a Never Even Had A Fumble Mary.

I focus on the door of Zach's office at the end of the room. As I approach, Keith With The Bad Teeth walks out. He's wearing drop crotch indigo jeans and a grey V-neck sweater. Diesel and Prada Sport, I bet. (Everyone in this building wears high end high street denim with designer diffusion knitwear separates.) He makes a pathetic yelping sound when he sees me then attempts to cover this up with a fake, eroded smile.

'Ashley! Oi oi! This is a surprise. A nice one, obviously. Yeah, looooo-vely jubbly. Been a while, been a while…how are you?'

'Fucking livid!' I reply, barging past him through the door. I don't bother shutting it.

Zach is sitting at his desk. The large Mac monitor in front of him is at an angle. I can see he is logged on to a specialist sneaker website. As I burst in, he jumps to his feet.

'*Ash?* What the hell are you d—?'

I cut him off. 'Doing a bit of online shopping, are we?' I snap. 'Nice to know that all that hard work I put in to saving up for, buying and creating the home of my dreams is going to be invested in your collection of statement leisure footwear. Please, do me a favour in return. Every time you tie the laces in that pretentious way you always do, by never quite pulling them tight enough so they look as if you are achingly close to kicking them off, *think of me*. No, think of that home I saved for, bought and created…and think of someone else living there so that you could buy…' I briefly attempt to control my breathing. 'Another. Pair. Of. Fucking. Hi. Tops.'

Zach's eyes are wide. He has never seen me like this.

'Woah. O-kay. *Caaaaalm* down, Ash.' he says.

'FUCK OFF! I AM TOTALLY FUCKING CALM!'

'The whole office can hear you.' He steps out from behind his desk and shuts the door. 'I will not have you causing a scene. Now, we can talk calmly here or leave and get a coffee…'

'A coffee? Do I look like I need a fucking coffee? I don't want a coffee, Zach. In fact, I'd say a coffee is currently lagging *way* behind on my list of priorities of things I need to concern myself with right now. It's behind my husband pissing off, missing Kat Moss so much when I think of her face my heart compresses, a possible drinking problem, being threatened with the sack, the death of my mother and, oooooh, there was something else on my mind too. What *was* it?' I rub my head. 'Ah, yes, working out how I am going to pay you thousands and thousands and thousands of pounds.'

He exhales loudly. 'Right, that. Listen to me, it's a fair deal, and I guarantee your solicitor thought the same. You know how much that flat is worth. We only had it valued at the end of last year. It will have gone up since then too. The area is booming.'

'Ah…so suddenly, it's "that" flat, is it? Last week it was "your flat, Ash".'

'Don't be naïve. You must have known we would need to approach the subject of the profit we had made somewhere down the line,' he says. 'I thought we could leave it for a bit, whilst we were both coming to terms with the situation, but ultimately this had to happen. Every couple who gets divorced has to divide their assets.'

'*Every couple?* It's us, Zach. *Us.* Remember who that used to be? The two people in that picture on the sideboard in the corridor. They were in love. One of those people is me. The other is you.' I cringe at my meaningless and mawkish words, but then add an equally embarrassing final flourish. 'You may not love me any more, but I love *my* flat. You can't make me sell it.'

'There are a number of ways you can pay me the money. Ask your solicitor. It's not my problem.'

'No, what you mean is *I am not your problem.*'

He doesn't reply to this. He doesn't need to. There is nothing further I can say either. No matter what I come up with, it will not change the situation or the opinion he now has of me. All this visit has done is confirmed the power shift. There is a knock at the door. Then it opens. A woman sticks her head through the aperture. I recognise her.

'Zach? Is everything okay? Keith said th—'

'That Zach's wife had nipped in for a visit?' I finish her sentence. 'Yes, she has—but *do* join us. It's nice to meet you again. Rachel, isn't it? You were dressed as an elf last time I saw you. My husband was dressed as Father Christmas. Well, you certainly turned out to be Santa's Little Fucking Helper, didn't you?' I bat away her attempt to speak. 'Oh, and can we just establish *now* that fancy dress is *always* a Crime Against Fashion? It's *so* Heidi Klum the Seal years…and even *she* never *quite* carried it off. This year I suggest you stick to what you know. Maybe add some pizazz with something *sparkly*. Ha! I *bet* you have a load of "larky" sequinned shrugs that only appear over the party season just in case you need to give an outfit some festive oomph. Or m—'

'Shut-*up*, Ash!' Zach interrupts. 'You should go. From now on, we communicate only through our solicitors, I don't want you coming here or to my apartment. It's the sensible option. Neither of us need any more of this…of this…' He hangs his head, his face is draining of colour. 'Of this bad, *bad* blood. It's painful.'

I stare at Zach—he actually looks *in* pain. I've only seen him like this once before. He came home after work on a Friday evening, kissed me, opened the fridge, grabbed a beer, flopped down on the sofa with the Chinese menu, read it subtly behind the *Evening Standard* so Kat Moss wouldn't get over excited, then flicked on the telly and shouted to me that I had better prepare myself for a boxset marathon this weekend because he was absolutely knackered from dealing with an increasingly tetchy Keith With The Bad Teeth who was being given the run around by a girl he actually liked, so Zach had suggested maybe a start in gaining her trust and respect would be not to refer to her consistently as 'poontang'…and that's when I sat down next to him, took a gulp of wine, and told him I was no longer pregnant.

I consider whether to reach out to him, but Rachel gets there before I can. She dives into the room and wraps her arms around him.

'He's right.' She glares at me. 'Leave now. You've caused enough upset and upheaval…'

I watch as Zach returns her embrace. It is the first time I have ever seen him close to another woman.

'…I won't let you break him,' she says.

'Oh, per-lease save me the very amateur dramatics,' I tell Rachel. 'Zach is more than capable of looking after himself. He doesn't need you to help him in any other capacity other than to help him get over me. Because you do realise what is going on here? You couldn't be more of a textbook rebound. You're both clichés! You've got a crush on your boss and he's even using a pair of fucking dumbbells as a door stop!'

Rachel says nothing. Neither does Zach. His face is now hidden in his hands. It's too late. He is broken. I can see that. I briefly deliberate whether I should ramp things up another level. Why not? When you have nothing, you'll say *any*thing.

'See? *See?* You both know I am telling the truth, don't you? Your silence speaks volumes. The fact is, Zach, you will always compare her to me. You'll be thinking of me whenever you're together. And yeah, even when you're *together*. You'll be looking at her but seeing me…' I almost choke on how vile this sounds. '…and wishing it was me, so you'll have to pretend. And afterwards you'll have to *lie*. Of course, the lying will take its toll. I give it a matter of weeks. I very much doubt the two of you will be together at Christmas.'

I pause and step back, thrilled I have attacked them so skilfully in exactly the right places. They are unable to defend themselves. This battle is over. The victory is mine. But as I feel my adrenaline levels decline, Rachel untangles herself from Zach and moves out from behind him. Staring me square in the eyes, she begins to talk.

'We will,' she says. 'We will be together. Zach and I will be very much together, Ashley.'

'Oh, yeah? What makes you think that?'

She walks up to me. She is centimetres from my face. Her lip curls.

'I'm listening, *Rach*.'

'…and I'm pregnant.'

I fall backwards, then stabilise myself.

'Pregnant,' she repeats. 'So, yes, there is a strong likelihood that Zach and I will be together this Christmas. And the following one. And the one after that. We'll be together. And just for you, I'll make sure I wear a 'larky' sequinned shrug in the pictures. Our family pictures.'

The expression on her face says one thing. That battle meant nothing…*I have won the war.* I glance across to Zach, expecting him to look victorious too, but also mortified. Despite everything, he would not have wanted me to find out this way. But he is staring blankly at Rachel. Then I realise, he didn't know either. He groans and punches the wall.

'Congratulations,' I say to him, my voice now entirely calm. I glance over to Rachel. 'Congratulations to you both.'

Then I leave. I don't slam the door. I never slam doors. I shut it calmly. I walk round the—silent—open plan office, and even when I step into the lift and hear the excited sniping and whispering start, I remain calm. Even when, as the doors close and I turn round to see Keith grinning I do not feel the need to charge back out, punch his teeth to the back of his throat, then force him to cough them up in order to make a witch doctor style necklace that I could present to my husband as a good luck token to wear at company pitches. I am still calm as I get the tube back into Central London and walk to a bar a few blocks away from the *Catwalk* office. Not any bar—the bar I met Zach in. I order a double vodka. Not that I need to 'take the edge off'. There are no more edges to remove. Instead, a definitive line has been drawn…with a thick, black, Sharpie marker pen. And now that the line has been drawn, I know what I need to do. I text Fitz and ask him to meet me.

Within ten minutes he is striding into the bar, wagging his finger.

'Oi, Jacobs! You SHREW! Where have you been? What's going on? And don't give me any more guff about lady issues.

Why aren't you at LFW? Why is Jazz? Why have you not
called me? Or worse, not liked any of my most recent pics
of me and Jesus on Facefuck? Guess what? I think we might
be *act-u-ally* dating. We've met up five times and not *once*
have I showed him the real me, so it's going really well. *And*
this is the best bit: I've lost three pounds. I can get into my
A.P.C. Mr Porter Japanese selvedge slim-fit denim. Finally!'
He pats his arse then notices my glass. 'Is that vodka?'

'It is.'

'It's also half-past eleven in the morning.'

'So? It's in my blood,' I mumble, inaudibly.

He examines me. 'Jacobs, you look like shit. I'm going to
ask you one more time. And if you don't give me an answer
I will break into your flat, steal your entire set of *The CR
Fashion Book* and put it through the shredder. Talk.'

So, I tell him. Firstly, that I have been suspended from
Catwalk. Secondly, that Zach and I have separated, he is
with someone else and *she* is…I use the term 'knocked up'. I
describe her. I tell him I have seen 'multiple men'. I describe
them. And I also tell him I owe money; to the bank and to
Zach. But that is where I leave it. Because where would I
stop?

As if sensing this, at the end of my monologue, Fitz says
nothing. He simply jumps up onto a barstool next to me, gets
out his mobile, taps it a few times, then scrolls and presents
it to me. He has logged on to Zach's Instagram, specifically
onto a picture of his company's trip to Bestival. The whole
team are sitting on a wall outside a club in the Isle of Wight.
They are dressed as sea creatures and wearing wellington
boots. Zach has captioned the photo: *Before the rain…and
carnage!* #festifun.

'Nice try at cheering me up, but I've seen that shot,' I

tell him. 'So bloody typical that they chose a festival which specifies fancy dress. Fuck knows when that office gets any work done. They must spend half their working hours scanning the Net for flammable costumes and acne-popping face make-up.'

'No! Look *closer*. The one who's going to reproduce... that's her, isn't it?' Fitz points at Rachel sitting next to Keith.

'Yep, it is. She's dressed as a prawn. I told you, I've seen it.'

'You need to zoom in.'

'What am I meant to be looking for?'

'Ahhh, you'll know.'

I scan down, past the pink shower cap which has been customised with bendy tubes, pink Lycra leotard, shimmery pink disco tights and then her...CHRIST! I burst out laughing with such force I almost snot over Fitz's phone.

'Hahahahahaha! She's wearing wedge wellies. *Wedge wellies*. WEDGE FUCKING WELLIES!'

Fitz giggles. 'I know, I know, I *know*...are you DYING?'

I nod. 'Almost. I've given up the ghost, for sure. You?'

'Already cashed in my chips. Have to dash though as I have an appointment...'

'Meeting your maker?'

'Yep! I'll be knocking on death's door any minute now. Ha!' As I am laughing, my voice cracks. I start coughing.

'I heard that, Jacobs. Decent attempt using the classic cough kaftan...a cover up, in other words.' He pulls a face. 'Are you upset? Actually, let me rephrase that. Are you going to get upset in front of me?'

'As if!'

'Good, because you won't get anything tactile. You know I don't do the whole personal space invasion thing. That picture is way better than a hug, anyway.'

'*Much* better,' I confirm. 'You couldn't have been any more supportive, Fitz. Unless you find me a picture of her wearing jelly shoes…or Crocs.' I look at him hopefully. 'No, *wedge* Converse.'

He shakes his head at me and sighs. 'You see! This is what happens when you give a *little*. People just want more. Oh, and now I've made light of the situation, don't be expecting me to get all serious again and reassure you that everything is going to be okay. Because let's face it, right now, your life is a mess.'

I smile at him. 'Oh, no, you're wrong there. It may *look* like that, but the mess—much like you—is superficial. Everything will be okay, because *I* am going to make myself okay.'

'How do you know?'

'Because I've had to do it before.'

I could see it coming, so when it happened I was almost prepared. I had a good idea of what I would pack and where I would go for the first few days. What wholly blindsided me was how calm it was, when it did happen. We were in the kitchen. No one raised their voices.

ME: *Can you not see what is happening, Mum? You're blaming everyone else for what he has done. He is the one who cheated. He is the one who lied to you. He is the adult.*

HER: *(Splashing Gordon's gin into a glass.) Why don't you hate HER?*

ME: *I do. I haven't said a word to her since she told me.*

HER: *But you hate him more.*

ME: *I'll always hate him for what he has done to you.*

HER: *And what about her? Will you always hate her?*

ME: *Do you want me to?*

HER: *If you can't say you will then that says everything I need to know.*

ME: (Shaking my head.) I'm sixteen, I can't say anything for sure. What I do know is that we both need to move on from what has happened.

HER: There is no 'moving on' for me to do. How would I do that now, anyway? What do I have to offer anyone?

ME: You don't mean that. You're saying it because you're pissed. Besides, I'm not talking about moving on with a man. What about the rest of your life? Your work? Those last designs you did were so on point. It's such a shame we didn't try to sell them. Why don't we try to contact s-...

HER: Shoosh! (Splashing tonic on top of her drink. Taking a gulp.) For God's sake, Ashley, you don't get it do you? I don't care about any of that. I stopped caring about all of that when I had you. Nothing else mattered. I had him and I had you, an extension of him. That was all I wanted. Ever. (Staring at floor.) I want him back, Ashley. He made a mistake.

ME: A single mistake?

HER: Yes.

ME: Mum, please, you're an intelligent woman. You honestly think this only happened once? There were always signs, you chose to ignore them. You shouldn't even consider forgiving him. You should be fucking defiant in that.

HER: (Looking up.) Don't swear. You're wrong, Ashley. I shouldn't be angry. I have no right to be. I caused this.

ME: Wh—

HER: (Interrupting.) I have no right to be, because this is what he warned would happen. He said things would change irrevocably because HE would have to change. I told him he wouldn't. I said that he could still have the career he wanted in the club scene, but deep down I knew that unless he was totally committed it couldn't happen. He could have done big things too. All he needed was his ambition and his...

freedom. But he lost that at seventeen years old. He lost that the moment I decided to keep it.

   ME: (Confused.) Kept wh—?

Then I stopped myself. Because I realised. She was talking about me.

   HER: (Staring at me.) I think it's best you leave, Ashley.

   ME: You don't mean that. I will not let you choose him over me. Or that. (Pointing to the bottle.) Tell me to go, but at least have the respect to back it up with a real reason. Give me the truth.

   HER: Fine. If you don't leave me you'll always be dissatisfied with your life. You'll always want more. You'll always be angry. Like him. And you have to expel the anger, otherwise it will make you sad. Go. I mean it, go now. I don't want you here. (Walking into the bedroom with her gin and tonic, muttering.) You'll be okay.

I went to my room and filled a large holdall bag with clothes; it was the first time I had ever gone anywhere. The packing process was comforting. I put together a selection of seemingly random pieces that I knew I could pull together on a daily basis to appear effortlessly collated; the perfect ratio of 'staples' and 'statements'. Then I zipped up my bag and sat down and wrote a letter. After that, I left.

'I'm going to be okay,' I repeat, and turn to Fitz. 'I am going to be okay because I am going to become the Editor of *Catwalk*.'

He clicks his tongue at me, then smiles. 'That is *so* what Donatella would do.'

Twelve

TANYA

I take the lift up to the fifth floor of The Rexingham Hotel and walk down the corridor. With each step I attempt to rebalance myself but I can feel it... the crazy. It makes me tense but jittery and hyper sensitive. This was how I felt every day on the estate as people started to find out. Each morning I would wake up with increasing levels of paranoia that I was being discussed. But then that paranoia would be totally justified by a small change in the way someone reacted the next time they saw me. "Hi... Tanya." That millisecond pause told me all I needed to know.

Outside Room 579 is a breakfast trolley with a succession of elaborate silver cloches still placed over the plates. I unlock the door and wheel it into the room. Then I see my fiancé. He is swaddled in a duvet at the edge of the bed. He has a flannel on his head and is clutching an empty bottle of Volvic. The clothes he was wearing yesterday are in one column – on top of his boots – by the bedside table. I pull back the thick, chintzy curtains, open the window as far as it will go before the safety lock kicks in. Then I breeeeeathe.

'Rise and shine, Princess!' I shrill. 'You've got a wedding to organise. I've bought down a variety of embossing techniques for you to look at it. We need to think whether we want to go down the lithography or thermography route. But if you don't like either of those there's always die-stamping, foiling or letterpress. Or, obviously…hand engraved. Those options are for the save-the-date card. The actual invitations to the day itself we'll have more options to assess because there will be extra inserts; map, gift list and also possibly hen/stag party info for a select few.'

Greg groans. Then he does a wiggly-waving motion with his right index finger.

'Very funny, babe. It's nice to see you.'

'You can't see me. You have a flannel over your head. So much for being out of bed, showered, Berocca-ed and feeling fresh…good gig?'

He nods and the flannel slips down his face. 'As far as I can remember, yeah. Think I might have overdone it. Ughhhhh. No, I *know* I overdid it. The inside of my head feels like… that theatre thing…musical…with the bin lids…tyres… aluminium…'

'I have no idea what you're on about.'

'The actors are all blokes…construction workers who happen to be tap dancers. You *do* know. I keep thinking *Stamp*?'

'Oh, *Stomp*.'

'Ha! Owwwww! Yeah! *Stomp*. That's what my brain is dealing with; a full production of *Stomp*. Have you got any paracetamol?'

'I should do…' I rummage in my bag. 'So, what time did you crawl in?' I attempt to say this playfully. I pass him a packet of Nurofen.

'Ah, you're a life saver…' He fumbles with the packet.

I take it back from him and pop out two pills. 'You're

pathetic. And yes, I will also get you some water. In your current state you're likely to be outfoxed by a tap.'

I take off my jacket, put my phone on the table and wander into the bathroom. It has dual sinks, a deep round bath with a whirlpool function, and in the corner there is a snazzy double shower with two shower heads shaped like hula hoops. A fluffy white dressing gown hangs from the door. It's the lovers' marbled aquatic playground I was expecting. It makes me feel even more tense. Jittery. And hyper sensitive.

'Don't be mean, babe…' Greg calls out, his voice is raspy. 'Remember, I'm suffering.'

'Well, it could be worse. Can you imagine how Rollo is feeling right now?'

Greg does not reply.

I yell loudly, 'I said, imagine how Rollo is feeling right now looking after six kids by him*self.* I keep imagining those scenes at the end of *Skyfall.* You know, where Bond's ancestral home gets annihilated by the baddies and all that's left is a few burning embers and exposed walls…' I don't pause for him to laugh, because all I want to know is the answer to my original question. '…it was a late one, then? You got back…*late.*' I grab a glass from the counter and repeat my initial question. My hand clenches around the glass as I fill it.

'Nope,' he calls back, immediately. 'I peaked way too early…during the support band. Pint, shot, repeat. I have *no* idea what time I got in, but I had to get another room card from reception as *obviously*, I lost mine. How do hotel keys disappear as soon as you leave the building? They must get swallowed up in a similar vortex to the one single socks vanish into en route from the washer to the dryer. In fact, even if you have a combined washer-dryer, they still manage to un-pair themselves, don't they? It's like a laundry Bermuda Triangle sponsored by Zanussi…or something.'

I am pleased by all of these extra—no, even better, *volunteered* pieces of information. But when I see my expression in the mirror I am appalled. I am smiling; but it is a *crazed* smile. My lips are dry, hooked up over the top of my teeth. Yvonne Atwal sometimes smiled like this. Ashley pointed it out to me for the first time when she was thirteen. We were eating biscuits in the kitchen at her flat. Mrs Atwal was having a 'lie down'.

ME: Is your Mum ill?

HER: (Shrugging.) She was fine when she left for the pub.

ME: Maybe she ate something.

HER: (Rolling her eyes.) Yeah, Scampi Fries or something. Duh! Tanya…she obviously drank something. A lot of something.

ME: Does your Dad mind? I don't think my Mum would dare get tiddled in front of mine.

HER: (Whacking me on the shoulder.) File 'tiddled' in the 'I USED TO ATTEND A WANKY PRIVATE SCHOOL' folder with 'tickety-boo'. (Pausing. Eyes narrowing.) He's gone in the van.

ME: Who has?

HER: Dad. Another road trip.

ME: And?

HER: It's not JUST road trip.

ME: What is it then?

HER: (Ignoring me. Whispering.) She knows it's not.

ME: (Confused.) Who? And what's not?

HER: Tanya! Keep up! Mum. Since he's left she's done no sewing…she's been down at the Red Lion the whole

time. Until he gets back on Tuesday, that's where she'll
be. Of course, she's trying to convince herself it is JUST
a road trip, but she knows it's not. You only have to
see the way she smi-...' (Stopping suddenly as Yvonne
Atwal enters.)
ME: Hello, Mrs Atwal. Thank you for having me over
again. Nice to see you...

She shuffled sleepily towards the fridge, first of all
acknowledging me with a floppy wave...then she fixed me
with *that* smile. Her dry lips were hooked up over the top of
her teeth. As she got closer, I could even see a deep crack in
the skin. It looked so sore.

I go back into the room and pass Greg the glass of water.
It sloshes over the edge because I am shaking.

'Are you going to be babbling nonsensically like this all
day?' I ask.

He swallows the tablets. 'Probably. It may even get
worse. Although, I can assure you that any nonsensical
babbling will be *more* than made up for by the fact we will
be spending our time in this *very* luxurious room—nice
choice, by the way—getting down to some *very* serious,
very focused, *very* thorough...' He glances up at me. '...
you know *what*.'

I act puzzled to continue the joke. 'What?'

'It begins with an "n" and ends with an "e"...'

'I thought you were feeling rough?'

'Nookie will help.' He pulls me down onto the bed. 'Ugh,
I stink of BO.'

I kiss him. More of a peck. 'And you taste of fags...'

'I only had a couple.'

'What happened to your electronic cigarette?'

'Well, I'd forgotten to pack my I'M A BELLEND! T-shirt to

wear at the gig, so I didn't bother taking my e-cig. The two go so well together.' He raises an eyebrow at me. 'I am stopping though, babe. *All* of it. I promise, when we get married I will behave.' He reaches up the back of my shirt and unclasps my bra. No fumbling. Ping. It's undone.

He pulls me down again to kiss him properly. I should kiss him back; a long slow lingering kiss to indicate that I'm ready to speed things up. Then I should be kicking off my shoes, wriggling out of my T-shirt, peeling off my trousers… and hurling them with lusty abandon, like you're supposed to in a room like this. I sit up. Then I stand up.

'Jesus, do I stink *that* bad?' He pulls a face. 'I should brush my tee—'

'No,' I interrupt him. 'It's not that. I've got a lot on my mind.'

'You know that the best cure for having a lot on your mind, is to let someone else draw the point of concentration to an entirely different body part?' He starts wriggling out of the duvet, grinning at me as he does.

'Really, *no*. I don't want to, Greg. Well, it's not that I don't want to. It's more that I don't think I *can*. Sorry.'

He flops onto the pillow and stares up at me.

'You *should* be sorry,' he says. 'I've got an absolutely *ra*ging hangover horn. In fact, I would compare the extent of my current horn to that of the Ankole-Watusi cattle, which are native to Africa. The horns on these beasts can reach eight feet tip to tip. And get this; the longest horn ever measured was on a bull called…wait for it: *Woodie*! Ha! How appropriate is that? *Woodie with his massive horn*. Get it?'

'Yeah, I get it.'

He laughs. 'I'm babbling nonsensically again, aren't I?

Okay, from now on I will try my best to initiate interesting, not to mention *coherent* conversat—'

'Stop. Stop laughing. Stop talking. I'm freaking out,' I interrupt him again. My voice is rising. 'I am f-r-e-a-k-i-n-g out. I'm freaking out…'

'Slow down, babe. Breeeeeathe.'

'I can't…I told you! I'm freaking OUT! I need to speak to you. I was going to ring you last night, but I stopped myself. And now it's worse…now, I am freeeeeak-ing. *Out.*'

'Shooooosh. Come on, whatever it is, relax and tell me.'

'Give me a break, Greg. I am always relaxed. Don't tell *me* to relax! I need this moment to freak out.'

He peers at me from the bed and I can tell he is wondering *who is this woman*? But this is not surprising because he never met the girl she used to be.

About what?' he asks, slowly.

'About Suze.'

He sits up. 'Suze? What about her?' His delivery is even slower.

'About what happened the other night…when you had that argument.'

'Oh…' He tuts at me. 'Do we have to talk about Suze again, babe? I thought we were going to have a nice weekend?'

'I will not have a nice weekend, Greg, not until I have stopped freaking out. You need to listen. Please do not say anything until I instruct you to do so.' I take a clipped breath and stare at the carpet. It is good quality. Lustrous. *Beige-y grey.* 'You lied to me. You told me that you went to A&E with Rollo to look after Kian when he got into that fight at the beginning of the summer. You didn't go to Casualty. You didn't stay with the boys. You disappeared and got back home at five in the morning. I know this because I had to tell you the alarm code.' *Mink? Fawn? Stone?* Another breath. *I think an interior designer would call it 'greige'.* 'Why did you feel it necessary to lie? Where were you? Who were you with? What went on? When were you going to tell me?' Even though I am looking at the carpet I can sense him about to butt in. I hold up my hand. 'Let me finish. I am not trying to *create* a "situation" between us. But I will not become the sort of couple who have issues but fail to examine them. I do not want to co-exist without really being *together.* I don't want us to be like that. Like my parents.' Another breath. *Ecru? Taupe? Putty?* 'So I need answers, Greg. Because right now, I am questioning you. Not just about *that* night, but *last* night too, which is absolutely ridiculous! Because all you did was get pissed and sweaty at a gig, which is what you told me you were going to do. With that ridiculousness in mind—or more specifically in *my* freaked out mind—I know that if we have nookie, I won't be thinking about *it*, I'll be thinking about all of my questions. And that I need…' I take a final clipped breath. *Mushroom.* The carpet is mushroom. I look up at Greg. '…*answers.*'

I stare at him. He says nothing.

'Aren't you going to say anything?'

He is silent.

'*Greg?*'

'You told me not to speak until instructed.'

'Oh, right, yes…well, you can talk now.'

'Thanks…' he says calmly—*kindly*—and pats the bed indicating me to sit down. 'Babe, there is nothing for you to be freaking out about.'

'Nothing?'

'Nope. That night, I was pissed. Met up with Jez. Got stoned. Threw up. Passed out. I told a porky pie because I hate you seeing that side of me. Everything about you is so measured—in a good way, and that always brings out the best in me…but sometimes when you're not there, I act like a doofus. I'll tell you the whole story if you want, but it's not pretty or very interesting.'

'Now?' I sit down.

'Why not? Let's order some food first, though. I'm *starv-ing*.' He peers over at the trolley. 'All that is going to be cold by now. What a waste. I ordered it before I went out last night thinking it would be nice to wake up to. Okay, where's the room service menu? I need a fat, juicy burger with bacon, melted cheese. And chips. Definitely chips. But first, a shower.' He swings his legs over me and hops out of the bed. 'Can you also order me a beer.'

'What sort?' I find myself asking. 'Peroni?'

'Perfect.' Just before the bathroom, he turns round. 'Anyway, shouldn't we be using this weekend to talk about something a little more important than me being embarrass-ingly unable to handle my drink in my thirties?'

'Like what? Fonts?' I smile, weakly.

'No. Something *way* more important.' Then he adds, breezily. 'Begins with a B ends in a Y, screams a lot, shits a lot, cries a lot…takes over your life.'

He winks at me, disappears into the bathroom and closes the door. I stand still staring at it.

'*Babies?*' I yell. 'You want to talk about babies?'

'Ha! Don't get too carried away,' Greg shouts back, laugh-ing. 'I said, ends in a Y!'

I laugh too as the relief jangles through me. As soon as I hear water start blasting out of the shower, I strip off my clothes and follow him into the bathroom. We make full use of the aquatic marbled playground. Afterwards, he puts on his jeans, I put on the complimentary dressing gown and we sit at the table to enjoy our room service. Greg knocks back his beer and then we have champagne. The first time we shared a bottle of fizz was also in the morning. I woke up in his studio flat above The Croft.

HIM: (Sitting on end of bed, passing me two glasses.) So, when am I going to meet your parents?

ME: Excuse me?

HIM: Maybe we could pop in later? I ought to let your father know that I very much enjoyed ravaging his daughter and am intending on doing it repeatedly over the coming weeks.

ME: Shut up.

HIM: (Popping cork. Pouring champagne.) So, come on, tell me…what's he like? The notorious Mr. Dinsdale…

ME: (Shrugging.) Set in his ways. There's no point airing an alternative opinion to his on any subject. I don't even bother now.

HIM: My father was the same. I remember when I told him I wanted to join the youth club and learn the guitar. He said it would distract me from school work, I'd spend my days having ludicrous pipedreams about wanting to be in a famous band touring the world and fall behind in all my academic subjects.

ME: And did you?

HIM: Of course. I flunked everything. But all he would have needed to say to me was. 'Why not, son? See if you enjoy it. If you do, let's work out a way you could combine being a star with getting decent GCSE results.' Would that really have been too much to ask?

ME: He was probably cross because he thought you weren't asking and had made up your own mind.

HIM: Yeah. True. But why would any parent not want

*their kid to have the freedom to express him or herself?
They say they want you to be a certain way for your own
good, but ultimately it's because they don't understand you...
no, worse...they don't want to get to understand you. Why?
Because they have shit going on in their heads that they
inherited from their own folks which they never dealt with.
And now? Well, it's less psychologically invasive for them to
simply inflict their way of thinking on you. They don't break
the cycle. I will break that cycle. When I become a dad I want
my kids to grow up as individuals. Being different is special.
Yeah, getting there will mean they'll screw up. But so what!
Bono once said, 'My heroes are the ones who survived doing
it wrong, who made mistakes but recovered from them....'
That's how I want my kids to think. Don't you?*

I stared at him, not sure of what to say because I had not
allowed myself to imagine anything to do with parenthood
in so long. Not that it was painful any more, it was not even
a dull ache, or even numb...it didn't hurt. It was a vacant
space. Greg wholly misinterpreted my silence.

*HIM: Shit! I just quoted Bono at you. Ha! How to make
someone instantly regret sleeping with you. (Grinning.) Your
face was classic! Look, it could be worse. I could have quoted
someone way more self-righteous and sure of themselves...
like, oh...okay, so I couldn't have! Does this mean we're
over?*

ME: I didn't know we had begun?

HIM: Well, erm. I hope we have. I'm up for it. Are you?

ME: (Smiling.) Yeah, I'm up for it.

*HIM: Okay, then I'd... (Exhaling deeply. Taking gulp of
champagne.)*

*ME:...better stop quoting behemoths of stadium rock at
me?*

HIM: Ha! Exactly. (Spoken laugh.) But also, I'd better… explain…to…Sadie.

ME: Explain what to Sadie? (Twisting sheet in my fingers.) I thought you'd split up with her?

HIM: Yeah. I mean, it's over…but we're still, you know.

ME: Really? Oh, right…

HIM: I need to get the rest of my stuff. And talk to her. Let her know…for sure…that we're done. You know how messy the end of a relationship can sometimes be…anyway! (Raising his glass.) Cheers, babe.

ME: (Tentatively. Raising my glass half way.) Yes, erm… cheers.

'Babe?'

I jump. 'Yeah?'

'Look at your robe…' He laughs.

I look down. There are two large blobs of ketchup on the front of the towelling gown. Right on top of the hotel logo.

'Well, that's attractive. You see, this is why I only wear black. White is way too high maintenance. I don't know how Elizabeth Hurley has managed to keep her jeans so pristine for three decades. Mind you, she probably doesn't ever enter high-risk soiling areas in them. Where's your one? I'll put that on.'

'You can't. There was only one in the bathroom, I think.' He shrugs. 'Shall I call down and get another?'

'Nah.' I don't want anyone to disturb us. 'I'll grab a towel. I'm only going to get undressed again, aren't I?' I wander into the bathroom. 'So, shall we start that conversation about the begins with a B and ends in a Y?'

'You want to start whilst you're hiding behind a wall?' he shouts.

'Actually, yes.' I throw the robe over the side of the bath.

'Because I want to confirm a few things before we talk face-to-face. I want to reassure you that if I do ever get begins with a P ends in a T, I assure you I will not be grizzly towards you whenever I am feeling tired and remember that we are both bearing a weight of responsibility in some way. In addition to this, I will not ask if I look fat, pat my stomach in public (or invite anyone else to), go berserk in overpriced baby boutiques, wear a BABY ON BOARD badge or any novelty maternity clothes; especially knitwear with arrows pointing to my growing stomach. And there will be no getting involved in any gestational/birth focussed chat rooms and giving myself a whimsical User Name. Maddie's was READYPREGGYGO. I kid you not! I am also anti any kind of social media presence for a baby or growing child. If you need any evidence of that you can read the section on my blog asking why a mother would want a stranger 'liking' pictures of their offspring? Oh, and that also means I will never be duped into the Cult of Competitive Motherhood. I will not feel it necessary to throw birthday parties headlined by Idina Menzel, where miniature Shetlands are drafted in and goodie bags are 'out sourced'.

'But before all of that…' I wrap a fresh towel around me. 'I will never refer to the growing foetus as anything other than the begins with a B ends with a Y. If I call it The Bump you are allowed to leave me. I will also attempt to remember at all times, that I am not The Only Woman In The History Of The World To Have Ever Conceived, even though I have a sneaking suspicion that this is a *resolutely* unavoidable part of being begins with a P ends in a T.' I am laughing as I leave the bathroom. Greg is looking at his phone.

'Tanya?'

'Eh? *Tanya?* Ha! You never call me Tanya.' But then I see

Greg's expression. There is no amusement there. 'What's the matter?'

I go over to him. He is not looking at his mobile. It's mine. He passes it to me. On the screen is a text message from Noelle. No reference to last night's 'episode', just...

What shall I say to Angus re: Greg. Does he wanna like, meet him or what? Let me know asap. These people—

...the rest of the message is cut off from the display screen.

'Can I see the rest of the message, please?' Greg's voice is calm, but not *kind* calm like before.

'Erm...yeah. Of course.'

'Now.' No, please.

'Greg? Stop being odd...I'll show it to you.' I take the phone from him, tap in my code and read the full text. '*What shall I say to Angus re: Greg. Does he wanna like, meet him or what? Let me know asap. These people don't hang around you know.*'

'What does she mean by that?' he asks. 'What sort of people is she referring to?'

'Ah, I know!' I click, and smile excitedly. 'She means music types. *Professional* ones.'

Greg does not smile back.

'Is she referring to Angus O'Donnell? The guy who has written the last two double platinum albums for Barbed Wire?'

'I think he's their producer. I thought that plum, Troy, and the rest of the band wrote all their own st—'

He butts in. 'They don't. O'Donnell is the mastermind behind their sound. Their first album without him—which they pretend never happened—is pitiful. How long have you known about this for?'

'Known what?'

'That Angus wants to see me.'

'Noelle mentioned something yesterday.'

His face tenses. 'When were you going to tell me?'

'I've only just got here.'

'Why didn't you call me last night? Or tell me when you arrived? This is serious shit.'

I burst out laughing. 'Did you just say "*this is a serious shit*"?' Greg does not respond. 'Come on, that *was* funny. Look, I didn't think she was being serious.'

'Because you didn't think I could be taken seriously as an artist?'

'No!' I ignore his use of the words 'as an artist' on the tail end of the last cliché. 'I've asked her to help you on numerous occasions and she's always fobbed me off. To be honest, I assumed that the offer she made yesterday was more about her looking good in front of Dad, as usual. Add to that, *apparently* this Angus guy fancies her so she was probably trying to involve him to make Troy jealous.'

Greg clicks and inhales on his e-cigarette, then chucks it down on the table. 'I need a proper snout.'

'Have I done something wrong?'

He shrugs. 'Other than assuming that no one could be *genuinely* interested in my talent and then not bothering to tell me, even though a major player had shown interest to the point of wanting to meet me? Oh no, nothing.'

'*Major player?*' I can't ignore this one. 'Stop getting so huffy. We can set up the meeting. Greg, really…now *you* need to relax, because this is getting sill—'

There is a knock at the door. He jumps up, marches over and yanks it open way too abruptly than is necessary. On the other side, a maid is holding a large bouquet of yellow roses. She explains that they were dropped off at reception for me.

Greg fishes around in his jeans pocket for a tip, thanks her, then shuts the door.

'Well, that was either the most perfect or the most awkward timing of a floral delivery *ever*. I can't decide which,' I laugh, in a bid to rescue the us-ness. 'Thank you, Greg, you shouldn't have done. Actually no, you *should*!'

'They're not from me,' he mutters. 'Did you tell your parents about the engagement?'

'Of course not. We agreed we would wait. Is there a card?'

He pulls an envelope from the cellophane and reads the card inside. '*To Tanya (and Greg obviously!), good luck with the…*'

My purple heat rash springs across my chest then leaps up my neck. Suddenly, I picture the information print outs scattered over the floor in the spare room at my parents' house. I thought I had picked them all up.

'*…IVF. I'm rooting for you both! Love, Mum AKA The Pomeranian Nanny.*' Greg places the flowers onto the dressing table. His back is to me. 'Well, now it *all* makes sense,' he says.

I nod to myself and smile tentatively.

'Thank you for understanding. I found out last week,' I begin. 'I wanted to check that everything was in working order…so that if and when we are *both* ready we knew that my machinery was too. Anyway, I went to see the doctor and she said my Fallopian tubes are up the spout and this means that I won't be able to get pregnant that easily—if at all, naturally. The younger you are, the more chance you have of IVF succeeding. Mum must have found some literature I'd been reading about it and jumped to conclusions that we were starting already, but I was only researching our…well, *my* issue. I should have told you after I had seen the doctor, but then we had that r—'

'No…' He butts in and turns round. '*No*, that's not what I meant. What I meant was it now makes sense that you didn't want to tell me about Angus O'Donnell.'

'*What?*'

'I'm not thick, Tanya. I bet you didn't even ask your father about using the garage for rehearsal space either.'

'Now we're talking about the *garage*?'

'See?'

'See *what*? You're acting like a child.'

'A child being the real issue, eh?' he snaps, nonsensically. 'You don't want me to progress with the band, because you want a family *now.*'

'Greg!' I reach out to him, but he pulls away. 'I would never stop you pursuing your dreams of a music career.'

'Dreams? It's my reality.'

'Not yet it isn't!' I snap back. 'But frankly…my medical condition *is*. Which is why I can't get my head round your reaction. I know you're shocked, but the least I expected was a little support. And there was me thinking Suze's reaction would be the most bizarre…'

'*Suze!* She knows too? Well, this is brilliant. You involved that opinionated hag before me? Oh, I'm sure she managed to take a stance on the matter within a hundredth of a second of you telling her.'

I wrap my gown tighter around me. 'She was concerned about whether you would be there for me through the treatment.'

'Oh, I'm sure she is *very* concerned…' he mutters.

'Greg, please, don't be angry. Why would I lie to you about anything?' I ask him. 'You're my *true* love.'

He looks down at his bracelet. Then back up at me for a few seconds. Maybe three or four, no more than that.

'I need some space. Please, give me some. I'll call you.'

'*Greg!*'

He doesn't answer. He leans down to open his Adidas hold-all, pulls out a fresh T-shirt, sweatshirt and socks, gets dressed and then strides round the bedroom and bathroom, chucking the rest of his clothes and toiletries into the bag. Once packed, he grabs the car keys off the dressing table then leaves.

I watch the open door, waiting for him to come back. When he doesn't, I dash out of our room and run down the corridor, but there is no sign of him. I arrive at the lift and watch the floors light up 4, 3, 2, 1…as it goes down. I slam my hand against the button to call it back, but it continues its descent to the foyer. I return to Room 579. The door has swung shut. I am about to slump down in front of it when a bus boy wheels a room service trolley out of the suite two up from ours.

'Are you locked out, madam?'

'I…I nipped out to…just needed to tell my…oh, it's cool, I can phone him.' My voice sounds strangulated. I indicate to the towel I am wearing. 'Actually, as you can see, I can't, my mobile is in the room…sorry…could you…'

The bus boy smiles. 'Not a problem, let me use the house key…' he offers, reaching into a leather pouch attached to his waist. 'And can I apologise for this morning…for waking you up. I was on "earlies" and you hadn't left the Do Not Disturb sign on the door. As there were some hot items on the trolley I thought I should persist in knocking…anyway, I left it outside as you instructed. I do hope you enjoyed your breakfast.'

'Sorry…what? As *I* instructed?'

'Yes. You asked me to leave the trolley by the door… unless you were sleep-talking, madam?'

Thirteen

Fitz slaps his entry pass against the door and we enter. It's always strange being in the *Catwalk* office when no one is in there. You can hear the photocopier humming, pipes gurgling, air conditioning whirring…and there is one light which buzzes differently to the rest. It's above the fashion desk. I figured this out on one of my weekend visits when things started to get difficult between Zach and me. Needing to 'catch up on some work' was my excuse to escape intermittently from the enforced couple-y togetherness that a Saturday or Sunday demanded. Forty-eight hours of me treading on eggshells and him walking on thin ice. We were living idioms.

'Right, we need to start by accessing the distribution figures,' I tell Fitz, chucking my jacket onto my desk. I notice that dust has collected on my unused keyboard. 'You could have wiped a tissue over my computer last week.'

'I did think about it, but I rather liked the idea of leaving it exactly as you did…as the days progressed it got a Miss Havisham vibe about it. I *die* for that anguished, uptight Victorian Gothic look.'

'Majorly Olsen…' I add, trying to get back into our routine banter. 'Every time they do it, I'm *literally* a pile of ashes.'

'Remember the cream lace high neck with a train Mary-Kate did at the Art of Elysium gala? I mean, I was already dead but with that frock I was basically ex*humed*. Okay, now…shoosh.'

'Why? This is not an episode of *24*. I can't believe you bought a torch. It's not even four o'clock.'

He tuts at me. 'God, you're dry, Jacobs. No sense of adventure. Anyway, why do we need to check those numbers? We know that the magazine is selling consistently. If this *was* an episode of *24*, Jack Bauer would be at a loose end for the next fifty-three minutes; filing down his acrylics, casting a critical eye over Rachel Zoe's new faux-fur line for QVC, nibbling on a half-fat blueberry muffin…more to the point, *anyone* can see the sales figures.'

'I said *distribution* figures. Not *sales*. I want to see *where* the magazine is selling.' I walk over to Catherine's office. It is locked but can be opened with a 'Slidie'. 'Have you got a credit-card-style card which isn't a credit card?'

'Only my gym card.'

'Pass it to me. I need one that I can potentially mangle.'

'But I need it for the gym!'

'You don't go to the gym.'

'I will do. I'm going to *have* to if I want to keep Jesus. He is ripped. I need to step up to the plate. No, get *on* the Power Plate. Or at least something to get rid of all those cocking cupcakes Jazz brings in. A serious exercise regime is required. It's all very well having a decent personality…'

'…but you don't have one of those either,' I interrupt. 'So face facts, your relationship is doomed. Now, hand me your card.'

Reluctantly, Fitz rummages around in his Dries Van Noten man bag.

'By the way, you better be coming to Lazare's bash tonight. I need you to turn up with *and* hang out with *briefly* before I spend the entire night pawing Jesus.' He passes me an out of date membership card for Fitness First. 'Yes?'

'Nah, Noelle will be there. That means her agent will be too, and on the warpath. I don't want to see either. I'm tired. I should stay in.'

'Tsk! *Me me me!* Jacobs! Two points to make. Firstly, you're stalling. I thought you were supposed to be turning a corner in regards to all of your *issues*. Secondly, you're being selfish. I'll protect you from Gopher Hag-Needy-C*nt. Look, just because your love life is on a bleak, downwards trajectory, I won't let you pull mine down with you. I need you to come to the party so I look as if I have friends. No one wants a clingy, lonely boyfriend. But if you do come, do me a favour and stay off the booze. It would do you good, but more importantly it will be better for me. If there's one thing no self-respecting gay wants more than a clingy, lonely boyfriend it's a clingy, lonely boyfriend with a pisshead fag hag bezzie mate.'

'I'm not sure whether I am more offended by you calling me your best friend or an alcoholic. Anyway, stop getting all Anne of Green Gables on me.'

'Fab drag name.' He giggles.

I ignore him and slide down the edge of the door against the lock. It clicks open.

'Ta-dah!'

Fitz gasps. 'Where *did* you learn how to do that?'

'Squatting.'

I sit down in Catherine's cream leather chair and turn on

her computer. To log on to the network requires her password. I know what it is. She asked me to change it to 'something I'll be able to think of instantly' when she returned from her most recent maternity leave. I stare at the white box on the screen as I hover over the keyboard, ready to hit the letter 'M'. As my finger hovers above the key, I think about the day Catherine gave me my job; the last day of my internship. She sat down in this seat, leaned back underneath the neon light installation on the wall behind her and eyeballed me.

HER: So, when were you going to tell me?

ME: Tell you what?

HER: That you were a, oooooh, I think the expression is a 'bullshitter'?

ME: A what? A bullshi—? (Clamming up. Knowing what is about to happen.)

HER: Yup. A bullshitter. (Reaching into a drawer.) Some-one who bullshits! You, Ms. Jacobs, are a bullshitter. (Pulling out a few pieces of A4 paper.) Or should I address you as Ms Atwal? Either way, your alternate CVs make for entertaining reading. To secure your work experience in this way is pushy, calculating and smacks of desperation.

ME: But you don't understand, I...

But I stopped. Because what was the point? I had been busted. I stared at Catherine in silence. I knew that if I said anything I would get angry and lash out…because that would be so much easier than showing her how upset I was. My heart was breaking. She stared back at me. The longer she did, the more upset I became. My heart was broken. So I got angry. And lashed out.

ME: Yes, I lied. I fucking lied. You know why I lied? Because it was the only way to get in here…to get past that obnoxious trust fund princess, Polly. I had to pretend to be an identikit version of her, because people like her only want to be with their own. She represents everything that this magazine should be trying to avoid. She doesn't breathe fashion. She just buys it. And she doesn't give a shit about her job. I guarantee you that to her the role of Editorial Assistant at Catwalk *is merely a (Putting on a bad home counties accent.) 'pretty coolio' way to pass the time before she heads off travelling with Ava, Tamara, Olivia, Victoria and Camilla to somewhere self-consciously spiritual to go and find themselves. Well, I also guarantee that they will discover everything they need to know between Customs and the Departure gate. And I also guarantee that before she goes, she'll make sure that her post is filled by another identikit version of her whose CV will be ready and waiting in her* DEFFO POTENTIAL *file. And in she'll come...the next Cressida, India, Arabella, Georgina or Ara-fucking-bella and the cycle will begin again. That is why I lied, Catherine. (Standing up.) Well, at least I tried. Oh, and the final thing I can guarantee you, is that I would not have stopped fucking trying. I would have tried harder at this job every day and worked my way up until I became that person who all the Editorial Assistants who followed wanted to try and fucking be. (Walking to the door.)*

    HER: *I know.*

    ME: *(Turning.) You...what?*

    HER: *(Calmly.) I know that, Ashley. Now, please. Sit down, brush off that giant, boxy Heston Blumenthal triple-cooked chip from your shoulder and listen to me. (Taking a breath.) As I was saying, what you did was pushy, calculating and smacks of desperation. It also showed commitment and passion. And because of that, I am going to ask you if would like to be our new Editorial Assistant.*

ME: (Quietly.) Sorry?

HER: Polly is leaving to go… (Smiling.)…travelling. With friends. To Bali. (Laughing. Raising her hand.) And no, you're not allowed to laugh. But I am, because I say what goes. And if you ever tell me what I should or should not be doing or swear in my FUCKING office again, I will kick you off the staff, immediately.

ME: (Dazed.) I'm going to be a real member of the team? On the masthead?

HER: You are. And I tell you why, it's because I do understand. More than you know. But I want you to remember one thing, Ashley. Don't ever try and bullshit a bullshitter again. (Holding out her hand.) Welcome—officially—to Catwalk.

'Come on,' says Fitz. 'My suspenders are killing me.'

I turn to him. 'I'm not sure we should do this.'

'Why? Catherine is ruining the magazine and seemingly doesn't care. We need to find out what she is up to. She isn't going anywhere unless we oust her. If you want to be Editor like you said, we need to do this. You do, don't you?'

'Of course, but she and I have history…'

'"History" being the operative word. Any good times the two of you shared are in the past. You're Madge and Gwynnie.' He delights himself at this comparison. 'Not even Kabbalah or The Tracy Anderson Method could bring you back together.'

'But she's pregnant,' I mutter. 'We don't want to stress her out.'

'Jacobs, all we are doing right now is investigating. If we find something that needs to be reported to an independent industry regulator, we can work out the best time to inform them. You know as well as I do that Catherine is never going to give up that position of her own accord. I understand! God, who in their right mind would choose to stay home Monday to Friday with four children *under four* when they can pay some Bulgarian student with a clean driving licence to do it at the minimal cost of one hundred and fifty quid a week and a Habitat sofa bed in the roof conversion?' He claps his hands together. 'Tap in her password.'

I hover over the keyboard for a few more seconds... then type MALDIVES. This takes me into Catherine's personal files. I go through them until I find the most recent spreadsheet detailing the distribution of *Catwalk*. I scroll down and down and down...the names of hundreds of newsagents', supermarkets and specialist shops appear on the screen. Next to each one: a number detailing how many were received, how many sold, how many returned. Then at the bottom; there is a list of 'bulks', signifying the amount of copies which were given away—and not paid for—as part of promotional tie-ins. I print out copies of the bi-annual distribution statistics for this year and last, then Fitz and I leave Catherine's office.

We have only sat at my desk for a minute to examine the stats when we both notice the same thing.

'Are you sure these figures are from separate years?' asks Fitz. 'They look exactly the same at each outlet.'

'I know. Even the promotional bulks are pretty much the same and those *never* are.'

He taps his torch against the palm of his hand. 'So either we've managed to entirely bypass the fluctuations experienced by *all* women's magazines in the last year and have sold exactly the same amount in exactly the same places across the nation, or the numbers are being bumped up at each unit so that it *looks* as if *Catwalk* is selling as well as it used to, despite it not being as good. It has to be something to do with Lazare. These figures tie in with his increase in advertising and the influence Ogilvy has allowed him to have on the magazine.'

'But he could have focused his resources on a much more commercial publication or digital platform to promote RIVA products,' I reply. 'Why choose our magazine?'

Fitz considers this seriously for a few seconds, then bursts out laughing.

'Yikes, listen to us…we sound so convincingly corporate! Actually, I can rather see myself in an eighties' Anne Klein boxy power suit and some spiky patent Ferragamo sling-backs. Handbag?'

'You'd have to go Gucci.'

'Tan with a horsey style snaffle clasp? Totally. Okay, so we need to access Ogilvy's emails…do you have the password for her inbox too?'

'Nope. A few weeks ago, I tried MALDIVES again when I tried to recall a message I sent her by mistake.'

'Bollocks. And it's unlikely to be one of her kids' names or she'd never remember it.'

'You could pump Jesus?' I suggest. 'For information, I mean. Obviously, you're already pumping him in the more biblical fash—' I stop, as I notice Fitz is doing something very strange. 'Are you *blushing*?'

'No.' He shrugs his shoulders. 'A little bit. The thing is, there has actually been no erm…' He takes a breath. '…pumping,' he says. '*As yet*. I want to…'

'Wait?'

He nods.

'Wow. You want it to be *special*!' I suck in my cheeks and whistle. 'You really do like him, don't you?'

'Maybe. Probably. Yes. But you know what, Jacobs, I like

all of them at the beginning because I'm so charged up on endorphins, hope, neediness and poppers. And we both know what happens? Within a week—no, five days tops!—the whole thing implodes and I'm deleting *another* number in my phone and I'm downloading *another* app to check out *another* queen's bathroom selfie. I've got to the point where I'm not even checking out the guy. I'm checking out their grouting. And I can tell you, there are a lot of gay men in the capital who could do with spending a weekend resealing their tiles if they don't want to get damp spreading up their walls.'

'Gosh, be careful Fitz.' I wink at him. 'You're sounding resolutely *non* one-dimensional. Almost like you have feelings.'

'Shut it, you shrew.' He points his torch at me. 'That info does not go any further than this room. As far as the rest of the fashion community is concerned I am still a heartless, soulless, wizened, bitter and fickle husk. Got that?'

'Your sordid secret is safe with me,' I tell him, and am about to continue winding him up when I notice a new message has pinged through into my work inbox. It is from *bookings@thecroft*. The subject box is blank. I click on it.

I'm in London. Should have listened to you, the journey was DRAINING. If by some chance you are checking your work emails on a Saturday, call me. I have JUST enough energy to meet up with my favourite one night stand. Jx PS. Not that you would need any encouragement...but I do have this!

He has attached a picture of my expensive bra, which I left in the budget hotel.

'How the hell did he know I worked at *Catwalk*?' I say out loud.

'Who?' asks Fitz.

'Oh, no one. Some guy I erm…you know, since Zach and I…'

'That doesn't narrow it down, Jacobs. From what you told me the other day, there have been rather a few 'erm' guys 'since'. What does he want?'

'To meet up later. He's in town. I don't know, though…'

'Was he a good shag and did he have a sense of humour?'

I shrug. 'Both, I suppose.'

'Then you should meet him. We can't have both of us giving it the big purity ring. Besides, there isn't anything else we can do here and I need to get home to prep for tonight. I was going to do a battered BOY London trackie with my Yeezy boots, but I don't know where Jesus stands on the Kanye West debate. He is *such* a cultural divider. Kanye, I mean, not Jesus. Although, actually he is too! Maybe I should play it safe with a suit. Aghhhhh, why is life so complicated? Jack Bauer has nothing on the shit I have to deal with. Anyway go…go and enjoy a frisson with this…'

'Jared. He's called Jared.'

'Sexy name.'

'And *he* is,' I admit. 'But…'

'But what?' Fitz clicks his tongue at me. 'Because if the next word after "but" is "Zach", then I will be forced to shine this torch into your eyes until you see sense. You owe Zach *nothing*. Well, apart from the shedload of money made on your flat—which, by law, you will have to give him. Ha!'

'Fitz! We're not laughing about that yet.'

'Serves you right for abusing my new status as a person with f-e-e-l-i-n-g-s. Anyway, I mean, *mentally* you owe Zach nothing. He should not even enter your thoughts. Let's face it, you won't be entering *his* thoughts as he and that welly wedge-wearing cow assess the latest range of Bugaboos on the sixth floor at House of Fraser? *Will you?'*

*

So, I do something I haven't done since 'it was decided'; I invite a man to 'The Home Formerly Known As Our Flat'. Of course, *partly* because I have that image which Fitz planted in my head. (In my version Zach and Rachel detour via women's shoes on the second floor so she can invest in some less offensive mid-price swampy terrain footwear.) But I also want to see whether I can do it; attempt functional interaction with a man in the place where it all went so dysfunctionally wrong with the last one.

At 9.33pm, Jared presses the doorbell. I stare at the intercom screen for a few seconds, examining what he looks like. The answer is: exactly how I left him. Alluringly dishevelled. I'm impressed. That's quite a hard look to pull off *authentically*, because the slightest noticeable effort in attempting to create it removes any sex appeal whatsoever. He points his key ring up the street, checks his phone, appears to switch it off and puts it in his back pocket. Then he loosens his watch and puts that in there too. I buzz him in.

'What was with the delay?' he asks me, as he jogs up the last few steps towards my door on the top floor. 'Having second thoughts?'

'I had to give you the once over. The last guy I met up with was with a dancer who insisted on meeting in a bar below street level so I couldn't see that he was wearing a bandana until I walked in.'

'What's wrong with a bandana? Is that another one of your crimes against fashion?'

'You have to ask?' I pull a face at him as he walks into

the flat. 'Admittedly, it was wrapped round his wrist, not his neck or his head. But still. *He was wearing a bandana.* Unforgivable post-secondary school, except hanging out a back pocket on low slung denim to signify US gang membership. Anyway…hello, *Jared.*'

'Hi, *Ashley,*' he says, pulling my Agent Provocateur bra out of his jacket and pinging it at me. 'You're glad I tracked you down for our first official date?'

'This is not a date,' I tell him, quickly. I stare at my underwear lying on the ground but I leave it there, *because I can*. 'I'm not a dating sort of person. All that browsing round local foodie markets and sampling street snacks. Not for me.'

'Ah, damn. I was going to suggest we take a late night walk to a local landmark that has some sort of personal resonance for you. It's a hook up, then?'

This makes me even more uncomfortable…sober sex. Half of me instantly regrets inviting him over. The other considers necking my decoy bottle of putrid white wine. I change the subject.

'How did you find my email address?'

'Erm…well, initially I Googled you…entered 'Ashley, fashion writer'. That told me an Ashley Jacobs worked at *Catwalk*, I checked it was you with an image search and emailed the address on the masthead. You're not as mysterious as you like to think. What are we drinking?'

'We're not. You're driving.'

'I think I preferred Hotel Ashley. Home Ashley is very strict. But hey, that could work…later.' He smiles flirtatiously at me. 'Nice place, by the way.'

Jared walks down the corridor—past a series of blank spaces on the wall where Zach has taken down pictures to put in his flat, and the sideboard which now contains our wedding photo—and into the lounge. I follow him and watch as he assesses where he should sit. His eyes rest on the corner section of the 'L' sofa. That was where Zach always sat.

'Take a seat,' I tell him, acutely aware I sound as if I am about to interview him.

'Thanks.' He chucks his jacket on the sofa and follows my instructions. 'So, are you going to explain yourself?'

'Explain what?'

'That little number you pulled the other day at the hotel. Disappearing without taking my number or even saying goodbye.' He makes a goofy upset face. 'Do you know how that made me feel?'

'You're about to tell me.'

'I felt wounded. No one has ever done that to me before. I woke up, naked…and alone. You used me then discarded me.'

I stare at the cushions next to him. Zach would pile them up behind him when he watched television. Not that he watched a lot of TV, but when he did, he fully committed himself. He would research a drama, download the boxset and view every show, sometimes multiple seasons—through Friday night to Sunday evening. He'd ask if I wanted to join him, but I always said no. Then he'd ask if I was *sure* because he wouldn't want to be explaining the plot to me when he was three series deep. I'd say yes, I *am* sure. Then I'd get on with my weekend around him, joining him for food or passing through the lounge on my way to exercise or go shopping. He'd be spreadeagled in various different positions, adding more props—duvets, pillows, blankets—as he clocked up episodes. Invariably, on Sunday morning I would flop next to him on the sofa, hungover, and start asking loads of questions about who the characters were and what was happen—

'*Ashley?*'

'Mmmm? Sorry…'

'I was saying you discarded me.'

'Don't take it personally.'

'What other way is there to take it?' He laughs.

'I didn't leave because of *you*. I left because I needed to see…'

I consider lying, but then I find myself imagining Zach's 'new' sofa; the artfully tattered and battered leather Chester-field. I imagine Rachel on it. *She* won't need any persuading to join him for a boxset weekend. She'll have already 'done' *all* the David Attenborough documentaries, *Band of Brothers*, *The West Wing*, *Mad Men*, *Breaking Bad*, *The Wire*, *House of Cards*, *The Killing*, *Homeland* and be a fully fucking fledged IMDB-bothering master fucking mind on every fucking epi-sode of *Game of* Fucking *Thrones*…

'…my ex husband. Well, soon to be *officially*. I'm getting a…' But I trail off.

'Divorce?' Jared's eyes widen. 'Ooooooh…'

'Yes, that. The ultimate conversation stopper.' I can hear the faux brightness in my voice.

He shrugs. 'Well, most people get divorced these days don't they? One in two?'

'I don't know, my solicitor and I haven't been going over the recent UK stats. We've mainly been concerned with my case.'

'Ha! Sorry, didn't mean to make you feel any worse. Not that you *should* feel bad, of course. Agh! I'm not very good at saying the right thing when it comes to stuff like this. I'm not meant to ask what happened, am I?' He grimaces at me.

'Christ, no. I think the best you could do right now is give me some formulaic words of support in the form of a meaningless back story and then we can move on to some subjects that are not so depressing.'

'I'm down with that!' He smiles at me. 'Okay, well…I'm sure you'll get through it. These things happen. Actually, my mother divorced my father. It was the best thing she could have done. He was controlling; stopped her from being *her*… and the person she could have been.'

'The back story is meant to be meaningless. That's way too personal. I'm sorry, though.'

'Me too,' he mutters. 'How about some more formulaic words of support? Some people are better off apart. Not everyone can live the marital suburban dream like your folks.'

'My folks are living the wha—?' I stop, remembering my pissed monologue in the hotel room. 'Oh…that.' I *squirm*. 'They're erm…not my parents.'

'Shit, you weirdo.' He laughs. Who the hell are they?'

'They're Zach's parents. Zach is my erm…ex.'

'At least they're real people, I suppose. That's a *little* less odd. But only a little. So, I'm guessing you preferred them to your real parents?'

I ignore the question. 'Bill was fairly pleasant and warm but Gwen was the opposite. I know every mother-in-law is *meant* to be frosty and cold towards their daughter-in-law, but I actually joked to Zach that she was the "something blue" at our wedding.'

He leans forward. 'So, what about your *own* mother?'

'She's dead.'

'That's a sick joke.'

'It's not. She is.'

'I'm sorry,' he says, gently.

'Really, it's…'

'Something you don't want to talk about. I get it.'

'I doubt it,' I tell him.

'I can assure you I do. My mum passed away too.'

'That had better not be a joke as payback.'

His face contorts. 'You think I would *joke* about my mother dying?'

'No! I *am* joking now. Of course, I know you wouldn't joke about it. Or at least, I hope you wouldn't. You wouldn't joke about something like that, would you?'

'NO!'

I cringe. 'That's a relief. We've confirmed that neither one of us is a sociopath. Which is a great start to our…whatever this is. Actually, I do know what it is. It's *awkward*.' I shudder and flop back in the sofa. 'Fucking awkward.'

'Nah.' He raises an eyebrow at me. 'I'm having a *great* time with you. It's easy. Conversation is flowing, so are the drinks…'

I smile. 'Piss off. What would you like to do?'

'Honestly?'

'Yeah.'

'Smoke. Do you mind?'

I do, but Zach would have minded even more so I nod at Jared. Then I open the window and pass him an ashtray. He flicks a lighter up to his cigarette and inhales deeply.

'And you? What would you like to do? Let me rephrase that. What would you normally be doing on a Saturday night?'

'I'd be at some painfully hot fashion party…being relentlessly cool.'

'Oh, yeah?' He waves his cigarette at me. 'Prove it.'

*

Whilst Jared showers, I get changed; adding a brand-new 'body suit' and some gold shoe boots to the pair of battered skintight suede trousers I am already wearing, then after assessing the outerwear section in my wardrobe for fifteen minutes, I 'casually sling' on a denim jacket.

Jared drives us to the party in his car. Well, it's more of a *runaround*. We arrive at Frédéric Lazare's riverside penthouse and step out of the entry lift straight onto the dance floor. A smoke machine blasts out a gust of cold white fog and we are sucked into the crowd of knowingly and flamboyantly styled guests dancing underneath a giant glitter ball to disco-tinged house music. As the smog clears I see a podium in the middle of the room where male and female models wearing only Lazare-branded underwear and baby oil are writhing and slithering over one another; a human viper nest. Jared glances across at me and grins.

'Case proven!' he shouts over the bass. 'If this is normal, now I know why the idea of eating a handmade tortilla on the pavement freaked you out. Bring. It. *On*. If I have a few beers and leave the car here, am I allowed to stay with you?' He gives me that flirtatious smile again. 'Pretty please…'

I recoil as I am forced to think it about *it* – sober sex – *again*. Even the last time with Zach, I was tipsy. When you get used to leaning on alcohol, all communication feels supported by it. Work relationships. Social relationships. Romantic relationships. Booze becomes a crutch. You know you'll stumble if anyone takes it away. And everyone else knows that too. So, after a while they don't make any *real* attempt to remove it.

HER: (Shouting from bedroom.) Ashley, can you make me a G&T? In one of those tumblers they keep giving us at the petrol station.

ME: (Shouting back.) Mum! They're not tumblers, they're pint glasses. Anyway, I thought you were going out?

HER: We are. I'm starting early. Oh, come on, it's the weekend! Aren't you doing anything with Tanya?

ME: (Deadpan.) Yeah, we're going to get the train down to London, stay out ALL night and come back with eyes like saucers.

HER: (Sticking her head out of the bedroom.) ARE YOU?

ME: (Tutting.) NO! Don't be silly. Our GCSEs start on Monday.

HER: Oooooh! SHIT! I knew that! (Entering lounge.)

She was wearing a strapless dress made out of patch work denim. I was shocked. My mother usually lived in her dungarees. I had never seen her in anything like this before. This look was so noughties, so cute and so American. It was the sartorial equivalent of Jennifer Love Hewitt.

ME: Wow, you look nice, Mum. Did you make that?

HER: Yep, decided to retire some of my old jeans and 'dungees'...ran it up this week. Shall I give you a twirl?

She turned on the radio (which was tuned into some pirate dance station) cranked up the volume and started to spin round the room, laughing her head off. I found myself laughing too. As she spun, I prepared her drink. Finally, she came to an untidy stop in the kitchen. I slid her the gin and tonic across the breakfast bar as if I worked in a saloon. Dizzily, she picked it up and tipped half of it down her front. My father arrived home from one of his road trips at exactly the same time. He stared at her from the doorway. His expression curled into one of embarrassment. Then fatigue. Then contempt.

HIM: You know what, I'm tired from the drive. Let's have a night in, Yvonne.

HER: What? I always have a night in. You always have a

night out. NIGHTS OUT. PLURAL! (Voice tightening.) I'm
ready. Let me get my bag and we'll g-...
  HIM: *No.*
  HER: *Sorry?*
  HIM: *I said, no. I want a night in.*
She stared at him for a few seconds. For the first time
ever, I thought I was going to witness my mother crying. But
then she took a breath and threw the tumbler at my father.
Hard. It hit him square in the forehead then fell to the floor
and broke into two equal halves. I remember thinking what
good quality the glasses were given that they were freebies
from the garage.

                                *

'Get me a drink,' I blurt out.
  Jared starts. 'What?'
  'I need...a vodka on the rocks. Or with grapefruit,
whatever. He'll have everything...in the kitchen. Now.' My
forehead is sweaty. 'I mean, c—'
  He steps back and interrupts me. 'You mean; 'please
could you get me a drink, thank you...' I'm not at work now,
Ashley. Or is that what you see me as, bar staff?'
  'Of course, not.'
  'Clearly, you do. Who barks orders like that?'
  'I didn't mean to.'
  'So, that's all you think I'm ever going to do?'
  'Okay, woah. No! Besides, what's wrong with working
in a bar?'
  'You clearly think there is.'
  'Christ, I can guarantee you I've worked in more catering
establishments than you have. Jared, it's no big deal. I'm
sorry if I sounded shirty.'

He exhales deeply. 'Where is the kitchen?'

'Downstairs,' I mutter, embarrassed. 'I'm going to get my mate, Fitz. We'll come and find you.'

I watch as he ricochets off through the shimmying guests and heads towards the stairs, doing a naff hands in the air 'woop woop' motion as he goes. Presumably, to amuse me and make light of what just happened. Was he *actually* offended? Or am I overreacting because the nuances of conversation have so much more impact when you're sober? I stand still for a minute or so, and attempt to let the repetitive baseline of the music bring me 'up'. When I made the decision that it was time to *live* again, this was something I often did at parties if I arrived sober or simply not drunk enough. It works but you have to let it happen. You cannot force the beat.

*

I find Fitz alone on the terrace, smoking a cigar and gazing out plaintively over the Thames. He is wearing a sharp suit with a roll neck.

'Oooooh, very Givenchy Pour Homme.'

'Hi, shrew, you came.'

'More intonation on the final word to show appreciation and excitement please.'

'Sorry, I'm on a Debbie Downer. And before you tell me to stop being a hypocrite and to cheer the fuck up, let me have my moment of self-pity.'

'Oh, God. This is going to be Jesus related, isn't it?'

'He's ignoring me,' sighs Fitz. 'All I got when I arrived was a "hey" and a peck on the cheek. Then he buggered off. I feel like such a cocking idiot. Clearly, I totally misread the signals and whilst I've been fantasising about us buying a cottage in the shires, owning our own chickens and having cosy home-cooked meals of fish pie and kale and possibly a chocolate-y Gü pot for pudding because he wouldn't mind me putting back on the three pounds I had lost—'

'He would only be *saying* that…'

'Jacobs! This is serious. I *know* what has happened. Jesus has been waiting for me to put out. And *now*, because I haven't, he's not interested. I thought he was different. I thought *we* as a couple—were different. I took an E to cheer me up, but it's done nothing.'

I grimace. 'Give it forty minutes. I hear that's when the fun kicks in.'

'I've always been very impressed at your anti-narcs policy, Jacobs.'

'I don't need them, I'm high on life,' I deadpan. 'Besides, I don't have the patience to wait forty minutes. A drink equals instant fun.'

Fitz turns round, leans against the railing and gazes at the throngs of people gossiping and hooting in the lounge.

'You know what, maybe there is only *so* much fun we can have. And can it be really classed as "fun" when having it takes so much effort…and *other* people; a decent dry cleaner, facialist, barber, bar tender *and/or* a dealer? I always thought one of the advantages of working in fashion was being able to wear "fuck-off" sunglasses with a larger lens surface area than welder's goggles at any time of the day *or* year, but maybe those lenses simply encourage you to hide the gradual increase in pain behind them.'

'Woah.' I smile. 'You're more Sally Suicide than Debbie Downer. Actually, Zach used to moan about these sorts of parties. He thought they were pretentious, full of people trying way too hard to show how unaffected they were by *other* people. And frankly, coming from someone who imported their trainers from Japan…'

Fitz manages a smile too. 'Good. I like the fact you've started griping about Zach. I had an awful feeling earlier that you may try to become one of those couples who end up divorcing amicably. All that, *"Oh, we still go on holiday together with our new partners…". So* naff!' He stops himself. 'Uh-oh…look who's here!' He points to the sofa where Noelle is being helped into a seat next to Frédéric by Jesus.

'Blimey,' I say. 'Look at the state of her. More to the point, look at the state of Jesus. Is he wearing his hair in a man bun?'

'He is…' says Fitz. 'But that doesn't mean I'm going to suddenly stop liking him.'

'Wow, you've got it bad.'

'I know.' He sighs. 'And look how kind he is too…helping that brittle praying mantis.'

We watch as Jesus encourages Noelle to drink a glass of water, but after a few sips she pushes him away and flops over Frédéric. He pulls her onto his lap, but she wriggles off and weaves through the room demonstrating some 'from da 'hood' dance moves as she goes. As she leaves she throws the room a gang sign. Everyone cheers and whoops. The loudest whoop is unmistakeable. It belongs to Noelle's agent, Sophie. My usual dislike of her is ramped up a notch by seeing that she is wearing a Lana del Ray tour T-shirt and a *bowler hat*. Surely, the most irritating millinery resurgence of recent times.

Fitz follows my line of vision. 'It's okay. Go round the terrace and get back in the other side of the lounge. I'll create a diversion and distract Gopher Hag-Needy-C*nt.'

'Do you mind? I haven't seen her since Noelle's book launch. Beeyatch'll get right up on my grill, yo.' I throw a gang sign too, to try and make Fitz laugh. 'Chins up, Sally Suicide. Meet me in the kitchen, I'm going to find Jared.'

'You brought him here? Nice! How's it going?'

'We just had our first row.'

Fitz giggles. 'You like him, I can tell. That body you're wearing is Maison Margiela, isn't it? Sample sale?'

'It is, but I'm not sure about him. He's so twitchy.'

'No, *you* are because you're not drinking.'

'Fuck, it's a dull existence. But I'm going to try…' I flick his arm. 'All that training I've had hanging out with someone as dreary as you for years has got to help, right? I'll see you downstairs.'

But when I get to the kitchen, there is no sign of Jared. The room is full of guests using the hard surfaces and precision lighting to divide and consume Class A substances, whilst the catering staff carry on around them—non-plussed—shaking cocktails, swirling spirits and mixers and popping corks on champagne bottles. I do a shot of tequila, then another and grab a can of 7-Up. Swigging it, I return to the dance floor, walk round and through it twice. Still no sign of Jared. I check the loo on both landings. He's not in there either. So, I jog up the stairs past the lounge to the top of the penthouse and find myself in the master suite.

In the centre of the room—on a black suede plinth—is a circular bed. Behind it is a canvas of the triple-headed dog, Cerberus, gnashing his (three sets of) teeth at the gateway to hell. On the ceiling above is a round gold-edged mirror. At either side of the bed are black gloss columns containing sprayed black lilies. The black velvet bed spread is embossed in gold with the Lazare logo. I reckon it would be safe to assume that underneath this counterpane there is unlikely to be a matching Orla Kiely pillow and duvet set. I see a door—not quite shut—at the edge of the room.

'*Jared?* Are you in there?'

I throw my bag on the bed and approach the door. I nudge it. It swings open to reveal an entirely mirrored en suite bathroom. A girl is lying on the floor; legs tucked up neatly, knees held in position by her hands. She is rocking back and forth making a gravelly humming noise. As she hums she clicks the heels of her shoes. They are monochrome, patent *brogues*. I know exactly who they belong to.

'*Noelle?* Noelle?'

'Mmmm…' she mumbles

But she does not stop rocking or look at me. Her eyes are glazed over, her eyelids flickering.

'Noelle!' I tap her on the knee. 'What are you doing?'

'Singing…'

'I can see that, I meant…what have you taken? You're on something.'

She bursts out laughing. 'I am not! I am Noelle Bamford. I'm high on life, I mean, like have you *seen* my life? Anyone would be high on like that shizzle, yeah. Read my book and see…it's HASHTAG ON FLEEK!' She pauses to make a gleeful gurgling sound. 'Oooooh, actually. Maybe I have taken a little *some*thing. But don't tell my squillion Insta followers. Or Diddoo! Or my sister. Deffo not my sister. She thinks drugs are for losers. But I know they're for winners! I'm winning. Noelle is a winner. She is. Are you? Are you winning?'

I almost laugh. 'No…not recently,' I tell her. 'Listen, you ought to sit up. The rocking is not a good idea, you'll make yourself sick.'

'Good!' she says.

'Don't give me attitude.' I put down my drink and lift her head off the ground. 'Let your legs go, Noelle. Sit. *Sit!*'

She slaps her hands down and pushes herself into a sitting position. The effort makes her head loll. I catch her as she slumps to the side. Her skin is hot and damp with sweat. I drag her to the side of the bath, plonk her against it, blast a towel with cold water, wring it out and dab her forehead with it.

'Sip this…' I pass her the can.

'What is it?'

'Lemonade.'

'Diet?'

'No. Drink it. You need the sugar.'

Her eyes become a little more focused. 'That's totally not HASHTAG thinspo.'

'Drink it. Now, try to concentrate. Do you know where you are and who I am?'

'I am at Frédéric's house and you…you…you are…' Her pupils dilate from kumquats to mangoes. 'You're like, that like BITCH from *C-c-c-atwalk*.'

'…and the penny drops,' I mutter. 'Narrowly missing the single brain cell. Excellent. We're getting somewhere.'

'You think you're soooo like, smart, don't you? Well, look whose earning more doing a personal appearance on the FROW than you do in three months. Er, meeeee! I suppose you're going write about this in your like, shitty magazine and make me look like a like, *tit*.'

'As if I would do that. We've had more than enough of you in recent shitty issues and unfortunately, due to some unfathomable decisions by my Editor, we have more of you planned in future shitty issues. You don't need me. As your career develops I'm sure you'll make yourself look like even more of a tit all by yourself. Now, *drink*.'

She drains my can of 7-Up and smashes it on the ground.

'Right, let's go. It's time for me to *like*, get out there and be Noelle: television presenter, model, DJ, style icon and author, *don't forget author*. This is my party…my people need me.'

'They don't. But what you need is to rehydrate, eat something, stop talking about yourself in the third person, have a shower, then sleep off whatever it is you've taken. And that means you're going home.'

She grabs my arm. 'I don't have a home. Not here, not anywhere…'

I smile at her. 'Leave it out, Noelle, the woe-is-me routine doesn't really wash after banking your first million qui—'

'He said I was fake,' she interrupts me. 'A made up person, lacking in auth-…auth-…authent-…depth.'

'Who did?'

'Troy. Tonight, He was here. I thought he had dumped that *dumpy* girlfriend, but he said they were even closer, that they had found a connection. She feels stuff, apparently, and wants to talk…about like, all the stuff. Constantly.'

'She'll be a fucking nightmare to live with, *trust* me,' I find myself reassuring her.

'…and *then* he said that, *I*, like, lacked a certain level of profund-profundacious-ness.'

'Profundity?' Now, I do laugh. 'That's rich. Troy from Barbed Wire doesn't exactly strike me as one of life's great thinkers. A great *wank*er, yes, but *think*—'

She interrupts again. 'That's why he left me. He said I wasn't real. That I wouldn't know how to be. But like, how could anyone be real if they were me? Noelle is not real. I wish she could be. I look at her Insta and think, I'd love to be that girl. She's like, *liked*. That's who Troy liked. The girl who gets the 'Likes'. The girl who thinks she deserves the 'Likes' because she likes herself. But then he realised that wasn't the real me. He had a realisation. Oh, my God…the word R E A L I S E. I never thought of that…when you realise something, you find out what is REAL. That's like, cool.'

'Yeah, I s'pose it is.' I clear my throat, unsure of what to add. 'Listen, Noelle. We should leave in case you come up on anything else.'

She stares at herself in the mirrored tiles on the floor. 'You know who the mostest realist person in the whole world is? My sister. Everything about her is real. Real friends. Real job. Real opinions. Real worries. Real boyfriend.' Her eyes flicker. 'I can see him in my mind now. Or did I actually see him? I'm not sure. Probably tripping.' She shrugs. 'But I saw Troy. Troy was here. It was Troy. Troy told me…you're not real, Noelle.'

'Let's not forget his real name is Eric.'

'Haaaaa!' She laughs briefly and manically. 'I'm scared though…of being real. The moment I get real is the moment it's over. *I* am over. Noelle is finished. No one wants the real me. And when she's gone, where do *I* start? How hard is it to begin again?' She grabs her Hello Kitty phone from her bag. 'Let's film a video for Insta…of me…being REAL. Let's show my fans who I really am…the "me" my book left out!' She starts filming herself. 'Hey, like, everyone, you may have read *This Is Me*, but *this* is me…call it the director's cut. No, the director is *half* cut. Haaaaa!' Her head lolls to the other side and her eyes glaze over.

'Okay, Noelle. Put down your mobile and look at me.' She looks *through* me. 'I'll be back in five minutes. Don't move. Stay seated and breathe deeply; in through the nose and out through the mouth…' I demonstrate inhaling and exhaling. 'I'll call a cab and take you to my place.'

'Who are you? Who *are* YOU? Who are *you* to take me anywhere? You're no one. Well, soon…' Suddenly her eyes are more focused. '…it'll be up to Frédéric to decide who *you* are. I wonder if he'll even keep your shitty column? You get me, sistaaaaaaaaa?'

'What are you talking about, Noelle?'

'He's like, skint to da MAX! Not a bowl to piss in.'

'*Pot*, and who is? Frédéric?'

'As if! He owns a squillion pound congl-…conglom- company. I mean Rhuarrr-Rhuarrrr-Rhuarrrrrrrrrridh… whatevz his name is. The posho who owns your precious rag. He's selling it. Byeeeee! Ugh. My head.'

She says this with clarity. But then she slumps to the floor. A globule of dribble tips over her lips and runs down her chin. I am about to mop it up with some loo roll when a spurt of thick and brown vile-smelling liquid pours out of her mouth. Then her body judders and she projectile vomits all over me. But I don't retch. I got used to the sound and smell of an adult expelling toxins a long time ago.

But this isn't just booze. Suddenly, Noelle's entire body goes floppy. I hear a noise behind me. I twist round. It's Frédéric.

'Thank fuck! Look! It's Noelle. She needs medical help,' I tell him. 'I don't know what she's taken. Do *you* have any idea? Call an ambulance and I'll put her into the recovery position. I know what to do. I've done it before.'

He presses a stubby, ringed finger to his lips. '*Arrête! Arrête!* Ssssshhhhh…you, how you say? Make the mountain from the mole. Naughty *bébé, elle adore les drogues un peu trop*. She okay.'

'She not okay!' I screech. 'Call an ambulance. Or I will. My bag is on the bed. Pass it to me.'

'*Vous ne comprendez pas,*' he snaps. Sweat prickles along his (artificial) hairline. '*Ma maison, mes reglès*. My house, my rules. We have party not paramedic! No siren. No wee-wah wee-wah wee-wah!' He waves a zip lock bag of white powder at me. 'Let her have some of Papa's coca…*c'est le meilleur*. Strong enough to wake *les morts dans la morgue*!'

'Christ, you're serious aren't you?'

'Everyone bloody relax…' A woman's voice from behind him. It's Sophie Carnegie-Hunt. 'I'm not having Noo-Noo go to hospital in that bloody state,' she says. 'It's too public. I'll organise an amaaaaazing private doc, I know. Discreet. Does all the VIP ODs. In the meantime, a glass of Coke should do the trick.'

I glance down at Noelle. Her face is becoming almost translucent. As I watch, her lips turn a spectral white-blue. My body momentarily freezes with panic, but then I see her phone on the mirrored floor. I grab it, jump up, dragging Noelle with me with one hand, with the other I push Frédéric backwards out of the bathroom. Then I kick the door shut, lock it and call 999.

Fourteen

TANYA

And *maybe that is the reason. Karma. What goes around comes around. The law of moral causation…*

I am sat on the bed in the hotel room. I have been in the same position all afternoon and all evening. Now it is 01:49. I am staring blankly at the feature wall the other side of the room. It is covered with a flock wallpaper which is decorated in alternating swirls of ivory and grey. The longer I have looked at it, the more images I can see *in* the wallpaper. Right now I am seeing faces. My face. Greg's face. 'Her' face. Whoever she is. Every time I 'see' her face, it winds me so hard I don't have the strength to get angry. Because that is what I'm meant to do, isn't it? *Get angry.* I should be on the attack; changing the security code at our house, having his belongings removed, cancelling joint future engagements, plotting some sort of social humiliation…at the very least, I should be slating him to my friends.

But all of the above would make it public, and there-fore—real. Even the most discreet locksmith or removals man would give me a 'seen it all before' nod when he arrived and a 'you deserve better' sigh on departure. If an affair becomes public, you will *never* be able to control it. And what

I obviously mean by that is *get back together*. Because right now, that's what I want. I think I could have the strength to mend our relationship—I will find it from somewhere—but I know that I would not have the strength to start again with someone else.

I get my ring from my bag and put it back on my finger. Then I flop back on the bed and close my eyes. It was tiring finding Greg. It is tiring for any woman to find their 'Greg'.

The 'sensible' first dates at a decent chain restaurant. The cocktail to start—something sugary (you need a boost as you didn't have lunch), the 'you choose no *you* choose' playful spat over the wine list (final decision: third one down), the post starter 'do you mind if I have a sneaky cigarette?', the 'no, go ahead!' lie which follows, the unfinished main which you'd demolish with an extra pot of mayo if girlfriends were at the table, the shared pudding (gooey but no pastry), the insistence on splitting the bill because you don't want to be one of *those* girls, the ironic second date at the zoo, the escalation of texting, Whatsapping, DM-ing, the first picture on Instagram, the official Facebook status change, the introduction to the 'mates'—including at least one suspiciously in-your-face female, the meeting of overly dominant mothers and faintly inappropriate fathers, the unsavoury but unavoidable firsts; first poo, first fart, first bat in the cave, first light spat, first deeply affecting row…the routine falling into place, the two nights at yours, the two nights at mine…but most exhausting of all, the first morning you wake up and realise that this is not the man you want to have a baby with.

My mobile rings. I take a breath and peek out at the caller ID, praying it will simply say 'T'. But it doesn't. Reluctantly, I press RECEIVE.

'Noelle! It's nearly two o'clock in the morning, for God's

sake.' I tell her. 'You have got to stop ringing me when you're off your head and th—'

'*This is not Noelle.*' A woman's voice. '*I found your number in her phone under* SISTA.' She spells it out. '*Are you her actual sist—*'

'Yes, I am her sister. Who are you? Why have you got her phone?'

'*She collapsed at a part—*'

'What? Can I speak to her?'

'*We're at Chelsea and Westminster Hospital Accident and Emergency. She seems okay. Doctor is running some tests. Can you get here?*'

'Yes, yes…I'm in London. I'll leave now. Who are y—?'

'*Good…*' She interrupts and hangs up.

*

A doctor pulls back the curtain. Noelle is lying—her upper body slightly elevated—on a trolley bed. Her chest is covered with a series of white pads. Each pad has a lead which is attached to a computer. A ream of paper decorated with graph-type patterns is spouting out the bottom of it. Noelle is lying motionless, staring ahead. She is pasty, clearly woozy, definitely sulking, massively indignant…but, thankfully, alive.

'Noelle? It's me.'

'You shouldn't have come, hon-eeey,' she mumbles, turning her face into the pillow. 'I told that woman not to call you. She tricked me. Got the code. Where's my Hello Kitty phone? I need to check my Insta and call Sophs.'

I ignore her and turn to the doctor. 'Could you explain what that machine is doing, please?'

'It's an ECG…electro cardiogram. It records the electrical activity of the heart, specifically the tiny electrical impulses which spread through the heart's muscle which make it contract. We're also checking her bloods too to make sure that N—'

'Noelle isn't a junkie?' suggests my sister, the pillow muffling her voice. 'Well, let's face it, yeah. I didn't like, come here because I'd OD-ed on Tangfastic Haribo, did I? Whevz. T'ink what you want, but I've got everyt'ing like, under control.'

The doctor—who is probably about the same age as my sister—gives me a smile, presumably thinking Noelle is putting on a stupid 'street' accent because she is light-headed and not quite sure what she is saying.

'There is no judgement here,' the doctor tells her, as she tears the most recent sheets of paper from the machine. 'We only want to make sure that you leave here healthy and will continue to be. As you can't provide us with an exact description of the toxins you have taken these tests are essential. That said, given you are awake, reactive and able to speak semi-coherently, I can't imagine we'll find anything too problematic. I know it all seems a bit scary…'

'I'm not scared,' snaps Noelle, pupils dilated.

'Don't be so rude,' I snap back at her. 'The doctor is helping you.'

'But what if someone in this place, like, sells their story?'

The doctor does not look offended. 'I can assure you that the entire medical staff in this hospital have the highest regard for patient privacy and confidentiality.'…*more confused.* 'But erm…sorry to ask…*should* I know you?'

'Oh, no.' I reply, quickly. 'She must be hallucinating.'

'Ah, okay. I'll be back soon with the bloods.'

As the doctor leaves the cubicle, Noelle emits an anguished whimper.

'Please,' I face her. 'Tell me you're not upset because the doctor didn't recognise you?' I sit down on the side of the bed. 'Look, your rise to fame probably coincided with her medical education. I imagine that focusing on qualifying in a highly demanding career in which she would dedicate her life to helping others might have distracted her from catching up on *Check Me Out, Sista!* via series link.'

Noelle glares at me out of one eye. 'You couldn't *wait* to tell her that I wasn't famous, though, could you?'

'I did that to protect your privacy! For God's sake, Noelle, let's not argue. You need to rest. This…' I wave my hand at the medical equipment. '…is your body's way of telling you enough is enough. I knew things were getting out of hand, but I had no idea of the extent.'

'Bet you can't wait to tell them,' she snaps. 'Especially *him*.'

'Who?'

'Mum and Diddoo. You've been waiting for a like, *drama—not* starring you—to happen for *years*. I don't blame you though, honeeeeey. I would probably be the same way if *I* was *my* sister…I'd be like, jealous.'

I almost laugh. 'Mmm…as you can imagine, what with you currently lying in a hospital bed attached to specialist machinery after a suspected drugs-related lapse into unconsciousness, the one overriding emotion I am feeling towards you right now is jealousy. And as for telling Mum and Dad, now you are being even *more* ridiculous. Of course I won't.'

'You won't?' She snorts. It is loud, phlegm-y and appears to shift something in her throat. 'Ugh, that was like, gross. You erm…promise?'

'Yes, I promise.'

She pauses for a few seconds. 'Thanks.'

We are silent for a bit as I watch the paper churning out of the ECG machine.

'Well, at least we now know you do still have one.' I say, watching the ink zigzagging up and down in time with the ventricular activity.

'Have a what?' mutters Noelle.

'A heart.'

My sister manages another—less huffy—snort at my joke as the curtain is drawn back again. I twist round. To see…*her*.

She is wearing an authentically battered, stonewashed and ripped denim jacket over a black top and skintight suede trousers. Gold shoe boots on her feet. She is holding a plastic vending machine cup filled with tea, taking care not to spill it.

'There are some *great* random looks out there,' she says. 'I actually prefer an "I grabbed the first thing I saw" style to a heavily pre-meditated "outfit". Victoria Beckham would look so much better if she got dressed pretending she was hotfooting it to A&E at one clock in the morning. Crimes Against Fashion Numb—' She looks up, sees me, gives me her emotionless, impenetrable stare…

…then laughs. Ashley Atwal is laughing at me. She would do this to other people at school and instantly, she had the power. No matter what was fired at her, she was bulletproof. Suddenly, the anger I should have been feeling earlier starts coursing through me. Noelle looks from me to Ashley and back again, her focus all googly.

'How do you two know each oth—?'

'It doesn't matter.' I interrupt her. 'What drugs were you taking, Ashley? The doctors need to know.'

Ashley ignores me and looks down at Noelle. 'Wow, WOW! This is too fucking much! No wonder you changed your name. *You* are little Nelly Dinsdale. Although, Tanya didn't call you that, did you?' She sniffs at me. 'She used to call you "Tiff", after the lead character in *Bride of Chucky*. Did you know that? Your sister used to joke that you were exactly like the maniac murdering doll, except more stressful to live with on a daily basis. Ha!'

'Shut up. Shut *up*, Ashley…' I seethe.

She ignores me again. 'I often wondered what became of Tanya's bratty sister who always got what she wanted and was never told "no". And here you are…overdosing. There must be a lesson for us all to learn there.'

Noelle shakes her head at Ashley. 'H-h-how do you know me? *Us?*'

'I lived on the same estate as you when you were little. You met me a few times but not many, as I wasn't welcome over at your place. On the other hand, Tanya was *always* welcome in our flat. And she took great pleasure in accepting any invitation. She was like one of the family.' She spits these last three syllables. 'I'm sure your own family have told you how…well, *cosy*, your sister made herself in my home. The Atwal home.'

Noelle gasps. She tries to sit up but is prevented by the leads attached to her chest. Her eyes dart back and forth between Ashley and me again, then rest on me. She sinks back into her pillow, and is quiet.

'Putting two and two together now, are we, Nelly?' asks Ashley. 'For you, I bet that would almost register as a brain teaser.'

'Ashley…' I step up to her. She turns to me, non-plussed. 'I am warning you. You do not want me to get angrier than I am already. And right now, I am seething. There is nothing you can say which will hurt me. I am immune to your poison…but believe me, I could tell you things that you do not want to hear. Now, relay what the medical staff need to know and leave.'

'Oh, please,' she replies. 'You think I've withheld information because I don't want to get "done" myself? Look, *Tanya*…it was a *fashion* party. I don't know what the drip- dry "knees-ups" you probably frequent are like, but the spread wasn't exactly going to be limited to some prawn vol-au-vents and some chicken tikka on sticks. I've already told the doctor there would have been the *usual* stuff available. Cocaine, ecstasy, mephedrone, GHB, ketamine, MDMA, skunk, poppers, liquid valium, possibly speed, but I doubt it…and I think a few people had taken LSD,' she adds. 'Right, I'm out of here. A little advice, Tanya. Your hair is much better tonight. Less *contained*. But please, wear less black. It's draining and a bit "meh", unless you style it *specifically*. It's the only colour that always requires a "look", otherwise you're a…smudge.'

She smirks. Directly at me. I square up to her, fury swelling and surging through me. I am ready to attack.

'Why don't you take your patronising advice and stick it up your hobgoblin backside. I'm not interested.' I scowl at her, then smirk too. 'In fact, I am not interested in anything you have to say. Is anyone? I haven't bothered with your column in *years*. I wouldn't be surprised if it is the least read page in *Catwalk*. No, make that *in the industry*. Mindless, vapid, random, precocious, badly executed, throw-away drivel of no consequence. You think you have a reputation and your writing has respect? That you have the sophistication of Emmanuelle Alt? The wit of Hadley Freeman? The bite of Bryan Boy? The authority of Suzy Menkes? The flamboyance of André Leon Talley? The quirk of Taylor Tomasi Hill? The boundary pushing of Katie Grand? The laid-back cool of

Leandra Medine? The reach of Susie Lau? The resonance of Robin Givhan?' With each name I spit, Ashley's eyes narrow. 'And as for your obsession with Carine Roitfeld, I can bet my house she has NO IDEA WHO YOU ARE!'

The curtain is yanked back again. The doctor comes in.

'Ladies, *please*! You are surrounded by sick patients… keep your voices *down*.' She goes over to Noelle and starts removing the patches from her chest. 'Your ECG results have come back fine. Bloods are too. I imagine your blood pressure is still a little over what it should be, but given what I and the rest of the ward—or rather, London—have just heard I would wager all of you…' She glances at Ashley and me. '…would get an above normal reading. I can discharge you now, Noelle. However, I do not want you to be on your own for the next forty-eight hours and during that period I want you to rest in bed. No alcohol. No drugs; over the counter or otherwise. You can shower—with assistance—but no hot baths. Is there anything else you would like to ask me?'

'No.' This time Noelle looks directly at the doctor as she speaks. 'But I guess, I am like, sorry, you know. For being such a…'

'Tit,' Ashley offers.

Noelle shoots her a look.

The doctor sighs. 'Like I said, I don't judge so no need for you to apologise…or self-flagellate. We can cure a lot of things, but as yet, we still have no medicine to alleviate wallowing. However, Noelle, I do have some groups I want to put you in touch with so this incident does not repeat itself.'

She folds her arms. 'I don't need help from someone I don't know or who doesn't know m—'

I interrupt. 'That would be much appreciated. And also thank you, for looking after my sister, doctor.'

'It's not really me who you should thank.' She nods at Ashley. 'Your *friend*…' She gives this word an awkward inflection as if it is (quite correctly) up for debate. '…here, stopped Noelle from choking on her own vomit, cleared her airways then put her in the recovery position, which thankfully encouraged her to release whatever else her system needed to. The paramedics didn't have to do much after that. Anyway, a porter will be in with your clothes, then we can get you discharged.'

As the doctor leaves, I turn to Ashley, my face twisting. Ninety-nine per cent of me still consumed with resentment. One per cent accepting that she has done something…kind. She looks back at me, then opens up her jacket to reveal a black top with a *mulchy* looking pale patch covering most of it.

'And before you call this *just* a black top, it's a leather panelled stretch jersey body suit by Maison Margiela. *This* season.' She tuts at Noelle, who is tapping her Hello Kitty phone. 'Put it this way, I was wrong about one thing. Turns out that some of the meals your sister posts on social media *do* end up in her stomach.'

Suddenly, Noelle screams.

'Oh, please, like, God, *no*…' She is reading a text on her phone. 'No! They'll get one of those vac-vac-vacu-brain-dead YouTubers who talk about their own lives all day. They will, I know they will,' she rambles. She clasps her head in her hands. 'I've lost. Lost to some med-med-medioc-boring teenager with her like, shitty skin and like, shitty wardrobe and like, shitty friends. What was the point? Everything I've worked for. *Gone. GONE!*'

I grab the Hello Kitty mobile…on the screen there is a text message from SOPHS.

You're collapse is all over the Internet. You don't need this. Call me ASAP.

I press Contact. Noelle makes a feeble attempt to snatch back her phone but she is too weak. My call to Sophie Carnegie-Hunt is picked up on the first ring. I tap the speaker phone facility.

'*Noo-noo!*'

'No, it's not 'Noo-noo', *Sophs*. It's her sister, Tanya. I'm here with Noelle and I'm calling to let you know there is one other thing *way* more toxic than a drugs overdose that Noelle doesn't need…and that's you.'

She laughs. '*That's a very basic attitude. You're over-reacting.*'

'And you're fired.' I am about to cancel the call. 'Oh, and that's spelt Y-O-U-apostrophe-R-E. The "your" in "your collapse" on the other hand, is spelt Y-O-U-R. *Very basic* spelling and grammar.' I hang up.

'What did you do that for?' moans Noelle. 'Where am I meant to go now? Sophs would have looked after me.'

Ashley interjects. 'Not that I care, but this may be the appropriate time to tell you that your agent witnessed you going blue and told me to give you a glass of Coke.'

'Then I'll call Frédéric,' says Noelle. 'He'll help.'

'Ah,' adds Ashley. 'He wanted you to do a *line* of coke, and at that point you were barely breathing.'

'He wouldn't do that. We're about to launch the "Noelle"clutch.' She stares at me. Her eyes are dry and matt. 'Where am I supposed to go? My hotel will be crawling with press. Any other hotel would leak my arrival. I can't go back to Mum and Diddoo's, it's where I did *Cribs*. Honey!' She taps my arm. 'You'll have to drive me back to your house.'

'My house? We can't…'

'Why not?'

'We can't…because…' *Greg will be there. He has cheated on me. He is cheating on me. Don't make the discovery public.* I stare at the floor. '…I haven't got the car, you know I hate driving. I came on the train.'

Ashley rolls her eyes at us both.

'Oh, for fuck's sake, the pair of you, stop being so dramatic. Come home with me.'

'Why?' I ask. 'Why would *you* do that f—'

Noelle interrupts me. 'I don't want to go back to *her* place.'

'In that case, given there are *no* other options,' Ashley points out, 'it looks as if you'll be doing something you don't want to do. Can you remember the last time that happened?'

I stop myself from looking even vaguely amused.

'As long as I can charge my phone?' says Noelle, bolshily.

'Yes, just stay away from my wardrobe,' continues Ashley, as she leaves the cubicle. '*Both of you.* I can't handle any more soiled designer tops.'

*

Noelle refuses all of the literature and helpline numbers which the doctor considered appropriate and is discharged. As soon as we get in the taxi, she falls asleep, her head resting on my shoulder. She looks shrivelled. *Sapped.* Even her skull seems shrunken. When we were kids, she used to love car journeys. It didn't matter to her where we were going because being in a moving vehicle meant one thing: liquorice and a captive audience. She liked to role play a scenario where a family were off on holiday; with (only) her taking on the parts of the father, mother, children and any extended relatives. 'A regular little Eddie Murphy, isn't she?' Dad would say proudly, as I stared down at the protective matt on the car floor counting the rubber ridges—there were thirty seven—over and over again. Inevitably, the multiple roles would take it out of Noelle and she'd flop across the back seat, her gangly limbs digging into me.

Neither Ashley or I speak on the journey to her home. We have the excuse that we don't want to wake up my sister. When we arrive, Ashley shows her where the shower is and slaps a pair of jogging bottoms, a sweatshirt, towel, bottle of water and a half-eaten bag of strawberry boot laces on the bed. Her home is not what I expected. For a start it is a small flat. I assumed that she and her husband would live in a house, and that it would have been architecturally designed with clean lines and a minimal interior with lots of 'things' (that don't have much function except to look stylish but only to those who know what *is* stylish) placed at exacting angles. Instead, it is cosy and cluttered, everywhere except the walk-in wardrobe which is precisely ordered. The only randomly placed piece of clothing in the entire flat was a bra lying in the hallway, which Ashley grabbed off the floor as soon as we came in.

'I've got the kettle on,' she calls, brusquely, as I tuck Noelle into bed. She is snoring softly. 'Do you want anything?'

I touch my sister's forehead to check it is not too warm, then go into the kitchen. Ashley is leaning against the counter eating the rest of the laces as she waits for the kettle to boil. She has got changed too, into an all-in-one. But it isn't a fashionably ironic 'onesie', it's a fleece-y blanket style overall. The sort you would see advertised in the back of the Sunday supplements alongside other specialist advertising (like knee supports for weeding herbaceous borders) for a more mature audience. But she makes it look cool. Of *course* she does.

'What are you staring at? It's a Snuggle Suit,' she explains. 'The most comfortable leisure garment ever created. In man-made fibres. In Taiwan. Anyway, tea?'

'Coffee, please…'

Ashley wrinkles up her nose. 'As if I'd have that muck in my home.'

'So, you found a husband who doesn't drink it either, then? You said you would.'

She doesn't say anything. I wonder if she is remembering one of the afternoons we spent planning Our Future. Never simply *the* future. It was ours. As soon as we became friends, we used to do this at least once a week. We'd sit on Ashley's bed with notepads, writing endless lists of what we wanted to achieve and by what age. After each session we thought we had it all *sussed*. Then the next week pretty much all our plans would change. But one day during our first Christmas holidays together, everything fell into place. And we shook on it.

HER: Look at this! (Brandishing the first issue of Catwalk *at me.) It's new. My mum got it. No one at school will have even heard of it, I guarantee. This is it, Tanya…this is what I am going to do with my life. (Solemnly.) This is fashion. These people know fashion. I've been reading the articles. When I'm older I will be a writer too and join them.*

ME: (Giggling. Flicking through.) Don't be silly. You're not one of them. It would be like me saying to you, "I'm going to become an international show jumper!' when I've only ever sat on a rocking horse.'

HER: Stop being so pessimistic… and posh. I know fashion.

ME: You customise your school uniform. To get a job like that you need to know people who work in that industry.

ME: I do! Mum does.

ME: Your mother sells clothes at the market in town, she's not an international designer like...erm...

HER: Duh! Ha! You don't know anyone, do you? Well, you'd better read Catwalk *VERY thoroughly, otherwise you'll never get a job there.*

ME: Me? Why would I want to work there?

HER: Duh! AGAIN! Because I will be. You didn't have a life before you met me, agreed? Exactly, so I'm not going to abandon you. And don't panic, by then I'll have completely sorted out your look. We'll work at Catwalk *together and share a house round the corner from the office.*

ME: In London? Do you realise how expensive it is there? My father says that the property market down there is moving at such a pace it could well be imposs—

HER: YAWN! Shoosh, Tanya, we'll have already saved up enough to get ourselves settled.

ME: How?

HER: By selling Mum's clothes on the stall, silly! By then, we'll know EVERYTHING there is to know about fashion, so we can tell her what to make in order to achieve maximum sales! I've already checked on the map for a good place for us to live in London. You know that famous shop where they do the big yellow shopping bags?

ME: Selfridges?

HER: We'll get a pad near there. It's not far from Catwalk and also mega useful...because that store sells everything we'll need. I went there once with Mum. We didn't buy any-thing but we had a good look around and she got one of the sales assistants to give me a bag for FREE! Anyway, they do clothes, food, electricals, homeware and they have a whole floor for mens stuff so we can get presents for our boyfriends' birthdays. Obviously, we'll have to meet them on the same night and start dating them at EXACTLY the same time, otherwise it might be awkward. They will need to be really into fashion...

ME: *...but not work in it.*

HER: *Agreed. And obviously, mine will only drink tea.*

ME: *But mine can drink coffee if he wants.*

HER: *Bleurgggggh. He'd have a furry tongue.*

ME: *I'd like someone slightly older.*

HER: *Furry tongue and bald. Yum!*

ME: *Not ancient! Just not like the boys in our year. They're so annoying and juvenile. I hate them.*

HER: *Is that because you are in love with me? (Laughing.)*

ME: *No. (Bopping her on the head with the magazine.) Idiot.*

HER: *(Nudging me.) Anyway, let's make a pact now... not to show* Catwalk *to anyone. We don't want other people thinking about wanting a job there too.*

ME: *Agreed. (Looking at her incredulously but excitedly.) You really think this is going to happen?*

HER: *Of course! Obviously, we need some experience, so we should start making fashion scrap books. In the meantime we should write to* Catwalk *and say we are both interested in positions after we leave school, that way they'll at least know we will be available.*

ME: *Well, it does sound like a solid plan. At the very least it's worth a go. (Pausing.) One question. How do you know we'll still be best friends by then? My dad says that at school you fall in and out of friendships so we could be with someone else by then.*

HER: *Duh! AGAAAAAIN! Who's the idiot, now? It's YOU and ME! (Holding out hand.)*

ME: *(Shaking it.) TRUE!*

She clears her throat.

'I'll make us both tea,' she says, her voice staccato. 'So, let's cut to the chase. There is a reason I asked you back. It's about the state I found your sister in. When I took the piss out of her at her launch, I didn't realise how out of control she was behind closed *bathroom* doors. She needs help. It's not about attention-seeking because she's doing it on her own. Do you know that?'

I shift from foot to foot, her concern making me uneasy.

'I do know that, but she won't listen to me. My opinion of Noelle's behaviour and where it could be heading does not interest her. I'm *way* down the list of those whose thoughts *do* count. That ridiculous agent is at the top, then that pervy designer, then her ex-boyfriend, other celebrities, Diddoo… and then come the TV producers, magazine editors, bloggers, nightclub managers, her 1.3 million Instagram followers… and Mum. Then me.'

Ashley selects two cups hanging from a mug tree—*she has a mug tree!*—by the sink, fills them with boiling water and plops a tea bag in each.

'That's not the impression Noelle gave me at the party,' she replies. 'She was rambling on about you being the only real person in her life.'

'If my sister said that she must have been completely nutted.'

'Maybe she's too scared and too proud of admitting to you she's fucked up…'

Ashley opens the fridge and reaches for a carton of milk. There is nothing else in there, bar a cloudy half-full bottle of white wine, and a couple of takeaway boxes. Clearly, she and her husband are one of those dynamic couples who are so busy with their careers and social life that they do not concern themselves with the minutiae of domestic life.

'...*is* fucking up,' she continues. 'Her team may be able to fix the problem superficially and *temporarily* with a damage limitation strategy, but it will still be there. And the longer it goes on, the worse it will get, the more mistakes she will make.'

'Why are you so interested in my sister's career?'

'I'm not,' she retorts. She pauses for a second as she adds milk to our drinks. 'Trust me, I would love nothing more than *never* having to write another word about "Brand Noelle". But Nelly needs to pack her trunk, say goodbye to the circus, then head to rehab. Look, Tanya, we are never going to see one another again after this. You know that, I know that. The only reason we bumped into one another after all these years is because of *your* sister. I am not retracting what I am saying about her being a moron, but she is *your* moron.'

I shift my footing again and scratch a non existent itch on my arm. 'Thank you for looking after her. You erm... you knew... I feel compelled to say it. 'You knew what to do because of all those times with your mum, didn't you?'

She says nothing as she passes me a mug of tea. I blow on it, then take a sip. We stare at each other. It is the first time I have allowed myself to properly examine her face since I saw her in the loo at The Rexingham. She has aged exactly as I thought she would. There are only a few tiny wrinkles around her eyes and a faint line in the middle of her brow. She is en route to ageing 'like Iman—the Somali fashion model, actress, entrepreneur and pioneer of ethnic cosmetics...' which was what she said would make her happy. I always said I would be happy getting older, if I was exactly that...

happy. Ashley would tut at me saying that going down the spiritual route was a cop out. As I remember this, I realise…

'You want to ask me why, don't you? Face to face…' I say. '*That* is why you told us to come back. It wasn't because of Noelle. You want answers.'

She shrugs. '…is that why you came back? To explain?'

I do not hestitate. 'No. I have nothing. I have nothing that I can tell you which won't sound as if I'm trying to make an excuse, or blaming someone else, or using hindsight or any of the other default methods that people employ in situations where they have made a mess that cannot be cleaned up. The last person I am going to try any of that with is you.'

Ashley stirs her tea and raises an eyebrow at me. 'Clever.'

'Why?'

'Sounds like *exactly* the sort of answer I would have formed.' She takes a gulp of tea. 'There is another reason… why I invited you back. It's been annoying the fuck out of me for *years*.' Although she is swearing at me, her voice is softer. 'How the hell did you get your work experience slot at *Catwalk*?'

I grimace at her. 'My father played in a charity golf tournament with Rhuardih Ogilvy.'

'Ha! I knew it would have been something like that. So, the rumours were true, then, about him making a shedload of money? Bet he couldn't wait to move out of the estate. He hated that place as much as I loved it.'

'You really did, didn't you?'

'Of course. It was the best training ground for me to join the industry I'm in now. Everyone knowing each other's business, gossiping and backstabbing de rigueur, relationships spiralling out of control with one misinterpreted word…that's fashion. So, how is "Diddoo"?'

I shrug. 'Well, you know how he used to be consumed by his social position and how others regarded him even if that meant that he didn't pay attention to the relationships that really matter?'

'Yes.'

'Well, he's the same…but richer.'

Ashley almost smiles as she leans back against the counter. 'His face when you had me over for tea the first week I met you. It was as if you'd pitched up for your fish fingers with a rattlesnake in a pillowcase. He would have much preferred you to be hanging out with one of the "nicer" middle-class girls from school…like Suze Lyons, that doctor's daughter. Remember her? Christ, butter wouldn't melt. Or rather Lurpak, in her case.'

'Actually, I, erm…see her a lot. She still lives back home… same village as my parents. She married a guy called Rollo, they have two children. Her husband is a barrister, Suze was training to be a legal secretary but got pregnant when we were at college and decided to stay at home to look after them.'

'My *God*…you hang out with Suze Lyons. Ugh.' She pulls a face. 'Well, that wasn't on our list, was it?'

I almost smile too, knowing she has remembered those afternoons.

'What do you do the rest of the time? For work, I mean. Or does Diddoo bankroll your undertaker's wardrobe?'

I ignore her sartorial dig. 'I work for a local firm writing copy for websites. Corporate stuff. And just to make you *really* jealous that I'm employed by a regional business-to-business set-up, I even have a boss who is a huge *Star Wars* fan. There is a poster of Yoda on the wall, saying, TO BE MAD YOU DON'T HAVE TO BE, BUT IT HELPS TO WORK HERE.'

Ashley doesn't bother laughing. 'So, how come you

know all those editors and writers you fired off at me in the hospital?'

'I write a blog.'

'Christ!' She rolls her eyes. 'You're a blogger?'

'Mmm…'

'Don't tell me you post pictures of pastel fairy cakes. Or anything pink. Or spongy. We have a girl called Jazz at *Catwalk* whose blog looks like she has the same dopamine response as a seven year old child.'

'No, mine is not that kind. It's a study of social media culture and how it effects all the major touchstones of how young women live today.'

'Get you…' She has a gulp of tea.

I shrug. 'Well, blogging *is* the future. Free information, pictures and thoughts written by people who are not constrained by advertising. Well, that is of course, if you are a *pure* blogger…'

'And you are?'

'Yep.'

'But then you don't earn money from it.'

'No, if I did that, I may as well be working for a magazine.' I half-smirk at her. 'The perfect magazine of the future will be almost like a blog. It will be interesting to see who fuses the two together and finds a place in the market where the content is wholly sincere but at the same time the product is making money. Less women are buying magazines because they are looking for real content elsewhere which allows unfettered images and unedited copy. Reliabil-…'

I pause, suddenly realising what I am doing. I am talking to Ashley how I always used to. We'd get on to a subject I had an opinion on and there was no stopping me. And she would let me continue. No, better that that, she would listen.

'Pfff! Who the fuck are you? The media oracle?'

I pursue my argument. 'Come on, you have to admit that the power of magazines is diminishing, Ashley. Not just yours. All of them. A lot of this has to do with accessibility; the Internet is free, at your fingertips and more varied. But personally, I feel women are now questioning what they are being told by these publications. They feel patronised.'

'Ex-*cuse* me?'

'All those endless articles on how important it is to feel confident and empowered. And to be sexy. No, REALLY-FUCKING-SEXY-ALL-THE-TIME. Since when? What's wrong with being slightly insecure, not too fussed about how much welly you have and getting your rocks off if and when the opportunity arises and you're not having a "bloated" day. Of course, the assumption is that the people who write those articles are already that way themselves. *Hurry up, readers! At least try to have a go at being as splendid as us. We know that it must be very hard. Especially as right now, you are sitting on a grotty bus flicking through the pages of our magazine, on your way to work at a uninspiring job where no one will EVER put you on the guest list for the launch of the new GHD tonging wand. Nor will you EVER be allowed to borrow some Tom Ford sunnies from the acces-sories cupboard for your freebie mini-break at a Mr and Mrs Smith boutique hotel in Northern Europe. Nor will you EVER be invited to the Skinny Bitch Collective, so you'll just have to watch Millie Mackintoshes sweating in hundred-quid wet-look Lycra leggings on Instagram.* And then…to bang on and on and on on Twitter about how exhausting this all is. What is? Sitting writing. Sitting in a features meeting. Sitting in an Uber en route to meetings and shows. No wonder half of them are on the Paleo and doing extreme Pilates on pulleys…if they didn't they'd be a size 16 with curvature of the spine. They don't even have to nip to Boots in their lunch hour to get essentials. They'll just ask the beauty editor what she's slinging out that week because she can't physically put any more cream on her own body without resembling a cross-Channel swimmer. A good blogger makes her readers feel included. She is authoritative without being smug… and will deliver something fresh over and above what they can find elsewhere on the internet. It's going to be tough for a magazine to do that on a monthly basis when a blog can update every minute.'

Ashley shrugs at me. 'Ah, another *classic* Tanya Tirade! And like all of the ones that you used to have, I'm pretty sure. No, I *guarantee*…you have *done* nothing and will *do* nothing about it.'

'God, why does everything always have to be about what you "do"? It is perfectly acceptable to have an opinion and simply "be", Ashley.'

She eyeballs me. 'Okay, so tell me. What would be on top of your list right now? What do you want to *be*, Tanya?'

A mother. Suddenly, I can feel my hands shaking. I place my mug on the counter, but the tea sloshes over the side as I make contact. Then the rest of my body judders. Like the early-warning signs of earth tremors that signify an oncoming tsunami, I know what is about to happen. My chin wobbles. My eyes well up.

'*Tanya?*'

I blink hard. 'What?'

'Are you about to fucking cry?'

I shake my head vigorously from side to side.

'Good. You know how I feel about that.' She eyes me suspiciously. 'Let's go in the other room.'

I nod, relieved for the moment to collect myself and follow her into lounge. Lounge being the operative word. All the furniture encourages slothing. A round leather pouffe the size of a whirlpool and a suede corner sofa covered in fur throws and tasselled woollen blankets fill up most of the space. I imagine Ashley and her no doubt equally (naturally) cool husband curled up in the couch together on a rare night in; a picture of chic upwardly mobile bliss.

I sit down on the sofa. On the coffee table in front of me there is a stubbed out cigarette lying in an ashtray.

'I thought you'd given up,' I mumble, pointing at it.

'I thought you'd given up reading my column.'

'Touché.' I find myself smiling. This time, at her.

She smiles back at me.

'I am sorry, Ashley.'

'I know.'

Fifteen

ASHLEY

I know because Tanya left me a letter.

She gave it to my mother, hoping that I would receive it. My mother did not pass it to me herself. I found it in the flat when I went home to the estate. It was my birthday. I was engaged. I wanted to ask if she would come to my wedding. There was no reply at the door so I let myself in with my old keys. The letter was not hidden. It was lying on a shelf in the kitchen with my name on it… in Tanya's handwriting. I was about to open it when Sheila arrived. She squirmed uncomfortably when she saw me, said she was getting 'a few bits for Yvonne'. I asked where she was. Receiving some treatment, apparently, but would be out in a few days. After that, she was moving to be with her new partner.

'*Would she like to see me?*'

Sheila paused, then looked away. I did not open the letter. I put it back on the shelf. So that when my mother returned she would have no idea I had visited.

*

I jump as my phone vibrates in the pocket of my Snuggle Suit. I check the caller ID. It's Zach. He must be out. His phone has gone off in his pocket as usual. No doubt, he and Keith With The Bad Teeth are quietly celebrating in a media hotspot. Keith has his arm looped over him and is offering up hackneyed platitudes. '*Couldn't be happier for you, mate. Yeah, yeah, I know it's not the best timing, but you can't plan these things. Que sera sera, innit, guvnor. And besides that, Rach is a tasty bit of poontang. The boy's done good.*' And Zach will roll his eyes at Keith's casual sexism but will also nod, because he is excited. He'll already be planning a move to a bigger flat, the purchase of a more suitable car, potential dates for paternity leave, just like he did with me. He could even use the same fucking checklist. I let the mobile ring out.

He rings again. I snatch the phone to my ear.

'Your phone keeps ringing me. Switch it off, n—'

'*Ash? I'm here.*'

'Oh. Right. What do you want?' I ask. No 'Hello'—which I guess, is how all non-amicably divorced partners end up answering the phone eventually. 'Do you know what time it is?'

'*I know it's late, but I...*'

Nodding to Tanya that I need to take the call, I go out into the corridor and shut the door.

'You *what*?' I hiss. 'If this is about the money then call my solicitor during normal working hours. Not *me*, in the middle of the night.'

'*Please, Ash...of course this isn't about money. I didn't know who to ring. No, no...that's the point. I did know who to ring. You...*'

'For Christ's sake, what's the matter?'

'*I have to talk to you.*'

'Me? Ha! What's Rachel doing? Is she not available for a cosy chit chat at...' I check my watch. '...four in the morning?'

'*She's on a hen weekend, but it's you I want to…well, it's you I need. I haven't told anyone, I can't tell anyone.*' He stops. '*It's Mum…*'

'What about her?' I realise saying 'what' a *lot* with a toddler-like petulance is an integral part of separation lingo. 'This had better be good. Because I am telling you now there isn't much you could say to me right n—'

'*She's got cancer.*'

I pause, staring at the mouthpiece of the phone. I know what I need to tell him. He needs to know that I am not the person he can expect anything from. Not sympathy, not kindness, not understanding. Legally, he is only allowed to expect money via direct debit. The rest he has no rights to. I take a breath.

'I'll see you in fifteen minutes.'

I throw some blankets and a spare Snuggle Suit at Tanya and tell her I will be back. When I get to Zach's flat, he opens the door before I get a chance to knock and grabs me. I rub his back. I don't need to see his face to know how exhausted he is, I can feel the strain in his body. He is wrapped around me, but there is no force in his hold. As if sensing that I know this, he tightens his grip. I don't know how long we are standing in the doorway but eventually I have to extract myself.

'Zach, I'm about to stop breathing,' I mumble. 'You need to release the pressure.'

'Sorry, sorry…' He steps back. 'I'm so sorry.'

'Shut up, put the kettle on. You remember how I like my tea, don't you?'

'I will die remembering how you like your tea, Ash.'

I go into his lounge and wait on the artfully battered and tattered leather Chesterfield sofa. The room is laid out the same way as when I last saw it, but with the addition of some boxes in the corner. Not random cardboard; branded storage company ones. On top of them are piles of neatly folded clothes. On the floor; a collection of women's shoes. I zone in on the worst offenders. Leopard print kitten heels—acceptable only if you are a government minister wanting to make an impact at your party's annual convention. UGGS—acceptable only for indoor use. ASIC trainers—acceptable only for running, *not* leisure activities across the board. Brown calf-length cowboy boots—acceptable (only just) in 2003 as clubwear with *bare* legs. High street copy Leboutin-esque nude high heel pumps—acceptable only at the *TV Quick* Awards. Without a doubt the top offender. I hope Kat Moss pees against one. Or even better, throws up a squidgy mouse intestine-infused fur ball *into* one.

Zach walks in, shuts the door and hands me a mug. I grip onto the handle to stop me making a barbed comment about Rachel *clearly* having moved in. He looks at me. I look at him.

'Were you going to ask if Rachel had moved in?'

'Nope.'

'Bollocks. I bet you were casting a critical eye over her footwear.' He gives me a very weak smile.

'Zach! Don't make me out to be some kind of obnoxious style fascist,' I reply sarcastically, but I don't smile back. 'Besides, I really don't give a shit about Rachel, and when I say that, what I mean is…I *really* do *not* give a *shit* about her.'

'About that. Listen, Ash, I…'

I hold up my hand. 'Don't. Anything that either of us have to say on that subject is pointless. Not to mention irrelevant, because that's not why I am here. Just tell me about Gwen,' I say.

He places his cup on the coffee table and sits down in the

velvet armchair opposite me. I examine him properly. His face is puffy. He rubs his eyes and takes a deep breath.

'She's got tumours in her ovaries and will need to be operated on,' he explains. 'The surgeons will try to remove what they can and then she'll have chemotherapy. They're hoping they won't find any cancerous cells in other parts of her body, but Dad is worried that because she didn't seek medical help until she was in pain, it may have already spread.'

'When is the operation?'

'Tomorrow.'

'Woah, that's fast.'

Zach sighs. 'The growths are prominent. So typical of Mum not have done anything about it until now. You know she can't "abide" hypochondriacs and feels that going to see your GP is a sign of weakness.'

I nod. 'I *do* know…remember that time she almost chopped off her finger with the gardening secateurs? She came in from outside, ran it under the tap then wrapped a kitchen cloth round it and cooked Sunday lunch. The cut was so deep that the top of the finger was actually flopping.'

'Yeah. Dad only persuaded her she needed stitches when she felt faint getting the date flan out of the Aga…and she still insisted on dropping off some slices to Tim and Barbara's en route to the hospital.'

'Did she purposefully ignore her symptoms this time, then?' I ask, drawing the conversation away from nostalgia.

'Sort of. But to be fair, apparently, ovarian cancer is not that easy to detect. She admitted to Dad her tummy had been feeling a little swollen, but had put it down to, I quote, 'a rather gaseous batch of kale…' she'd been growing in the garden. She only organised an appointment at the doctor after the swelling got so bad she couldn't button up a specific pair of trousers.'

'I bet they were those Herringbone ones she always wore. They were a bit snug. See? Who says fashion can't save lives, eh?' I sip my tea. '…and she will be saved, Zach. The doctors have clearly got a plan for h—'

'They have to save her,' he interrupts. 'She has to live, because she is my mum. I can't imagine a world in which she isn't here.' He stands up, his bottom lip is quivering. 'Sorry, I don't mean like that when your…'

'This isn't about me. I understand, Zach. Of course I do. Look, if there is anyone that is going to survive an up-against-it diagnosis it will be *your* mother. In fact, I bet she rebuilds herself post-surgery and comes back even stronger—smarter at bridge, faster at tennis, nippier in the John Lewis sales—like some kind of middle-class Transformer.'

'But what if she doesn't? I can't…I just can't…'

He walks out of the room. I hear him go into his bedroom. I stay seated, because I know he is going to cry and will want to be on his own. He cried three times during our marriage. Happy tears twice and one sad lot. All were directly caused by me, and on each occasion after he had released them privately, it was me who comforted him. After a couple of minutes, I creep down the corridor and press my ear to the door. He has stopped. I knock gently and go in. He is lying on the bed with a pillow over his face. I remove it and he smiles at me gratefully.

'Thanks for coming over here so quickly. You would have been quite within your rights to hang up on me.'

'Swear at you, and *then* hang up.'

'So why didn't you?'

I shrug. 'Because it takes less energy to be nice, I suppose.

I do not have the reserves for any more anger. I'm done. I don't even think I could get angry if I tried.'

He takes my hand. 'Listen, Ash, about the flat. *Your* flat…'

'Enough. Merely watching your mouth form the opening "fl" of the word "flat" makes me want to punch it.'

He rubs his eyes. 'I understand that, but given the circumstances—everything that I have put you through…I only want you to start paying me *when you can*. If you can't start immediately, then we'll work out a schedule for next year.'

'You mean that?'

He nods and stares up at me through painfully bloodshot eyes.

'When was the last time you slept, Zach?'

'Thursday night. I found out on Friday about Mum. I can't sleep.'

'Well, walking around like a zombie and being over-emotional is not going to help the situation, is it? To support your parents properly, you need to look after yourself. I don't want to see you like this.'

He sits up. 'You *always* look beautiful, Ash.'

'Zach!'

'It's true. I knew that you would from the moment you sat down next to me in that bar—I can picture you now—even though you were in a *vile* mood.'

'Seriously…enough.' Suddenly, I feel tired too. My temples feel as if they are being nudged together in a vice. 'You're tripping on lack of sleep. Concentrate on the times I was in a huff and looked ugly. Like that night Keith was round at ours and got so drunk he decided to wee in the kitchen sink. Fuck, I could have killed him…'

'…but instead you dumped the litter tray over his head.' Zach laughs. 'You know that was the turning point for his decision to go to rehab? I guess when you wake up with a woodchip-studded cat turd in the hood of your sweatshirt there really is only one place to go. Very funny, though.'

'Even your mum found that amusing. Our hatred of Keith With The Bad Teeth was the only thing we had in common. You know *she* made up that name for him? She didn't think he was good enough for you either.'

Zach sighs. 'I'm sorry she made things difficult for you.'

'So am I,' I agree. 'I still can't figure out if—when we first met—she intended to give me some sort of chance but I simply didn't live up to her standards on any front. Or that she was always going to take issue with me no matter what I did or said because of my background…that I wasn't from "decent stock".'

'God, I can't believe she actually used those words. More to the point, I can't believe you heard her *say* those words.'

'You had her on speaker phone.' I nudge him. 'I bet Rachel is from "decent stock"…a nice home counties girl, I imagine. She *is* from the home counties, isn't she? Kent? Surrey? Sussex?'

He nudges me back. 'Surrey, but she's only based there half the week. The rest of the time she's…erm…here. So, yeah, she *has* moved in.'

'…and I *was* assessing her footwear. And *yes*, very much in a critical way.'

He flops back on the bed and stares up at me. 'I meant that, you know. You're beautiful. I'll always think that. Actually, it worries me that I will always think that.'

I stare back at him. 'But there is no point saying it, Zach. Why? Because it doesn't matter what we *think* any more, as that has no bearing on what is actually happening, in *real* life. What goes on in our heads is redundant. The time when we should have said what we were thinking is gone.' I shake my head. 'You used it. I didn't.'

'So, what would you have said?'

I shrug. 'I still don't know how I would have worded it, because I would never have wanted to hurt you.'

'How would you have hurt me? You weren't just my other half…you were half of *me*. I would have understood anything.'

Except the truth. I look out the window. It's getting lighter but there is no sunshine. It's going to be another rainy day. As the first drops of water plop against the glass, I realise there is one thing I can do, which *is* true and which won't hurt him. I can do what Tanya did and apologise.

'Zach, I am sorry. I'm sorry you are here in front of me right now as half the person you used to be. I'm sorry I have cut your life in half. I'm sorry that you let me be half of you. I'm sorry.'

We look at each other and without either of us saying anything else, we lie down next to each other on the bed. Our hands shoulders, arms, hips, thighs and feet are touching. The last time our bodies were as close as this was the night 'it was decided'. Zach didn't leave immediately. We slept in our bed together one last time. When he turned out the light I remember thinking there was no way I would be able to sleep, but I did. I know why. It was because I thought—no, I *knew*—there would be another time, *because he would come back*. So, when I woke up in the morning, I didn't regret not trying to stay awake. I rolled over and asked Zach how he had slept. He said he hadn't. Not a wink. All night. It was *him* that knew, not *me*.

But now he is asleep. And soon, as I listen to the rain battering down against the window, so am I.

A woman's voice wakes me. She is shouting from the corridor.

'Ugh, it's peeing it down. I made the big mistake of walking from the tube to try and burn off some of the three trillion calories I have consumed in the last forty-eight hours…'

Tanya? Noelle? My head is foggy.

'…I advise you to stay in your room until I have a shower or risk never fancying me again. I currently look like a panda. But that does make me a pregnant panda, which is kind of special…as they rarely mate, do they? I should live in a Chinese zoo and be called Yang Yang or Ying Y—'

My head is clear. *It's RACHEL.* I sit up. I shake Zach then slap my hand over his mouth in case he yelps…and point at the door.

'SHE'S BACK!' I mouth at him.

He jumps up from the bed, his legs wobbling beneath him as his feet hit the floor.

'Shit. Shit…*hide!* Hide! She must *not* see you,' he hisses. 'Not like this, not because…but because, oh shiiiiit. Ash, I'm sorry. I'm not being an arsehole but I can't deal with any of this right now, it's all too m—'

'Calm down…sssssshhhhh,' I hiss back. 'We haven't done anything wrong so she c—' I stop myself. As if the truth would matter if *she* saw *me* in here. 'I'm not going to stitch you up. Go into the kitchen. Distract her. Tell her I have come round to discuss something to do with Kat Moss, and am in the lounge.'

'Mmm…yeah.' His eyes don't meet mine. 'Okay…thank you…really.'

I slip out of the bedroom, down the corridor to the lounge and in through the door not connected to the kitchen, which is still shut. I hear Zach greeting Rachel and her returning his greeting like…well, like someone who has not seen the person they are in love with for a couple of days.

'…I'm so glad to be home,' she says. 'I got a much earlier train. Hen weekends are a nightmare when you can't drink. I can now confirm, you need to be one hundred percent sozzled to have a laugh doing karaoke. I took it way too seriously. So embarrassing. It was as if I was auditioning for *America's Got Talent.* Anyway, I wanted to get back…I've been so worried. You look knackered, poor love.'

Disconcerted – I thought Zach hadn't told anyone else about his mother? - I sit down on the velvet armchair.

'Listen,' says Zach. 'I know this is going to sound weird, but Ashley is here.'

'Here?' repeats Rachel. 'In the flat?' She sounds a little taken aback but not surprised. Definitely not shocked. 'Oh. Okay.'

'Yeah, she's in the lounge. I know I should have told you th—'

She interrupts him. 'It's fine, Zach. I understand. I wouldn't have expected you to have met up in some public place. If you remember I did suggest you call and tell her as soon as we knew.'

The door opens. She nods at me.

'Hi, Ashley…'

'Hi…' I say, scanning her face. I can't read her expression at all.

'You probably heard us talking. I'm glad you're here.' Her voice is gentle. The way she is looking at me is too. 'We needed to tell you at some point, it was hard to know when. I know this is the last thing you—or either of you…' She glances over her shoulder at Zach. '…need. But we're hopeful. Zach said that it has happened before and everything turned out okay.'

'It's happened before?' I repeat.

Seeing the confusion embedded in my face, Zach steps up. He taps Rachel's arm lightly.

'Rach, Ash has only just arrived. I hadn't told her yet.' He takes a breath and hangs his head. 'Kat Moss is missing.'

'It happened about five days ago,' explains Rachel. 'She went out overnight as usual and didn't come back in the morning.' She looks across at Zach to elaborate but he says nothing, so she continues. 'We didn't want to worry you, so we decided to search for her first. We have been thorough, I promise. I've knocked on the door of every resident in the surrounding roads to ask if they can check their houses and gardens. If there was no answer at any of the addresses I put a poster in through the letterbox or stuck one on their railings or dividing wall.'

Again, she glances at Zach, but he adds nothing. He stays staring at the floor…exactly as he did the evening I told him I was no longer pregnant. I watched him move around the flat, from the entrance hall to the bedroom to the bathroom to the kitchen to the sitting room. At each stage I thought… do I do it now? But I stopped myself. It was as if I already knew that the moment I chose would be *another* end. I took that gulp of wine.

ME: *Zach…*

HIM: *(Glancing across.) Mmmm… (Doing a double take.) What's happ—? No, oh, no…*

ME: *Yes.*

HIM: *But…no. No.*

ME: *I'm sorry.*

*

I was sorry. I said it then. I've said it again tonight.

'Zach covered all public places,' adds Rachel. 'He looked under stationary cars, hedges, any sort of sheltered space… then covered the entire park. He also asked all shop owners to put posters in their windows too.'

I stand up, walk past both of them and out of the room.

'Ash…' Zach calls. 'Ash! Come back, please…'

'Leave her, Zach,' I hear Rachel tell him. 'You can't make this better. It'll be too emotional for both of you. Let me talk to her…I want to. Please, stay in here for a few minutes.'

I hear the sitting room door shut. Rachel pads up the corridor to where I am fiddling with the latch. She puts her hand on my shoulder as I am about to open it.

'You don't have to say anything, Ashley, but I want to reassure you I will not give up looking for Kat Moss. It wasn't ideal I had to go on a girls weekend, but I'm hoping that in the last forty-eight hours someone may have seen her. I've taken tomorrow off to resume the search.'

I turn round. She stares at me plaintively, and I don't think…insincerely. I stare back.

'I also want to apologise…' Her voice drops to a whisper. '…deeply, about what happened in Zach's office. Divorce is bad enough—God, I should know—when just two people are involved, let alone three. Well, four…now.' *She's wearing frosted eye shadow…and it wasn't applied with a setting primer underneath. That's why she's got panda eyes. Who wears frosted eyeshadow on a Sunday? Unless you're falling out of a nightclub or entering a teen beauty pageant. I scan down to her scarf…'* The way I told you about the pregnancy, it was unforgivable. And please, believe me…I had no idea what had happened to you. Zach told me afterwards. Although this is not any excuse I want you to know the reason it came out like that was because I was scared. I'd been panicking since I found out.'…*a paisley patterned silk one, tied loosely round her neck. Crimes Against Fashion No. 76: Country-pursuits-style accessorising in the city. Guilty: K Middy (the Waity Katy years). She is wearing it with a cashmere jumper. A baggy one. Not necessarily unacceptable but definitely unnecessary. She has no bump…yet.* 'I've worked with Zach long enough to know his entire world revolves around you. I never thought you two would split up, and despite being crazy about him for years, I never wished you would. Actually, I imagined if you *ever* did, he'd never get over you anyway so what would be the point?' *At the moment, it's an embryo and is able to grow in the tissue surrounding it. If you do feel bigger round the middle at this stage it's because the uterus is thickening out ready for the expansion required later…* 'But then we got together and for a few weeks I thought that maybe he could. Now, I think he was only trying to convince himself, because the way he was looking at you in the office—the effect you had on him—anyone could see that he hadn't stopped loving you. No…worse, he may even love you more.' *Even when she does start to show, she should never go 'loose'. Only the Olsens can truly master voluminous chic. No one else should try. I scan down to her jeans…* 'In that moment, I was terrified I would lose him. I'd waited so long for him. And now there were two of us that needed him. I'm older than you and this might be my last chance to have a family…'…*and give her the benefit of the doubt in assuming they are NOT boot cut. That would be unimaginatively mean of me. The reason why I cannot make an exact call on their style and acceptability is because from the knee down they are tucked into her…'*…not that I'm expecting you to understand how that must have felt but I wanted to tell you the truth, even if you can never forgive me.'....*socks. I glance across to the doormat. There are her wellington boots. Her wedge wellington boots. HER WEDGE WELLIES. But there is nothing funny about them now.*

Because they are staying. I am leaving.

I look up and into Rachel's smudged eyes. I don't blink. As mine start to well up, I shut the door behind me. I don't slam it. Slamming the door would imply that I am feeling victorious in some way. But I am not. I wasn't the winner when I left home at sixteen. Nor when I left Zach's office. Or now. I was the loser. I am the loser. And because of that someone else is lost too. Kat Moss. She lost her home and now she is lost.

I may have insinuated this was Zach's fault, but it isn't. It is mine. When he left, Zach insisted on taking Kat Moss because he felt it was what he deserved. I let him take her because I wanted him to leave. I knew he needed to leave *in order to come back*. There was never a discussion about what was right for her. She should have stayed with me. Our home was her kingdom. Kat Moss was queen. Overnight, her kingdom was taken away from her. She had to start again. I made her start again. Just like I had to. I knew how tough it was but I still made her. It's my fault. *It's my fault. IT'S MY FAULT!*

IT'S MY FAULT.

As I run home, I don't even realise I am screaming. I know it is raining harder and I am slumped in the middle of the pavement at the bottom of the steps leading up to my flat. I am beating the concrete with my hands, eyes streaming, face burning and aching, snot dangling out of my nose, throat hoarse and sore...and I can hear a hideous high-pitched wailing, but I have no idea that the noise is emanating from

me. I want the noise to stop. I want it to stop. Stop. *STOP!*
But it won't.

'Ashley? *Ashley?* Look up. Are you okay? Okay, stupid
question. Clearly, you are *not* okay.'

I don't answer. I would if I could but I am crying so hard
I can't develop any words, just strangulated choking sounds.
I look up. Through the blurry film of tears I see Tanya. The
expression on her face is not anywhere near as awkward as
mine would be if our roles were reversed. She places a hand
on my arm. I push it away, but she puts it back and with the
other she gently pulls me off the ground and encourages
me to walk up to my front door. She sits me down under
the lead parapet. As she lowers herself next to me, the rain
develops from heavy droplets into hard shards. My tears fall
as aggressively. I don't even attempt to stop, I simply hang
my head in my hands…*wailing and sobbing*. I wail and sob.
I keep going until I am whimpering. I whimper for a while.
After some time, Tanya prods me.

'Like you always used to say, "*I never cry*".'

'You're not the funny one, remember?' I croak.

'Fair point,' she mutters. 'Do you want a tissue? Actually,
let me rephrase that…you *need* a tissue. You have major *gunk*
issues going on.' She reaches into her pocket and passes me
a Kleenex. 'Do you want to talk about it, whatever it is?'

I shrug and wipe my nose.

'I don't blame you, if you don't. Sometimes things are too
big for words. You know, my father tried to get me to talk
about what happened back then…not to him, obviously. In
therapy. I was presented with a succession of people I had
never met before wanting to know how I felt. It's only now
that I am realising I told them what they wanted. I didn't tell
them how I really felt. The only person I had ever told how I

felt about anything was you, so ultimately, with you out of my life...' She shrugs too. 'I know why I didn't want to let these people in though, it wasn't because I didn't know them. For a long time, I used that as an excuse. It was because talking about your feelings makes them real...even when you are not ready for them to be.'

She sighs and stares ahead. I examine her side profile. The edges of her eyes are pink and underneath bags have formed. I wonder if she slept after I left.

'So do pregnancy tests,' I say, looking down at the concrete.

'Pregnancy tests do what?' Her voice is thin, papery.

I pull my jacket around me and watch the rain splash down on the steps. Then I exhale deeply. I feel a rushing sensation as I breathe in again, because I know I'm about to tell her. For the first time since it all happened, I am about to let it all out.

'Pregnancy tests make everything real when you're not ready for anything to be. Those double fucking lines. DOUBLE FUCKING LINES. I bought two tests to make sure. One of them said it would show the result in pink. The other in blue. *Pink and blue?* I found that offensive...as if there was an assumption that you wanted the end result to be an *actual* girl or a boy. What about the women who are hoping they are *not* pregnant? There should be a test you can buy that has a skull which appears if you have been inseminated and a smiley face if you haven't. The wording on the instructions would also be re-written. If a result is "positive" then you are not pregnant. If the result is "negative" you are.'

'You never wanted a baby?'

'Tanya! You know I didn't. It was never on my husband's list either. Zach and I both knew from the day we met we were on the same page. No, we were the same word, in the same sentence, in the same font on that page. And that word was NO. Because we were so united in our decision we could have fun with it. We even used to play this silly game on the way back from his parents' house. His mother would *always* have made some snide comment about not having a grandchild, so we would list off all the reasons we didn't want to produce one.'

I can see us now stuck in traffic on the M25.

HIM: You start.

ME: Okay. We like to sleep.

HIM: You had that last time.

ME: But it's a big one.

HIM: Fine, then I'm allowed we like to have sex whenever and wherever we want.

ME: Erm...having one would really piss off Fitz.

HIM: (Sheepishly.) NOT having one would really piss off my mum.

ME: You can't have that. It's WHY we're playing the game. Anyway, my turn...I don't want to make a mockery of my crockery.

HIM: (Grinning.) Your crockery is a ceramics sensation... and should stay that way.

ME: You don't like to say 'no'.

HIM: You don't like to take 'no' for an answer. Take your feet off the dashboard.

ME: No! Ha! I like to be alone.

HIM: I like seeing you on your own.

ME: Ditto.

HIM: I need my emotional, spiritual and physical strength to get through the day.

ME: I need my look to be strong at Fashion Week.

HIM: You think Disneyland is where people go when they've lost all hope.

ME: (Laughing.) You think a smudge on your laptop is the end of the world.

HIM: I find dolls creepy and lack patience with all brands of plastic building bricks. I also lack assembly skills.

ME: Most importantly of all, we have Kat Moss.

HIM: She has us. The three of us have each other.

'The double lines appeared?' asks Tanya, slowly.

'Yes. One line deleted the agreement we made. The other through 'us'. Suddenly, a baby was *all* Zach had ever wanted. I'd never seen him so...*alive*. It felt as if the entire time we had been together, he'd been operating on what had appeared to be his highest plain of contentment, but actually, there had been an even higher level of happiness—no, *exhilaration*—that he hadn't realised could be attained. Once he'd had a glimpse of that. Once I had glimpsed *him* like that...' I trail off. Not because I don't want to continue but I am suddenly bewildered I have got this far. 'Once I had glimpsed him like that, I had to...' Finally, I look up and turn to Tanya.

'Keep...' She begins. 'You had to keep...'

'It. Yeah, I kept *it*.' I watch her physically balk at my depersonalisation. 'I ACTUALLY REFERRED TO IT AS AN 'IT',' I shout. 'The more Zach humanised it, the more pressure I felt. And I was feeling compressed. Suddenly, I was responsible for the future health and happiness of a child *and* a husband. Everything depended on me.'

'But why would you have thought that?'

'Because Zach had jumped way ahead. Within a fortnight he had let the news slip to his mother and they were giddily imagining blowing out candles on milestone birthdays after the presentation of a tricycle, scooter, bicycle, moped, car...

meanwhile the thing inside of me wasn't even the size of a poppy seed. He was pushing for change; in my life, Kat Moss's life, our life... he saw it as planning for the future but he was also boxing off the past. I felt as if I was going mad. But what I did next, was thought up, deliberated on and carried out in a series of totally sane moments.' I cough then clear my throat, so I can say it with the necessary clarity. 'I went to the clinic.'

I look at Tanya. Her eyes immediately divert from mine.

'The clinic....' she mumbles.

'Yes, Tanya, that's what I said. The clinic. The CLINIC.'

'Oh my god, Ash-...'

I jump in. I need to get it all out. 'Yes. I went to the clinic to get rid of it.' Now, I turn away from her because I don't ever want to see anyone's reaction to this. 'I didn't tell Zach. I didn't tell my husband I was going to abort his baby. I didn't tell anyone. I researched where to go and arranged the appointment. And I didn't cancel it... not until seven minutes before as I was sat in the reception. By then the guilt was so unbearable I felt as if I was dying inside. Oh, the irony of those words…because, it did. It died. A few days later. No reason. *Just one of those things. These things happen. Things weren't meant to be.* Insert your own banal truism.' I sense Tanya about to attempt an offer of support or sympathy so I shake my head. 'Wait. But then the guilt turned to anger. I was angry. Because no-one wanted to deal with what I had lost, only when that space would be filled again. And what got me even ANGRIER was the assumption that it would not be possible for me to morph back into that woman I was before I got pregnant. That I would automatically want another as if there was now something missing. But what got me FUCKING LIVID is that they said I was "scared".

I was not scared. I am not scared! I have never been scared of anything. Not anything in my life. Ever.'

I twist to face her. There is moisture in her eyes too.

'How do you feel now?' she asks, quietly.

'I feel like a bad person. I feel like my father.'

Sixteen

TANYA

I sit up with a start. Surely, *surely* Ashley's father did not tell her I was pr-...

'I felt relief.' Her tone is aggressive. 'Relief.'

'God, I don't know wh-...'

She shuts me down. 'I'm explaining! He would have felt relief if my mother had gone ahead with an abortion, which is what he wanted her to do.'

'Oh. Oh, right...'

'He made it clear that he was not ready for parenthood. But she had me. Imagine that, she loved him so much that she couldn't give up something of his, even though he didn't want it himself. She risked the only person who she had ever loved. For me. Someone she had never met. She told me that herself, you know. And I never thanked her. She died thinking I wasn't grateful.'

I swallow and stare out to the road, unsure of how Ashley will react. 'No, she didn't.'

'What? How do you know?'

Deep breath. 'Because I told her. Sort of. The last time I saw her. She wasn't well. When she asked if I had seen you... I lied. I had a feeling it would be the last time she and I would have any contact. It was as if she needed to hear something. She didn't ask me but I could feel it. So, I said that you and I were back in touch; you had a big job at a fashion magazine, had got married... and that you were happy.'

Ashley nods slowly.

I don't push her. 'I know it wasn't my place to have said any of th-...'

'No, no...' She interrupts me again. 'I'm glad...well, not glad, but I understand. When someone is ill, it changes everything, doesn't it? I'm sure I would have done the same for you.'

'I hope you would have dropped the words 'business to business' and 'regional' from my job spec. Not exactly death bed lingo.' I giggle and nudge her.

She manages a smile too. 'Did she ask any questions after you'd said that?'

'One. She asked what you wore on your wedding day. I told her vintage Versace.'

'Ah, so that's another issue of *Catwalk* which you secretly purchased, then.'

'Ashley, you always planned to get married in vintage Versace. It was the only non-negotiable on your list. You whittled it down to those fifteen dresses, didn't you? Were they A/W 1995? You found that archive shot on line of the 'supers' hanging out backstage in Milan all wearing that season's metallic look. Christy, Kate, Naomi, Claudia, Helena, Linda, Carli, Shalom, Amber, Nadja...you were obsessed.'

'You've forgotten Yasmeen Ghauri, Lucie De La Falaise, Emma Sjoberg, Eve Salvail and Trica Helfer. And the picture was from the S/S 1994 catwalk...' She corrects me. 'Nice try, though.'

'So, which one did you go for in the end?'

'Ironically, given her legs are probably longer than my entire body, the one worn by Nadja Auermann: shimmering gold, floor-length with a 'cut out' rib cage. I tracked one down at a seconds store.' She sighs. 'I bet she thought Gianni was a really pretentious choice.'

'Your Mum? Not at all. When I told her she just smiled.'

Ashley pauses. 'So, what about you? Have you lined up your frock yet?'

'For what?'

She taps my left hand. 'Duh! Your wedding I clocked the sparkler. You're engaged. Congratulations. I'm obviously *thrilled* for you. Well, as much as anyone could be on the tail end of a bitter separation about to finalise a divorce. What's he called?'

'He's... he's called... Greg.' As the tears fill my eyes I drag my sleeve across my face.

'Christ, are you serious?' Ashley balks at me. 'Happy tears are naff. At least I was crying because I've fucked up my life…no, more importantly, my cat's life. And let's get this straight. Me crying is like a total eclipse of the moon or Poppy Delevigne *not* looking really pleased herself; it can only be witnessed once in a lifetime. Come on then, have you bought a dress?'

I bite my lip. 'Oh…erm… I haven't thought ab—'

'Shut *up!* Of *course*, you have. Don't pretend you're going to be one of those 'it's not about what you wear, it's about the sentiment' brides. One day, you may be thankful you put more effort into the former rather than the latter. And no, you can't wear black, because for you that would not be making an avante garde statement, it would simply be playing it safe.' Suddenly, she jumps up. 'Hey, I have something which may inspire you. Come back upstairs.'

Two minutes later, I am in the kitchen watching Ashley wheel in a fake Louis Vuitton suitcase. She is smiling at me. I gasp awkwardly and grip onto the oven behind me. She misinterprets my reaction.

'Don't worry, I didn't wake up Noelle. She's snoring her empty little head off. So, remember this?' She grins again, almost manically this time. 'It's the case which we used to t—'

'That we used to take your mum's clothes to the stall in. I know. Ashley, listen, I don't think this is a good idea. We both have too many mem—'

'But you never got to see what was inside this load. You have to see what she made. Look…'

She flips open the lid. As it always was, the case is immaculately packed with tissue paper dividing each of the garments, but the designs are different. Ashley starts lifting them out and placing them on the table. Everything is body conscious. Foil leggings, PVC mini-kilts, lycra bodies, faux fur bras, snakeskin hipster shorts…

'This was what we would have been selling. Finally! She had started to create something for the new generation of clubbers. These are the looks all the fashionistas were doing in the *Catwalk* party pages back then. This is my favourite piece,' she says. Gently, Ashley unfolds a white lurex backless catsuit with bandaged legs that has a matching white lace veil and bustle. 'It's a wedding outfit. How cool? It's a little bit Pam Hogg, a little bit Jean Paul Gaultier and a little bit Herve Leger with the tubular effect. What do you think? I mean, I know it's all so dated now, but…'

'Actually, I think it looks a lot like the work I've been seeing recently on the Japanese fashion blogs,' I say. As it always did, Ashley's enthusiasm instantly has the same effect on me. 'There are specific Tokyo fashion tribes who love throwback Western influences and are really experimental with how they wear it. This would be every day street wear for them. You should check them out, see if you could take these designs somewhere. Your Mum would love that.'

'But she's not here, Tanya.' Suddenly, Ashley's voice is clipped again.

'No, but I'm sure sh—

'Yeah, I am sure that *you* are sure. You have the luxury to be sure of what she might have thought. Be thinking. Because you saw her, you spoke to her. And she saw you. She spoke to you.' Ashley starts grabbing the designs from the table and shoving them back in the suitcase.

'Slow down, slow down…'

She shakes her head. 'I can't…' she mutters.

'Can't what?'

'Do any of this. She was *my* mother. It's not fair that y-…'

'She was ill, Ashley. *Really* ill. Alcoholism is a disease. She did not want your life to be diseased too. She thought she would cause less hurt that way.'

'But that should have been my choice. She took that choice away. She did not give me a chance. Why does no-one give ever *ME* a fucking chance? It's so unfair!' she shouts. 'Her. *Him*. It. All of it. ALL OF IT! It's so FUCKING UNFAIR' She chokes and pulls away from me. 'I'm g-… I'm going to look for my cat. I'm sorry too. I am. I'm sorry, Tanya.'

Ashley picks up her keys and leaves the kitchen. I hear her open the door and run down the stairs. For a while I stand staring at the clothes, picturing the precinct where for most of our youth we would attempt to sell Mrs Atwal's collections. It wasn't a buzzy concentrated fashion market, but a soulless collection of 'gift' stalls. We were positioned between the handmade candles and discounted perfumes. Both stalls reeked of exactly the same smell: a sort of chemical fruits of the forest. The stall owners would be burning and spritzing their wares all day. Ashley and I always joked that by the end of trading hours we needed to have one of those toxic decontamination showers they use at nuclear power stations. One Saturday morning, I remember sitting under a pungently synthetic blackberry-and-raspberry-scented cloud as I waited for Ashley to bring the stock. In the past, I would have helped carry the load from her flat. But for a while, I had made excuses and said it was easier we met at the precinct. I was seventeen. I had been best friends with Ashley Atwal for seven years. I had been having sex with her father for one. I never planned to tell her in that moment. Until now, I don't know why I did. And now I know why. When she arrived she was so excited. Not just for her Mum. Or herself. Or for me. It was for us. She thought it was the start of Our Future.

That's when I said it.

'*I need to tell you something.*'

Delicately, contemplatively, I re-layer the suitcase with tissue paper and place the clothes back inside. As I am zipping it up, my phone bleeps. It's a number I don't recognise, but I snatch it to my ear, just in case…

'Greg! Hello? GREG!'

'*It's your father.*'

'What? This isn't your number, Dad.'

'*I'm using a Pay As You Go…in case.*'

'In case of what?'

'*Where the hell is your sister?*'

'With me.'

'*I'm sending a car to pick you both up.*'

'Why? What's happened?'

'*Tell me where you are!*'

'At…at…someone's house.'

'*Whose house?*'

'Just a…' I trail off. 'Nobody you know.'

*

Bar a moment of extreme anguish upon realising she has left her Hello Kitty phone charging in Ashley's living room, Noelle is calm all the way back to our parents' house. We devise a plan. As we pull up to the gates at the top of the driveway, I brief her again.

'So, stick to the story we rehearsed. Tell them whatever they've read on the internet is wholly over-exaggerated. You fainted at the party because you hadn't eaten. Paramedics were called to be on the safe side but they couldn't find anything wrong. You're embarrassed at all the hoopla surrounding the incident. Oh, and you could add in something sarcastic and self-deprecating about never liking a fuss to be made on your account. Finally, if there is one positive to come out of this, you've realised you need to relax and take a dip into Lake You…for God's sake, don't say you're suffering from 'exhaustion'. It's a cliché. It won't wash with Dad.'

'You don't think he is angry with me?'

'As if! His little Nelly could go on a violent killing spree of an afternoon and return home swinging the severed heads… and her Diddoo would welcome her in for tea with open arms.'

But as the gates open and the Mercedes glides over the gravel and stops next to Dad's Hummer, I see him standing in the porch. His arms are folded across his chest. As we come to a halt, he does not approach, wave or even nod at us.

'Howdy, Diddoo…' says Noelle, getting out of the car. She

does a weak skip towards him. 'Your little Nelly is here! Soz about what you've like, read. Safe to say, it's all been blown waaaaay out of proportion. No need to press the *hashtag* panic button. I've sussed out that eating is a pretty useful tool for like, staying upright. Have to say though, the whole episode has really made me think about addressing my maje hectic sched-u-leeeee…'

'Your *schedule*?' Dad retorts, abruptly. 'You think *you* have a hectic schedule, Noelle?'

She visibly smarts at Dad's use of her proper name, and walks up to him, arms elongated, ready for a hug. He does not reciprocate.

'*Diddoo?* Why are you b—'

'I think it would be appropriate to remind you,' he interrupts, 'that when I was your age, I was working seven days a week. Some nights I didn't even bother to go home—I grabbed a few hours' kip on the floor in the building site office. And when I'd built up my company only to watch it go bang, I started again…this time doing *physical labour* through the night, so I wouldn't have to pay anyone else. So, don't talk to me about a "hectic schedule".' He wags his index finger at my sister, then at me. 'And this will probably come as a surprise to you both, but I didn't do it for the money. Nor did I do it for the leisure time it would reward me or your mother with one day—believe me, I could quite happily go without seeing her hack another expensive golf course to pieces. I didn't do it for the recognition either. I did it so that I could set an example to my daughters. To inspire them to work hard too.'

Noelle shifts from foot to foot, the gravel crunching underneath her. 'And you erm…*did* Diddoo. That's why I do work hard.'

'Yes, you do,' he mutters. 'The difference is my nose was to the grindstone. Yours is to the back of a cistern.'

He turns and walks back inside.

'No, Diddoo, wait!' shouts Noelle. 'You *have* to believe me. I wouldn't do anything that could jeop-jeop-jeopodate…'

'Jeopardise…' sighs Mum, as she steps outside. The Pomeranian follows, skipping close to her ankles. 'Noelle, shoosh, shooooosh, you're making things worse. You were filmed at that party. That stinky pillock has emailed Howard the footage.'

'No!' Noelle howls 'NO! *Nooooo!*' She stumbles forward and collapses into Mum's arms.

I rush past them, into the house and up the corridor to Dad's study. I knock on the door.

'Go away, Noelle,' he says.

'It's me, Tanya.'

I turn the handle and peek in. Dad is sat in front of his computer, his back to me.

'It's from that Troy character,' he mutters, without turning round. 'He sent it.'

A frozen frame from 'it' is displayed on the screen. It must have been taken before Ashley found her. Noelle is leaning over the back of a lavatory, with a rolled up bank note dangling out of one nostril. A fresh globule of blood is hanging from the other. Her forehead is shiny with sweat, her eyes bulging, her mouth is set in an inane grin that if you continue to stare at, starts morphing into more of an expression of abject terror. Even with my limited knowledge of doing 'gear', I imagine this is not how it should be done… or how anyone would set out to do it. It is the sort of image that—if it didn't star my sister—I would encourage to be paraded around the UK's secondary schools to put off kids from getting involved with drugs. Or indeed, despicable emo rock front men.

'He wants quarter of a mill for it.'

'Oh, my God…' I walk into the room. 'Are you going to pay him?'

'No!' snaps Dad. 'I thought I would let him sell it on to one of the tabloids and in doing so flush my reputation and hers down the very toilet she is snorting cocaine off. And your mother's. And yours.' He adds these last two sentences as more of an afterthought. 'Of course, I'm going to pay him. I will not have people gossiping about this family. *Again*.'

'But Dad, listen, you don't know how much Troy has got on her. He could continue to blackmail you even after you've paid him. We could speak to someone in his team. Noelle knows the producer for Barbed Wire. Remember she told us about him at supper? Angus O'Something. She has his email address. He may be able to h—'

'Let me deal with this, Tanya.'

'You don't have to deal with it on your own. I know you're disappointed. I can tell Mum is too. So am I. But you should know that the person who is most disappointed is Noelle. At the moment, she is in too much shock to be disappointed for anyone other than herself. But as she comes to terms with everything, she will realise how much she has let everyone else down, especially you…and she is not strong enough to handle that. Either mentally or physically. You think that the problem is this guy asking for money, but it's not…the problem is Noelle. She has *problems*. You know that. Mum knows that. She knows that. I know that. I've known it for a while, if I'm honest. Now, *we* have to be honest with her and each other.'

'Like you're always honest with me?'

He swivels round on his chair and taps his chin with his index finger as if giving me an opportunity to reply. But I know he isn't. He does this to Mum too sometimes. I used to think it was a foible. But it's not. It's a control mechanism.

'I asked you not to have any more to do with that Atwal girl and you promised you wouldn't. My driver picked you up from her home this evening. I had the address checked. I suppose it was her that gave Noelle those vile drugs.'

'Yeah right, Dad! Because, exactly like when we lived on the estate and Ashley's flat was the drug dealing epicentre of the South West, where she lives now is the key to the underground movement and flow of narcotics in the capital. I mean, when Noelle and I were there she was cooking up illegal highs in the bathtub as if it was totally normal.' I throw my hands up. 'For God's *sake*!'

'Then what were you doing there?'

I take a breath. 'Ashley saved your little Nelly's life, made sure she got the treatment she needed and *then* let us stay at her home so she wouldn't get papped.'

'You still lied.'

'Stop it, Dad.'

'Stop what?'

'Judging me as the person I was back then. I am an adult now.'

'I seem to remember that was your argument back then too. You insisted on making your own decisions. But it wasn't a decision, that would imply you had weighed up the pros and cons…it was simply a succession of selfish acts.' He rubs his forehead. 'You had no concern for anyone other than yourself. Every single day I would—and I still do—ask myself how you could have cared for that man so much,

when clearly he did not care about you. That much became
blatantly obvious, didn't it?'

'What do you mean?'

He taps his chin again.

'*What do you mean?*' I repeat.

'Well, he left, didn't he?' My father swivels back round
to face his computer. 'Now, let me get on, please, Tanya.'

I shut the door and go upstairs. Noelle is lying on her bed,
staring at the ceiling. I sit down by the window on a padded
seat that Mum has had covered in the same floral print as the
curtains, which also complements the pinky base colour of
the bed linen. All the new décor in this house matches, but
that only emphasises the disordered state of the people in it.
I stare out into the night. I wonder how much longer I can
keep everything in.

'It was Troy, wasn't it?' Noelle mutters.

'Yeah.'

'…and it's bad. Be straight with me.'

'If it gets out you're unlikely to be awarded that MBE.'
I sigh. 'Unless it was for services to the exportation of
Colombian plant derivatives. Don't worry though, Dad is
on the case.'

'He'll never forgive me, though. I know he won't. I'm not
his little Nelly any more.'

'Don't be silly, he *will* forgive you…and I'm sure you'll
be his "little Nelly" again soon. But hey, if not, that might
not be such a bad thing. After all, he did start calling you
that when you born. You're a grown woman with a business
empire now. Actually, I reckon one of the reasons he's so
cross is because he is cross at himself; for *still* treating you
like his "little Nelly"…even though he knew you weren't
her any more.'

'Has it been that obvious?'

'He can't have thought you were boshing Liquorice All-sorts at all those glitzy parties you go to. Sometimes you'd turn up here for Sunday lunch with your jaw at a ninety degree angle to your mouth. Admittedly, what was coming out of it wasn't necessarily as ridiculous as what has always done…' I raise an eyebrow at her. '…but it must have been pretty obvious what was going on. Don't you think?'

'No,' she replies, plainly. 'Not surprisingly, though…given that I don't do that much.'

'Do much what?'

She rolls over and faces me. Then I realise her face is not so much sapped…as aged. My younger sister. My kid sister. My baby sister. She's gone.

'*Think*. Not like you. You think about everything. *I* talk. *You* think. Maybe if I was more like you, I wouldn't have got myself in this mess.'

'But you also wouldn't be famous.'

'I could do without that.'

'Oh, come on, Noelle, it's what you've always wanted.' I pause. 'Out of interest, why *did* you always want it?'

'I was thinking that, in the bathroom, before Ashley found me.' She rolls back to face the ceiling and clears her throat before continuing. 'When you're made to feel like you're perfect, you feel as if you *have* to be perfect…to achieve perfection. Diddoo always said I was perfect. One of my first memories is being on the swings in the playground on the estate and him asking anyone who went by, 'How perfect is my little Nelly? Well, he wasn't asking them was he? He was telling them. It was one of those rhet-rhet-…'. She holds up her hand knowing without even looking at me that I am about to help her. '…*rhetorical* questions. They all nodded, clapped…even cheered, but I was thinking, even then—and I must have only been four or five—that those people don't really mean it, because I was only swinging. *All children know how to swing.* They were showing their appreciation because Diddoo told them too. That's my career in a nutshell. Ashley was right. I don't *do* anything to deserve congratulation. I have a team of people around me telling other people to appreciate me doing *some*thing, but I am not doing *any*thing. I read the autocue but I don't write the script. I wear the headphones but I don't mix the tracks. I model the clothes but I don't style them. I hold the "Noelle" tote and I *will* hold the "Noelle" clutch; but I have contributed nothing to the design of either. I party hard but I wouldn't even consider leaving the house without a concoction of uppers to get me in the mood. I'll be the Guest Editor on *Catwalk* soon, but I can't write! I didn't write my book. I didn't write that break-up poetry—my stylist, Kenny, did…pissed. I don't even write my own Twitter feed, Sophs does, and I have no idea if she uses "YOU'RE" and "YOUR" the wrong way round. The only thing I do—and this I *am* perfect at—is taking endless selfies to ensure my make-believe perfection seems real. To prove that I am perfect…that all the people around me *are* right. That Diddoo *was* right. At bedtime he would say goodnight, then whisper to me, "Who's my perfect girl?" I know you heard him too. And I would whisper back, "Me, Diddoo." But I knew I wasn't. I knew I was perfectly replaceable. I have spent my entire life trying to hide that truth.'

I smile at her even though she can't see me. I can't remember the last time I heard her speak without any annoying affectations.

'You see? You *are* a thinker, Noelle…and a talker, *obvi-*

ously…but you're a thinker too. For the record, you're not perfectly replaceable, not to the people who matter.'

'Does that include you?'

'Of course. You know it does.' But I can hear the ingrained awkwardness in my own voice as I try to reassure her. 'Maybe I should tell you that a bit more…'

'I should tell you too.' She sighs. 'So, are you okay? About everything…seeing her? Ashley.'

'I'll be fine,' I reply, brusquely. 'It was a long time ago… everything is…everything is different now.'

'Yeah, you've got it all. Funny isn't, I have *a* life two million girls *think* they want but you have *the* life I *know* I want. Solid job, solid home, solid man.'

I feel my eyes prickle again. 'You *will* find someone, Noelle…but let's hope he isn't quite such a keen amateur filmographer as the previous.' I get up to leave.

'Can't you stay with me?' she asks. 'Bring a bed in here. Make it like our old bedroom.'

'I can't.' I flick the light switch. 'I've got stuff to do. Get some rest. By the morning, Dad will have sort—'

She interrupts me. 'Don't think I'm not aware that it was hard for you when we were like, kids…Diddoo focusing so much on me. I sensed it was unfair. Especially when it all like, kicked off... with everything.'

'It's not your fault, Noelle. There was nothing you could have done.'

'I did try though. That's why I told him.'

I stop in the doorway. 'Told who what?'

'Diddoo. I told him because I thought his attitude towards you would change if he knew what had actually happened.'

'What do you mean, what had *actually* happened? What did you tell him?'

'That you'd had…had a…well, that *operation*. That you fell ill afterwards. That you needed to see Dr Lyons. One night, I heard you talking to Suze on the phone about it and… Mr Atwal. I was worried, but I didn't know how to be there for you myself. I was confused as to what it all meant anyway…I was so young. All I knew was that you sounded scared.' She takes a breath. 'All, erm…that.'

I flick the light switch back on. 'Dad knows *all* of that?'

'Yes.'

I stand still for one second. Maybe two…

'*You always have a choice, Tanya. You always have a choice to be who you want to be and how you want others to treat you.*'

…then I return to my father's study. I don't knock. As I open the door, he spins round.

'Tanya, I told you th—'

'You knew.' My voice is clipped, raspy. 'YOU KNEW!'

'Knew what?'

'That I'd gone to the clinic.'

'The wh—' He stops. 'I'm not discussing this right now.'

'I don't want to discuss it. I want you to apologise.'

'As if I wouldn't be sorry you had to go through that.'

'But you didn't think of telling me that at the time? Or maybe being there for me?'

'I wanted to keep it contained. I thought it would be better for you if the least amount of people were involved. Not your mother, not your sister. Not me.' He shakes his head. 'I did the best I could, Tanya. I encouraged you to have therapy afterwards. And in the first instance, told that… that *woeful* excuse for a man to take you to the best place for the best treatment.'

My body judders. 'Oh, my God, you *paid*?' I hold onto the

door frame. 'Right. For the forseeable future, I don't want us to communicate,' I tell him. 'The relationship between you and me has never been easy, but it is now too difficult for me to be part of. Obviously, I will continue to see my sister and my mother.' I am about to shut the door, but then I add. 'Oh, and on the subject of Mum, be careful, Dad. Be *very* careful.'

I tap my chin as if giving him an opportunity to reply, but I have no intention. Then I walk back up the corridor to the utility room, grab my mother's Puffa jacket, a torch and an umbrella in case it starts raining again. Mum peers out of the kitchen, cuddling the Pomeranian.

'Where on earth are you going, sweetheart?' she asks. 'It's almost one in the morning.'

'I'm not staying here tonight.'

'But you don't have your car here.'

'I'll walk.'

'Don't be silly. It's dark and wet out there. Tatiana and I were about to have a sneaky protein-based snack. Stay. You might catch a chill. That's the last thing you want if you're taking all those hormone thingies for the IV-wotsit. By the way, did you get my flowers?'

My jaw clenches. 'Yes, thank you.'

'Now, I know why you were a little fretful the other night. Maybe tomorrow we could talk properly about it all. I'd like to be there for y—'

'Mum, leave it. I'm going.'

'But *where*?'

'To see Suze.'

'Why do you need to see her *now*?'

Because Suze will make everything okay. Just like she did back then. And at that time I didn't even know her too well. We'd never bonded at school. The moment Ashley and I became friends, Suze was off limits. At college we'd only reintroduced ourselves when I fainted in the student mini market. But a few weeks later she was the only person I wanted to talk to.

HER: *(Answering phone. Confused.) Tanya? Tanya Dinsdale?*

ME: *Yes. I know it's late…I'm sorry.*

HER: *Don't worry, I'm wide awake. Unlike my boyfriend who's SNORING REALLY LOUDLY BESIDE ME. Nope, nothing. Can't wake him up. He's like a reverse Gremlin. If he has anything to eat or drink after midnight he's so BORING. I m—*

ME: *(Interrupting.) I need to see Dr Lyons.*

HER: *Mummy? Why? Have you keeled over again?*

ME: *No, but I…I n-n-eed her to see me.*

HER: *Now?*

ME: *If it would be at all possible…she knows me… the thought of going to to A&E…I can't bear any more questions…I know I shouldn't ask out of surg—*

HER: *Tanya. Slow down. What's the matter?*

ME: *I had an operation and I don't feel well.*

HER: *What sort of operation?*

ME: *An abortion.*

HER: *WHAT?*

ME: *Last week. That was why I wasn't in class. I was pregnant. And now…now I'm not. I'm not any more. It's over. It's gone.*

HER: *(Brief pause.) Shitting HELL. Did you have someone with you?*

ME: *Yes. He took me, then he left. He left the clinic. The clinic. THE CLINIC.*

HER: *Calm DOWN…who left the clinic?*

ME: (Dazed.) The father. Her father. Ashley Atwal's father.
HER: Why the hell did he take you? (Gasping.) ARE YOU
TELLING ME IT WAS HIS? (No pause.) I'll wake up Mummy
now. Stay calm, text me where you are, and we'll pick you up.
ME: Thank you, thank you…I feel so bad for calling you.
HER: Shut up. I'm glad you did. And listen to me, eve-
rything will be okay. I promise. Everything. Will. Be. Okay.

I jog down my parents' driveway, let myself out of the
gate and then march briskly for a few minutes up the road,
pass the village pond and the church before I come to the
junction. On the other side, behind a well clipped hedge is
where she lives. I pull out my phone from my jacket pocket.

'Suze! Oh, God, this has gone straight through to voicemail so you're probably asleep. Listen, I know we aren't
talking right now, but I would like to start again. Starting
from now. So much has happened this weekend and I want
to see you. No, I *need* to see you. Look, I'm erm…outside
your place. I know, I know…that sounds weird. But I…just
please…please, call as soon as you get this message.'

I hang up and wait a few minutes, but Suze doesn't ring
back. I walk up to the house. The garage door is shut. The
Range Rover is not in the driveway. I knock on the door.
Gently at first. Then harder. No response. I press the bell.
Still, no one comes to the door. I wonder if she is even back
from her spa weekend. I go round the side of the building
and up to the kitchen window. All the lights are off except
for the spotlights over the cooker. But then I make out an
empty bottle of wine and four empty bottles of San Miguel
on the table. That could well have been *just* for Rollo after
his weekend of childcare. But then I see an ashtray. Suze
must be there. And she must have been more than a bit tipsy
when they went up to bed, because she hasn't emptied it. The

children will see the cigarette butts in the morning. I look up, there is a glow coming through the curtains in the master suite. I find myself panting with relief. I approach the back door and thump my hand against it. Not long afterwards, I hear steps approach and then…her voice.

'What the *hell*! Who is it?'

'It's me…'

Silence.

'*Suze?*'

Silence.

'SUZE!'

'T. *Tanya*.' Her voice is stiff. 'I was sleeping.'

'No, you weren't. Your bedroom light is on. Look, I know it's late and you're slightly worse for wear…and I'm pretty sure I am the *last* person you expected or wanted to see but I would really appreciate it if we could talk. I need *you* to tell me that everything is going to be okay, like you did. Remember that time wh—'

'I told you, I can't talk now…'

'Don't be like this. You've come down now. At least open the door.'

She unlocks it, but only pulls it ajar, so I push it hard with my hip and hold it back. Suze flinches. Her eyes dart from me to the floor. She is in a white fluffy towelling dressing gown, which has got foundation on the collar. Her hair is mussed up and she hasn't removed her make-up for bed. She is definitely drunk. As she acknowledges me she makes a strange gasping-snarling noise and tightens the belt on her gown.

'Can whatever it is not wait until morning?' she snaps, flicking her hair. 'Rollo is asleep, so are the kids…they've had a long weekend. We're all effing tired.'

'Suze? It's *me*.' I wave my hand in front of her face. 'It's me, finding you in the middle of the night because I need to tell you something. My life is a fucking MESS. Yes, I fucking swore and I will be swearing a lot more…and I need you to listen to me fucking swearing. There will be nothing you can do to help, but I want to tell you because I have to make it real. I have to accept it. And unlike all those years ago, I am not even going to attempt getting through it on my own and screw myself up. I am going to talk to my best friend. Because this time I have one. You.'

Her face contorts. She doesn't gesture me in. 'Seriously, Tanya, I would prefer it if we spoke tomorrow. I haven't exactly had the best time of it either lately.' She lowers her voice to a whisper. 'Things aren't great with Rollo and I. I'll explain everything at some point. I agree we need to sort things and I do want to, but now is not the time for us to do that. I've had enough arguing for one day.'

'But I don't want to arg—' I attempt to tell her, but I can't manage the second syllable. Because I can't breathe…

Suze has flicked her hair again and now it is all behind her shoulders. I can see an embossed crest in gold thread on the front of her dressing gown, and underneath this logo, the name of the establishment it represents: THE REXINGHAM HOTEL.

She sighs and clicks her tongue. 'Great. So, let's *not* argue *in the morning*. Thing is, Rollo and I have had a bit of a falling out. I need some space to get my head around…*stuff*. Rest assured I *do* want us to be mates again, but right now I want my bed.'

That dressing gown is from a bathroom in The Rexingham Hotel. I nod and gulp some air. I expect my chest to start prickling with my purple heat rash, but it doesn't. It—like the rest of my body—is cold. I look past Suze at the hall table. Lying on top of it, next to a pile of mail, leaflets and an unopened Amazon package is a set of keys. They are attached to a mini-Fender Stratocaster guitar.

'Okay, I understand,' I somehow reply, but I can't feel myself annunciate any words. 'I'll go, but I walked from my parents. Can you…call me a cab to go back to erm…my own house…please?'

'I'll drive you…' she says.

'You're over the limit.'

'Wait *there*, I'll get a number.'

She turns right and moves off in the direction of the kitchen. As soon as she disappears round the corner I dash into the house, turn left and run up the stairs. I march past Evie's and Jasper's bedrooms. Their doors are open. The curtains aren't even shut. They are not in their beds. I reach the master suite and push the door.

'Who was it, babe?'

'It was me, Tanya…' I reply.

I step over a black Adidas bag and walk into the centre of my best friend's bedroom. I stare at him lying in bed, smoking a cigarette. A real one.

'And there you are…' I continue. 'My true love.'

Seventeen

'We'll be working for that over-accessorised frog with the appalling hairpiece? This can *not* be happening…' Fitz rages down the phone at me. 'Unbelievable.'

'Unbe-weave-able, in fact,' I deadpan, without smiling. 'But unfortunately, true. Rhuaridh Ogilvy is selling up. He needs the money…I reckon it must be to support the family pile. Those massive stately homes need millions purely to keep them operating and that's before you've fed the Labradors and clothed the children head-to-toe in Boden.' I swap my phone into the other hand to bite off a length of masking tape with my teeth. 'The magazine will be *another* RIVA product…that I am pretty sure of.'

'How did you find all this out?'

'Noelle Bamford.'

'*Noelle Bamford?* I don't get all this. Why hasn't Ogilvy sold to a publishing company where the infrastructure is already in place? Also, why would Lazare want to buy a magazine he has been propping up financially already? And just before you think 'corporate me' is back, *most importantly* can I ask: how am I meant to work in the same building as Jesus? Every day…reminded of the shame. The *shaaaaame!*'

'Come on, there's nothing to be ashamed about. So, he ignored you at the party and your fling came to an end. He doesn't *know* that you were really into him, and it's not as if you've pursued him since then. Have you?' I fix the masking tape to the top of another laminated LOST 'KAT MOSS' poster. I am trying to be positive, but with each one I attach to a lamp post or bus shelter even further away from Zach's flat than the last, my hope is fading. '…have you, Fitz? *Fitz*, are you still there?'

I hear him exhale deeply.

'Yes, I am, but only just. Aghhhhh, Jacobs, I sent Jesus a text the next day, almost the *same* day. It was half-six in the morning. I wrote, '*Had to leave early, catch up soon sometime, yeah?*' Which, of course, actually meant, '*I haven't slept because of YOU! Why, why, whyyyyyyyyyy are we not together? I miss youuuuu! Pleeeeeeeeeeease, like meeeeeeeeee! I'll chaaaaange. Tell me what to dooooo!*' and he obviously interpreted it as such, because…'

'…he didn't reply.'

'Again, worse. He replied with a happy face emoji. *A single one.* I only send single happy face emojis when I can't be arsed to reply…to people like you. It means *BORE OFF!!*'

I smile at the phone. 'Obviously, it's my natural instinct to make you feel worse, but I do have a positive theory as to why he ignored you.'

'Please, give it to me. Something! *Any*thing!'

'Well, given that on your previous dates you and Jesus were lolling over each other and capturing every clingy, mawkish moment on social media…there has to be a reason why he went cold so quickly. I think he found out about Frédéric's takeover shortly before the party and felt bad. I saw him looking furtively over at us *both* when we were at the penthouse. Maybe he doesn't agree with what Frédéric is doing and feels conflicted between his personal and professional life.'

'Ie, he hates me.'

'For fuck's sake, Fitz! Yes, probably. No, almost certainly. Just think about the man bun. Either way, finding out about the content of the magazine and what our jobs will entail after the takeover is far more important than your tragic personal life, so you're going to have to get over the *shaaaaame*.'

'Oh, I'm sure I will…by about the year 2036.'

'I'm afraid you need to get over it a *lot* quicker. You have a few hours, in fact. I phoned up the *Catwalk* office, pretending I was one of Lazare's assistants, saying I wanted to confirm Catherine's next meeting with him as there had been a diary issue. They are seeing each other this afternoon at RIVA HQ. We'll be pitching up unannounced. So, the good news is that you *will* get your Jack Bauer moment. The bad news is that we need to get the entry number. All the staff have individual codes…so you need to contact Jesus and ask for his.'

'That's an absolutely ridiculous suggestion.'

'Why is that ridiculous?' I touch the picture of Kat Moss and shut my eyes. Then—as I have done with every poster I have taped since six-thirty this morning—I silently pray for her to be safe, warm and *clean* somewhere. 'You've already embarrassed yourself with Jesus, this isn't going to make the situation any worse. Go into work as usual, then meet me at the entrance of Oxford Circus tube station on the dot of 3pm. Okay, that's it, I'll s—'

'Woaaaaah! Not so fast, Jacobs, I want to know about *your* tragic personal life. What happened with that Jared bloke?'

Now, it is my turn to exhale deeply. 'I have no idea.'

'What do you mean?'

'He disappeared from Frédéric's party. Said he was off to get a drink…'

'…and never came back?'

'Yup. I must have really offended him during this silly spat we had when we arrived. After that I was dealing with that batshit crazy Bamford. He certainly wasn't there when I left with the paramedics. Well, no one was.'

'He didn't call you afterwards?' Fitz hoots. 'Oh, Jacobs. You're doubly as tragic as me. See you later. *Winky emoji.*'

I hang up and walk home, taping the last posters en route. Back in the flat, I tidy up…then I do it again, but more thoroughly. Then I clean to a high standard; wiping, dusting and Hoovering. Then I make a cup of tea, adding milk to the mug first, then boiling water. I let the bag rest until the liquid turns a dark beige. On the cusp of a shift into more caramel territory, I remove the bag, and add a level teaspoon full of sugar. Then I add another half. And stir. This was the precision science which Zach followed to make my tea. I have time to do it now. Too much time. I go into the lounge and sit down. I don't hear anything except for distant shouting and whooping coming from the school playground up the road, a mild flow of traffic and Noelle's Hello fucking Kitty phone intermittently beeping. I switch it onto silent and stay seated on the corner sofa, sipping my tea. This is what Monday 8.47am feels like when you don't have a job to go to. Correction: this is what Monday 8.47am feels like when you don't have a job to go to, *you are sober* and can't spend money. All you can do is sit and think. About yourself. No one else comes into it. It's just you.

I had a lot of time to think like this—by choice—when the news broke on the estate. I didn't want to engage with anybody. Neither did my mother. I knew how the residents around me were reacting from the messages they left on the landline and the 'just thought I'd pop in and see how she's doing' visits. I could keep these brief as she was never usually there. It was bizarre how the reaction of her friends changed. At first they were horrified by what had happened, but when neither she nor I elaborated on the story, their interest became more questioning, then suspicious. As if by keeping quiet about it, we were hiding something. I don't think my mother noticed this. If she did, she didn't care. She'd get up at lunchtime and sit in the Red Lion until closing not saying a word to anyone other than Sheila.

Then one day, it must have been about three weeks afterwards, there was another knock at the door. I didn't bother getting up to answer it as I couldn't face another gawper. And besides, I was watching the MTV Awards which was being presented by Lindsay Lohan, fresh from the success of *Mean Girls*. In the opening sequence her look was bang on point for a seventeen-year-old ingénue. A studded white crop top and shorts with white boots. She was all 'freckles'n'frolics'. It was *so* her. And it made me think. That is what fashion should be. It should be YOU.

Then a key turned in the lock. I jumped off the sofa. The person pushed the door open.

HIM: Ashley.

ME: (Stepping back. Breathing hard.)

HIM: You could say hello.

ME: You want ME to say, 'Hello DAD!'?

HIM: (Holding up his hands.) Just don't start shouting.

ME: I wouldn't waste the energy. Leave now.

HIM: Hear me out, hear me out…is your…is… Mum here?

ME: No. And I will start yelling my head off if you don't get back down the hole you've crawled out of. You're not welcome here. No one wants you. More to the point, no one needs you.

HIM: (Sighing.) Please, Ashley, I'm not going to stand here and expect you to understand what I did. You know what? I don't even understand totally why I did it. I've spent the last few weeks thinking why the hell didn't I b—

ME: Bang some other WOMAN your own age like you always used to? As opposed to selecting a GIRL the same age as your daughter? Yes, I'm sure that's been tough to figure out. Maybe it's because you're a dirty pervert. Or maybe it's because you're a PATHETIC dirty pervert. Either way…

HIM: Don't talk to me like that, I'm still your father.

ME: (Loudly.) Ha! (Even louder.) Ha ha ha!

HIM: Stop it, Ashley, I'm trying to explain. Like I said I don't fully understand why I did it, but I have an idea. I think there is a reason why I chose T—

ME: Don't say her name.

HIM: …it's because I wanted to press the self-destruct button. I can't cope being with Mum. She's screwed up and she won't get help. I had to get caught doing something that was so unforgivable she would never take me back. And then it would be the end of us.

ME: Ah, so there's the answer. You're a PATHETIC dirty pervert. (Pausing.) Well, you even fucked up being pathetic too, because she still loves you. See? You fail at everything. You can't even get someone to hate you properly. You're a failure.

HIM: (Scowling.) What? And you think you're going to amount to anything? Give me a break, Ashley. Look at where you are. Look at who you are. You'll screw up too one day, trust me. You'll be screwed up. Just like her. And you'll force someone to leave. Trust me.

I looked at the expression on his face for a few more seconds. His scowl mutated into something I couldn't decipher. I looked away at the television. Lindsay was accepting the award for Breakthrough Female. She was wearing a fresh frock—an electric blue dress which had been hemmed in a 'rag' style. As she was already hosting, she came out from the wings not the audience. The first person she thanked was her 'Mom'. Then her siblings. Then some movie bigwigs. Then the studio. Then hair and make-up. She didn't thank her father. I turned back to mine.

ME: Get out or I will call Mr. Dinsdale and tell him you're here. (Leaning down. Reaching for the hands-free telephone on the coffee table.)

HIM: Don't be silly, Ashley. I need to see your mother. We have to talk…I have to explain…I have to insist that we are over and why we are over. Don't you want to give her that chance to say goodbye? It's the least she deserves.

ME: (Tapping out the digits.) You have three seconds. Three…two…one…

He left. I sat back down on the sofa and watched Lindsay leave the stage with her popcorn-shaped award. I remember watching the 'rag' hemline swishing on her electric blue dress and thinking that neither was 'me'. I'd never done experimental hems or primary colours…but again, it was *her*. And right now I am thinking that Lindsay Lohan's current look—Studio 54 meets *101 Dalmatians*—is *still* her. You *know* it hasn't been contrived in a meeting between her management and a stylist with a directional haircut and a statement Harajuku back pack. I love that. Lindsay knows what Lindsay wants to wear. So Lindsay wears it. *Done*.

And then I stop thinking.

I jump up and start pulling the throws off the sofa. There is so much more that needs to be done; all those domestic jobs which go under the radar on regular cleaning days. Uphol- stery! Windows! Skirting boards! Unblocking! De-scaling! Mattress flipping! I start with the sofa cushions; the covers could do with a once over in the machine. Cool wash…

*

When I meet Fitz at the station he is wearing a Katherine Hamnett CHOOSE LIFE T-shirt under a black leather jacket.

'You do know that wearing a copy of any classic eighties slogan tee is a heinous and dark Crime Against Fashion?' I tell him. 'Jazz has a RELAX one she had printed herself.'

'Per-*lease*, Jacobs. This is an original, first batch from the factory…1983.'

'Wow, I didn't know you had one of those.'

'I bought it a charity auction. Cost me a fortune. Had to beat off every knackered old stylist, door whore and model booker in London. I thought we needed to add a certain air of authenticity to our arrival.'

'You got the code from Jesus, then?'

'Yep. He didn't push for further convo. Either because he was worried about his job or worried that I hadn't got the hint with that smiley emoji, I wager the latter. Anyway, he said take the lift up to the fifth floor, turn left and walk to the end of the corridor where we will see a grey door. That's where they're having the meeting. He can't be seen with us at any point, but wished me 'best of luck!'.'

'*Best of luck?* Oh, God, really?'

'I know, I know. That's up there with any facial emoji.'

'Still, not as bad as 'take care!' …'

'Those were his next words.'

Fitz and I stop talking after that. We approach the RIVA

building, with its stucco Georgian façade and metal plate on the left pillar bearing the company logo. Fitz punches in the code, we enter, ascend to the appropriate floor and stride purposefully up the corridor—past various offices, making sure we look as if we *should* be here. We get to the grey door. I can't hear any voices. It must be soundproofed. Fitz looks at me. I place my palm on the handle, then twist.

The boardroom is as gauchely decorated as Frédéric's bedroom at the penthouse with black velvet padded walls, a black carpet and gold chandeliers hanging from the ceiling. Sat at a gold table decorated with a black lily centrepiece, is Catherine Ogilvy, her husband Rhuaridh, a woman in a well cut grey suit who I don't recognise, and Frédéric Lazare. Catherine gasps and grabs her husband. He looks at us, confused. As does the woman. Frédéric's surprise is only momentary.

'*Bienvenue!*' He waves—jewellery jangling—and gives us both a nod. 'Come, come, join us for our *petit tête-à-tête.*'

Rhuaridh turns to Frédéric. 'I didn't realise we were being joined…'

'Neither did I,' he replies. 'But far be it from me to turn away guests when I am having a party.' He winks at me. 'And as *you* know, *ma chérie*, I am *all* about the good times.'

'We're not here to celebrate, Frédéric,' I tell him. I look across at Catherine, immediately her eyes drop to the table.

Frédéric shrugs. '*Non?* That is a shame. I do hope you are not planning to—how you say?—piss on *ma parade*, because myself…' He motions to the woman in the grey suit. '…Miriam, *la directrice des resources humaines à RIVA, et Monsieur et Madame Ogilvy* are *sur le point* of taking *Catwalk* into its next exciting—*et plus important*—money making chapter. Can I assume you are both here *pour découvrir les détails*? If so, I am happy to sh—'

Fitz interrupts and points at Catherine. 'An explanation from our editor would be more appropriate…'

She looks up and exhales deeply. I notice her hair is not immaculately coiffed and her make-up is not as polished as both would normally be. Maybe morning sickness has kicked in.

'…a *full* and frank explanation, without any cack-handed extended metaphors.'

Rhuaridh Ogilvy coughs. 'Excuse me! Don't you dare make chippy demands of my wife. You have no right.'

'Oh, Mr Ogilvy, with all due respect I think I do.' Fitz walks over to the table and sits down. 'I have worked under your wife and *for you* over the last seven years; but…' His voice is measured. 'Let me add, I have only been on the payroll for six of those. The first year I provided my services for free across every department. There were no full time positions available, but I was too terrified to leave in case another intern came in and got the job. To support myself, I unpacked boxes in a supermarket every night and every weekend. I had no support from my parents. My father called *Catwalk* a "fag rag", i.e., *it* was a *rag* and *I* was a *fag*. But I stuck in there and I got that job. Last year, I won an award from the Fashion Council for my writing and when I accepted it, I only thanked two people. My father for making me want to succeed and in doing so annoy the *fuck* out of him…and your wife for giving me the opportunity. So, yeah…that… *that*…gives me the *right* to demand an explanation.'

Fitz leans back in his chair, his eyes are focused on Catherine. She stares back at him.

'Look, erm…Mr Martin, we've always got on, you know

that,' begins Rhuaridh, his face pink. 'I—and Catherine—are both grateful for what you have done at the magazine, I can assure you of that. But you shouldn't be here. Neither should you, Ashley. I'm sorry, but…' He tails off and turns to Frédéric. 'I'm not comfortable continuing this meeting, I think it best if we have a break and then concentrate on the contracts in private as originally planned.'

I shake my head at him. 'Rhuaridh, come on…if you're making a decision that affects our future, we deserve to know. What is the difference if we find out now or later?'

'I agree,' says Frédéric, and gestures for me to sit down. '*Mais s'il vous plaît…*' He nods at Fitz. 'Remember this is a *business* meeting to discuss a *business* decision…*c'est ne pas un* reality show. I am afraid that any back stories, however moving—I mean that *sincèrement*—*tout simplement pas pertinents*. They are simply *not* relevant. With that said, I believe it best if *I* explain, not Madam Ogilvy. As you can see…*elle est un peu pâle, aujourd'hui.*'

Catherine gives Frédéric a noticeably pinched smile. Her forehead is sweaty. He smiles back at her and reaches for a remote control. As he directs it at a monitor embedded into the padded wall, an appalling hi-energy dance track fills the room. Catherine's eyes drop to the desk again. I look up at the screen. A CGI image appears of a girl dancing round her room then flopping onto her bed with her phone. A clock in the corner says it is 10am. She selects an app called *Catwalk* and a *very* copy-light version of the magazine appears on screen. She swipes left repeatedly, whizzing past a selection of shoots and small features until she comes across an image of a model wearing a Tory Hambeck neoprene tunic and holding the 'Noelle' tote. She sighs dreamily and taps a barcode on the screen. The clock leaps forward to 6pm.

The girl is seen answering the door. Behind it is a courier with a parcel. She unwraps it to find the dress and bag she was admiring. The last image is her in a bar showing off the new purchases to friends. Giddy with envy, they get out their phones, then tap onto the *Catwalk* app. Frédéric zaps the screen. The music stops.

'*That, mes amis…*' says Frédéric, standing up. '*…est le nouveau Catwalk*. A virtual world where everything you see or read about, can be bought simply by tapping your Smartphone. Do this by midday, and in some cities, you can wear it that night. This "*tap et acheter*" technology is not original *dans le monde du* publishing, *je sais*. The difference is, *Catwalk* will now, *only* be available as an app…and it will *only* be selling *my* products. It is not—how you say, the science of rockets?'

Fitz balks. '…and you think *that* is what our readers want? A cocking app?'

'It is all *any*one will want soon,' Frédéric shrugs. 'The future is in images and promotion. In fact, the present is already, the words merely lure the consumer into a false sense of meaning. Because that is what your reader is; a consumer. *Pur et simple.*'

'Bullshit!' I tell him. 'Whoever buys a copy of *Catwalk* is looking to be entertained, turned on, celebrated, teased, *inspired*…and that takes words too.' I surprise myself at how much I actually mean what I'm saying. 'Our sales have been falling over the past year under your influence. Fitz and I *know* you've been bulk-buying magazines to make it look as if sales are steady.'

Frédéric nonchalantly waves the remote control at me. '*Absolument*. We simply didn't want to draw any attention to the magazine before we were ready to announce our news.

I am not interested in your readers, *ma chérie*. I am not interested in inspiring anyone. All that I am interested in is the name; *Catwalk*...and what *that* means.' He sits down between Fitz and me. 'Let me give you an analogy... I have a villa in Ibiza, bought it in the eighties. Back then the island was a heady playground where exotic, mysterious, bohemian beauties danced *toute la nuit et dans la journée*. Time was of no essence. Now, it is a place where loud hen parties creosoted *dans le* fake tan wear *les bikinis avec les* wedge heels and attend champagne spray parties that finish strictly at 2am, before they are herded back home on a budget airline. But on that flight? Ah, they feel like they have been touched by the same magic as their predecessors. Ibiza does that. *By association.* My brands are becoming that loud hen party. They need Ibiza! They need *Catwalk*. I make sense?'

I turn to Rhuaridh and Catherine. 'So, what's really happening is that you're selling us out. And can I add here, selling us out to a man who will have no duty of care to his staff whatsoever. I know this because he can't even look after his own muse. Noelle overdosed in his penthouse and he refused to call an ambulance.'

Rhuaridh swivels to look at Fredric. 'Is this true?'

'As if!' Frédéric rolls his eyes.

'I was there,' I insist.

'Do you have evidence?' He snorts. 'Non. Exactement! Besides, Noelle and I are about to launch the 'Noelle' clutch. As if I would endanger ma petite vache de cash! I jest, she is precious to me, you all know that.'

'Listen to me, Lazare,' says Rhuaridh. 'I will not have the Ogilvy name in any way associated with illeg—'

Frédéric laughs. 'Pfffff! This is getting silly. You...' He points at me. '...are cuckoo. And that we *have* seen evidence of. But—getting back to business—let me reassure you this: neither you, Monsieur Martin, nor your team will be sold out. That is why Miriam is here.' He motions to the woman in the grey suit.

'As Frédéric said, I'm the head of human resources at RIVA,' she says. 'We're working out the basic figures.'

'Figures for what?' asks Fitz, his jaw clenched.

She takes a breath. 'The redundancy packages for everyone currently working on the editorial side at *Catwalk*…'

I feel as if my mind is caving in on itself. I try to compute what is being said.

'…we will be keeping Mrs Ogilvy and the advertising team,' continues Miriam.

'…and *that* one,' adds Frédéric. 'The one *avec le* social media presence. She will also be joining us.'

'*Jazz?*' Fitz yelps. 'But she can't write!'

Frédéric shrugs. 'I disagree. *J'adore* her hashtags.'

'What limited copy that is required…' adds Miriam '… will be written by the advertising team. This makes sense as every aspect of the magazine will now be sales driven.'

'And our in-house web designers will duplicate the *Catwalk* feel,' continues Frédéric. 'So, it looks like *Catwalk*, even though lurking beneath is a very different product. *Je suis sûr que vous comprenez*, given your love of fashion… it's what's on the outside that counts!'

Miriam grimaces awkwardly at Fitz and me. 'As I was saying, naturally, RIVA will be honouring all your original contracts in terms of redundancy packages. We wish to make the transition as smooth as possible, so please, any other queries you have moving forward, I would be happy to answer them, Ms.…erm…apologies, I didn't catch your name?'

I glance across at Fitz. His eyes are squeezed tight, as if

hoping this is a nightmare he will wake up from. I have heard enough. I jab him and push back my chair, ready to leave.

'Her name is Ashley Jacobs...' says Catherine, finally speaking. Her voice sounds strange. *Wobbly*. '...and *she* should have been the one Fitz—my brilliantly talented senior writer—'

He opens his eyes, and sniffs, sulkily accepting the compliment.

'...thanked when he won that award, because although I may have put him on the payroll, it was Ashley who gave him his internship. It is she who has selected every member of staff on the current editorial team—bar one—and overseen their development. She can be difficult. She still is difficult. She doesn't let me or anyone else on the magazine have it easy. But this is because she cares. I could see that in her at the beginning. I have seen that in her with every promotion I have given her, because I cared too. But now she cares *way* more than I do. I haven't cared about *Catwalk* for a long time.'

Rhuaridh reaches for his wife's hand. 'What are you saying, darling?'

'I'm saying that I need to go to where I *do* care.'

'Another magazine?' asks her husband, horrified.

Catherine takes his hand. 'No, I'm not going to another magazine, I'm going home.'

'She is not thinking clearly,' says Frédéric to Rhuaridh as if Catherine wasn't at the table. 'She has—how you say?—the baby brain.'

'I'd rather you didn't patronise my wife, Frédéric. Darling...' He turns to her, his voice dropping to a whisper. '...you can't back out now. We're about to sign the contract and you're part of the package. The magazine is in no condition to be sold to anyone else but Frédéric. We must pursue this.

We'll lose the estate. Fifteen generations of Ogilvys have lived there…'

'…but it's the *next* generation I care about and it doesn't matter where they live when they're older as long as they invite me round. Right now, I'm not sure they will.' She flops back in her chair and sighs. Her face has developed a yellowy green tinge. 'I have three children and another one on the way. I barely know the three that are here already. They barely know me. That needs to change. I want them to experience how rotten I am as a cook, driver, nurse, counsellor and mathematician. I want to wipe their faces with the nearest bit of fabric that comes to hand irrespective if that is a dish cloth, Alexander McQueen skull scarf or exfoliating mitt. I want to be the one who helps them with their paintings and drawings so that when they come home from school and hand me those pieces of A4 paper covered with incoherent blobs of paint or random scribbling, I can only blame myself. I want to *really* endure the mind-numbing tediousness that is watching my sons go down a slide for the seventy-ninth time. I want to put aside all that Camille Paglia has taught me to read my daughters a fairytale about a princess whose only life goal is to get married to a dishy landowner. I want to piss off other mothers at the school gate by wearing my eye-poppingly expensive cashmere lounge wear. And always with Isabel Marant fleeced boots or her wedge trainer, which is the original and *only* acceptable "invisible" wedge shoe in a market flooded with wedged footwear…'

I almost smile. She has made a good point.

'…I want to dress up my children in wholly pretentious designer clothes for school photo days,' she continues, caught in the moment. She is now the colour of mould but she sounds brighter. 'I want to feel a growing sense of dread that morphs into pride as I realise they are becoming brighter, wittier and sharper than I ever was, am now or will ever be. I want to be the person they call for when they fall over, instead of an Elena, Ivanka, Rosica, Gergana or Petja. But most of all, I want to stand naked in the mirror, witness my spaghetti junction of stretch marks, spaniels' ears bosoms and serial killer scars slicing across my lower abdomen and not even stop to question if it was all worth it.' She looks at everyone, one by one. 'That's what I genuinely want. But when you've "got it all", and all your peers have too, it's hard to admit, you'd be happy without *some* of it…as if in some way, you've lost. But as I will be teaching my children, as long as you tried your best—and looked stylish doing it, obviously!—it's not the winning that counts. I have tried my best. And I have looked *very* stylish doing it. Now, if you'll excuse me…' She glances down at her Longines silver and rose gold watch. 'I need to go and be sick. Then I need to pick up my eldest two from nursery.'

Rhuaridh touches her arm gently. 'Darling, Marijka will have already done that…she fetches them home at two forty-five.'

'Oh. I still need to be sick though.'

'Go, then…' He shakes his head, but he is smiling. 'I'll sort this out.'

'Are you sure?'

'Yes, don't you worry. Go home and be with your babies.'

'Thank you,' she says, her voice breaks. She kisses her husband on the cheek, then nods at Frédéric. 'Apologies for pulling out, but you have the perfect editor sitting at this table. She has far more respect in this industry than I do. I couldn't recommend anyone else more highly.' She touches my shoulder. 'Offer the job to Ashley.'

Catherine walks out of the boardroom. Before the door has even closed, Frédéric turns to me.

'Well?'

My brain re-engages. I don't pause either.

'Only if you can guarantee that content is not driven by your merchandise and the editorial team keep their jobs.' Even as I'm saying this, I know my request is futile.

Predictably, he laughs. '*Ma chérie!* Have you not listened to anything? *Catwalk* as *you* know it, is finished. The last tangible magazine issue will be the one currently in production. This will be announced at the grand party celebrating *dix-huit ans* of the magazine. *Ce sera une grande fête!* A celebration of the new, and of course, the old. *Une nuit fabuleuse*…it is the very least I can do for your departing colleagues. But like I say, that does *not* have to include you. Join RIVA. Come, be cuckoo *avec moi*!'

'Ha!' I laugh too. 'If you think that I would even consid—'

Fitz jabs me hard. 'Owww! What the f—'

'Jacobs. *Shoosh*. We need to speak.' He yanks me from my seat and marches me to the door. He nods over his shoulder to Frédéric, Rhuaridh and Miriam. 'Ignore what she said. Give us two minutes.'

We step outside into the corridor. Fitz grabs me by the shoulders.

'Okay, Jacobs, what I am about to say, you must never repeat to anyone who we work with. You swear?'

'I swear.'

'No, really *swear*…swear on the memory of Gianni Versace.'

'Christ, pulling out the big guns. No, the *cannon*! I swear on the memory of Gianni Versace.'

'Good. Take the job. *Take the job*. TAKE THE JOB! It will

come with a whopping salary. You need the money to pay off Zach so you can keep your flat. The rest of us are going to be unemployed whatever, so there's no point trying to be a hero. Artistic integrity is all well and good but that won't secure your home. I won't be naff with you…well, no more than I am already. The others will understand too. They have their redundancy package.'

'But what about the ones in the more junior roles? They have a two-week notice period, not even a month.'

He shrugs. 'That won't change if you don't take the job. They'll *still* be skint and jobless. Yeah, it sucks, but…'

'…but all that stuff Catherine said about me…' I cringe at the word. '…*caring*. I wouldn't if everyone else didn't care too. That magazine is a team effort. If I accept that job I may as well return to the office with 'scab' written across my forehead.'

Fitz shakes his head at me. 'But, *I repeat*, they will still get the bullet!'

'True, but what does it say about me if I am seen rejecting all that the magazine represents, in exchange for a pay cheque?'

'It says, 'I'm a woman who is in the middle of a divorce and in debt, and have therefore been forced into a position where *how* I earn my money cannot be the priority, but how *much* I earn…'. This is life, Jacobs…*real life*…YOUR LIFE…it's serious.'

'Yeah, I know. But I'm sick of everything being so fucking serious. I've been dealing with serious for longer than I can remember.'

For once, Fitz does not joke back. Neither do I. I sigh at him.

'Talking of real life, you never told me your father disapproved of your sexuality.'

'And *you* never told *me* it was *you* who selected me for my internship.'

'It's irrelevant.'

'And so is the Rev. Martin. Oh, go do the maths, Jacobs. He's a man of the church. The last thing religion does is promote kindness, unity and acceptance. Pops wasn't exactly going to be giving me a leg up onto my first float at Pride. Anyway, enough reality. God, it's dry! Let's go back in…' He reaches for the door handle.

'What for?' I slam my hand on his. 'Admit defeat and let them take more pleasure in their victory? No, thanks. Besides, there are some far more important people who we need to talk to.'

*

So, we leave RIVA HQ, go to the *Catwalk* office and gather the other longest-serving members of the editorial team, Bronwyn, Dixie and Wallis, in the boardroom. Fitz drops the blinds so that no one outside of the room can see their faces when we deliver the news. Bronwyn is the first to speak.

'You do realise that between the five people in this room we have given over forty years' service to *Catwalk*?' she seethes. 'And *this* is how they treat us? More to the point, this is how Catherine has treated us. I don't care if she's been missing her brats, that woman has come into this office every day—looked each one of us in the eye—knowing she is betraying us. I've got kids too but I also have morals.'

'Looking for a new job is going to be so depressing,' adds Dixie, her tone uncharacteristically deep and flat. 'Booking roles on fashion magazines never come up. I'm going to end up working for a celebrity weekly…the nearest I'll get to even dealing with fashion is contacting Michelle Keegan's "people" for an "in" on her new range for Lipsy. Oh, God.'

Wallis is pale. 'That puts you in a better position than me. It's unlikely I'll even get employed after this. Over the past few months, Catherine has forced me to put aside my creative principles. I should have refused to use all those RIVA labels she insisted on. I'm meant to be an avant garde fashion director, but in the last few shoots you can almost see my creativity curled up in the corner of the shot *crying*. And as for the one scheduled with Noelle dolled up in Tory Hambeck's cookie cutter designs…well, when the industry sees that, I may as well forg—'

I butt in. 'Hang on, they don't have to see that. Or anything else we don't want them to see. Where's this issue at?'

'Just over halfway,' replies Fitz. 'Catherine has approved early copy, images and layout. Cromalins will be in soon. It's too late to reformat.'

'No, it's not,' I reply. 'We can re-shoot and re-write anything we're not happy with before it goes to print. Catherine isn't coming back into the office so she won't be checking anything again.'

Fitz claps his hands together. 'Oooooh, Jacobs, you *shrew*! That's the kind of underground thinking I expect from you.'

'What's the point?' shrugs Dixie. 'If we're all losing our jobs anyway?'

'For our dignity. And our portfolios,' says Wallis, cheering up slightly.

'Jazz will tell Catherine, though,' says Dixie. 'For *sure*.'

'She won't notice,' I reassure her. 'She's only just crawled out from Markus Lupfer's arse after LFW. I'll set her a project to keep her occupied. Besides, when has she *ever* looked at anything being sent to print that hasn't got her byline pic attached to it? We'll have to get everyone else onside though: juniors, subs, designers…but not the ad team; they're safe so there's no need. The editorial staff need to know so they can start looking for work. I don't want them to find out at the party. Imagine their faces…the shock.'

Fitz sucks in his cheeks. '…like when the frow benches collapsed at Balanciaga S/S 2011. Anna Wintour and Mario Testino went down like a sack of spuds. And Carine Roitfeld.'

'She did not!' I tut. 'Carine slipped as the bench began to bend but she didn't fall.'

Bronwyn steps back. 'Er… rewind. The party? You're not seriously thinking of still going? You couldn't pay me in La Praire Cellular Crème Platinum…and trust me, that makes Crème De Le Mer feel like Nivea.'

'I'm not going either. It would be way too emotional,' says Dixie.

'I'd have to invite my girlfriend and you know she'll make a scene, even if it is on my behalf,' adds Wallis. 'Count me out too, for sure.'

'Are you all kidding?' Fitz balks. 'I'm certainly going to attend and I shall be drinking the free bar as dry as a nun's gusset. And I will be inviting all the people who *should* have been invited in the first place: the young designers we championed, the ones we were planning on championing but never got to, the fashion students who literally *live* on our web forum, the interns, the stylists, the freelancers, the hair and make-up artists, the models and…warning! I am going to fist pump. Here it is.' He punches the air. '…the readers who have *never* missed an issue. They need to be rewarded too. We should invite every single person who has subscribed to *Catwalk* from issue one.'

'Wow!' I smile. 'From evil queen to people's princess in the space of an afternoon. Does that mean we're all in?' The girls nod.

'I couldn't be more "in"…' Fitz grins. '*Unless* I was an Ashish sequinned silk-georgette gown worn under a vintage Loewe leather biker jacket with Brian Atwood shoe-boots, accessorised with—wait for it—*no* jewellery, bar a loose-fitting eighties men's chunky diving watch.'

In unison, we gasp, then burst out laughing. But as we do, no one dares to look at each other in the eye. Our sadness is palpable. *Catwalk* is over.

By evening, I have worked out what needs overhauling in the issue and produced a detailed production schedule to work to. There is no more I can do today, but I don't want to shut down all the documents on my computer because as each one closes, more of my screen saver appears. And the more I can see of Kat Moss. I can see her left whiskers, the end of her tail, the tips of her ears…

'Jacobs? *Jacobs?*' Fitz taps me on the shoulder. 'Everyone has left. You should get home too.'

I blink and check the time on my monitor. 'You're right, I should. My husband will be wondering where I…*oh*…' I manage a sarcastic smile. 'What about you? Hot date with an M&S Fuller For Longer Chicken and Pistachio Kofta Salad in front of *Fashion Police Live From the Red Carpet* on E!?'

'Nope, it's not the same without Joan. NOTHING is the same without Joan. Hey, that could be my new T-shirt! Actually, I'm meeting…' He slaps his hand to his forehead. '…*him*. The perpetrator of the smiley face emoji. Do I look as if I am cacking myself?'

'Following through as we speak. Pull yourself together, Fitz. Try to focus on a good outcome and how great it will feel when you can ring up the Rev. Martin to say, 'Things are getting serious with Jesus…'.'

'A-*men*!' He laughs.

'I'm impressed that you've decided to bite the bullet.'

'…and *I* am verbally shackling myself right now not to make a double entendre. But yeah, thanks, Jacobs. Well, I thought about what you said. Maybe Jesus had his *own* issues going on to have behaved that way. I always assume everything is about *me*.'

For once I consider what Fitz has said. After he has left the office, I reach for my mobile and make two calls.

Eighteen

'Aren't you going to answer that?'

Maddie stares at my mobile phone. It's on my dressing table, ringing. *Again*. It takes longer to ring off than it used to. In the early hours of Monday morning, I reset my phone from its usual short alert pattern to the longest one possible.

'No,' I tell her, as I sit down at the mirror. 'I want to be consistent.'

'How many times has she called?'

'Since Sunday? At least twenty-five, maybe getting on to thirty now…'

'What about him?'

'Zero.'

'But you haven't answered any of hers?'

'I told you…' I rummage in my new (bulging) make-up bag. '…consistency is key.'

'Key to what? Driving you crazy? *Crazier?* You look wired.'

'Sleep deprivation tends to have that effect. Actually, after a while you get a buzz from it.'

'I don't remember it being enjoyable at *all* when I had Carter.'

'Maybe you didn't push it as far as you could.'

Maddie peers at me and plonks herself down next to her son who is wriggling around on my bed chewing on a rubber teething duck. It is odd speaking to her. I have not had any verbal communication with anyone in a fortnight. Finally, the phone stops ringing.

'If you're not going to pick up her calls, why don't you block her?'

'Because, with each "beeeeep beeeeep" she hears, I want her to *hope* I am going to answer. And each time the beeeeep beeeeps run out and my voicemail kicks in, I want her to acknowledge that hope fade. Then I want her to hear my voice asking the caller to leave a message and as she does I want her to be forced into thinking of something she hasn't said already. Then, as she is leaving the message I want her to wonder whether the only time she will ever hear my voice again is by ringing my mobile to hear an impersonal voicemail message…*which it is, by the way.* Finally, I want her to hang up, and as she puts down her phone be already wondering what she is going to say in her *next* message, whilst at the same time knowing that whatever she comes up will be pointless. And hopeless. And then I want the hopelessness of the situation to consume her for the next hour, hour and a half…until she makes that call again and the cycle is repeated. Hope to hopelessness. Over and over again.' I start applying a matt base to my freshly moisturised face. '*That* is why I haven't blocked her.'

'Ah.' Maddie sounds uncomfortable. 'Is that erm… primer?' she asks. 'You never even usually wear foundation. Tell me you're not going down the wronged woman who needs to reinvent herself route?'

'Give me some credit' I snap. 'I'm simply changing things up.'

'Putting a barrier up, more like. A cosmetic one *and* a mental one.' She sighs again. 'God, Tanya, I don't know how I would react if Kian, aghhh...I can't even say it. I don't know *what* I would do—what *we* would do...' I watch her in the mirror as she tickles her son. '...but don't you think that this is all getting out of control?'

'By *this*, you mean *me*?'

'Well, yes,' she agrees, quietly. 'When you hadn't got in touch with me, I called your office. I know you've quit your job...'

'And this means I am out of control? Actually, Maddie, if anything I am getting more *in* control. Something I certainly wasn't when *they* were fucking each other whilst *we* were at Center Parcs with *her* children. I also wasn't when *they* fucked in *my* hotel bed before I arrived. And I've been in even less control all the times *they* have fucked without *me* knowing...or been planning to fuck whilst *they* have been outside fucking smoking at *my* suggestion.' I dot spots of foundation on my T-zone. 'The control needs to fucking shift! It *is* fucking shifting, I can feel it! And I like it.'

Maddie winces. 'You never swear either. This is not normal.'

'Good. I don't want to be normal.' I pick up my eyeshadow applicator and exhale deeply. Not just because of everything that has happened, but I am about to start the laborious process of a smoky eye. 'I tried to create a normal life for myself and it has imploded. All of this...' I wave my hand around. '...all the things I thought I wanted, maybe I only wanted them to try and be normal. Even having a baby, maybe I only wanted that to feel normal.'

'You wanted a baby because you loved him,' she says, simply. 'You wanted to share that love with a child.'

I spin round to face her. 'Or maybe I needed to validate where I am in my life…the final proof that I had achieved maximum normality. But would I have been *genuinely* fulfilled?'

'Maximum normality after *what*? Why? Were you not normal before? You're not making sense.'

I don't reply. Maddie is silent for a few seconds. She picks up her son's teddy bear and puts it to her face as if about to play peek-a-boo with him, but she doesn't peek or boo. He continues chewing his rubber duck. I chuck the sponge applicator back in my make-up bag. I can't be bothered to do my eyes now, I'll do them on the train. Maddie puts down the bear.

'Sorry,' she says.

'Eh? What are *you* sorry for?'

'For being part of your 'normal' world. But hey, maybe recognising that you are destined for something far more is the one positive that will come out of this truly dreadful experience. Now you can move on and be 'genuinely fulfilled'.'

Irritated at myself for sharing this with her, I direct my irritation back at her.

'Oh, please, you know damn well that wasn't aimed at you nor does it have any bearing on our friendship. I understand this is hard for you, Maddie, being the only person who knows, caught in the middle…and I'm also well aware that the situation has affected your life too.'

'All of which I'm perfectly capable of handling,' she fires back, her cheeks reddening as she gets up. 'Stop talking to me as if I'm secondary. You always do that. Suze does it too. No, in fact, I'm tertiary. It's as if my role in our friendship group is simply as a mediator or buffer between the two of you. You may have shared more of your *past* with Suze, but it is me standing here…in the *present*. Anyway, I want Carter to have a proper nap, so I'm going to take him home now.' She pops her son's toys in a striped bag embossed with his initials, swings it over her shoulder, then picks him up and heads for the door.

'Let me help you put him in the car.'

'I'll be fine. Not that this is of any interest to anyone but me, but I can now get him in the baby seat without him trying to alert anyone in a three mile radius for help.'

'That's good.' I mutter.

'No, it's *great*.' She is about to walk out, but then stops and looks straight at me. 'Oh, and if when Carter and I get home he lets me put him down to sleep without acting as if I'm putting him up for adoption, then eats all of the savoury mush part of his tea without looking at me as if I'm attempting to poison him, then gets in the bath and allows me to wash his hair without insinuating I am trying to drown him, then lets me apply ointment to his sore gums without screaming as if he is visiting an Elizabethan dentist's surgery and *then* lets me put him in his cot for bed without peering through the bars as if I'm imprisoning him for a minimum twenty-five year jail term…then *yes*. I will feel genuinely fulfilled. *That* I know for sure. Enjoy your party.' She leaves.

I let her go. All the way down to London on the train, I could call her to apologise but I don't. Instead, I concentrate on my smoky eyes. I layer the product until the combined force of sleep deprivation and MAC cause them to shut.

*

When I arrive at the hotel Noelle is staying at, I am expecting her to be ready for the party, but she is shuffling around her suite in pale-pink cotton pyjamas adorned with a unicorn print. I have never felt less like dealing with…well, with *her*.

'You'd better hurry up and get changed,' I say. 'I only need to put on my dress. We should call a cab.'

'Loops has organised a driver. He can wait. I want to leave it till the last minute.' She taps the tips of her fingers together and glances at me, furtively. 'People will be looking at me. And talking about me. All of them, I know they will.'

'I thought that was why you wanted to go.'

'I don't want to go, I *have* to go…to promote the Noelle clutch. But that's not what anyone will be like, checking out. They'll be *assessing* me, wondering why I haven't been out.'

'It's only been a fortnight.'

'Which is about three months in celebrity years.'

'Why are you being so paran—' But then I stop. 'For god's sake, Noelle, do not tell me that you've been doing *that*.'

She snorts at me. 'If I had done *that*, honeeeeey, I would *want* people to look and talk about me. That's the whole point of *it*. It's also the whole point of *me*.'

'Do you realise how disturbed that sounds?'

'That's because I *am* disturbed.'

I breathe out slowly, buying time to decide whether agreeing with her or aiming to put a positive spin on things will cull the conversation quicker.

'Oh, come on, Noelle, you're making progress,' I say, choosing the latter. 'You haven't done any drugs since you collapsed.'

'Ha!' She laughs, bitterly. 'D'you know *why* I haven't?'

'Erm…because you've accepted that your life is so much better without cocaine? And you are now looking forward to an existence free of all artificial highs because you know they'll be replaced by genuine emotions. And even if those emotions are sometimes low ones, at least the *real* you will be confronting them and dealing with them, not the chemically altered you.'

She snorts at me. 'No. No, hon-*eeey*. That's not why I haven't taken anything. I haven't taken anything because I still haven't got my mobile, have I? All my numbers are on there. There is a reason why they call it a drug "habit" Because it is *habit-habitu—*'

'Habitual?'

'Don't do that, it's annoying. You're not the only one who has a decent voclab-voclablua-…who knows words. Anyway, what were you expecting? That because of *one* episode where my life and the lives of those closest to me were almost left in like, tatters, that when I faced up to what had happened I would not want to do any more drugs? *I want to do more!*'

'Then go to rehab, like I suggested. You can afford it.' I stare down at the floor. The hotel carpet is similar to the one at The Rexingham. *Mushroom.*

'It's that easy, is it? It's as easy as being able to afford it so you do it? You simply get clean. You ring up the Priory. Or alternatively, YOU RING YOUR DEALER! Hmmm…I wonder which is the easiest call to make. Ha! But like, cheers for your 'see the light' pep talk live and direct from a faceless search engine.' She jumps up. 'I'm here, honey. *HERE!* I'm a human being. I'm not simply a "case" or a "condition". Why are you such an auto-…automa-…automat-…*robot*. Look at me, say something to me.' She thumps her chest.

I stare at my sister, but then my eyes drift to the left. There is a polite no-smoking sign on the back of the hotel door. I picture *him* in *her* bed, waving his cigarette, then tapping ash into a pottery ashtray. He looked up. His eyes met mine. But it took him at least two—maybe three seconds—for his brain to confirm what he was seeing. That was when I looked away, and stared at the ashtray in his hand. It was the one I had bought as a seriously intended joke present for *her* birthday a few years ago. It was moulded in the shape of lungs which had been painted to look as if they were covered in tar. In the middle of the lungs where you flick the ash, it says: 'THANKS!'

HIM: *Babe...no. Oh no. No! No, no...no...(Shouting.) NO!*

HER: *(Running into room.) Oh god, T...oh T...I'm...I'm...T! T?*

HIM: *Babe? (Scrabbling around at side of bed for his jeans.)Please say something...*

HER: *Shut up! She needs to speak to me. T, come downstairs. I'll make you a drink We'll talk. You! (Pointing at him.) Get dressed and get out of here.*

HIM: *No! She needs me. Babe, listen to me this means nothing...*

HER: *He's right. It means...meant...nothing to either of us. This was going to be it...the final weekend.*

HIM: *As soon as we got engaged I told her. That was it. I still want to marry you...*

HER: *Oh, T, I swear it was only a few times. I know that does not excuse it any way but you have to believe me. It's just sex.*

HIM: *She's right. Say we're going to be okay, please... say it. Say it...*

HER: *Don't be so effing ridiculous. She'll need time. You're meant to be her fiancé... T, I'm your best friend. Talk to me...*

HIM: *(Voice choked.) I'm so sorry, I'm so sorry. (Yanking jeans up. Approaching me.) Babe, I want you to breathe. Breeeeeeeeeeathe. Now look at me... (Grabbing my face.)*

Please, please, say something. Please. Say. Something. To. Me.

I said nothing.

Because if there is one thing I had learnt by the age of sixteen, it's that silence is by far the most perfect weapon. You never run out of ammunition. *She* never did. I was defence-less. And I could not attack back either.

'See!' shrieks Noelle. 'You can't, can you? You can't say anything from here.' She slaps her chest again. 'Because there is nothing *in* there. You almost did, the night we went home, but then you like, pissed off and I didn't hear from you. And *I* am the one with issues? At least I have *some*thing inside of me. Even if I don't know how to handle it.' She walks into the bathroom. 'I'll be ready in half an hour. Help yourself to the mini bar.'

'Thanks.'

THANKS! I stared at the word in the ash tray. I remained silent even though they were both still shouting at me on either side. Then I pushed them both; her to my left, him to my right…and walked through the gap I had created in the middle. Then I left. Both of them followed, but neither of them could get me to say anything or even focus on them. Their panicked, desperate pleas for me to 'listen' blurred together as I made my way out of the house and headed for the road. That was when she told him to come back because he would make things worse. She said I would want to be on my own. He told her that he knew me better. And then, as I noticed our car parked up on a grass verge, their voices faded. My journey home took an hour. I made my way across the fields and along the country lanes with my torch and umbrella. I was in a trance-like state. Almost high…on uncut, pure, clean betrayal.

When I got home, I kicked off my muddy shoes outside the house, then showered, put on a tracksuit and trainers and started retrieving all of Greg's belongings from each room in the house. I was calm. I stacked up everything neatly in the reception room. Then at 8am, I ordered a 'large van with a nice man,' who I found on one of those locally recommended websites. He arrived at 10am. We loaded all of the stuff. We had a cup of coffee. He left at 11.30am. At 12.27pm, he called me—as I had asked him to—to say that everything had been delivered and offloaded at The Croft. One of the barmen had helped carry everything up to the studio flat.

There is a knock at the door of Noelle's suite. I answer it. A man in geeky spectacles and a smart, tapered suit is standing the other side.

'Hi,' I say. 'Ah, we're running late. Can you park up, please? We'll be down in half an hour, no more…'

He grimaces at me. 'I didn't drive, sorry.'

'What? How are we meant to get to the venue?'

'By taxi? Tube? Bus? Rickshaw? Personally, I think London's travel network is the finest in the world. And I've lived in New York and Paris.' He grins at me. 'I'm Gus.'

'Gus?'

'Noelle invited me tonight. To say cheers. She knows my studio is round the corner. You must be Tanya? I believe it was your idea that your father emailed me to, erm…help, the other week.' He offers his hand to shake. 'Angus O'Donnell.'

'Oh, God! I'm so sorry, come in, come in… I wasn't thinking. Noelle is getting ready,' I tell him. 'It was so generous of you to stand up for her. Thank you.'

'Really, it was no problem. I'd like to say that I was shocked that Troy—or Eric, as I like to call him—was capable of being such a, well, *prick*, but I'm afraid he has proved himself to be a prize one on multiple occasions in the five years I have known the band. They tolerate him because he's such a great showman on stage. Eric lives like Axl Rose circa 1991. Financially, that is. Artistically, he's merely a loose, spare cog. Of no use in order for the wheel to turn…'

I manage a smile. 'How did you persuade him to retract his threat?'

'Easy. Told him I would stop writing for Barbed.'

'I thought you were their producer?'

'Given that I'm a fortnight away from submission of their third album to the record company, and Eric owes two hundred grand in unpaid tax, he took all of seven seconds to say he would apologise to your father. Before I hung up, I reminded him that when we delivered the second album every executive who heard it at the playback, rejected Eric's *one* attempt at a song. They thought I had put it on there as an April Fool. I shouldn't laugh, but…'

'Really, you saved her career.' I lower my voice. 'To think the Western World might not have got another series of *Check Me Out, Sista!*.'

'Actually, I quite enjoyed that,' says Angus, sweetly. 'It was a guilty pleasure when I was locked up in the studio on the boys' second LP. So, speaking of careers. Noelle sent me a demo…from your other half? He's pretty on point in terms of tone and pitch but could really do with defining his sound. He doesn't seem to have settled upon *who* he is, as an artist. I thought, maybe we could have a jamming session? And, yeah, I am *quite* aware of how heinous that suggestion sounds if you don't play an instrument. Will he be joining us later?'

'Not tonight. No. But…*thanks*.'

*

The Catwalk Coming of Age 18th Birthday Party is being held at a nightclub in Central London. There are layers of paparazzi at the entrance, their cameras flashing whenever someone of note makes their way in. I watch as a succession of them pose, their grins becoming more forced and position of their limbs becoming more awkward. But Noelle makes it look effortless. She makes sure that the 'Noelle' clutch baring her initials is captured in all its oblong-shaped, gold snakeskin effect, gilt-chained glory and stares into the glare of the lights. Unblinking and steady, the booomsht booomsht booomsht of dance music reverberates through the doors behind her. To the onlookers she looks like a winner. But I know my sister is lost.

Inside, Angus takes our coats to get checked in at the cloakroom whilst I follow Noelle down the stairs into the bowels of the club. I can see she is tensing up. Her collarbones jut then squeeze together with each step.

'Noo-Noo!'

Sophie Carnegie-Hunt bounds up the stairs towards us. She is wearing a sequinned beret and a Daft Punk T-shirt.

'Where the fuckety-fuck have you been?' she squawks at Noelle. 'I was going to send Loops over to your hotel. The party is kicking *off*. Bloody a-*ma*-zing vibes. Frédéric ETA twenty mins. Get yourself in the VIP pronto. They're a-c-t-u-a-l-l-y calling it The Noelle Lounge. Isn't that amaaaaazing! Bloody love the word "lounge". Except when used to replace sitting room.' She sees me. 'Ah. It's *you*. Tamara, isn't it? Listen, I wanted to apologizzle about that sticky little episode the other week. I'm sure you do too. It's hard for civilians to understand *that* part of the biz. I'm not surprised you overreacted.'

'...I overreacted?' I glance at Noelle. She looks away.

Sophie pulls me towards her. 'But please, don't give yourself a hard time. I would have done too. I love Noelle *like* a sister. But unlike an *actual* sister, we have no deep-rooted issues with each other and I only want the best for her. Ha! I jest!'

Now, Noelle looks at me—with the same mindless stare she was giving the paparazzi. Irritation jangles through me. I extract myself from Sophie's embrace and march to the main bar, where I order a double vodka with orange juice. And then a shot of tequila with a lemon wedge and a lick of salt. I do the shot first. As it slides down my throat I gag. Then the bitter tang of citrus makes the muscles in my face distend involuntarily. I look round the club. It is packed with guests having fun. No...*revelling*. I order another shot. And a double vodka and orange to follow.

'Tanya!' A voice shouts my name over the music.

Ashley approaches. She is wearing a shimmering gold floor-length dress with a 'cut out' rib cage. She assesses my black heels and strapless black dress but doesn't quite look up any further to meet my eyes. Which is fine by me.

'Hi.' I dab salt from my mouth.

'Hi. I'm erm...surprised to see you. I bumped into Noelle and she said you were here,' she says, finally scanning my face for a reaction. 'You never replied to the voice mails I left, so I assumed that you didn't want to...' She drifts off. 'I ended up giving my plus one to this guy I'm seeing but I wanted to give it to you. Despite everything, I thought...' She doesn't finish her sentence again. 'Like I said, the way I left things. Left *you*. Agh. Anyway, now that you're, erm... here, I guess, we sh—'

I zone out. She is rambling awkwardly, which is so not her. I consider butting in to tell her to *relax*, it's not as if I think *any*thing has changed between us, that I only came because Noelle asked me to support her, and after tonight we'll go our separate ways again…but I am distracted by how tired she looks. Or is it *my* tiredness that is influencing everything I see? It feels as if there is a greasy, mottled film of exhaustion over each pupil.

Ashley exhales deeply and leans back against the bar.

'Just to let you know, since I left that last message, there has been a further *monstrous* development in the fate of *Catwalk*,' she says. 'Jazz, that blogger I was telling you about, is going to be the Editor of the new format. Which goes to show that anyone wanting to get ahead in fashion publishing these days should forget about actually *writing*. You simply need to get one hundred and forty two fucking thousand hits on YouTube for your video on five ways to wear harem pants. I feel bad I couldn't save the magazine. Bizarrely, I feel worse for them, though…' She points over to a group of people—mainly women—on the edge of the dance floor. I recognise them as *Catwalk* staffers from their picture bylines. '…the team. *My* team.'

She pauses. I have no idea what she is going on about. I think it could be my cue to congratulate her on having some sort of feminist epiphany. But frankly, I now have no desire to celebrate anything about modern women. In fact, I think that the Disney princesses I mocked as backward have it sussed. Concentrate on winning and keeping your man at all costs whilst only tolerating friendships with mice, teapots and elderly fairies.

Ashley continues rambling. 'So…you decided to stay a pure blogger, then? Not sully yourself by getting involved in the Machiavellian world of Being Paid For Writing Something? It's a shame. I wanted to use that piece you wrote on

Insta-couples. My favourite line had to be, "*...and as for the use of the word 'bae' when referring to your partner on social media? Surely, a crime so heinous that any previously liberal thinker would reconsider their views on the death penalty, and yearn for the comparatively halycon days where 'boo' merely made you want to kill yourSELF...*" Fucking ace! And the fashion angle you gave it with the reference to couples taking "up-close-and-digitally-altered selfies to celebrate their matching beanies/parka hoods/overly-plucked-overly-arched-eyebrows" delete as applicable...' So on point. I really wish you could have recon—'

Suddenly, I re-engage. 'Reconsider what?'

'Me using your work in the final issue of *Cat*—' She stops herself. 'Hang on, did you not listen to my message explaining that the magazine has closed? About Frederic buying it to flog his over priced, over exposed, over logo-ed tat...'

I shake my head.

'Or the other one?' She steps forward. Now, she appears thrown. Or possibly *concerned*? No, nervous. 'Tanya?'

'I haven't listened to any messages for a while. Not yours, not anyone else's. I didn't even know you called. I've had... I've not exact— I've been really busy...' It is still to raw to even contemplate sharing. '...with stuff.'

'Agh! SHIT!' Flustered, Ashley throws her hands up in the air. 'That means I will need to repeat what I said... Christ, it was hard enough first time round. But if I tell you again, you have to promise that the message I left will be deleted. As the thought of it lingering in the ether as evidence that I have become a total...god, I don't know what the word is. Me, not knowing a word. I *know* words! Okay, listen to me, Tany—'

We both jump as Angus arrives and passes me a yellow ticket.

'For your coat, Tanya. Sorry, I didn't realise you were talking to someone. Angus…' He holds out his hand to Ashley. 'Angus O'Donnell.'

'Oh, hi! Actually, I sort of know you. We've featured you in *Catwalk* before,' she says, effortlessly slipping back into professional mode. 'Ashley Jac—'

'Jacobs,' he interrupts. '*I* know. The writer.'

'*A* writer. But you're *the* music producer,' she replies. 'Although, I imagine you usually keep that quiet in public… just in case you get badgered into some impromptu listening.'

He laughs. 'Actually, I was saying to Tanya earlier that as long as I'm allowed to be brutally honest, I'm up for it. I've got her man's demo. Fortunately, it was more than alright. Anyway, let me get you two a drink.'

'I'm fine, thanks,' she replies. 'I'm not drinking tonight.'

'I am.' I butt in. 'Vodka and orange, please…' Then I drain my first one. 'Thank you, Angus.'

'I'm going to try the other end of the bar,' he says. 'More gaps up there.'

As he walks off, I turn to Ashley.

'I'm listening…'

She turns to me too. But she doesn't say anything. She doesn't have to because she is smiling at me. And I realise, just like I did by the end of lunch in the school canteen on the first day of that Autumn term…

'You want us to be friends?'

She nods.

I step back. And I think, *this is it*. This is the moment I am released from all of it; the guilt, the loss, the shame, the fear, the desperation…the past. The moment which I hoped would happen but then—after time—forced myself to stop hoping for. Because hoping would only make the guilt, loss, shame, fear and desperation so much more acute. I want this to be it. But it isn't. I may be thinking this. But I am not *feeling* it. What I am feeling is *this*. I now know what it feels like to feel how you did, Ashley. What he did to me. What she did to me. I will *never* forgive *either* of them or forget what they did. I look at her smiling at me. She may want to believe she has forgiven and forgotten, but we will never be equal. What happened will haunt us forever: tipping the scales of friendship; *the spectre of judgement*. Therefore, it is over. *Again*.

'Listen Ashley…' I begin. 'We shouldn't t—'

'Oh, I *know*! We can't talk now. It's too noisy. More to the point, neither us need an emotional *scene* tonight. Not with me saying goodbye to my career and you potentially losing that ultra intense smoky eye you've got going on. I mean, seriously Tanya, you'd drown in a pool of Maybelline. Listen, I need to go and check if my guy has arrived,' she adds, clearly mistaking my silence for some kind of agreement. 'Before I forget, I found some of your jewellery behind the cushions on my corner sofa. It must have come off when you were staying.' She picks out a folded up piece of tissue from her vintage Fendi baguette and places it into my left hand. 'I've given your sister back her phone.'

'The what? You gave her th—'

'Hello Kitty phone, yeah.'

'Oh, God,' I mutter, more to myself. 'That has got all of her numb—'

But then I stop. Because a silver chain with a disc attached to it has slipped out of the tissue. I dangle it in front of me. It does not belong to me. It belongs to him. It is *his* bracelet. But it is *my* inscription on the inside: TO MY T. T = TRUE LOVE. I close my hand around it.

Ashley taps me on the shoulder. 'Tanya?'

'Thanks,' I say, without looking at her.

'No worries.'

'Thanks, thanks, *thanks*…'

I don't say it again. My hand tightens around the bracelet. Suddenly, my head feels heavy. The music sounds distorted. People swaying on the dance floor merge together. Lights start to flicker. Ashley's head looks as if it is lit up by a halo. I grip onto the bar behind me.

'JACOBS! JAAAAACOBS! Oi! You SHREW!'

I glance to the side. Fitz Martin is yelling as he approaches us. His face is blurred. His speech is sludgy.

'Jacobs! It's all kicking off in the VIP. Quick! Major DRAAAAAAAAAAAMA. You have to check it out. Noelle Bamford is going loony at Gopher Hag-Needy-C*nt! It's handbags at dawn! Or rather, tackily monogrammed clutches. Follow meeeee!'

Somehow, I move. But not as fast as Fitz and Ashley. When I get to the VIP area it is surrounded by people gawping giddily at Noelle. She is standing on top of a steel table screaming and waving her phone. Her face is pale but sweaty. Her agent is reaching out to her.

'Noo-Noo, calm down, caaaaaalm down…' she says loudly, but not shouting. 'You don't mean any of this. We're bloody amazing together, and you know that. I tried to sort out the situation as best I could. You can hear me quite clearly on that video saying that I was going to sort it. Like I always sort everything…'

'Look at me!' Noelle brandishes the mobile in Sophie's face. 'Do I look like I needed a hit of sugar? I was DYING! I didn't think Ashley was like, telling the truth, but she was and now everyone else should know.' She taps at her phone, then reveals it to the room. 'This is me overdosing, and this is her…' She points at Sophie. '…offering me a glass of fizzy pop.'

Guests lean in, trying to get a glimpse of the screen. Sophie flaps her arms and steps in front of them.

'Oh, come on, Noo, you only needed to chuck up. It was a simple case of when the good times go bad. Now, I suggest you chill the hell out. Frédéric is upstairs…'

'I don't care about him,' screams Noelle. 'He doesn't care about me. Neither do you. You don't care at all. You've never cared about me. I thought we were like, friends. Now I realise you never even liked me. You only liked how much cash I could like, make you. It's because of *you* I don't know how to be *me*, only the *me* who *you* invented.'

I know this should be my cue to jump over the velvet rope, but this time I can't move. The only energy I have is being channelled into my left hand.

Sophie squares up to Noelle. Suddenly, she doesn't look as concerned about the scene they are making.

'And you think I can be me?' Her voice is getting louder. 'Ha! *Of course I can't.* Every day, I have to pretend you are a dream to work with…and not the Wes Craven-directed nightmare you really are. But I get on with it to make YOU *and* ME very wealthy. Trust me, I know some seriously hardened and wizened crones who have been in the industry since public relations was invented—when it was just called "turd polishing". And I know for a fact that you would push anyone to their limits. Demanding, rude, bolshy, intolerant, dense, short tempered, picky, vain, desperate, vacuous…I expect my clients to have at least one, two, maybe three of these character traits—that is why they need me. You? You have them ALL. *And* on top of it all your breath could rouse a corpse. Base fragrance of animal protein with a top note of bile and an undercurrent of Smints. But you know what? I would be quite happy putting up with all of this if you were grateful. But not once have you said "thank you". Not once! YOU NEVER SAY THANK YOU. Ever. And it's not as if you can't express yourself. Oh, no. The endless verbal sewage that flows from your mouth! Every time I hear you say "honeeeeey" in that preposterously contrived transatlantic accent you have acquired, I want to clap my hands over my ears. But even that is more bearable than your attempt at being "street". The first time you said "t'ing" I almost had to leave the room. But none of the above comes close to you saying "like" every other bloody word. It makes me want to slice off my ears, place them in a piping hot pan with olive oil and chilli, squeeze lemon juice over the top and sautée the pair of them until nothing is like, left in the like, *pan.*' She exhales deeply. 'The thing—sorry, t'ing—is…without me putting up with all of that, no, simply without me; you *know* what you would be.'

Noelle is staring at her, almost hypnotised.

'What would I be, Sophie?' she mutters.

'A Nobody,' replies Sophie, rearranging her beret. 'And *that* is why you shove that dirt up your nose because deep down you think that is what and who you are. I have tried so hard to make you change your opinion of yourself, Noelle, because despite all of the above, I think you are A Someone, and I genuinely hoped that if everyone saw that, eventually you would too.'

'Well, I…I…' She stalls. 'I haven't, so, like, screw you!' screeches Noelle. 'And him!' She points across the dance floor.

I turn to see Frédéric Lazare. He is happily chatting to

another man, oblivious to the commotion. They walk towards the VIP section. Noelle jumps off the table and over the velvet rope, then throws herself in front of her Svengali. She is screaming at him. I can't hear what she is saying. My head feels heavy again. The music sounds even more distorted. This time the people on the dance floor don't so much merge together as swim. The lights fade. I am aware of each link of the bracelet embedded into my left hand. With my right I am squeezing something else. I remember I am holding my glass. I feel it crunch. My palm feels damp and then cold as it closes in around the ice cubes. It is a satisfying sensation. A rush of relief. My breathing becomes rapid. I squeeze harder. The nightclub floor hurtles towards me. I remember standing at the top of the yellow tower. The one which looked like dirty Lego. Then everything goes black.

'*Tanya. TANYA! Wake UP! Christ. How long has she been out now?*' Ashley's voice.

'*Medic is on his way.*' Fitz's voice. '*Good grief, what a drama! Now THIS is a party!*'

'*Hon-eeeeey, I'm here!*' Noelle's voice. '*It's okay...I'm like, fine! I'm like, liberated! Awwwww! That's so sweet that you got so upset, about m—*'

'*Shooosh, Noelle.*' Ashley. '*She didn't faint because of you. She cut her palm on some glass. Look...it's bleeding.*'

'*Aghhhhhhhhhh!*' Noelle.

'*Medic is here.*' Fitz. '*Stand back every one! STAND BACK!*'

'*Get out of her face, Noelle.*' Ashley. '*NOELLE! Let the guy do his thing.*'

'*My sister, my poor sister.*' Noelle. '*Nooooo! No! It should have been, like, me!*'

'*She is not going to die from a superficial wound.*' Ashley. '*STOP lolling over her…look, she's awake.*'

'*Oh.*' Fitz. Sounding disappointed. '*Show is over every-one.*'

The medic stems the bleeding and insists that he supports me as I leave the dance floor. I keep mumbling that I am fine, that I haven't slept in days, that I have a history of fainting, that stress can bring it on, that this is what I do…but he refuses to let me go. He manoeuvres me through the club. My body feels rigid with embarrassment the way it did the first time I collapsed on my first day in the college mini mart. We go through a series of swing doors and I am taken into a private room; the sort of sumptuous enclave with womb-like décor that would be used by elite guests getting up to no good. The medic lays me down on a sofa and removes glass from my right hand. Then he checks my left. It is no longer holding the bracelet. He bandages both hands and tells me to rest. I tell him it is fine to leave me, but he refuses, saying he'll wait for my friend. I tell him I don't have one out there.

Forty minutes later, Ashley sticks her face round the door. Instantly, my purple heat rash crawls over my upper body. The medic gathers his equipment. I thank him as he leaves, but then get up. Ashley waves my bag at me.

'Where's Noelle?' I ask, groggily. 'I want to go.'

'You can't leave.' Ashley grins. 'The celebrations are about to start. Your sister has been *very* useful—words I think we both thought would *never* have a reason to be said. Rhuaridh Ogilvy was shown the footage of her OD-ing at the penthouse. Or to be more precise, he was shown the footage after everyone else had seen it. And Fitz videoed him watching it. There is more chance of Anja Rubik having a bad hair day than him selling the magazine to Frédéric now.'

She pauses, and mistakes my look of agitation as one of piqued interest.

'Yeah, yeah, it's blackmail. But it's *contained* blackmail. That's the best thing about the 'bubble', no one in it will tell *any*one outside of it, but it means *every*one in it will know. If Rhuaridh goes into business with Lazare there's no way Catherine will get another job in this industry, if her new earth mother routine doesn't work out. It's all about association, and no one wants to be associated with the near-death of a *model-come-DJ-come-It girl-come-presenter-come-entrepreneur-oh, come off it!* Ignoring an overdose always reflects badly, but especially in fashion. It's quite literally *not* a good look.' She laughs at her own joke. 'Obviously, Rhuaridh is going to need to sell the magazine elsewhere, and he will have to take a hit on it, but I believe that with some restructuring and poss—'

'Shoosh, Ashley.' I push her to one side and reach for my bag. 'Give me that. I'm not well, I'm going.'

She snatches it back. 'Woah! Did you just shoosh me? Man up, Tanya, it was a minor accident. You fainted and cut your hand. Christ, you haven't lost a limb. Admittedly, sewing crystals onto couture for Dior could be out of your capabilities for the next few weeks, but at least you've still got the tips of your fingers to flick through your—our—favourite magazine. Anyw—'

I interrupt her. 'Stop playing games with me, Ashley. You're sick. SICK!'

'I'm *sick*? What are you on about?'

With each second I look at her, my purple heat rash intensifies. My neck is so hot it is itching. I rake my fingernails down it. Up and down, up and down...

'Tanya, re-*lax*. You're being odd—and not odd as in

Daphne Guinness or Anna Dello Russo *achingly stylish* odd. Sit back down. I reckon you hit your head when you fell. You must have fallen harder than I thought.'

'Harder than you thought? How much harder did you want me to fall, Ashley? I don't think you could have pushed me harder if you tried. Oh yes, I fell, Ashley, I fell *hard*! And now, it's all over for you, isn't it? You have done what you set out to achieve.' I go to clap her but I can't.

She steps back. 'Okay, this is too much. Stay there, I'm going to find that medical guy…he can't have gone far. You need help.'

'HELP!' I fire back at her. 'I'm not the one who needs help. That's you. You're the one who has been quietly plotting her revenge. But I have to hand it to you, this is about as coolly premeditated and brilliantly calculating as it gets. I suppose it had to be, given what I did to you. It had to be something that would make us equal.' The blank—almost amused?—look on her face fills me with so much anger I feel nauseous. 'Don't look at me like that! STOP IT! ENOUGH!' I'm screaming now. 'Or is this the final flourish? Offering your friendship. Mocking me too. Making me mad. Is that what you want? FOR ME TO GO FUCKING MAD! Did you really have to do it? Did you really have to go this far? Yes, Ashley, I had sex with your father. I did it. I DID IT! BUT I HAVE SAID SORRY! So why? WHY? *WHY* DID YOU HAVE SEX WITH MY…MY…FIANCÉ?'

Ashley squints at me and steps back. She pauses for a few seconds, her eyes tracing mine. Then she bursts out laughing so hysterically, I feel her spittle land on my bare shoulder. Before she can say another word I whack her across the face with my bandaged right hand. She raises her clenched left one to protect herself, but my swipe is so violent that on impact she staggers back then falls onto the couch. I am shocked to see the mark on her skin, a raw, jagged bruise directly under her eye socket. Suddenly, a pain so sharp and intense I actually yelp, shoots up my arm.

'Owwwww!' I flop down into the couch and start to weep. I'm not crying. That would take too much effort. All my strength has been used up being *silent*. 'Owwwww...my true love.' I whisper to myself. 'You. Gave. Me. It. You gave me it. You gave me it. I gave him that because I loved him. I thought he loved me but it was all a lie. All of it. From the very start it was false.' The pain is no longer in my limb. It is all over my body. 'Owwwww.'

'Ow, my cheek bone,' mumbles Ashley. 'Pick on some your own size next time.'

'Leave me,' I manage.

'No.'

'No?'

'No. The old me would have left... happily so. But I want to see this through. I do not want any more pain, Tanya. Not physically...'

I glance sideways at her—the mark on her cheek is turning the colour of my heat rash

.'...or mentally. Not for you or me. The new me.' She inhales deeply and slowly. 'We need to be honest with each other if we are going to begin again or simply to end it. Now, I'm going to assume for a few seconds that you are capable of listening to me. Please, answer the following questions with a YES or NO answer. Got that?'

'Ashley, enough. I don't w—'

'Oi! YES or NO only! Okay, so when you say "that", are you referring to this?' She pulls her hand away from her cheek and drops the bracelet onto the floor.

I stare at it. 'Yes.'

'And would I be right in assuming that *you* bought this for *him*? Your fiancé?'

'Yes. Yes.'

'And you think that because I found it in my living room I slept with him?'

'Don't wind me up, Ash—'

'Oi! YES or NO!'

'Yes. The "T" stands for "true love" I had it made for him.'

'Ouch. Shit. I'm *almost* getting it now. But your fiancé is called Greg. You told me that. And I am telling you that there has been no one called Greg in my flat. I swear on my missing cat's life that the only man who has been in my home since I split up with Zach is called Jared.'

As she says this, I slump. I know exactly who Jared is.

'Okay, your turn. YES or NO only.' My voice is quivering. 'Did you meet Jared in a bar near the train station called The Croft?'

'Yeah, it's about ten minutes from the estate. It was called something else back th—'

'YES or NO. Does Jared have dark hair which he wears in a purposefully undone style, a well-toned body, a decent amount of stubble but not quite a beard and a fairly progressive but not too daring fashion sense?'

'Mmmm, I guess…'

'Did you see his car? Was it a Ford Ka?'

She shrugs. 'I don't know anything about car labels.'

'They're called *makes* not labels,' I mumble. 'Was it a small, blue runaround type thing?'

'Oh, yep. It was definitely a *runaround*.'

I nod slowly to myself. 'Ashley, you slept with my fiancé,

Greg. He wanted to change his name because he didn't think Greg was cool. Clearly, he chose Jared.'

'Oh my god. But I sw—'

I interrupt her. 'Wait. I want to know whether he gave you any indication that he was in a relationship?'

She chews the inside of her mouth. 'Not really. Well, there may have been a few hints. He never fully admitted to anything.'

'But you didn't ask him…to make sure?'

'It wasn't like that. I didn't think about anyone else.'

'You didn't think about anyone else?'

I sense her building up to retaliate in the only way Ashley Jacobs can, and Ashley Atwal always could. That mocking tone. That sense of superiority. That overwhelming belief in herself. Ready to chuck back in my face whatever I say, because nothing will ever be as bad as what I did back th—

'You're right. I didn't think about anyone else,' she repeats, but her voice is shaky. 'Unsurprisingly. Because that is what I do, isn't it? I never think about anyone else and that means I destroy…stuff. Love, trust, ambition, confidence, hope…I'm a human wrecking ball. Did you see the ones they used to knock down our estate? You can watch the buildings collapse on YouTube. They aimed the ball at the lower part of the structure, because the nearer the foundations the more of the building gets destroyed. I started young too, didn't I? I only had to be born to wreck my father's life. Then I wrecked Zach's. Then Kat Moss's. And now I have wrecked yours. I could have asked him. I could have found out. I could have done the right thing but, no, I j—'

I butt in. 'Ashley…'

'No, let me finish. This is important. For once, I need to take full reponsibil—'

'Really, enough!' I raise a bandaged hand at her. 'That is not what happened.'

'It is. I didn't ask him anything because I was too busy being angry.' Her voice is now hoarse with bitterness. 'I have so much anger inside me, Tany—'

'It wasn't you,' I interrupt her again.

'She warned me, you know…my mother. She warned me that unless I let the anger go it would burn me up ins—'

I pretend I am going to slap her again. She ducks and cowers.

'Okay, you have to SHUT-UP. *SHUT UP!* It wasn't *you*. It wasn't you who wrecked my relationship. It had already been destroyed.' I flop back in the sofa. 'He'd been sleeping with someone else.'

She rubs her eyes. 'Yeah, me.'

'No, someone else.' I exhale loudly, my lips trembling. 'I know about multiple specific occasions *for sure*…but, probably throughout the entire time I was with him. I'll never get the whole story but I don't want it.'

'What…the…f—' Ashley mutters. 'Do you know who she is?'

'Yes.'

'WHO?'

'Suze.'

'*Suze*?' Ashley gasps and sits up. '*Suze Lyons*? SUZE LYONS tried to steal your fiancé? That cheeky tea-leafing bitch! Correction! That SHIT cheeky tea-leafing bitch! She can't nick anything without getting caught.'

'Why what else has she stolen?'

The corners of her lips edge upwards.

'She nicked a load of clothes when we were kids. Blamed me. And I wouldn't have been seen dead in any of it. In fact, not even the last flimsy plumes of gases leaving my corpse would not be seen wearing a single item. All jersey separates in black or white…in exactly equal amounts. What? Was she moonlighting from school as a fucking chess piece?'

That's when Ashley starts to giggle.

So do I.

And then we laugh. We laugh a *lot*. We laugh like we used to when we were kids, sitting on Ashley's bed, flicking through magazines and planning our ridiculous futures…and everything was funny. Just because it was. She was funny to me because she was so full of herself and thought she had everything figured out. And I was funny to her because I was the total opposite. We never laughed *at* each other. It was always *with*…because back then we were totally equal. But after a while we stop and look at each other. Both of us know that even if we laugh longer we will never reach a point of full acceptance or resolution. But we also know we have laughed long enough to acknowledge the hurt. Ashley speaks first.

'Am I allowed to ask how you found out? Please, don't tell me you caught them in bed, because that would be too much of a cliché.' She nudges me. 'But pleeeeease…tell me if you did, you walked away. In *silence*.'

'I did…and of *course*, I did. It was hard. It still is.' I nudge her back. 'It all seems to surreal though now, though. As if it didn't happen to *me*, but it was the opening sequence of some lame chick flick…one where the heroine spends the rest of the movie building up her self worth thanks to some cute guy she randomly meets en route to dumping her fiancé's suits in a rubbish tip.'

Ashley snorts. 'Obviously, the random cute guy does not own fancy tailoring – he has no need as he works with animals. *Really* fluffy, lonely ones.' She sighs and leans back. 'Christ, Tanya…this is a tough one to make a joke out of. You'll get over him, though. I promise you. Maintain your silence, avoid contact and do not surround yourself by anything to do with him in any way. That's what I'm doing. It's the only way to move forward.'

'Ashley!' I point at her. 'You are wearing your wedding dress.'

We burst out laughing again. But this time when we stop, I pick up my bag.

'Okay, I'm out of here.'

'Where are you going?' she asks.

'Home.'

'You can't. Not now.'

'Really, I don't feel like celebrating. But you should. It's *your* night. Besides, I need you to keep an eye on Noelle. Would you mind? I dread to think what effect that moment of self awareness might have on her over the next few hours.' I smile. 'I'm going to get the last train and sleep. Then tomorrow, I need to sort out the house. There are a few things in the garage I need to bring inside…oh, and then I want to see my friend Mad—'

'No, Tanya, you're not getting it. I mean, you cannot even go out into the main room.' She sucks her cheeks in sharply. 'Jared. I mean, *Greg*. He's here…'

I scrape my neck. '*What?*'

'…well, out there in the club,' she continues. 'The guy I'm seeing, dating, sleeping with! My plus one. Same fucking person. Fucking Jared. Fucking *Greg*. Fucking HIM! I wangled him a gig for tonight. SHIT!' She pauses then grabs my arm. 'Look, you're going to have to have a little faith, which I can imagine—right now—is not something that will come easy, but *please*…it will be worth it. I have a plan. I promise he won't see you.' She checks her watch. 'Do *not* move from here until *exactly* midnight. Then go to the central dance floor—not the VIP. Stand at the back facing the stage. I'll send in a barman to bring you a drink, but *stay* here.'

As she heads to the door, it opens. Noelle screeches and pirouettes into the room.

'What a like, *night*!'

'Noelle, where's Angus?' asks Ashley.

'Out there somewhere. Why?' Grinning at me, she doesn't wait for an answer. 'Hon-eeeeey! OMG, you're like, alive! And no, I am *not* going to accept an apology, so don't even try! You don't need to say sorry for timing your fall, with like, the most defining moment of my career *so far*. Kidding! I still can't get my head round what happened tonight. What happened to me. What happened to Noelle. It was like, she, like, met the real me. I guess I had a, like, epi-…epi-…epiph-…saw things for what they really were. But I don't regret a single second of anything Noelle did, said, experienced…because she is part of me. She has to be. And always will be. But if there is something that I do regret, it is this…and believe you me, I never thought I would have the fort-fort-*FORTITUDE* to admit it, but I never actually ever, like, liked…' She fixes me with a solemn stare. '…the Noelle tote. Anyone can see it is a rip off of the original Hermès with the buckles of the Mulberry Alexa. And as for the Noelle clutch…when I saw the finished article tonight, I like, *physically* recoiled. The shine! Way too in your face and attention seeking…know what I mean?'

Ashley and I look at one another and smile.

'Trust me…' she mouths, then leaves the room.

As she shuts the door, I decide it's time to do something I have never done before. I'm going to talk to Noelle Bamford as if she were my sister. I tell her everything.

*

As instructed, at midnight I go back into the main club. Noelle follows me, intermittently touching my arm. As I walk through the corridor I realise the DJ has stopped playing. There is no boomsht boomsht boomsht just a few cat calls and whoops. The dance floor is rammed. Everyone in the crowd, those standing by the bar and in the roped off VIP section are all facing in the same direction towards the podium in the middle. It is lit up by a single spotlight. I walk past the bar and check myself in the mirrored walls. I have washed my face. I look more like me but I still do not *feel* like me. I wonder how far back I will have to go. As I hear Ashley's voice, magnified by a microphone, I wonder who that *me* even is.

'…and as you know, at *Catwalk*, we are all about exposing fresh talent and that doesn't just apply to fashion. Tonight we will be showcasing some unsigned artists and DJs from around the UK, who we're really excited about. Our first act is a singer songwriter…*he calls himself Jared*. Please, make some noise!'

I walk slowly to the edge of the dance floor and watch him jog up the steps—holding his guitar—to the top of the podium, where Ashley is waiting for him. He is wearing the jeans that he was wearing the night he came back from The Croft and didn't want to have 'nookie'. The same ones he was wearing that afternoon we rowed at The Rexingham. The same ones I watched him pull on as he got out of *her* and her *husband's* bed. With these jeans he is wearing a grey low V-neck T-shirt. I bought him that. It's from ASOS. I got him six—three grey and three white. When I packed his stuff, they went into a box marked TOPS-CASUAL. I picture him sliding his finger under the cellophane to open it. Putting it on. Checking himself in the mirror. Taking it off again, crumpling it up a bit. 'That's better…' he would have thought. I lurch towards the stage…

'*No!*' Noelle leaps in front of me and spreads her arms. 'Don't, honey, you'll regret it…' she insists. 'He doesn't deserve to see the pain he has caused. If you let him see that, he'll always control you.'

'Yeah, you're right.' I breathe deeply. 'Thanks.'

'Don't sound so surprised. I'm talking from experience.'

'Troy?'

'Mmm…' she says, then smiles at me. 'Like I said in my monol-…monal-…monil-…speech I made on my own, I am a like, human being, you know.'

'No, you are a human being, not *like* one,' I tell her, as the applause dies down and I watch *him* soaking up the last few claps. 'For God's sake, what is Ashley doing? After everything he did…and look, she's giving him his moment of glory.'

'Oh, it will be a moment.' A voice from behind me. Angus. 'That's for sure…'

'What's going on?' I ask him.

He nods at the stage. 'Watch.'

'So, Jared,' says Ashley. 'You're going to perform one of your own tracks.'

'Pretty please!'

'But before we do, would you like to tell us a bit about who you are…as an artist.'

'Well, erm…yeah, sure!' He nods, enthusiastically. 'I can

do that. As with any artist, I like to think I'm one of a kind and have no direct influences…'

He turns to the crowd to give them a goofy smile. The supportive whoops that they return with make me want to clench my fists, but my bandages are stopping me.

'…but of course, I do,' he continues. 'I'd say the more contemporary British alternative artists like Jake Bugg, Jamie T, Alex Turner from the Arctics…they all have an unmistake-able, instantly recognisable vocal. As far as songwriting and production is concerned, I worship Angus O'Donnell. The man is a genius…'

I sense Angus and I cringe in unison.

'He's also here tonight,' grins Ashley.

'*What?*' He claps his hand to his forehead sarcastically and gives her a knowing wink. 'No way!'

'*Way!*' she confirms. 'So, Jared, the song you're going to perform tonight is called *Tanya*… what does this track mean to you?'

He swallows. And sighs. Then swallows again. His eyes are glassy. Finally, he is thinking. I know he is. He is being forced to think. Exactly as I have been forced to. He is think-ing about his actions, the repercussions…not only what has happened up until now, but what will happen after tonight when he realises that he has lost what we had, what we could have had. I can feel it. I can feel *him*. He is feeling what I felt. Guilt, loss, shame, fear and desperat—

'Doesn't really mean anything!' He shrugs. 'But I *love* the melody.'

Both Noelle and Angus grab on to each of my arms to constrain me.

'Well…' Ashley steps away. 'Introduce your song, then, *Jared*.'

The spotlight centres in on him. It is so bright I can see the sheen of sweat on his forehead and the purple-white glow on his knuckles as he grips his guitar excitedly.

'Everyone, this…' He smiles proudly. 'This is *Tanya*…'

On the 'ya' of Tanya, the guitar chords kick in through the powerful nightclub sound system. I look down at the floor then shut my eyes. As his vocals kick in, I keep my eyes closed, and even I have to admit that my true love has never, *ever* sounded so… *OUT OF TUNE*. At first it is his inability to hit the high notes that is more obvious, but as the song continues I get to appreciate the lack of skill he is applying to the rest of his range. I open my eyes.

'It was her idea to use it as a backing track,' Angus explains, pointing at Ashley. 'I only twiddled a few knobs.'

'Knob, being like, the appropriate word.' Noelle giggles.

I look back at the stage. 'Jared' only lasts a few more seconds in the spotlight, before he makes an anguished yelping sound.

'That's not me, it's not me,' he shouts, trying to grab Ashley's microphone. 'Kill it, now. This is a twatting stitch up! STOP! Stop. Let me do something acoustically. I can show you! That's not me. Turn that shit OOOOOOOOOOFF! I'm an artist!'

He attempts to riff on his guitar but is drowned out by the hideous wailing coming from the speakers and the extraordinarily, eerily loud white noise of five hundred fashionistas not quite knowing how to react. He scans their faces, then twists to stare at Ashley. As he does, I sense his switch *flicking*. He turns back to the crowd.

'Piss off the lot of you!' He screeches. 'You think you're all sooooo special, don't you? But where's your actual talent, eh? OTHER THAN GETTING DRESSED? What do any of you *actually* DO?'

He has never looked more arrogant. Or pathetic. I have never felt so relieved. That man could have been the father of my baby. The room fills with giggles – no, far worse, cackling. I glance to his side. Ashley is laughing so hard she has tears running down her face. I am not laughing, but I have tears in my eyes too. I don't want to say goodbye. So, I'm not going to.

I walk away from the dance floor, go up the stairs to the cloakroom, collect my coat and leave the club. Once outside, I make a call. As I hear the ring tone, I can't wait to hear her voice. I need to talk…and she always wanted to talk, but I never did. And I need to change that. The phone connects. She picks up after three rings.

'Sweetheart? It's gone twelve…everything alright?'

'Hi, Mum. Nah, not really. But it will be.'

Nineteen

Most people consider packing to go away irritating. I usually find it relaxing. I pack by 'outfit'. But it goes without saying that all these outfits are a collection of (seemingly) random pieces that I pull together ultra-carefully to appear effortlessly collated. The key is to strike the perfect ratio of 'staples' and 'statements'. It goes without saying that I would never go down the *capsule* wardrobe route for a trip. As if *any* woman was *ever* going to use their swimming costume as a base for evening wear, knot a beach wrap round their waist and slip their feet into some dress-them-up-dress-them-down jewelled (barf!) flats. I have never met a female who packs a suitcase with efficiency of volume in mind over style. If there is one out there, I can guarantee our paths will never cross. Thinking about this makes me want to call someone. I grab my phone.

'So, I'm organising…okay, *stuffing* my suitcase…and obviously thought of you. How much did you pay in excess baggage on the way back from fashion week in Italy last year?'

Catherine laughs. 'Ashley! How lovely to hear from you. You've caught me mucking out the cage. We have a gerbil! She's called Donatella…you'll have to tell Fitz. Bright

orange with impressive razor-sharp teeth and a fabulous
bitchy resting stare; the gerbil, that is, not Fitz…actually,
both of them. Ha! And I have no idea how much I spent. I
just passed over my AMEX, like I did every year. When in
Rome, eh? Well, Milan. Listen…' Her voice stiffens. 'I've
been meaning to call you. I wanted to pop into the office to
see everyone, but I didn't know if, well…'

'…you would get a decent reception? Don't be silly. You
know what media people are like, never ones to dwell on
an issue or hold a grudge against someone. Oh, hang on a
second…'

'Exactly. But even if they are sticking pins into a voodoo
doll wearing a silk polka dot pussy bow neck blouse, I'd like
to tell them how impressed I am with the re-launch issue.
The new direction is absolutely on point. I knew you would
be a great team leader, Ashley.'

'Me too,' I joke, because I know this is what she is expecting me to do.

I pull out a wicker drawer full of sunglasses. The final
items I need to pack. Six pairs? No, five. It's not as if I can't
buy more. I feel my body tense then flinch, so I shake my
shoulders. I thought packing would relax me.

'And what about you? I bet *your* team are pleased you're
back in charge.'

'My kids? Mmmm…not really. My au pairs were so efficient and calm under pressure, and that rubbed off on the
children. I'm not efficient *without a PA* and I'm somewhat
highly strung. Last week, my eldest son swore at me—in
Bulgarian, I hasten to add—because I'd forgotten to order
food for the aforementioned vermin. I didn't realise we even
owned any pets.'

'But leaving work was the right thing to do?'

'Do you want the answer I give to all the hugely successful and mentally well balanced working mothers I am friends with or do you want the honest answer?'

'Both.'

She sighs. 'To the former, I say that I couldn't have made a better decision. But the truth is I question it every day. I go to sleep each night feeling as if I have taken part in one of those oriental game shows designed to push the contestants to the edge of their physical and mental endurance. Between you and me, I've got Marijka back three days a week. I told everyone it was because the children missed her, but it was me. *I* missed her!' A long sigh. 'I also miss the magazine. Rhuaridh and I had the new investors over for dinner the other day…I felt like a spare part at the table, and got teary. Pathetic really.' She sighs again. 'I don't know when it will seem less upsetting.'

'When you have your new baby. You'll be too tired to feel, think or function generally.'

She giggles. 'I can always rely on you for an optimistic perspective, Ashley. So, I hear you've lined up a new Deputy Editor…'

'Well, kind of. We've decided on a fresh title to fit in with what we're doing.'

'What's she like?'

'Different. Doesn't live in the bubble. Not one to make snap judgements about people, which apparently, isn't always necessary or accurate. News to me.' I know Catherine is smiling. 'The only glaring negative is that she wears too much black. Draining…'

'…and contrary to popular opinion,' continues Catherine, '…does not hide all stains. Only grown up ones like coffee, wine and squid ink ravioli sauce. Not kiddie ones. It highlights all those phlegm-y mucus-y substances that they permanently excr— *aghhhhh*! Oh, my God! Sorry, Ashley, I have to go… Donatella is…BLOODY *HELL*…no wonder she was looking fed up…she was full term…and now she's having…a…*baby*. No, bab*ies*. Aghhh! Push, Donatella! PUSH!'

'Go get some hot towels!' I laugh, but I am stiff. 'Hey, you'd better insist that Donatella has to go back to work if she wants an au pair as you're not sharing Marijka. Good luck with the rodent midwifery and please, email me soon, Catherine.'

'Of course, I will. Bye, Ashley. I was going to say good luck, but that's one thing you'll never need.'

'Why do you say that?'

'Because you're a get out there and create your own chances kind of girl.'

I hang up and replace my mobile next to my passport in the zipped compartment of my bag. Then I slam the lid shut on my suitcase and zip it up. As I do, I flinch. Again. These flinches are becoming more regular since I made my decision. This morning at 4.37am, I woke myself up with an actual *spasm*.

The intercom buzzes. I go down the corridor, check the screen and press the audio button.

'Hi, Tany-aaaaaaaaaa!' I wail. 'I want yaaaaaaaaaa…to come in.'

She rolls her eyes at the camera.

'Still haven't come up with any new jokes, then?'

'Why find a new one when this one keeps getting funnier? Repetition is humour.'

'You're sick,' she says. 'Anyway, you need to show me a bit more respect now I have a fancy new title. Especially as you gave it to me…'

I press the buzzer and let the new Future Media Editor of *Catwalk* into the building. She arrives at the top of the stairs wearing a well cut, long coat with epaulettes on the shoulders. I'm pretty sure the coat is from Zara, part of their new season's collection. They *always* put a military twist on at least one item of 'outerwear'. Imitative army wear is o-*kay*, I suppose. But wearing the real thing if you have *not* served a period of your life in the forces, is not. *Especially* if it is embellished. If you'd defended your country, wouldn't it piss you off seeing the clothes you fought in decorated on the arse with Swarovski crystals in the shape of Bambi?

'Ashley?'

'What?' I shake my shoulders again to release the tension.

'Don't worry…' She tuts at me, misreading my body language. 'I wasn't going to hug you…what with us not being friends and all that.'

'Where's all your stuff?'

'Being driven down in a van. I visited Noelle in rehab earlier. Family day…'

'Ah right, how's she doing?'

'Well, initially she was a little surprised by the whole, in her words, "*like, medical angle of it all…*". I think she was expecting to be welcomed by the staff and residents as if she was presenting a *People's Choice* award. But now she's relishing it. All that talking about herself in a closed environment. Her new agent is encouraging her to stay in as long as possible. They're concocting a plan for her to be seen as the UK's answer to Demi Levato when she gets out. There's been talk of a new series on teenage depression.'

'Her *causing* teenagers to be depressed, you mean?' I laugh, mainly to encourage myself to be more *present*. 'Sorry. I am glad it is working out for her.'

'Yeah, me too. I'm proud of her. I told her that in a session we had—just the two of us—with the therapist. *And*
she said it back. 'I'm proud of you, Tanya.' Apparently, this
is what is known as breakthrough moment. It felt good…'
She considers this for a moment. 'No, it didn't. It felt very
awkward. My toes were *curling*.'

'Good!' I tell her, as I walk through to the kitchen. 'There's
nothing wrong with finding all that touchy feely stuff awkward. Remember that, or you'll end up like Fitz. He's become
such a sap. He Tweeted a video of him and Jesus eating a
chocolate Gü pot last night with *one* spoon, so I un-followed
him. He used to hate couples who didn't use separate cutlery.
Anyway, your emotional stuntedness is part of your appeal.'

'As is your physical stuntedness,' she adds, and glances
down at a ring binder on the kitchen table. 'So, is that my
'How Not to Destroy Ashley's Flat' manual?'

'Something like that. Just remember, in case of a fire,
rescue all of my remaining clothes first, then move my accessories to safety. Then focus on saving yourself.'

'Got it.'

'And do not under *any* circumstances borrow—or let *any*
visitors borrow—*any*thing from my wardrobe. You'll also
find all the instructions for appliances and their associated
warranty forms which I never filled in…and also codes for the
wifi and cable and…' I rub the back of my neck. '….details
for the direct debit for…well, to pay into…and all the contact
details: mobile, email etc,; in case you need to get in touch
directly. With…' I check the time on the kitchen clock and
flick on the kettle. '…him. Tea?'

Tanya peers at me. 'You haven't spoken to…him?'

'I asked if you wanted a cup of tea.'

'I asked if you had spoken to him.'

'No need,' I snap.

'I just thought that maybe y—'

'Why would you?'

'Think about it? Well, obviously *not* because we are friends, because then that would mean I would be thinking from a place of empathy. Ashley, there is nothing wrong with admitting that your past has shaped who you are today and sharing that.'

'Ha! Was that from Noelle's shrink or one of your old ones?' I tut at her. 'Either way…drop it. Now, did you want tea or not?'

'Okay, *yes*…tea. And don't worry, no one will be plundering your wardrobe as no one I know is a Hobbit. Actually, I have a friend—of normal stature—from back home coming to stay this weekend.'

'Suze?' I raise an eyebrow.

Tanya gasps. 'Oi! *Too soon!* And no, repeating it will not make it funnier. It will be years before you can make a joke about *her*. Even when you're wheeling me around in our retirement home it will *still* be too soon.'

'Christ…' I get two mugs from the cupboard. 'What a terrifying thought, listening to your drip-dry waffle right up until the day I die.' I raise an eyebrow at her. 'Well, let's get one thing straight. *You* will be pushing *me* in the wheelchair not vice versa.' I clear my throat to distract myself from another flinch. 'So, what's the SHIT cheeky tea-leafing bitch up to?'

'Still staying at her mum's with the kids. Apparently, she and Rollo are doing couples counselling. They want to patch things up.'

'Patch things up? As if! *Quilt* relationships never work out. No matter how much they talk about what happened, her husband will never get over it. He will always watch his wife, no matter what she is doing; washing her hair, hanging out in the pub, driving to the South of France, taking the kids trampolining, giving him a hand job…and remember what she did. At least you'll always have that purely negative thought to cling onto, Tanya. Even if you never find love again yourself, she won't be *truly* loved either.'

'Cheers,' she says, giggling. 'I admire Rollo though. It takes guts to at least attempt to forgive…' She trails off. 'Anyway, it's my mate, Maddie. who's staying. She called me up in a panic, saying she desperately needs to get away from her attentive boyfriend and easygoing toddler for a few days. Turns out functional set-ups are equally as exhausting than our dysfunctional ones.'

'No, they are *more* tiring. If you're dysfunctional like us you don't have the pressure of expectation.' I pour hot water into the cups. 'Oh, and, erm…speaking of dysfunctional set-ups, a card arrived for you, it's at the front of the file.'

She pulls out the envelope and examines the handwriting. 'From my dad…that's weird.' She pauses. 'How did he know your address?'

'He ordered a car for you and Noelle…that night, remember?'

She eyes me suspiciously. 'But why would he think I am here now? *Ashley?*'

'Okay, *okay*…he called the magazine. We chatted.'

'You *what*? He has no right to discuss me with you. Or you, about me with him! What did he say?' She looks panicked.

'Calm down. We didn't discuss anything in detail. Your mum had told him about your new job and he wanted to congratulate you.'

'…no, Mum told him he *ought* to congratulate me.'

'Either way he made the effort to pick up the phone and

had to endure a conversation with me. He assumed you had already started but I told him you'd be in next week.'

'So that was it?'

'That was it. Well, it would have been, but then he told me you and he were going through one of your 'patches'…'

'But he didn't say specifically wh—'

'No! I told him that whatever it was, he should simply apologise and be done with it because you were his flesh and blood. To which he said he couldn't think of a worse person to give him advice on family unity. Which was fair enough, so I laughed. And so did he. Me and your dad…laughing. Imagine that. Anyway, he's away for the next week, taking your mum on a "non-golfing holiday", apparently. Ring him after that, maybe? Look, I'm not getting away from the fact that he is less ventricularly challenged than the Tin Man, but he does look out for you.'

Tanya stares at me. 'I thought you hated my father?'

'Of course I don't *hate* him! Not in an adult way. I hated him when we were kids which is a totally different type of hate. Look, in a sliding scale of crap fathers he's on the *mid* not *lower* end of the sliding scale, no? He's a social climbing plum who lacks communication skills and prefers your sister. All of that will never change. So, you have two choices. Say what you need to say to him and move on; either in his life or not. Or churn over what has happened over and over again in your mind and never release yourself from the internal dialogue.'

She pauses then nods at me. 'Then why don't you do it?'

'Excuse me?'

'Take your own advice. 'Say what you need to say to him and move on; either in his life or not.''

'We were not talking about me,' I snap at her. 'And frankly,

I have nothing to *say* to him. Not when everything has been made clear by his actions.'

'As long as you think that's the truth…both his…and yours.'

'I have everything figured out, Tanya.'

'Of course you do. When have you ever *not* had everything figured out?'

I add milk to our tea, remove the teabags and pass Tanya a mug. She has this look on her face; as if she is saying what she knows she *ought* to because otherwise I will lash out. She did this the first time I met her. I was ten years old and it was Day One of the autumn term. Two weeks prior, my parents got a call from Dr. Lyons. She had found the stolen jersey separates hidden in Suze's room… then Suze had blamed me. I was grounded for a fortnight, and as such was forced back to school without the two most essential components: bang-on-trend accessories to jazz up a fresh uniform… and a best friend. I was in the canteen, pushing my tray along the self-service. Piling powdered mashed potato on my plate, I heard a voice behind me.

HER: *You live on the estate, don't you? The one with the yellow Lego tower…*

ME: *(Turning round. Looking her down then up.) Yeah, why?*

HER: *(Smiling.) I moved in a couple of weeks ago. My name's Tanya. I'm in your year. Pretty sure I saw you in the square next to The Red Lion with a girl from my class. Which block do you live in?*

ME: *Anything else?*

HER: *(Confused.) Sorry, are y—*

ME: *Naffed off. Yes. What do you want?*

HER: *(Still enthusiastic.) I thought it would be nice to*

hang out. I don't know anyone on this side of town. I've got a little sister called Nelly. She's cute...well, that's if you like bumptious yet mysteriously powerful little show offs who are never told 'no', and I don't. Secretly, I call her 'Tiff'...she's the doll in Bride of Chucky.

ME: (Wrinkling my nose.) Bumptious. Where did you get that word from? And where did you get all that from? (Pointing at what she was wearing on her lower half.)

HER: My Mary Janes? Or my culottes? I got both from the same place as where I got the word 'bumptious'...my old school. It was the uniform.

ME: Where did you go? Hogwarts?

HER: (Giggling.) It was private.

ME: (Not smiling.) Word of advice, if you want to fit in here I'd get the regulation gear as soon as possible...and then customise the FUCK out of it.

HER: Why would I do that?

ME: It's called having identity.

I made a well in my potato mountain and squeezed a splurge of economy ketchup into it. Then I took my tray and sat down at the far end of the hall. I could see Suze joining the queue. She was holding hands with the twins from my form. They lived in her cul-de-sac, were spoilt with weekly TopShop vouchers and had once been to New York. Both Suze and I had always thought they were so 'meh'... especially when they wore their WE'RE TWINNING! T-shirts on games day. At least I thought we did.

HER: Can I sit here?

ME: (Looking up. Seeing Tanya again. Muttering.) If you want to.

HER: (Placing tray on table, sitting down.) So, if it's so important, how come you haven't customised YOUR uniform?

ME: I couldn't get to the shops. Parental issues.

HER: So erm...what would you have done?

ME: Towelling wristbands, Aertex shirt with the collar up and knee socks all from a leisure label. Preferably one that peaked in the seventies. Sergio Tacchini, Ellesse, Dunlop...

HER: Why? Do you play tennis?

ME: (Rolling my eyes at her.) Don't be stupid. It's called athletic chic.

HER: Ah, where did you get that idea from?

ME: (Snorting.) Does it matter? Nowhere. Everywhere. Wherever. Whatever. Fashion is about absorbing influences from around you. I work on my mum's stall, earn money and each term I arrive sporting a new look.

HER: 'Scuse the pun!

ME: 'Scuse the... (Gazing back over at Suze and the twins.)...what?

HER: Pun. It's a play on words. I learnt it at Hogwarts. You said 'sporting' a new look...and you wanted to do athletic chic so I s—(Stopping suddenly.) You look like you're about to cry, erm... are you? Are you okay erm...? Sorry, what is your name?

ME: Ashley. And I NEVER cry.

Then she twisted to follow my line of vision. Suze and the twins were now sat down two tables away from us. They were laughing and talking in overly loud voices. It was obvious they were taking the piss out of my accent.

HER: (Grimacing.) Well, now I can see why you're so upset. Sorry, 'naffed off'. Apart from not being able to accessorise, I mean. Those girls are making you feel bad.

ME: (Sitting up, shaking my hair.) No, they're not. You always have a choice, Tanya. You always have a choice to be who you want to be and how you want others to make you feel.

Then I smiled at her. She looked back at me with an expression as if she knew I was not strong enough to believe what I was saying. But she was not going to say differently because otherwise I would lash out. She didn't think I was 'naffed off' about my styling issues at all, she thought I was 'upset' about sitting on my own. Which I wasn't. I was fine... on my own.

Another flinch. I take a sip of tea.

'Anyway, when is your van arriving?'

'Later today,' replies Tanya. 'I'm using the same one who dropped off all of Greg's stuff at The Croft.'

'Wow, you're saying his name again?'

'Yes, because I know he hates it and I hate him. In the *adult* way...' She sighs. 'Oh, and get this...according to Maddie's boyfriend, Kian, he already has a new girlfriend.'

'So? You've moved house, got a new job, exorcized your demons—well, demon...*me*. You've risen like a phoenix from the flames. All he's done is gone and got another bird. Big deal! At least his singing career hasn't taken off. That would have been absolute worst case scenario. Imagine, his grinning face all over the press? Actually, no, don't imagine. I'd pass you the razor blade. Anyway, now you're in town, maybe you should start getting out there again. Get on some dating apps. You never know there may be a guy waiting for you to exchange a series of perfectly pleasant messages with, then be thoroughly disappointed within minutes of meeting him in the flesh for a drink when he makes a laboured joke at the barman's expense when ordering the first round of cocktails.'

'God, how depressing does that sound?' She shakes her head.

'Very, but not any way *near* as depressing as being with a

man who *actually* made up a new name to be a more attractive proposition to a record company. I often wonder why he changed that before his car. I mean, seriously, I'm not a motor enthusiast but that vehicle said "handy for nipping to Waitrose" not "I straddle the world like a rock colosuss".'

She giggles. 'Actually, I already have a dinner invitation. Angus texted me…but I made up an excuse. It could be difficult.'

'Tanya!' I wag a teaspoon at her. 'Angus O'Donnell is your cheating ex-fiancé's idol! Christ, have you learnt nothing from our non-friendship? If there is the opportunity to make Greg's soul feel so ragged and burnt with jealously it may as well have been ripped out, bashed with a rusty bicycle chain then set alight, you must take it!'

'I thought you were all about moving forward?'

'I am! But this is different. In this case causing extra suffering first is beneficial to your own trajectory. In other words, if you don't call back Angus to rearrange, I will. This is easy, not difficult. You know he likes you.'

'I don't mean it could be difficult in that way…more because of something else. Potentially someone else.'

She looks down at her tea, but I can make out that uneasy but defiant expression returning to her face. Her grip tightens round the mug causing the veins in her hands to stick out.

'I haven't poisoned it. I'm hardly like to employ you then murder you. Tanya, what are you on about? Are you already seeing someone?'

'No…well, yes.' She looks up. 'I'm seeing a fertility specialist.'

'Oooh, get you. Is he hot?'

'No! I'm not seeing him like that. I'm seeing him for… *treatment*.'

'Treatment for what?'

'Artificial insemination…to have a baby.'

'Fuck!'

'Or *not* as the case may be.' She laughs.

I laugh too. This time properly, for the first time since I started getting those flinches.

'You lunatic!'

'I know, it seems crazy, but like you said, why fight being the way we are? Look where being "normal" got me. *I want a baby.* So, I need…sperm. Don't worry, I've already told Fitz. I wanted to be upfront that I could potentially need a period of time off before I accepted the job. He was really encouraging. Started regaling me with his take on the cycle of life and that it was *very* Monica Cruz of me…oh, and how he and Jesus have already discussed looking into adoption one day.'

'Christ…' I shake my head at her. 'To think that his top movie icon used to be *Penelope* Cruz, nine months pregnant in a Halston jumpsuit doing cocaine in *Blow*. Well, sounds like you've got it all figured out.'

'Yeah…finally. I now know what it feels like to be you.'

I find myself gripping onto my own mug. I grip harder and harder until the handle snaps in my fingers and smashes on the tiles. Tanya jumps up.

'God, Ashley. Are you okay?'

'Yeah, yeah…' I bend down to pick up the broken pieces of china. 'Pass me that cloth by the sink will you?' I place the broken china in the bin and grab the cloth from her. As I stoop down to wipe the floor, I can feel her watching me. 'Don't worry, there are loads of mugs in the cupboard.'

'I'm not worried about the mugs. I'm worried about you. You look…' She trails off.

I know how I look. There is something in my eyes. I saw it last night when I went to the bathroom after my 4.37am spasm woke me up. I stared right into the inky dark pupils. In that moment, I thought about all the different collections those eyes had seen. A decade of shows. Hundreds of catwalks. But the same themes coming round again and again. Deconstruction, urban glam, vintage, grunge, gothic, Grecian, preppy, minimalism, avant garde, rock chick, power dressing, futuristic, bondage, boudoir, boho, Victoriana, punk, disco, eco, ethnic, excess…even sports luxe, which was meant to be the look of the new millennium was just nineties athletic chic with a heel which was eighties sportswear with a more rave-y edge. If you didn't get it right first time, you always got another chance. You lost one of the defining pieces that looked too 'obvious' the first time round and added something else. So, you did it better when you got another chance. Fashion allows you do this. It is not like life. Because even if you are '*a create your own chances kind of girl*', eventually, you run out…of chances.

The intercom buzzes.

'That'll be my cab.' I throw her the cloth, walk out of the kitchen and up the corridor. 'Can you bung the china in the bin? Thanks.' I shout.

'Ashley! Talk to me.'

I don't reply. I go into my wardrobe to get the suitcase which I have packed, and the other one which was already stocked. I swallow hard. Then I take one last look at the framed picture of Carine Roitfeld. At the bottom of the photograph is my favourite quote of Carine's: 'Fashion is not about clothes it is about a look.' I take a photo of this on my phone, add a single smiley emoji…and send it to Fitz. He sends a winky emoji back with a message.

'*Best of luck! Take care!*'

I manage a smile, then wheel both suitcases into the corridor. Tanya is waiting by the front door. She takes my hand luggage. We walk down the stairs and step out of my front door. At the top of the stone steps she turns to me.

'Listen, Ashley, before you go…' Her purple heat rash shoots up her neck. 'You said we needed to be honest with each other to begin again…' She takes a breath. 'I need to tell you something.'

I shake my head. 'Really, don't…'

'But you don't know what I was going to say.'

'Whatever it is, I don't want to hear it. Remember what happened last time you said that…exactly like that?'

'Yeah, I remember.' She exhales deeply. 'Okay, then at least let me say, thank you. *Thank you.*'

'Okay, you've said it.' I smile back at her.

As we look at each other, she nods at me, as if I should be adding to what I have said. But what else is there for me to say? There is absolutely nowhere for us to go. Not in a bad way. Not in a good way. But in a *real* way. I can tell that she is trying to give me one more chance. She wants to be that person. But I don't know how to be that person who takes it.

'*Meeeeeeeeee…*'

I jump. 'That noise…'

'What noise?'

'That 'meeeee' noise…I swear I heard it. It sounded like…'

'*Meeeeeeeeee…*'

'There it is again. Where is she? It's *her*…'

I run down the steps and check either side of the neighbouring walls, but she isn't there.

'I heard her.' I twist to face Tanya. '*I heard her!*'

She screws up her face. 'Who?'

'My cat. Mine... *our* cat.'

'But, Ashley, she's been missing for weeks...no, months. It was probably someone else's.'

I throw up my hands. 'No, it was *her*...'

My cab driver beeps and winds down his window. 'Think you should know...' he shouts. '...the traffic heading towards Heathrow isn't flowing too well. We should get going.'

'Hang on, please...I'm coming, I just need to...'

My eyes dart up and down the street. Then I look up towards my flat. Sitting on the lead parapet which hangs over the entrance to my building, licking her front left paw, is Kat Moss.

'Kat! Kat Moss! KAT MOSS!'

'Meeeeeeeeee,' she says again, entirely non-plussed by my display of emotion. 'Meeee.'

She jumps down onto the wall and trots over to me. I grab her and squeeze her. Then I check over her coat. It is immaculate. She is not underweight. If anything she has put on a tiny little bit, but that doesn't matter because her human namesake has too and still fronts major global fashion and beauty campaigns. I bury my nose in her fur and inhale.

'You came back, you came *back*. Oh, Kat, Kat, *Kat*...' I look up at Tanya. 'What am I going to do? I can't go...'

'Can't go or don't want to go?'

I ignore her question. 'I promised I would always look after her. I've already let her down once.'

'She certainly doesn't look as if she holds it against you.' Tanya rubs my shoulder. 'I'll look after her, I promise. You can Facetime us whenever you want.'

'Please, will you take her to the vet later and get her checked over? She goes to the one next to the park. You'll see it when you walk to the tube station.' I bury my nose into Kat's neck and inhale again. 'Remember you're the furriest and purriest super-meow-del in the whole world.'

'I'm going to pretend I didn't hear that. I thought you were cool.' Tanya laughs and gently pulls Kat Moss from my arms.

'I am cool.'

'Yeah, I know, I know. Now, go. Or you'll miss your flight.'

I cover Kat Moss in one last flurry of kisses and get in the cab. As I am driven off I turn to wave at them, the two most important females in my life, but then I turn back round, because I am thinking about the most important. My mother. Because it was *her* who taught *me* to be out there on my own. And I'm off again. Out there. On my own. But this time it feels different.

*

The queue for the British Airways check-in at Terminal 5 is long. But I don't do what I would normally and mooch around WH Smith 'assessing' (AKA carping to Fitz on the phone about) rival magazine covers whilst the line gets shorter. Not that I know it won't be enjoyable—pleasure will *always* be found in bitching about the use of over-zealous skin lightening on an ethnic model or a case of freakishly limb withering Photoshop. I simply don't want to see *Catwalk*. I've not gone into a newsagent all week. The moment Catherine gave me my job as Editorial Assistant, I imagined what it would feel like to produce my first issue of *Catwalk*, with me as Editor, on sale…but now that I have I am not sure I want to read it.

One thing I *am* sure of is that it's a good magazine. Noelle is on the cover. She is not wearing any make-up or clothes but her nudity is hidden by two words in pink neon letters:

FAKING IT. There was no airbrush and Noelle's interview was about as real as it could be. I managed to catch her at the tipping point between genuine questioning of her place in the universe and feeling *jolly* sorry for herself. If I say so myself, it was a 'moment'—getting picked up by national and international press, which got everyone very excited. And fortunately took the focus of attention away from my Editor's letter.

Not long ago, I was asked why I first wanted to work at Catwalk. *I was embarrassed to give my answer. It was because of the 'bubble'. That was why I thought I loved fashion. Because it meant living in a bubble unaffected by the real world. It was escapism. My mantra was DON'T PRICK THE BUBBLE. But I have realised that it was me who didn't want her bubble to burst. I wanted to escape me. I didn't want people to know the reality. But I faced my reality thanks to fashion. Fashion is real. It has power. It has guts. It has sex appeal. It has humour. It has sensitivity. It creates controversy. It is competitive. It inspires. It emotes. It is accessible to all. It makes money but it contributes positively to humanity. It also makes you feel fucking great. But the best thing is that it is constantly changing, moving and evolving. This means that every issue of* Catwalk *is a new story and each one has to be confident that it will be better, wiser and more compelling than the previous, exactly as the years of your life should be.*

Ashley Jacobs

Editor

I glance over at WH Smith and cringe. Partly, because I wrote the words '*contributes positively to humanity*' but mainly, I am embarrassed because if anyone was faking it, it was me. It *is* me.

Forty minutes of queueing later, I receive my boarding pass from the BA staff member and watch my suitcases juddering down the conveyor belt. I head towards passport control, stopping at the designated area to chuck away the bottle of water I haven't finished. A girl next to me is transferring her make-up into a transparent bag. Moisturiser, primer, foundation, concealer, clear eyebrow gloss, light filtering powder, under-eye serum, tinted lip balm, highlighting pen and lowlighting pen. Extensive contouring tools. Use each one of these properly, taking time and care with each application…and it will look like you are make-up free. She has done an astonishing job, I think. That's assuming she is wearing each product and not waiting to apply it on the plane. Maybe that is actually *her*. I stare at her. I am still staring when I feel someone behind me. It is him. I know it is.

He does not move. He stands still as if he too is aware that I can sense he is there. When I do turn round I don't say anything. For a few moments I want to look at him in the way I always used to. So that he understands everything we have been through is *done*. There is no more negativity. As he looks back at me, I know there is only positivity emanating from him too. This was exactly how it was. Every day. For so long. He smiles at me.

'Zach.'

'Ash.'

'How did you know I was here?' I ask, but I already know.

'I got a call from a T—'

'…anya.'

'Erm…yeah. You've never mentioned her before. She said she was your cat sitter. Well, at first, she did, but…oh, Ash, she told me about Kat Moss. I can't believe it. I'm so pleased she found her way home. How is she?'

I smile at him. 'She looked great. Tanya is going to take her for a check up, but I doubt anything will be wrong. She looked a bit tired. But then it was midday so she'd probably not slept since yesterday.'

Zach shakes his head and steps forward. 'I'm so happy for you, her…us. I crucified myself about the way you found out. I was going to call you the next day and the day after that, but I knew there would be nothing I could say that would make the situation better. But listen to me, I want to say to you that I nev—'

I butt in. 'Stop, Zach. My flight leaves in an hour and I've already put my suitcases through. I can't request any extra emotional baggage.'

'Thank you for making a joke.'

'It's okay. So, tell me, how's Gwen doing?'

'Well, the tests showed that the tumours hadn't spread, but she still needed chemo…and she is having more treatment moving forward. The docs say that this is the best case scenario we could have hoped for. Before you ask…' He pulls a face. '…even undergoing the effects of brutal cancer blitzing drugs Mum has not become less critical of others or interfering of me. Which is truly wonderful. I'm praying that she always will be.'

'Ah, I don't think you have anything to worry about there. Please, send her my best wishes…I mean that.'

'I know you do…and I will.' He gesticulates towards the entrance to Customs. 'So, where are you off to?'

'Tokyo.'

'Really? To buy me some rare eighties hi-tops?'

'No. Actually, I'm talking to a clothing manufacturer over there about my mother's designs. Sheila sent me a suitcase of her final work. I forwarded them some samples, they liked them and now they want to reproduce them. I'm taking the other pieces which they haven't seen over today.'

'Seriously? That is such brilliant news. *You* are brilliant! I'm…I'm proud of you…really.'

He smiles at me again and takes another step. He is now close enough for me to reach out and touch him. But I know that if I do, I will unravel. Tanya sent him here with good intentions, I know that. She wanted to give me *that* chance. But now it is here in front of me I do not know how to deal with it. Then I realise, that's why it feels different being out here on my own this time. I'm scared.

Zach breaks the silence.

'Hey, I was wondering, maybe we could meet up properly, when you get back. For a coffee or something? Or a drink, if that's what you erm…want. I'm not implying that I think you're a…or were a…' He laughs, nervously. 'No offence meant.'

'None taken. I'm not an alcoholic. I could stop, thank God.' I raise an eyebrow at him. 'I think the main thing that put me off was potentially having something in common with Keith. Enough to put *any*one off, I would have thought. But, yes…I guess…it would be nice to meet up for a hot beverage or a single unit of wine. I'll email you when I get an idea of the next time I'm coming back to the UK and we can arrange someth—'

He interrupts me. 'What do you mean when you 'get an idea'? Surely, you have a definite date to return from your trip? How long have *Catwalk* given you off?'

'I've left, Zach.'

'But I read it in the *Press Gazette* that you were made Editor?

'And I enjoyed every second of the short time I was. I

restructured everything. From this issue, only thirty thousand tangible hard copies of the magazine will be produced every month as a collector's item. The *Catwalk* website is now the hub. Everything that is happening in fashion happens on there. News, sales, live catwalk shows, interactive blogging and vlogging by the staff and readers, you can watch all our shoots. But this is the best bit, it even has a portal for buying clothes from all the fashion colleges. Students can sell their exam pieces to the public or retail units. It's a whole new...' I realise I'm rambling. '...direction.'

Zach shrugs at me. 'But you sound so excited about it? Why would you leave?'

'Because I thought a clean break was better. I'm going to Tokyo and then I'm going...*travelling*. I still haven't figured out where yet. I didn't want to turn into one of those Lonely Planet bores planning everything down to the last sushi roll. I'll stick to cities but am going to try and avoid any mega shopping opps though as I've got more than enough clothes in my suitcase. I couldn't face a rucksack...such a cliché.'

As I say this I watch his face contort.

'Don't panic, I'm not doing a runner!' I reassure him. 'I've sorted out all the payments on the flat. Tanya, the erm... cat sitter—is going to live there. She's setting up a monthly direct debit to put her rent into your account. It's exactly the amount my solicitor arranged with yours. The money will be going in on the first of every month.' I exhale. 'There is something I need to ask you though, and I know this is a big ask...but if it's okay with you, I'd rather Tanya look after Kat Moss. Is that okay?'

Now, his face crumbles.

'No...' he mutters.

'Zach, please don't be like that. I know you've missed her, but Tanya will give her the attention she needs. You're—quite rightly—with your mum in any spare time you have at the moment and you've got a…well, there are going to be *three* of you living in your flat soon. You know Kat Moss's routine. She likes to sleep during the day, which she won't be able to do when you've got a b—'

'No,' he repeats, a little louder. '*No*.'

'Come on, it makes sense. You know it does.'

'No, no, no…' His voice quiet again. 'I mean, no…you… you, *you*…shouldn't.'

'Shouldn't what?'

'Go travelling.'

'I need to, Zach.' I drop my head. 'I need to get out of here. Look, I'm under no illusions…this is not going to be an *Eat, Pray, Love* adventure of spiritual awakening. There is a strong possibility that if the fashion is as barmy as everyone says it is, I may stay in Tokyo for a few years.'

'Don't.'

'Why? Remember what you said, about being presented with Big Ben instead of a carriage clock when I eventually left *Catwalk*?' I smile at him. 'Fitz has had a personality reboot and is taking over the top job. It *is* time for a new adventure.' I say, overly brightly. 'You were right.'

'But I was wrong about so many other things,' he says. 'I know that now. Tanya…she told me she wasn't *just* your cat sitter. And she didn't *just* tell me that Kat Moss was home. She told me…' He takes a breath. 'She told me a *lot* that you had never told me. And for god's sake don't flip out at her. She was coming from a good place.'

I deliberate this for a few moments, then shrug. 'I know that. Trust me, we both know what it is like to be in a bad place…and we aren't ever going back. She told you because she wanted to give me a chance.'

'And everything she said made perfect sense,' he continues. 'I hate myself for not realising there must have been valid reasons for the way you acted, just like there were valid reasons for the way I acted. Maybe I would have understood you eventually, but I needed to sort out myself first. But before I could even start that process I got together with Rachel and—' He shakes his head.

'But Zach, it's happened. There is no going back. We have to move on.'

'I don't want to move on.' His voice cracks on each syllable. 'I want to be with you. I want us to have what we did before. Exactly like you said. We could even have a better life because we will always know what we almost lost. I will be the best father I can be to my baby and I will be the best support I can be to Rachel, but it is you who I want to grow old with, side by side, you and me. I love you, Ash.'

I look at him, then find myself gazing round the airport. The first time I ever came here was for a flight to New York. It was the start of the Spring/Summer fashion week collections. Slithering up to the BA check-in desk was the expected impeccably dressed snake of style journalists and columnists from the UK's biggest magazines and newspapers. Catherine had decided to take me as her assistant as, at the last NYFW, she had taken Polly… who had got smashed before Anna Sui, shagged a cameraman from the Fashion Channel, lost the invites to Vera Wang, forgotten to tell her that Jeremy Scott had changed venues and bitched that Tommy Hilfiger 'wished he was a ghetto Ralph Lauren' in earshot of his PR. It was a week of firsts for me. First time travelling by air.

First time I really felt this world was where I belonged. First time I had told Zach, 'I love you' and meant it.

The first time I'd merely *said* it, was the same minute we met. I went to the bar round the corner from work for a glass of wine. It was the same day Tanya had turned up for work experience. The drink I ordered was the only one in an *actual* drinking establishment I allowed myself in the entire time I was saving for my flat. A man was sitting at the bar. He glanced sideways as I plonked myself down on a stool next to him.

HIM: Well, someone is in a bad mood.

ME: The guaranteed way to tip a person in a bad mood into a worse one. And don't even think about asking if there is anything you can do.

HIM: I bet I can help.

ME: You can't. Unless you can make people disappear so that they can never EVER come back into your life again.

HIM: That would be murder.

ME: Don't try and make me laugh, it won't work.

HIM: For someone so young you are very serious.

ME: Maybe because my life is serious.

HIM: Okay, well… I tried. I'm off to meet some friends. (Getting up from the bar stool.)

ME: Have a nice life.

HIM: Have a nice life, too. What was your name?

ME: Ashley.

HIM: Mine is Zach. Goodbye, Ashley..

ME: Goodbye, Zach.

HIM: I love you, Ashley.

ME: (Smiling.) Shut up!

HIM: Told you I'd make you smile.

ME: Bye.

HIM: Is that it?
ME: I love you too, Zach.
'I love you too, Zach.'

I lurch forward into his arms and hug him. He squeezes me tight. His body is shaking. The vibrations soothe mine. I know there will be no more twinges, flinches or spasms. I am no longer scared. Gently, he takes my head in his hands and kisses me. I step back and look at him. This time my focus is only on him. I need to take the chance that has been provided for me. It's the least I can do for Tanya. It's the most I can do for me. I take a breath. He speaks before I can.

'Then let me give you a second chance,' he says.

'Sorry?' I genuinely think I have not heard correctly. 'What did you say?'

'I said, let me give you a second chance. I forgive you, Ash.'

I pull back and find myself making a strange noise. Half-way between choking and laughing. He misconstrues my reaction and smiles at me.

'I do,' he says.

'You do?'

'Yes, just like on our wedding day… I do.'

But here's the thing. *Do I? W*hen I said 'I do', I meant it. I would *do* anything for you. I loved you enough to have a baby because it was *your* baby. But you did not love me enough to stay with me without one. He is still talking.

'…I've tried so hard to make it work with Rachel, but I know she can tell I'm trying. She doesn't want to admit it to herself and neither do I, because then I will have made a mess of her life too. But both of us know we're over. When I received that phonecall from Tanya, so much of what happened between you and I fell into place. Maybe even down to the reason we got together in the first place. You needed someone like me. You'd been let down by everyone. Your mum, dad, best mate. It was no wonder you felt so much pressure not to let *me* down. Or our child. I get it. How *could* I blame you anymore?'

'You blamed me?'

'Just like you blamed me.'

'I never blamed you, Zach.' I almost mutter this because I have heard all I need to know. 'I blamed *me* too.'

'Then don't, because, like I said, I forgive you. More than that, I respect you again. I should never have lost respect. I should have recognised you were screwed up for real reasons and given you time to sort out those issues. I accept that now. But look at you! Exactly like Tanya said, you've got everything sorted. You're not that person anymore. You're strong now.'

'Is that what she said? That I am strong *now*?'

'Yeah, but then she said you *always* have been…that you have never, ever been weak. Even when you had to survive not wearing sporty towelling accessories on the first day of a school term when you had planning your look all summer.' He laughs and shrugs. 'Whatever that means.'

'It means everything,' I tell him. 'It means every-*fucking*-thing.'

I step to the side. I can see the girl with the contouring equipment as she stands in the line of passengers waiting to go through the security check. She is gripping onto her plastic bag of camouflage. Why do we do this? Why have we invented a way to cover up blemishes that not only hides the signs that we have lived *and are living*, but more than that… tries to entirely reshape the person we are? No, not why are 'we' doing this. Why am *I* doing this?

'I love you, Zach. I do, I love you.'

I say it again, so that he knows I do not regret a single time I said it after that very first time, and I kiss him. Then I lean down to pick up my bag and head to the queue. I don't look back. As soon as I am through, I check the live departures board. Ace. There's more than enough time to nip into Burberry in Duty Free. I am *literally—dy*ing—for the new collection. Am *totally* terminal. (Ha! *Get it?* TERMINAL. In the airport? #pun) Christopher Bailey is back to his edgy best. All those whimsical silk shirts covered in hearts he did a few seasons ago? Not keen. After all, Crimes Against Fashion No. 1: Wearing your heart on your sleeve. Guilty: Okay, *okay*…right now? Ashley Jacobs.

But it's time to get changed. I know what looks good on me.

* * * * *

SHOUT OUTS!

First up, she quite lit-erally got da power! Monumental gratitude to Anna Power @ Johnson and Alcock, my top notch agent. . .and also, mad respect goes to publishing whizz, Sally Williamson @ Harper Collins. If I'd made a pop/R'n'B crossover album (with an experimental edge) I'd be saying I'm #blessed and #humbled to work with you #laydeez.

In addition, I'm much obliged to Ben Mason, my original mentor @ Fox Mason, who signed me up back when I wore pleather as daywear. . .and taught me how to be ruthless when getting rid of overly verbose jokes. 'Ollie! Just do it. They're random words not your cats!'

I should also muster some sort of enthusiasm towards this bunch of glamour/sour pusses. . .who bring constant drama, a soupçon of entertainment and the very occasional laugh to my life. That's Sean 'Tits, Tan, Teeth 'n' Jump Seats' Varley, Hugh 'G★★i and B★★★a are not models' McPhillips, Minnie 'Swipe the f★★★ left' Frangiamore, John 'Bombs, TRX 'n' Wet Wipes' Tippins, Suzette 'Fast track' Allcorn, Ryan 'Invention test' O'Hare, Sandra 'Problems with the vendor' Carter, Faris 'Billowing kaftan' Khaliq, Oli 'Yellow rose on the hand towel as standard' Tretheway, Josh 'She's gone international' Caffe, Peter 'I'm only on 89%' Thompson, Peter '#NW3lifestyle' Grant, Micheal 'Parlour game' Gillespie, Fiona 'It's all about the icing sugar' Carlisle, Alex 'My PA might get back to you' Sapot, Scott 'Am I rich? Am I pretty?' Sapot, Val 'I've eaten!' Sapot. . .then last and obvz least, my (lacking in soul) sista; Martyn 'I'll bung it in your account next week' Fitzgerald. But not forgetting Charlotte and David Quain AKA 'Chaz 'n' Dave'. Oh, and of course, the non-invasive cosmetic legend that is Dr. John 'You may be slightly red tomorrow' Quinn.

Plus, maje respect to Pete 'Princess' Liggins and Jamie 'J Wizzle' Wilson. . .the brains, brawn and perennially well bronzed beauties behind Box Clever, West London's finest boxing gym. And big ups to my fave punch bag beeyatches;

Sinead 'Pitbull' McIvor-Cook, Laura 'The Lozz' Scott and Andrea 'Plank' Williams.

Y muchas gracias por ayudarme en mi aparatosa mudanza a la isla de Ibiza; Noelle y Anneke @ Engel & Völkers, Lucía y Jose @ Bufete Frau, Jason Ham @ Lucas Fox, Chiara Clark at Premier FX, Gerardo Vidaurre, Bruno Grasas y Monkey el gato. . .y especialmente a Víctor Sánchez Francés y su familia. Oh my gosh, I'm effing fluent en Español! Skillz, si?

And hola too in the direction of some small humans who are almost as cool as Eddie but still have a lot to learn from him; Noah Sapot, Jack Sapot, Ruby Griffiths and Jess 'J Kitty' Quain.

And finally, to Mummy Q. You is splendid, innit.

Is there such a thing as the *perfect* size?

Vivian Ward is in total control of her life. Actually,
scrap that—she's thirty-five, estranged from her
family, a failed actress and working in a London
members' club to pay the bills. Truth is, the only
thing she's in control of is what's on her plate...

But then she meets movie star Maximilian Fry,
who's just as screwed up, and journeys into a world
of celebrity even faker than the one she was already
living in. Will image triumph, or will she realise
that some of her answers lie within?

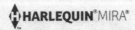

Bringing you the best voices in fiction
🐦 @Mira_booksUK

'**A whirlwind of glitz and glamour... an
entertaining debut for chick–lit fans
everywhere.**'
– OK *magazine*

Jess has all but given up on her dreams of
becoming a star – until she meets gorgeous record
producer Jack, who finally spots her talent and
offers her a job with his label.
Plunged into the crazy world of show-biz, Jess's
life is transformed. But as her star rises, she begins
to lose touch with her roots... Jess's dreams of
stardom may have come true, but at what cost?

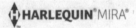

Bringing you the best voices in fiction
🐦 **@Mira_booksUK**

*A fast-paced, fun-packed rummage
through the ultimate dressing up box.*

When fashion boutique worker Amber Green is
mistakenly offered a job as assistant to infamous,
jet-setting 'stylist to the stars' Mona Armstrong,
she hits the ground running, helping to style some
of Hollywood's hottest (and craziest) starlets. As
awards season spins into action Mona is in hot
demand and Amber's life turned upside down.
How will Amber keep her head?

And what the hell will everyone wear?

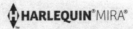

M439_TS

Loved this book?
Let us know!

Find us on **Twitter @Mira_BooksUK**
where you can share your thoughts, stay up
to date on all the news about our upcoming
releases and even be in with the chance of
winning copies of our wonderful books!

Bringing you the best voices in fiction

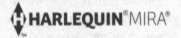